KU-503-582

THE PERFECT
FAKE DATE

NAIMA SIMONE

THE BAD BOY
EXPERIMENT

REESE RYAN

MILLS & BOON

All rights reserved including the right of reproduction in whole or in part in any form. This edition is published by arrangement with Harlequin Books S.A.

This is a work of fiction. Names, characters, places, locations and incidents are purely fictional and bear no relationship to any real life individuals, living or dead, or to any actual places, business establishments, locations, events or incidents. Any resemblance is entirely coincidental.

This book is sold subject to the condition that it shall not, by way of trade or otherwise, be lent, resold, hired out or otherwise circulated without the prior consent of the publisher in any form of binding or cover other than that in which it is published and without a similar condition including this condition being imposed on the subsequent purchaser.

® and ™ are trademarks owned and used by the trademark owner and/or its licensee. Trademarks marked with ® are registered with the United Kingdom Patent Office and/or the Office for Harmonisation in the Internal Market and in other countries.

First Published in Great Britain 2021
by Mills & Boon, an imprint of HarperCollins*Publishers* Ltd
1 London Bridge Street, London, SE1 9GF

www.harpercollins.co.uk

HarperCollins*Publishers*
1st Floor, Watermarque Building,
Ringsend Road, Dublin 4, Ireland

The Perfect Fake Date © 2021 Naima Simone
The Bad Boy Experiment © 2021 Roxanne Ravenel

ISBN: 978-0-263-28314-3

1221

MIX
Paper from
responsible sources
FSC™ C007454

This book is produced from independently certified FSC™ paper to ensure responsible forest management.

For more information visit: www.harpercollins.co.uk/green

Printed and Bound in Spain using 100% Renewable electricity at CPI Black Print, Barcelona

USA TODAY bestselling author **Naima Simone**'s love of romance was first stirred by Mills & Boon books pilfered from her grandmother. Now she spends her days writing sizzling romances with a touch of humour and snark. She is wife to her own real-life superhero and mother to two awesome kids. They live in perfect domestically challenged bliss in the southern United States.

Reese Ryan writes sexy, emotional love stories served with a heaping side of family drama. Reese is a native Ohioan with deep Tennessee roots. She endured many long, hot car trips to family reunions in Memphis via a tiny clown car loaded with cousins. Connect with Reese via Facebook, Twitter, Instagram, TikTok or reeseryan.com. Join her VIP Readers Lounge at bit.ly/VIPReadersLounge. Check out her YouTube show, where she chats with fellow authors, at bit.ly/ReeseRyanChannel.

Llyfrgelloedd Caerdyda
www.caerdydd.gov.uk/llyfrgelloedd
Cardiff Libraries
www.cardiff.gov.uk/libraries

CAERDYDD
CARDIFF

ACC. No: 05213897

Also by Naima Simone

Billionaires of Boston
Vows in Name Only
Secrets of a One Night Stand

Blackout Billionaires
The Billionaire's Bargain
Black Tie Billionaire
Blame It on the Billionaire

Rose Bend
The Road to Rose Bend
Slow Dance at Rose Bend
A Kiss to Remember
Christmas in Rose Bend

Also by Reese Ryan

The Bourbon Brothers
Savannah's Secret
The Billionaire's Legacy
Engaging the Enemy
A Reunion of Rivals
Waking Up Married

Discover more at millsandboon.co.uk

THE PERFECT
FAKE DATE

NAIMA SIMONE

One

"If you think I don't know that my purpose here tonight is being your beard, then you've seriously underestimated my role as your best friend. And my intelligence."

Kenan Rhodes glanced down at Eve Burke, the petite woman on his arm and the woman who'd just called him on his shit. And with a smile. She was classy like that.

He snickered, nodding to a black-suited server as he nabbed two flutes of champagne from the man's tray. After passing one to his best friend, he sipped from the other.

"You have such a suspicious mind. I think it's a by-product of being a high-school teacher. So used to having kids lying to you about homework and bathroom passes."

He smiled at yet *another* person staring at him, his mouth pulling tight at the corners. The older woman, draped in more diamonds than Cartier, dipped her head in acknowledgment before turning to the man next to her and whispering behind her gloved hand. Irritation prickled under his skin, and he deliberately turned away from the couple.

"What's wrong?" Eve demanded, studying him through narrowed, dark brown eyes.

"Nothing."

She arched an eyebrow. "You're rubbing your thumb over the scar on your jaw. Do I really need to point out you only do that when you're contemplating world domination or when something—or someone—is bothering you?"

He dropped the hand he hadn't even realized he'd lifted to his face down to his side and shot her a disgusted look. Sometimes he *really* hated having someone in his life who knew him so damn well.

"Fine." He paused, annoyance and frustration crawling through him again. "It's been six months. Six. Months. Eve. And still they're staring like I'm a sideshow act in a circus. Like we all are. As if we're all in their midst for their entertainment."

Admittedly, his entire world had been flipped on its ass when he'd received a certified letter requesting his presence at the reading of Baron Farrell's will. Baron Farrell. The longtime CEO of the international, multi-billion-dollar conglomerate Farrell International with the reputation of being a brilliant businessman and a ruthless bastard. Why he'd wanted Kenan, a marketing vice president in his family's successful commercial-real-estate development company, to attend his will reading had been a mystery. A mystery that had been quickly resolved when Kenan discovered he was Baron's illegitimate son. According to the will, Kenan and the two half brothers he'd had no idea existed had to stay together and run Farrell International together for a year or else the company would be broken into pieces and sold to the highest bidders.

Brothers.

Cain Farrell, the acknowledged heir Baron had kept and raised. And Achilles Farrell, a computer software designer and tech genius from Tacoma, Washington, whom Baron had abandoned, just as he'd done with Kenan. But Achilles had been raised by his single mother while Kenan had been adopted by his parents and raised in Boston.

Oh, yes. For the last few months, since the story had broken, Boston society had had a field day about the Farrell Bastards, as they'd dubbed Achilles and Kenan.

Eve's hand wrapped around Kenan's and squeezed, drawing him from his morose thoughts.

"They're small people with small lives who breathe for any hint of scandal or gossip to brighten up their existence. And let's face it, *the* Baron Farrell of Farrell International fathering two unknown sons? Sons he grants co-ownership of his company on his death? That's the kind of drama these people *live* for. But just because they're staring at you like a sideshow act doesn't mean you have to perform. You're Kenan fucking Rhodes. You don't dance for anyone."

Clearing his throat, he lifted his glass. "Drink your champagne," he murmured.

Smirking, she did as he ordered. But then responded, "You're welcome."

He glanced away from that quirk of her wide, sensual mouth on the pretense of scanning the crowded ballroom. Either that or risk letting Eve glimpse the secret he'd managed to keep hidden for fifteen of his thirty years.

It wouldn't do to reveal in front of God, country and all the guests attending the annual Brahmin Arts Foundation gala that he was in love with his best friend.

Unrequited love.

His hold tightened on the glass, matching the constriction squeezing his chest. Such a fancy, completely inadequate way to describe the hell of having your heart broken day after day when the person you crave more than air looks at you with wholesome…affection.

It killed a part of him.

And every time she brushed those soft, almost too-full lips over his cheek in a platonic kiss, or pressed her sexy, lush curves against his body in an amicable hug, another piece of him died another death.

"So tell me—" Eve nudged him with her elbow "—what overzealous socialite am I warding off tonight?"

He inhaled, taking in her earthy musk of cedarwood, roses and the shea butter she'd massaged into her skin for as long as he'd known her. If he was blindfolded and shoved into a warehouse filled with thousands of open perfume bottles, he would still be able to select her erotic, hedonistic scent. It teased him when he was awake and haunted him in his sleep. He couldn't escape it—couldn't escape her.

Even when he prayed to. And, God, sometimes he did pray that he could exorcise this damn love for her from his heart, his soul.

Sweeping his gaze over the packed ballroom of the former turn-of-the-century hotel, which was now an art museum, he quickly located a woman who would provide a suitable scapegoat to satisfy Eve's curiosity. Fortunately—or unfortunately, depending on the point of view—the woman seemed to sense his scrutiny and smiled in his direction, the invitation in her gleaming eyes clear and unmistakable.

"Never mind." Eve snorted. "Question answered. And I should've known. She's just your type, too."

"My type?" Even knowing he'd probably regret asking, Kenan did, anyway. Because one of the prerequisites of being in love with an unavailable, oblivious woman? A healthy dose of masochism. "What does that mean?"

She shot him a look that might as well have had the caption "Seriously? Is this what we're doing?" underneath it.

"Almost as tall as you. Size two, or hey, I'll be generous, a three. I'm betting on hazel or green eyes. And I'm not accusing you of colorism, mind you, but I *am* saying she's passing the 'brown paper bag' test. Also, her hair is ruler-straight either by a great keratin treatment or with the best Brazilian weave money can buy. And she's flawless. Like, 'a blemish would be too humiliated to do something as plebian as mar her face' flawless." She arched an eyebrow. "Ring a bell?"

Yes. In other words, the women he dated—he fucked—were anti-Eves.

Tall where Eve was petite. Slender where she was curvy and thick. Light, multihued eyes instead of a chocolate, nearly black shade that he could fall into. Fairer-skinned instead of a smooth mahogany that he hungered to drag his fingers over. Straight hair instead of the explosion of beautiful, dark brown natural curls that framed Eve's fascinating assembly of delicate bone structure and large, bold eyes, nose and mouth.

There was one area she wasn't their opposite—one area those other women couldn't compete at all.

Flawless?

Eve Burke was incomparable.

He bowed his head over hers, adopting a smirk. Pretended he wasn't affected by this fragile dance of innocuous flirtation and friendship. He was a pro, after all.

"I didn't know you paid such close attention to who I…entertained," he teased. "I have a question, though. Why do you care?"

She shrugged. "I don't. But it doesn't bother you to be so...cliché?"

Her criticism was a bee sting he couldn't dig out from under his skin. Because it was her. Because she had no fucking clue.

An unreasonable anger stirred within him, goading him to push, to sting back.

"Bother me?" He leaned farther down until their foreheads nearly brushed, until he could almost taste her champagne-flavored breath. Could feel the hitch of her swift intake of air on his lips. "Why should it? I'm not marrying them, Eve. Surely, you've heard the rumors about me. I know I'm your friend and you might consider yourself to be on the periphery of Boston society, but you're not deaf. You're smart. You read gossip columns." He dropped his voice to a murmur, narrowed his eyes on her mouth and studied the plump, overripe curves, before lifting his gaze to her eyes. "You know what those women use me for just as much as I enjoy being used."

Silence and a tension that damn near hummed sprung up between them. She didn't move, and neither did he. In a sea of people, they were statues, the tides of the crowd flowing around them as they stared at each other.

His words echoed in his head, over and over, the taunting tone growing louder, and an ugly part of him—the part of him that resented her for not *seeing* him, not *wanting* him—rejoiced at the shock that parted her lips, darkened her eyes.

But, God... His cock thickened, hardened behind his tuxedo-pants zipper. Lust and wonder, one a demanding howl, the other an awed whisper, twisted and purred inside him. Clawed and petted. Left him struggling not to reach out and stroke the tender skin beneath those beautiful eyes.

Eyes where desire glinted.

For…him.

Fuck.

Yearning pumped through his veins, piping hot like the strongest coffee, and it shot through him with the same kick of adrenaline.

"Eve…" he murmured.

"Kenan. Eve. I thought I saw you two."

Kenan stiffened at the intrusion of the new but familiar voice that doused him in a frigid wave of reality. Slowly, he stepped back from Eve and turned to face his older brother. Forcing a smile to his face, he pulled Gavin Rhodes into a hug, clapping a hand to his shoulder. He didn't glance back as Gavin greeted Eve—couldn't.

Not when he grappled with the truth and couldn't risk allowing either of them to glimpse the pain tearing into his chest before he managed to conceal it.

Because with Gavin's appearance, he got it.

That desire in Eve's eyes hadn't been for him.

God, how could he be so stupid, so foolish, to forget?

The only thing worse than being secretly in love with his best friend was for his best friend to be in love with another man—his brother.

"Eve, you look beautiful," Gavin said.

"Thank you, Gavin."

Kenan didn't have to peek down at her to catch sight of the pretty blush that undoubtedly painted her graceful cheekbones, or how the fringe of her lashes would sweep down and hide the adoration in her eyes. He'd witnessed her reactions to his brother's presence so many times they were branded in his brain like scar tissue.

He also didn't need to look at his brother to know Gavin would take in the thick curls brushing skin bared by her off-the-shoulder, deep red, mermaid-style dress and only see their father's executive assistant's daughter, and not a sensual, gorgeous woman who stared at him with need in her eyes.

Gavin might be heir apparent to the Rhodes family business—groomed to be even before they'd adopted Kenan—but he was still a "blind as fuck" idiot.

Bitterness, hot and caustic, crawled through Kenan. And he hated himself for it. Especially since he should be used to it by now.

Coming in second in a father's love was an old, sad story. Spare to the heir? So unoriginal.

Yet, it was the reason he couldn't bring himself to reveal the truth about his feelings to Eve. He might be second best in love and in business to his father. But he couldn't bear to be second best with her.

Not with Eve.

"Where are Mom and Dad?" Kenan asked.

"Dad was held up by Darren and Shawn Young. They wanted to talk about a possible new project in Suffolk Downs." Gavin cocked his head to the side. "Just a heads-up. Darren mentioned your name and what it would mean to have you involved. I think Dad intends—" He broke off the rest of the sentence, nodding and smiling over Kenan's shoulder. "Be right back. Duty calls," he grumbled, still wearing what Kenan labeled the "social smile." Gavin clapped Kenan on the shoulder and strode away.

Leaving Kenan with a hollow pit in his gut.

"I heard what he said." Eve stared after him. Hell, did she even realize that she couldn't hide the hunger, the longing in her eyes?

He slid his hands into the front pockets of his pants to hide his fisted fingers. When she turned back to him, tilting her head, yearning still shadowed her gaze, and a lesser, pathetic part of him wanted to pretend that yearning was for him.

Pride insisted he not tumble down that slippery slope.

She tucked her hand into the crook of his elbow, and even though the ever-present tingle of awareness, of need, tripped over his skin, so did the soothing comfort of her touch. That calming essence that was pure…her.

"Don't let that…omen ruin your evening, Kenan. If you decide not to talk business with your father tonight, then that's your choice. And he'll have to respect it."

"Will he?" He shook his head, arching an eyebrow. "You have met Nathan Rhodes, right?"

"A time or two." She waved her glass in front of his face. "I usually reserve this for emergency situations, but if the evening calls for it, I will pull out the 'it went down the wrong windpipe and now it's triggered an asthma attack' shtick. I haven't used it since Christina Nail's wedding reception five years ago, but I'm willing to bite the bullet."

He widened his eyes, issuing a mock gasp. "For me?"

"Page three, paragraph six, clause A, line two of the friendship pact demands I be willing to surrender my pride and lungs to the cause."

They looked at each other, then snickered.

"I'm almost afraid to ask what the two of you are up to," his oldest half brother, Cain, drawled as he stepped up next to them with his fiancée, Devon Cole, on his arm.

"I'm voting for no good." Devon grinned, and with her beautiful green eyes sparkling, she reminded Kenan even more of a lovely mischievous fairy than usual. "It's the only explanation why you appear to be having the most fun of everyone here."

"Behave," Cain admonished, but a smile tugged at the corners of his stern mouth—it was a miracle that most of Boston society still marveled at. Cain Farrell. Smiling. Devon Cole didn't walk on water, but she did perform other feats of wonder.

Kenan shrugged a shoulder. "She's not wrong."

"Who's not wrong?" Achilles Farrell, his other half brother—or "Jan" as Kenan called him just to irritate the bearded giant since he was the middle Farrell son—asked as he approached their group. "If it's Devon, I agree. She's right. If it's Cain, Devon's still right."

Cain shot Achilles a narrowed glare while Devon smiled at Mycah Hill—now Mycah Farrell—his wife. "You've trained him well, I see."

Mycah nodded sagely, then sipped from the glass of water Achilles handed her. Since she was nearly five months pregnant, she couldn't indulge with the rest of them. "It's all about positive reinforcement."

"Sex," Kenan stage-whispered to everyone else. "She's talking about sex."

Laughter erupted in their small group, and the knot of dread that had twisted his stomach at Gavin's announcement about their father loosened. In spite of a rocky beginning, he, Cain and Achilles had grown closer. He trusted these men—thought of them as brothers, not just half, not strangers whom he'd only found months ago.

That heaviness thickened in his chest again, pressing against his sternum as he lifted his head and found Gavin. Even if the price of that closeness with his found family had been the relationship with his adopted family.

"Kenan." Achilles hiked up his chin at him. "A minute?"

"Sure." He squeezed Eve's hand, which was resting on his elbow, then shifted to the side with his brother.

Cain nodded, indicating he would watch over Eve, and another wave of wonder uncurled inside him that now he and his brothers had evolved to unspoken communication. Shaking his head, he followed Achilles, who only moved several feet away, far enough that they could talk privately but close enough that he could keep an eye on his pregnant wife.

Kenan didn't bother stifling his snort. Just a couple

of months ago, Achilles had been one of the most emotionally shut down men Kenan had ever met. Breaching a heavily guarded medieval citadel would've been easier than getting through to him. But Mycah had accomplished it. And she'd given Cain and Kenan all of their brother.

"I have some news for you," Achilles said, lifting a dark brown beer bottle to his mouth.

"Seriously?" Kenan snapped, jabbing at the beer. "Where'd you get that?"

Achilles smirked. "Jealous?"

"Hell yes."

"This—" Achilles pointed at the bottle "—is a perk of being one of the common folk attending these pretentious events. You bond with the other common folk at the bar and they hook you up." His grin flashed in his thick beard. "For once, being the Feral Farrell has its benefits."

Kenan clenched his jaw, trapping the curse threatening to escape at that fucking nickname so-called polite society had given Achilles.

"I'm kidding, Kenan." Achilles nudged him with his elbow, the blue-gray eyes that identified him, Cain and Kenan as Farrell offspring soft with understanding. "You know that shit doesn't bother me anymore. Let it go. I have."

"Yeah." Kenan rubbed a hand down his clean-shaven jaw. And he'd try. Seeing his brother so happy would help, but he still resented the hurt the people in the world Kenan lived in had caused. "So what's going on? What did you need to talk to me about?"

"It's about the search for your biological mother. You're still certain you want me to work on that, right?"

Kenan drew in a breath, held it. His pulse echoed in his head like the steady pounding of fists against a heavy bag, fierce and powerful. It vibrated through him, and when he released his breath, it trembled.

"Yes."

The answer resounded against his skull, shaking as well, but sure.

He needed to know where he'd come from, who he was. Because his brothers had been raised with their natural mothers, they possessed that very basic, vital information, but Kenan was missing that part of himself. His adoption had been closed, and regardless of his desire to know, all his life, Kenan's parents had been stubborn about keeping it that way.

But Baron's will had toppled that mandate. At least as far as his biological father. Yet, Nathan and Dana Rhodes had remained firm regarding his birth mother.

So Kenan had turned to his brother. His brother who was something of a genius when it came to computers and research.

Guilt slicked through him, as it always did whenever he considered how he'd violated his parents' wishes regarding his birth mother. Since he'd been old enough to understand the concept of adoption, he'd weighed his complicated, tangled feelings of betraying his love for Dana against his desire to know about the faceless woman who'd given birth to him.

He'd tried to bury this insatiable hunger to unearth his identity. God, he'd tried. Out of loyalty to his parents. Out of self-protection for himself. Even for the woman who'd given him up. But with the introduction of his brothers into his life...

Yeah, he had to know.

"Once you open this Pandora's box, Kenan..." Achilles studied him. Maybe this man, who saw way more than others because he spoke so much less, recognized Kenan's resolve, because he nodded. His mouth firmed.

"Okay. But have you at least tried to talk to your parents about this again?"

Kenan shook his head before Achilles even finished speaking. "There's no point. They've been adamant about my biological mother not wanting to be identified or found. And they're determined to respect that. Besides they feel, rightly, that they are my parents, not the woman who abandoned me—"

"She placed you for adoption. Sacrificed to give you a better life. She did not abandon you," Achilles interrupted on a growl.

"I agree." Kenan paused, waging that aging, dusty battle of loyalty versus knowledge. "But there's no point in getting into it with them. Especially when there's nothing to tell. There *is* nothing to tell, right?" Kenan asked.

"A little more than nothing. I just needed to make sure this is what you want before I shared because there's no going back once we start." Achilles sighed. "I'm pretty sure I located the lawyer who facilitated the adoption for Baron. You already know from Baron's PI that he was aware of you and me all along and did nothing to claim us until it suited him. So your mother was free to give you up without any interference from him. And I think I found the attorney who handled that process with your parents and your biological mom. I'll do some more digging and keep you updated."

Relief, excitement and—God, he couldn't lie, not to himself—fear barreled through him, and he closed his eyes against the power of it. A big hand cupped his shoulder, the strength of it bracing him, and he leaned into it.

"It's okay," Achilles murmured. "We got you. Whatever we find."

Kenan nodded. Couldn't say anything else.

"Let's get back. Eve keeps glancing at us, and I think she's about to plan an intervention if I keep you over here any longer." Achilles squeezed his shoulder, and Kenan glanced at his brother, who cocked his head, his narrowed scrutiny almost uncomfortable. "Just out of curiosity… You plan on ever telling her you're in love with her?"

"What the hell?" Kenan's head jerked back so fast, a twinge echoed in protest at the back of his neck.

Achilles shrugged a large shoulder. "Just asking."

"You…" Kenan shook his head. Tucked his trembling hands into his tuxedo pockets. "I don't know what you're talking about."

Achilles stared at him for a long, silent, even more un-comfortable moment. Then said, "Ah." He rubbed a hand down his beard. "Sorry. I'm a people watcher."

"Damn." Kenan briefly closed his eyes. When he opened them and met his brother's sympathetic gaze, he fought not to wince. "Please don't look at me like I'm dying of an incurable disease."

"Since I was in love with a woman and didn't be-lieve she returned those feelings just months ago, I can't help it."

In spite of the pain and humiliation punching a hole in his chest, Kenan chuckled. "That's fair." He hesitated. "Am I that obvious?"

"No." Achilles held up his hands, palms out, when Kenan tossed him an incredulous look. "I'm not lying to you. Like I said, I've spent a lifetime watching people and I was right where you are. Which is why I can ask, why not put yourself out of this particular hell? You two are best friends and from what I can see damn perfect for each other. Why not just tell her?"

A humorless smile twisted Kenan's mouth. Spoken like a man who'd found his happily-ever-after and wanted the same for everyone else. On the other side, it seemed so simple. When it was so far from it.

"Because she's in love with my brother."

"Well, fuck."

A bark of laughter slipped free at Achilles's blank, wide-eyed expression of horror. Followed by another laugh. Achilles blinked, then after a second, a chuckle rumbled out of him.

"That's screwed up."

"It is what it is." Kenan sighed, his humor disappearing as quickly as it had arrived. "Thanks, Achilles. For…"

"You're welcome."

With a dip of his chin, Kenan turned and the two of them headed back to their small group. When they reached them, Eve immediately stepped close to him, her gaze searching his. And he reached for and found the familiar mask he'd donned since he'd been a teen and realized the girl he'd called friend for most of his life had become so much more. He *wanted* so much more. He wanted *her*.

She brushed her fingers over the back of his hand. "Everything okay?"

"Fine. Just a couple of work things he wanted to go over with me." The lie rolled off his tongue. Because that was another thing he'd become proficient at over the years with her—lying. Every day he made the decision to conceal the truth, so it'd become second nature.

"Kenan," Cain said, his voice threaded with warning. "Incoming."

He hadn't needed that heads-up. Not with Eve's hand wrapping around his and squeezing. Not with the snarl of love, unease and frustration tightening inside him until he couldn't breathe past it.

Just as he'd done with Eve, he donned another mask; that was his life, after all. One for the charismatic playboy that charmed Boston society. One for the serious businessman that worked with his industry associates.

Another for the wise-cracking, carefree younger brother of Cain and Achilles.

And one for the adopted son trying to prove himself worthy of being chosen by his parents.

That last mask had so many cracks and fissures from his many failures, sheer will and hope were the duct tape keeping it from falling apart.

"Mom. Dad." Kenan moved forward, greeting Nathan and Dana Rhodes as they approached. Pride and love swelled within him, temporarily eclipsing the tendrils of dread weaving through him.

Handsome and distinguished, Nathan Rhodes cut an imposing figure through the crowd. In a ballroom full of multibillionaires, he might not be the wealthiest, as a mere multimillionaire, but he was definitely one of the most respected. He helmed one of the oldest, most successful real-estate-development companies in the state, and Rhodes Realty Inc. enjoyed a solid national reputation. Kenan's mother, beautiful and elegant, might be one of Boston society's ruling matrons, but she also sat on the family company's board and helped run it.

Google "power couple" and his parents didn't populate just one definition, but the top three.

"Kenan." His mother extended her hands toward him, gripping his, and drew him forward to brush kisses over his cheeks. "You look handsome. But then, you are my son."

He grinned and kissed her cheek. "Of course. I get it from my mother." He turned to his father, offering him his hand. Nathan grasped it. "Dad."

"Son. I thought you were coming by the house for dinner before the gala. We missed you." Guilt speared Kenan as his father's gaze flicked over his shoulder to Cain, Achilles and their women. Nathan's eyes chilled, then returned to Kenan. "You were probably too busy."

The guilt crystallized into diamond-bright anger—hard, faceted and gleaming. His aversion to returning home had everything to do with Nathan, and Kenan's choosing not to deal with another of his father's lectures about loyalty and family. He was a grown man, yet minutes in Nathan's company could render him a boy seeking his father's unattainable approval.

That was all on Kenan and had nothing to do with the men standing behind him.

But neither his father nor his mother would hear him on that—they wouldn't listen to him on anything having to do with Baron Farrell or his brothers. His leaving Rhodes Realty was nothing less than a defection in their eyes, an unforgivable betrayal, and the only absolution he could receive would be if he returned to the family business.

Didn't matter if his chances of advancement in his own family's company were hobbled by the mere circumstances of his birth.

Didn't matter that every contribution he made was either dissected and discarded, or grudgingly accepted then credited to another.

Didn't matter that his creativity smothered and died a slow, painful death.

All they saw was his perceived abandonment.

"Not at all," Kenan said, the same ice in his father's gaze filtering into his tone. "I just didn't have time to stop in. Which is why I promised to try instead of saying I would." He smiled, and probably shouldn't have bothered if it appeared as forced as it felt. "Of course, you two know Eve."

"Nice to see you again, Mr. and Mrs. Rhodes," Eve murmured.

"You, too, Eve." Nathan nodded.

"Eve. You look beautiful." Dana's eyes narrowed

slightly. "Your mother didn't mention you were attending the gala tonight when I saw her at the office earlier."

Eve's lips twisted into a small rueful smile as she shot Kenan a sidelong glance. "It was a bit of a last-minute invite."

"Ah. I see."

Kenan waved an arm toward his brothers. "And you've met my brothers, Cain and Achilles. I'd like to introduce you to Cain's fiancée, Devon Cole, and Achilles's wife, Mycah Farrell."

Dana nodded, all warmth leeching from her expression, leaving her beautiful features cold, hard. His father didn't bother with even that small acknowledgment, and just demanded, "Can I speak to my son alone, please?"

Humiliation and fury lodged in his chest. "Dad—"

"We'll see you inside for the auction." Cain cupped his shoulder, squeezed. But the reassuring message did little to cool Kenan's temper, to assuage the pain. His brother meant to relay that they were fine, but nothing about this shit was fucking *fine*. "Sir. Mrs. Rhodes."

You don't have to go. Don't leave. Stay.

The demands, the pleas, crowded into the back of Kenan's throat. He detested how vulnerable they sounded, even in his own head. Hated more that he dreaded the thought of being alone with the two people who'd raised him.

"Kenan." Eve tugged on his hand until he tore his gaze from his father and lowered it to her. "You don't dance," she murmured. "Remember that."

Delivering the reminder of their previous conversation, she left with his brothers. Left him.

"It's not enough that you walked out on your family business to join the company of a man who did nothing for you but donate sperm. It's not enough that you've made it clear to us that you prefer those...men you dare call brothers by not even attending dinner. But now, you're announcing that preferential treatment by publicly aligning with them over the family that took you in, raised you, when that bastard and his son wouldn't even acknowledge you until it benefited them."

"Careful, Dad," Kenan warned, stepping close to his father. *He's speaking out of anger, out of hurt.* He repeated the words to himself, but the unfairness of his father's accusations pummeled him, leaving emotional bruises that wouldn't heal as quickly as physical wounds would. "You sound very close to blaming the son for the sins of the father. And since we both know Cain is as much of a victim of Baron's manipulations as me, I can't imagine that's what you meant."

"Kenan, don't twist your father's words," his mother snapped.

"I'm not," he said, not removing his gaze from Nathan's. "I'm just clarifying. Just as I'm sure he didn't intend to imply that I've chosen anyone over my family. Unless that is what you meant, Dad."

"What's going on over here?" Gavin appeared at Nathan's elbow, his gaze shifting from their father to Kenan.

Concern darkened Gavin's brown eyes, and guilt seeped inside Kenan like water creeping through a crack. Guilt because even as Kenan loved his brother, he resented Gavin because the only woman Kenan ever wanted could only see him.

"Ask your brother. And while you're at it, ask him to define *loyalty*. From his company tonight, I think he might have forgotten that his last name is Rhodes. Maybe he wants it to be Farrell."

Pain barreled into him. Staring at his father and mother with their almond skin and dark eyes, and his brother, who was a perfect combination of their features, he'd never felt like more of an outsider. They stood, shoulder-to-shoulder, an unconscious united front against him. The adopted son with the blue-gray eyes that proclaimed him different. Announced that he wasn't...theirs.

That he didn't belong.

"Nathan," his mother said, laying a hand on her husband's arm, "please." She shot Kenan a pleading look.

"Can we not do this here?" Gavin demanded, voice low, urgent. "People are staring and talking. That's not good for us as a family, and it's not good for business. Let's table this until later. Kenan." He lifted a hand toward him. "Are you joining us for the auction?"

Kenan stepped back. "I'll see you in there," he said, not committing to it. "I'm going to refill my champagne." He held up his half-full glass, then turned and strode away before they could call him back.

He headed in the opposite direction of the room that held the charity auction. The tall double doors that led to the exit beckoned him, and he answered, shoving through to the quieter hall. Several guests milled about, but he easily skirted them to escape...

Escape.

Fuck, how he hated that word.

Didn't change what he was doing, though.

The corridor ended, and he stood in front of another set of towering doors. He briefly hesitated, then grasped the handle, opened them and slipped through to the balcony beyond. The cool April night air washed over him. The calendar proclaimed spring had arrived, but winter hadn't yet released its grasp over Boston, especially at night. But he welcomed the chilled breeze over his face, let it seep beneath the confines of his tuxedo to the hot skin below. Hoped it could cool the embers of his temper...the still burning coals of his hurt.

"For someone who is known as the playboy of Boston society, you sure will ditch a party in a hot second."

Slim arms slid around him, and he closed his eyes in pain and pleasure at the petite, softly curved body pressed to his back. "All I had to do was follow the trail of longing glances from the women in the hall to figure out where you'd gone."

He snorted. "Do you lie to your mama with that mouth? There was hardly anyone out there."

"Fine," she huffed. "So I didn't go with the others and watched all of that go down with your parents and brother. I waited until you left the ballroom and went after you."

"Why?" he rasped.

He felt rather than witnessed her shrug. The same with the small kiss she pressed to the middle of his shoulder blades. He locked his muscles, forcing his head not to fall back. Ordering his throat to imprison the moan scrabbling up from his chest. Commanding his dick to stand down.

"Because you needed me," she said.

So simple. So goddamn true.

He did need her. Her friendship. Her body.

Her heart.

But since he could only have one of those, he'd take it. With a woman like her—generous, sweet, beautiful of body and spirit—even a part of her was preferable to none of her. And if he dared to profess his true feelings, that's exactly what he would be left with. None of her. Their friendship would be ruined, and she was too important to him to risk losing her.

Carefully, he turned and wrapped her in his embrace, shielding her from the night air. Convincing himself if this was all he could have of her—even if it meant Gavin or another man might have all of her—then he would be okay, he murmured, "You're really going to have to remove 'rescue best friend' off your résumé. For one, it's beginning to get too time-consuming. And two, the cape clashes with your gown."

She chuckled against his chest, tipping her head back to smile up at him. He curled his fingers against her spine, but that didn't prevent the ache to trace that sensual bottom curve.

"Where would be the fun in that? You're stuck with me, Kenan. And I'm stuck with you. Friends forever."

Friends.

The sweet sting of that knife buried between his ribs.

"Always, sweetheart."

Two

Eve smiled at the security guard as he handed her a visitor's badge in the lobby of the downtown Boston office building where Rhodes Realty occupied the fifteenth floor. She had been coming here to see her mother for so long—twenty-three years—that this place seemed like a second home, and she probably should have her own employee badge by now.

"Thanks, Mr. Leonard. Make sure you tell your wife I asked about her," she said, waving to the older man as she headed toward the bank of elevators.

"I certainly will. Take care of yourself, Ms. Eve, and have a good afternoon."

After flashing him another smile over her shoulder, she pushed the call button and, once the elevator arrived, stepped on and let it carry her to the offices of Rhodes Realty. Seconds later, she exited, and even so late on a Monday afternoon, the familiar sounds of the clatter of fingers on keyboards and the hum of conversation amid the ringing of telephones greeted her. Yet, as comforting as the soundtrack of this work environment might be, it'd never tempted her to join its ranks. No, her dream had led her in a different direction, and now she taught ninth-grade history in the Boston public-school system.

But in the last three years, that dream—her vision of her future—had changed.

Not that she could admit it to anyone.

Well, anyone other than herself and Kenan.

Always Kenan.

She couldn't contain the smile that tipped the corners of her mouth. The reaction came naturally whenever thoughts of her best friend entered her mind. This very floor had been the scene of the crime, where their friendship had started. At seven, he'd been visiting his father, her mother's new boss. And at six, she'd been stashed in the employee break room by her mother, his father's new executive assistant, because she'd been unable to find a babysitter for Eve after school. Kenan had sneaked out of his father's office and into the breakroom, sneered at her Powerpuff Girls T-shirt, then offered her half his candy bar. The rest was history.

Her mother hadn't been thrilled about her friendship with her boss's son then, and nothing had changed in two decades—Yolanda Burke still disapproved. Her mother might have encouraged Eve to pursue her education, to never allow anyone to dictate her worth or her identity— she'd pushed Eve to achieve her goals and to go further than she'd been able to in her own life—but Yolanda still possessed some of her old-school beliefs. One of those was that a line existed between employer and employee, and one did not cross it. And that included the children of said employer and employee. The two worlds didn't mix.

That Eve refused to adhere to her hard-and-fast rule remained a sore point between them.

But today wasn't the day to dwell on that old argument. Not when she had great news to share.

Making her way through the labyrinthine maze of cubicles, she approached the separate set of doors that led to the executive offices. Pressing the button on the intercom, she announced herself and waited to be buzzed in. Moments later, she strode through the quieter, more expensively appointed suite. Several closed doors bore the gold plates and names of the presidents, vice presidents and senior officers of the company, including Nathan, Dana and Gavin Rhodes.

Her belly dropped, then rolled as if a fire alarm had been tripped.

Gavin.

Just the whisper of his name through her head and she reverted to being that high-school girl who'd begged Kenan to use his extra football tickets so she could watch Gavin play.

Just a glimpse of the man who could be the younger doppelgänger of actor Morris Chestnut, and the heat that danced and flickered inside her had nothing to do with girlhood and everything to do with what the woman she was wanted from him.

His touch. His love.

Hell, just his notice as someone other than his younger brother's best friend.

She sighed. Yep, she'd put that aside for now, too.

The plush, pale blue carpet silenced the fall of her heels as she approached the long circular desk that guarded Nathan Rhodes's inner sanctum. And behind the intimidating piece of furniture sat Yolanda Burke.

Love swelled in her chest at the familiar sight of her mother. And underneath, like shadows of lurking predators, swam murkier feelings. Frustration, fear. Feelings she shied away from. Feelings she hated admitted possessing.

"Hey, Mom," she greeted.

Her mother looked up from her computer monitor, smiling. And Eve stared at herself in another twenty-three years. Petite and rounded, dark brown skin, straight hair instead of natural, brown and sprinkled with gray. Eve hoped to look as youthful in her early fifties.

"Eve. When they called from downstairs to let me know you were on your way up, it was a surprise. A lovely one, though."

"I have news I wanted to give you in person. Can you take a small break?"

Yolanda glanced at her screen. "I suppose so." She pressed a couple of buttons, then rose from her chair. "I need to refill my coffee, anyway."

Eve wrinkled her nose. "Mom, really? It's four o'clock in the afternoon."

"And I still have two more hours of work to go. At least." She arched an eyebrow. "Are you forgetting I've seen you working on lesson plans at eight o'clock at night? With a travel mug of coffee when the only place you were traveling was to the kitchen table."

"All right, woman, point made," Eve grumbled, but she grinned.

"That's what I thought."

Yolanda led the way to the employee break room, and though the furniture and appliances had been updated— a one-cup coffee maker instead of the pot, a high-end refrigerator with French doors—it still remained the same room she and Kenan had spent many hours in.

"So what's this news?" her mother asked, jumping right to the point as she dropped a pod into the coffee maker.

"Well…" Eve paused dramatically, and when her

mother glanced at her over her shoulder, she grinned. "I was named teacher of the year."

"Honey." Yolanda whipped around, beaming, her brown eyes glittering. Pride. Yes, pride shone there. She crossed the small space separating them and pulled Eve into a tight embrace. "Eve, that's wonderful. Congratulations. I'm so proud of you."

Closing her eyes, Eve returned the hug, inhaling her mother's no-nonsense, light-gardenia soap fragrance. The scent of her childhood. Pulling free to cup her mother's elbows, she smiled at Yolanda.

"Thank you. I'm thrilled and honored."

"You should be." Her mother squeezed her arms. "It says what your peers and administrators think about you as a teacher and person. It also shows that hard work is acknowledged. You deserve this award, Eve."

"Thanks, Mom."

That's not my only news. Not the only honor I've received.

The words loitered on her tongue as her mother patted her shoulder and returned to her coffee cup. But as much as she longed to say them, she couldn't. Couldn't tell her mother that she'd won the Small Business Award from the National Association of Women Entrepreneurs.

Because that would mean Eve would have to reveal to Yolanda that she owned a small business.

Eve smothered a sigh, guilt over her deception warring with sadness and anger for the necessity of her deceit. No, she thought, and shook her head. She could try to justify it all she wanted, but a lie was a lie. It all came down to her not having the courage to own up to the truth.

Most mothers would be delighted to discover their daughters weren't just business owners, but were wildly successful ones. But conservative Yolanda Burke, elder in her church and firm believer in all the tenets of her strict

Baptist upbringing, would never support Eve being the owner and designer of Intimate Curves, an online lingerie boutique catering to plus-size women.

Not happening.

"Do you have any plans to celebrate?" her mother asked over the hiss of brewing coffee.

"Kenan offered to take me out to dinner this weekend, but that's it."

Yolanda turned once more to look at her, her dark gaze steady, sharp.

Eve just managed not to roll her eyes. She might be twenty-nine, but she wasn't crazy. "Mom. Don't."

"You're twenty-nine, Eve," she said, pretty much plucking the words from Eve's head. "You should have a boyfriend to take you out to dinner and celebrate this kind of occasion, not a—" her mouth twisted "—best friend."

"Well, I don't. And he is."

"Mr. Rhodes mentioned seeing you at the charity gala he attended with his family this weekend."

It pierced something inside Eve that even after twenty-three years of working for Nathan Rhodes, her mother still called him by his surname. Knowing Yolanda, she probably insisted on it. But still, after so long, shouldn't Nathan have demanded even more strongly that she not be so formal? They'd been together longer than some marriages, for God's sake.

Eve shook her head.

"Kenan asked me to go with him at the last minute, and I did." Eve crossed her arms over her chest, and immediately regretted the gesture. She had nothing to be defensive about. "It really wasn't worth mentioning."

"Apparently Mr. Rhodes doesn't agree." She turned around and reached for her mug, then lifted it to her mouth for a sip. "Eve, I've said it before, and regardless that you don't want to hear it, I'm going to say it again—

this friendship with Kenan Rhodes isn't healthy for either one of you. He should've taken a woman he's dating or interested in dating, not you. And you should be out there looking for a man who can be a partner to you. Instead, you two are in each other's back pockets, and therefore in each other's way. I'm not the only one concerned about it. So are his parents."

What exactly did Nathan and Dana object to? That their youngest son still continued to dominate gossip columns and tabloids as Boston's most eligible bachelor and flagrant playboy, and he refused to settle down? Or that his best friend happened to be the daughter of his secretary?

How would they react if they discovered she was in love with their oldest son?

Her mother would take her name to prayer intercession then proceed to lecture her on boundaries and learning her place. There were separate worlds that coexisted— one inhabited by people like the Rhodeses and Farrells, and one for everyone else. They might work together, but they didn't mix socially, financially, geographically and definitely not romantically. Those were immutable laws, according to Yolanda Burke.

"What would you advise, Mom?" Eve quietly asked. "Cut Kenan from my life? Even when he eventually finds the woman he wants to marry, and I have a family, we'll still be friends and in each other's lives."

A curious twist wrenched her chest, and she tightened her arms. The thought of not seeing Kenan, of not confiding in him, hearing that low, wicked chuckle, or just sitting with him and letting that comforting scent of sandalwood and citrus wrap her in its familiar embrace… A dark longing yawned wide inside her, and it ached. It ached so deep she swallowed a gasp against the phantom pain.

But even more curious was the odd jerk in her belly as she mentioned Kenan falling in love and marrying another woman... Another woman who got to brush her fingertips across the sprinkle of cinnamon freckles scattered across the bridge of his nose and the high blades of his cheekbones. Another woman who was allowed to see the devilish humor light the startling beauty of his blue-gray eyes. Another woman who could curl up against that tall, lean, powerful body...

A murky swirl of emotion curdled in her belly and she scrambled away as it bubbled and hissed rather than analyze it. Heart pounding and mouth suddenly dry, she dropped her arms to her sides, mentally and physically turning away from—from herself. She strode to the window that looked over the street below, teeming with late-afternoon traffic.

"Look, Mom. I came over to share my good news with you, and to see if you had plans tonight. I wanted to treat you to dinner to celebrate, not rehash this old argument."

"Eve." Her mother's heavy sigh fell on her shoulders like a concrete shawl. One Eve had worn for so long that she barely felt its weight any longer. "I just want the best for you. And not just with your career. But for you, personally. I don't want you to be lonely."

The "like me" wasn't spoken, but it might as well as have been shouted because it echoed in the break room.

Yolanda had sacrificed so much as a single mother, had ensured that Eve remained on a path that included a stellar education, top grades and college, even steering her daughter away from her frivolous interest in art and fashion. Her mother had insisted Eve concentrate on acquiring a degree in a field where she would graduate from college and obtain a reliable, respectable job so Eve could provide for herself. So if anything happened—such as her becoming unexpectedly pregnant or a man abandoning her—she could easily take care of herself and anyone else who came along.

Her mother could've had relationships—Eve had witnessed men flirting with her—but Yolanda had remained single, focusing on work and her daughter by choice. And now, with Eve out of her home and on her own with not just one career but two—one Yolanda would consider above reproach and the other not so much—her mother was alone. And that saddened Eve. Because a woman who'd given so much deserved even more in return.

"I'm not lonely, Mom." Eve went to her mother and hugged her. "And because I don't bring anyone around you doesn't mean I don't date. Maybe they're not worthy to meet you yet. Ever think about that?"

Yolanda snorted. "Just how many of them are you seeing?"

"Tons," Eve drawled...and lied.

Because the only man she wanted didn't seem to notice she'd grown up past the age of fifteen.

"I'm praying for you."

Eve laughed, squeezing her mother's shoulders and planting a smacking kiss on her cheek.

"Abe and Louie's?"

Her mother nodded, stepping out from under her arm and lifting her coffee mug to her mouth for a sip. "You got it. Seven?"

"I'll meet you there and grab a table." She paused. "Love you, Mom."

"I love you, too, honey."

As her mother left the break room, Eve stared after her. And after watching the glass door close, she whispered, "I wish you could be proud of all of me."

Three

Cain tapped the screen on his tablet, then looked up at Kenan and Achilles, who were sitting across from him on the leather armchairs in his office's sitting area.

"That's the agenda for the board meeting next week. If there aren't any changes, I'll have Charlene finalize it and email it to everyone," Cain said, referring to his long-time executive assistant.

"Looks fine to me."

Kenan didn't have to glance at Achilles, who was older than him by a mere seven months, to see him shrug one of his massive shoulders. He didn't care much for board meetings, or meetings of any kind, for that matter. More often than not his head was buried in one of his computer programs or consumed with managing the tech company Farrell International had recently acquired to design video games geared toward at-risk youth.

"I don't think I have to remind you two that we're at

six months of our—" Cain huffed out a wry chuckle "—agreement."

No, he didn't need to issue that reminder. Not to Kenan, at least.

In those six months, Cain had stepped up as the heir and successfully helmed Farrell International. He'd shown the board that although Barron had created chaos with his stunning revelation of his sons and the unorthodox stipulation in his will, he was a force of strength and stability. And Achilles, the son everyone had expected to have the most trouble acclimating to Boston and this cutthroat world of business, had discovered his niche and excelled in it.

No, it was Kenan, born into this elite world of wealth and high society, who hadn't made his mark. Who hadn't done anything of note yet. And it grated, because hadn't this been why he'd left his family's business? To not just bond with his newly discovered brothers, but to prove that he belonged here, that he could be an asset to this company, this legacy?

That he was worthy.

"I also don't think I have to tell you that our 'anniversary' will be on the minds of everyone in that meeting," Cain continued. "They'll be looking for any chink in our armor. For any hole in our solidarity."

"They can look all they want." Achilles crossed his arms over his chest. "They won't find dick."

"Ah. And they wonder who the poet is among us." Kenan sighed, sprawling his legs out in front of him and linking his fingers over his stomach. "Are you worried, Cain? As eloquently as Achilles puts it, I have to agree."

"I'm not worried. I just..." He spread his hands wide, palms up. "Six months ago in that library, if you had told me the three of us would be here, I would've told you to stop hitting the bottle. I would've never thought..." He broke off, shaking his head. "And I damn sure know no one else believes this was possible. So I want to make sure we're all good. Consider this a check-in. Achilles?"

Achilles jerked his chin in the universal sign of "fine." When Cain arched an eyebrow in Kenan's direction, he nodded. Even as he swallowed back the urge to confess that no, he wasn't good. That he battled guilt daily for not pulling his weight in the company. For failing them.

For failing himself.

But in the end, he did what he always did. Wore another mask and said nothing.

"Good." Cain leaned back against couch. "All right, if you see any problems with the agenda, just email me, and I'll let—"

"Wait." Kenan scrolled down the screen on the tablet, his fingertip hovering over a line near the bottom of the agenda. "This item right here under 'new business.' Is this right? We're going to discuss selling Bromberg's?"

"Yes, we are."

Kenan slowly straightened in his chair, shock sliding through him like a droplet of freezing ice down his spine. "You're kidding me. They're one of the oldest, most established and well-known national department-store chains."

"And for the last three years, they've been falling in profits. It's becoming more of a financial albatross than lucrative. We have to at least discuss it. And it's likely that the board will vote to sell it."

Kenan blindly stared at the tablet, his mind shuffling through his memories and landing on the countless shopping trips to the downtown store with his mother as a kid. And then later with Eve, when they both went for prom—her for a dress and him for a tuxedo. The place claimed a special place in his memory. And the thought of it being sold and possibly disappearing under the umbrella of another company…

Excitement flickered in his chest, dancing, whirling, until it gleamed brighter. What if…? What if he could do something to save Bromberg's? This could be that opportunity he needed to prove he belonged here. That he wasn't just charming window dressing, but he brought something to the table. And he could do it by turning around a failing business. That it happened to be a business he cared about was just icing on a very profitable cake. And he could accomplish it all by doing what he did best—marketing, promotion, persuading people they wanted what he was selling.

An idea sparked like a struck match in his head, then caught flame. And it required every bit of self-control he possessed not to jump from his chair and stride out of his brother's office to get started. His heart thudded against his rib cage, pumping adrenaline in his blood like a drug.

Gripping the tablet as if it was the only thing keeping him tethered to the ground, he lifted his head and met Cain's gaze. "I have a favor to ask." When his brother dipped his chin, he said, "Could you remove the item about Bromberg's from the agenda? Just for this board meeting?"

Cain frowned. "Kenan—"

Kenan held up a hand. "I know it's a big ask, and I know it's business. But I would like time to present a proposal to revitalize the chain and turn around profits to prevent the sale. If you don't approve it, fine. But if you do, then it's possibly an opportunity to save an iconic chain and earn a profit, as well."

Several long moments passed, and Kenan held his breath as Cain studied him, his fingers steepled under his chin.

"Okay," his older brother finally murmured. "I'll have Charlene remove it from the agenda. I'm looking forward to seeing what you propose."

Four

Kenan parked his black Lexus at the curb outside the brick building in Cambridge. As he switched off the ignition, he glanced at his watch. Five thirty. Eve should be home by now, and he'd called her ahead of time to make sure. Anticipation foamed inside him like a freshly poured beer, and only part of it had to do with the idea he had to present her.

Jesus.

He pinched the bridge of his nose. Dogs eager to greet their owners had more decorum than him. Just the sight of Eve's quiet, residential street, which wasn't far from both Inman Square and Union Square, had excitement humming through him, and God, how pathetic did that make him? Yeah, he refused to answer that.

Cursing under his breath, he pushed open his car door and stepped out. He'd had so much practice at this scene, at assuming this role of platonic best friend, he slipped in and out with the blink of an eye. But by no means was it effortless. With each passing day, month, year, it required more and more...effort.

But he did it. Because losing Eve wasn't an option.

He didn't need to sit on anyone's couch to figure out his own issues and why he clung to her presence in his life. His parents had chosen him, and yet, especially with his father, he'd never felt accepted, loved without strings, without that ever-present "but."

Yes, you're a Rhodes, but not by blood.

It'd never been a secret in their household that Nathan preferred Gavin, his firstborn, natural son, the son with his DNA. Sometimes, Kenan wondered if his father regretted the adoption...or had even wanted it at all. He'd had no control in choosing his family.

But with Eve... He'd chosen her.

And she'd chosen him right back.

That had sealed both of their fates.

And, yeah, he bet his hypothetical therapist would have a field day with that.

Shaking his head, he headed up the walk to the first floor and knocked. Sliding his hands into his pockets, he impatiently waited the several moments it took for Eve to answer the door. When it opened, he braced himself. Why, he had no idea. Just pointless. Because after all these years, he hadn't managed to prepare himself for the impact of her *yet*.

And that smile.

Christ.

It lit up her face, lifting her full cheeks, and in turn, it lit up his chest. He glanced away, that smile threatening to burn down his facade as if it was a planet drawing close to the sun.

"Hey." She stepped aside, waving him in. "Come on in. You sounded so mysterious on the phone, and now I'm supercurious. Which was probably your goal."

It had been.

He entered, closing the door behind him. And as always, a sense of peace and comfort surrounded him, seeped into his skin, his bones. With the high ceilings, gleaming hardwood floors and wealth of windows throughout the wide, airy rooms, and decorated in Eve's eclectic blend of Bohemian chic meets rustic country meets thrift-store classy, her home was a haven.

He moved into the living room, taking in the nest of colorful blankets on the couch and her laptop on the coffee table next to her usual wind-down cup of peppermint tea. It was Thursday, which meant she was either working on lesson plans or updating her website with sales, new designs or any additional products she sold online at Intimate Curves, such as musk, lotions and jewelry from local merchants and artists.

She could've hired someone to maintain her website, but Eve had a bit of a problem with control. As in, she wanted all of it. Hell, it'd been a battle to convince her she needed a clothing manufacturer instead of continuing to sew her lingerie by hand. She'd argued for the personal touch; he'd countered with the creative freedom to produce more inventory. She'd said it'd be more risk; he'd come back with it meaning a bigger brand and more money.

Eventually, he'd won, and Intimate Curves, which had already been successful, had exploded. But it'd meant her loosening the reins of her control and placing that element of her business into someone else's hands. If Eve wanted, she could leave her job at the school and focus fully on the company, but she wasn't ready for that step.

Yet.

Hopefully, what he was prepared to propose would push her in that direction.

"Can you sit down? I have something I want to talk

over with you." He lowered to the chair adjacent to the couch as she settled back on the couch, her gaze on him.

A small frown wrinkled her forehead as she curled a leg under her. He resolutely kept his attention on her face and not the obvious sway of her unbound breasts under her thin, dark blue hoodie, or the sexy thickness of her toned thighs revealed by the pair of faded pink-and-blue sleep shorts. Not for the first time, he wondered if she kept pieces of her inventory for herself. Imagined how those strips of lace and silk cupped her curves...molded to soft, vulnerable places he'd sacrifice every cent, every account and his damn reputation to touch, to taste, to goddamn drown in.

God. He ground his teeth together, silently and deeply inhaling through his slightly parted lips in an attempt to quell the lust wringing him tight. This might be a new low. He was fucking jealous that scraps of material enjoyed a pleasure, an honor, that he was denied.

"What's going on?" she asked, dragging his thoughts back from a place he had no business going...especially in front of her.

"Eve," he began, leaning forward and propping his forearms on his thighs, "I need you to hear me out completely before you reply or make any decision. Promise me, okay?"

Her frown deepened, but she nodded. "Okay."

He paused, let the excitement and nerves roll through him. One shot, and he needed to get this right. Eve was the linchpin of this proposal. If she said no... If he couldn't convince her, then the rest of his plan wouldn't work—

"Kenan."

He jerked up his head, not realizing until this moment that he been blindly studying her hardwood floor.

Head tilted and eyes narrowed, she studied him. "It's just me," she said softly. "Talk to me."

"Right." He exhaled. "I had a meeting with Cain and Achilles today, and we discussed the potential of selling Bromberg's department store."

"Seriously?" She shook her head, leaning back against the couch. "That place is an institution." Her gaze went over his shoulder, seeming to go unfocused. "Remember when we went shopping there for prom?" She laughed softly. "You found your tux in thirty minutes but stayed with me the two hours it took for me to pick a dress."

"I remember," he murmured. "And you're right. It is an institution. It has history, not just here in Boston but across the nation. We're losing established businesses left and right—ones that mean something to our communities—and if I can do my part to save this one, I want to try. Cain has agreed to give me the time to come up with a proposal to present to the board."

"That's wonderful. It speaks for his confidence in you. And I'm sure whatever you come up with is bound to be amazing. You're brilliant at what you do, Kenan."

Warmth suffused him at her unconditional belief in him. Even when his family had downplayed his contributions, Eve had always encouraged him, supported him.

"Thanks, Eve. I appreciate that." He straightened and exhaled slowly. "I have an idea on how to completely rebrand and relaunch Bromberg's. It includes updating their image, retaining some of the established stores while bringing in newer, fresher clientele. My goal is to meld the classic with the modern without losing who and what Bromberg's has always represented—class, fashion and luxury. But I want to add accessibility and affordability to that without losing the luxury. That's where you come in."

She didn't speak, but he didn't miss the tension that invaded her body, stiffening her shoulders and drawing them closer to her ears.

"I want to include in my proposal an exclusive partnership with Intimate Curves."

Her full lips parted, and her sharp gasp echoed in the living room, but he pressed on. He knew Eve—knew her well. Her initial response would be a swift and emphatic "no." Fear of something new, unknown, so huge and out of her control… Whatever. He needed to work fast to make her see how this could be beneficial to both of them.

And if he needed… If it came down to it, he still had his trump card.

"You promised to hear me out before you made any decisions." He held up a hand, palm out. "Intimate Curves has fast become one of the most popular and successful online lingerie companies for plus-size women. And it's just won the Small Business Award from the National Association of Women Entrepreneurs, which is huge. But Intimate Curves is still *online*. Here is a chance to move to a brick-and-mortar store inside one of the most well-known and respected department-store chains in the nation. That would take your company to another level. It means more recognition. And exclusivity, because you can offer select designs and products in this store that aren't available anywhere else. Which means more profits. It would also bring a fresher, more modern, woman-positive image to the chain. And, of course, we're not even touching on what Intimate Curves does for size and sex positivity overall."

He rose, the pulses of excitement too much for him to remain seated. It got like this for him when a new project started forming. He vacillated between extreme focus and bouncing around like a kid on a sugar high. Right now, he paced the length of the room, striding over to her built-in bookshelves crammed with everything from texts on ancient Roman emperors, to the Civil War, to her favorite romance books. Then, he whirled around and ate up the distance to the massive fireplace on the other wall.

"Kenan." Eve released a short chuckle that carried a note of disbelief, and when he glanced at her, she stared at him, her hands fluttering in front of her. "I have no idea what to say here. Other than what the hell do you want me to say to that?"

"Say yes, Eve. Say *yes*."

Okay, so he couldn't hide the desperation in his voice. But then again this was Eve, so he didn't try. There was no point, anyway. She could ferret out every one of his emotions, every hint of a deception. Unless it pertained to her, that is. It seemed when it came to her, he was a fucking master of illusion.

"What is this really about, babe?" she quietly asked.

Shit.

He nearly winced. Nearly. And he *nearly* confessed the truth to her. But there were some things he couldn't even admit to his best friend. Well, other than the obvious. He couldn't tell her that he *needed* this. He needed to prove to the board, to his brothers, to his family—to his goddamn self—that he'd made the right decision in leaving Rhodes Realty. That incurring his parents' anger and disappointment hadn't been in vain. That he was worthy of being at Farrell International.

That he was worthy of being a Farrell.

He despised the weakness in himself for even thinking that last one.

Hated even more that he meant it.

"I know you enjoy teaching, Eve," he said, walking over to the couch and lowering down beside her. He met her beautiful brown eyes, saw the shadows of uncertainty in them. He hungered to reach for her, curl his hand behind her neck and draw her into his body. Offer himself as a resting place, a haven. But that's not what she needed from him. Not now. "But you *love* creating, designing. You're never more alive than when you're sketching out a new creation. You even crave the challenge of running your own business, of besting your own self every month when those numbers come in. This—" he jabbed a finger at her laptop with the Intimate Curves logo on the screen "—is what you should be doing full-time. If you would just take that leap of faith."

"That's easy for you to say." She glanced away from him, thrusting her fingers into her thick curls, fisting them.

"Is it?"

She flinched. "Shit. I'm sorry, Kenan. I didn't think."

"Doesn't matter." He waved off her apology. "Tell me your objections."

"You know them." She sighed, and the weariness in the sound settled on his chest like two-ton weight. "They haven't changed. Even while I'm so damn proud of this award, do you know what one of my first thoughts was while reading the email? 'I hope I won't have to accept anything in person.' The idea of Mom and the school finding out? Jesus." She shook her head, letting loose a dry laugh. "I'm twenty-damn-nine. Too old to be worried what my mother is going to say about my life choices, and yet—" she stretched her arms wide, her fingertips grazing his arm "—here I am," she drawled. "Rationally, I recognize I can't live my life for her, but seeing that disappointment on her face when she's done so much for me, sacrificed so much…"

"Yes, but for how much longer? Until next year? And then until you're thirty-five? Forty? When is enough, enough? When do your dreams become more important than someone else's comfort?"

She parted her lips and was about to reply…but no

answer came. He didn't need one. He spied the yearning for what he described in her eyes.

"Six designs. Six Eve Burke designs exclusive to Bromberg's that I can promise will roll out with the re-launch. Just give me that commitment. I'm looking at six to eight months for this, so you have that long to deter-mine how much you'd want to be involved beyond the stores. I can find a team to manage the store division, so if you're adamant about protecting your identity, con-tinuing to teach and focusing on the online arm of the company, then that's an option for you." He paused. "I have another offer."

She arched an eyebrow. "I'm almost afraid to ask."

He didn't smile at the teasing note in her voice, though. Not when tiny razor blades left him so wounded by the offer it was a wonder he could still sit upright on her couch.

"If you agree to my proposal, I'll help you with my brother."

Fuck, those words scalded his throat, his tongue. Even as he said them, part of him roared that he should re-scind them. But he didn't. And they hung between him and Eve like ripe fruit on a vine that she was probably dying to pick.

And damn if another part of him didn't resent her for that, too.

She blinked. Stared at him. "What the hell are you talking about?"

His mouth twisted into a wry half smile. "I'm talk-ing about Gavin, served up on a platter. Or maybe you serving yourself up on a platter to him. I don't know how you prefer it. Equal opportunity and all that shit. Doesn't matter. I've spent thirty years with him. I know him bet-ter than anyone. Understand what grabs his attention in a woman. I love you, Eve, but your flirtation game when it comes to him is woefully inadequate. You want an 'in' with him, I'll give it to you. I can't promise you you'll be the next Mrs. Rhodes—" *fuck me* "—but with me as your…love coach, you'll have a chance."

"Love coach?" she sneered. "Are you serious right now? If you could've helped me with your brother, why are you just doling out these jewels of wisdom now? Why not before?"

Because I didn't want him to have you before. Not when I still held a delusional hope that I could.

But he no longer held that fantasy. At some point, between leaving Cain's office and driving over to her Cambridge apartment, he'd come to a hard but final decision.

Eve didn't want him. She never had.

It'd always been Gavin for her.

So he had to let go of the dream of her.

No matter how it hurt.

Not the friendship; never that. But he was giving up the fantasy of ever being more. For fifteen years, he'd secretly loved and lusted after a person who had only seen him as a friend—or worse, a brother. He had to face reality, and not waste another year, another month, another damn day on a fruitless wish. Besides, if by some miracle, Eve actually returned his feelings, he would always question if she was settling for him because she couldn't have Gavin.

He'd been second best all his life. Being that for Eve? His gut twisted with a howl of pain. Jesus, no. Not with her.

What he could do, though, was pour all of himself into this vision of his future. And in doing so, he could help his friend obtain her own dreams—the career of her heart and his brother.

And in return, he'd cement his place in Farrell International, proving he was more than Barron's bastard. He'd prove he was needed and that he belonged there.

It would have to be enough.

Even if right now it didn't feel like it.

"Because you never asked me before. And I'm a self-serving son of a bitch, and it benefits me to hook you up with him now." It was a lie, but with just enough of a grain of truth that she might go for it.

Please go for it, Eve. I can't emotionally afford for you to dig deeper.

She tilted her head, eyes narrowing on him.

"So let me get this straight. I give you six designs—"

"Exclusive designs for an Intimate Curves flagship store in Bromberg's."

She paused. "I give you six exclusive designs with the extent of my involvement in a flagship Intimate Curves store to be discussed at a later date, and besides a partnership agreement, you will coach me in how to win the attention and affection of your brother."

"Yes."

"Why?" she whispered.

If she hadn't asked with that note of insecurity and pain in her voice, he might have deflected with a flippant answer. Instead, he thumbed a big "fuck you" at his control, leaned forward and cupped her cheek. He shoved, not nudged, the friendship boundary, and brushed his thumb under the curve of her bottom lip. Back and forth. Back and forth. Until the need to trace that path with his tongue became an all-too-real urge and he stopped.

"What are you asking me, Eve? Why am I helping you? Or why do I think Gavin will want you?"

"Either." A pause. "Both."

Yes, he'd decided to move on, to let her go, but that didn't mean the streak of masochism had disappeared. Only that could explain why he tunneled his fingers into her dark brown curls, their rough-silk texture dragging a groan from deep in his gut. Only by sheer force of will did he lock it down. But nothing could keep him from imagining it grazing his bare chest, his stomach…his thighs. Could stop him from envisioning his hands buried in it up to the wrists, holding the mass of it away from her face as she took him…

Damn…

Sweat broke out on the back of his neck. He dropped his arms, flattening his hands on his legs, hiding the prickling of perspiration on his palms.

She'd asked him a question. About his brother. The man she wanted. The man she'd always wanted.

Not you. Never you.

He jackknifed from the couch and stalked over to the window, staring out onto her quiet street and the gathering shadows. With his back to her, he could affix his mask and hide the erection thrusting against his zipper from just having touched her hair, as if demanding her hand, her attention.

He closed his eyes. "I'm helping you because you deserve every happiness, every desire, every goal—you deserve everything, Eve. Not that you didn't before. But maybe it was me being selfish then. Not wanting to share you. And this is me realizing I can't do that. Holding you back is holding me back, too. I meant what I said. Your dimmed light shouldn't be at the cost of someone's comfort. And that includes mine." Wasn't that the fucking truth? Bitterness coated his throat, burned in his veins like corrosive acid. "As for Gavin." He turned around, sliding his hands in his pants pockets. "My brother might not have noticed the beauty right under his nose, but that's not your fault. It's all on him. He's a fucking idiot. Worse. A blind fucking idiot. But if that's who you want, I'll help you grab his attention. He won't know what hit him, sweetheart."

She inhaled a deep breath, slowly exhaled it. Then she

stood and crossed the room, approaching him. He resolutely kept his gaze on her face, as he'd done earlier. And so he noted the acceptance there before she extended her hand toward him.

Loss shouldn't have wrapped around his throat and squeezed. Shouldn't have filled his nostrils, sat heavy on his tongue until the acrid flavor was all he smelled, tasted.

She stood right there, her small, dainty palm pressed to his. Her chocolate gaze smiling into his. And, yet, he couldn't get rid of the sense that things had changed for them with the excitement in her eyes. The excitement and the agreement.

"Okay, I accept. Let's do this."

"We have a deal then."

He shook her hand.

Sealing both of their fates.

Five

Eve stood on the sidewalk outside the hair salon and scanned Dorchester Avenue for a glimpse of the familiar black Lexus through the heavy foot traffic.

On a late Saturday morning, near the riverfront and with Fenway Park not far away, people teemed outside, enjoying the unusually warm spring day. And by unusual, she meant sixty degrees. Didn't stop people from wearing everything from sweaters to shorts as they strolled in and out of the book café next to the hair salon, or the tattoo shop and restaurants along the street. Already, music was pouring from some of the bars. Some people bought and enjoyed fresh lemonade from the cart parked on the walkway. To a tourist, it probably seemed like a big block party, but no. This was just… Boston.

She glanced down at her watch, impatience streaking through her. No, not impatience. Well, maybe just a little. But mostly, nerves. Because she was doing this. Taking this step. Making a change she'd been contem-

plating for a while but had been hesitant about doing because… There were so many reasons. Now, in the week
and two days since Kenan had arrived at her house and
presented his proposal, those reasons had gradually al-
tered in her head, becoming excuses. And they all boiled
down to one thing…

Fear.

*For God hath not given us the spirit of fear; but of
power, and of love, and of a sound mind.*

Second Timothy, chapter one, verse seven.

One of her mother's favorite scriptures. When Eve had
been terrified about standing up in front of her class to deliver her first speech on Crispus Attucks in history class
in the fifth grade, Yolanda had quoted that verse. When
Eve had confessed the night before she'd left for college
that she was afraid to leave home for the first time, her
mother had whispered the same passage in her ear, while
hugging her close, tears thick in her voice.

When Eve had called her mother from her car on
her first day as a teacher, scared as hell of walking into
that high school, her mother had reminded her of this
scripture.

It seemed kind of sacrilegious to murmur the verse
to herself now, when she was praying over gathering the
courage to pursue a man who had shown zero interest
in her beyond that of acknowledging her existence. But
what was the scripture about God giving her the desires
of her heart?

Oh, Lord, she was going to hell.

"Eve."

The sound of her name and the touch at her elbow
jerked her from her thoughts of imminent damnation.
She glanced up at Kenan, who arched an eyebrow. Rather
than answer, she ruefully shook her head.

"Hey." Lifting her cell phone, she tapped the screen. "You're late."

Showing a marked lack of remorse, he shrugged a cream, cable-knit-covered shoulder. "Since you didn't deem it important to share what I'm late for…"

"Does it ma—"

She narrowed her eyes, really *seeing* him. As in the five-o'clock shadow that ticked closer toward six, since it didn't appear as if he'd shaved since the night before. It'd been a week since they'd seen each other—the longest they'd gone without being in each other's company since college. Silky, light brown hair dusted the sensual bow of his upper lip and a small patch dotted the dip beneath the almost ridiculously full bottom curve.

Either he'd been burning the candle at both ends, which was definitely a possibility, given she didn't know anyone who worked harder than him. Or… Or, he'd just rolled out of a woman's bed and hadn't taken the time to go home and shave but had come straight to Eve. Another distinct possibility. Because as hard as Kenan worked, he played equally as hard.

If she leaned in, would she catch a whiff of the other woman's perfume or the musk of their sex on his skin?

A blaze, like a hundred fire ants, streamed through her, rippling across her scalp and down her spine, before reversing course and pouring into her chest. Her breath caught, and that went up in smoke under the flames of… Of what? Anger? Yes, but it didn't feel as…clean, as simple as that. But she refused to latch onto the other word her mind seemed so eager to supply. No. This was stupid, silly. Why did she care who Kenan fucked? She *didn't*. It wasn't her business. Never had been.

Then why are you squeezing your phone so hard? The address book is going to be imprinted on your palm.

Deliberately, she loosened her grip.

"Does what matter?" He cocked his head.

"Nothing." She waved a hand. "So the reason I asked you down here…" She turned and looked at the beauty salon in back of her. "I've scheduled a makeover."

He stared at her. "A what?" he asked, voice low Almost… menacing.

She shivered.

Then ignored it. She was being ridiculous.

"A makeover," she repeated. When he didn't say anything more, just continued to stare at her with that unblinking, bright stare, she stumbled on, even though she didn't owe him an explanation. "Look, I can practically see what you're thinking. And, no, I'm not changing for a man."

"No?" He crossed his arms. "Then what do you call it?"

"Changing for me." She tapped her fingertips to the middle of her chest. "I've been thinking about this for a while. Don't do that," she snapped, when his full lips pressed into a thin line. "I'm not lying. There are things I've wanted to change. My hair." She reached up, touched the ends of her thick spirals, then dropped her hand and glanced down at her form-fitting but plain green V-neck sweater and dark blue skinny jeans. "My clothes. I want… different."

She wanted to stand out. To be noticed. When she entered a room, she wanted men to stop in midsentence because they forgot their train of thought, and women to glare in envy.

Was that so wrong? Shallow maybe, but wrong?

Possibly, but at this moment? She didn't care.

"And you just now decided to do something about it? Out of the blue," Kenan drawled, skepticism dripping from his tone like condensation from one of those cups of cold lemonade.

"I know what you're getting at, and so what?" She

threw her hands up between them. "Your proposal about Gavin might have been the push I needed, but he isn't the reason. Why can't this be about me?" she demanded, frustrated and more than a little annoyed. "Of course, *you* wouldn't understand that."

He frowned, slowly loosening his arms and lowering them to his sides. "What the hell is that supposed to mean?"

"Please, Kenan. You have a mirror. And even if that wasn't enough of a clue, the women climbing all over you would be another one. You don't know what it is to be…invisible."

"And you do?" He studied her, that blue-gray gaze roaming her face so intently she stifled the urge to duck her head, hide from him. And that wasn't them. They didn't hide anything from each other. "You could never be invisible, Eve. Not even if you tried."

"Spoken like a true friend." She shook her head, briefly smiling. "But also spoken like someone who's never had cause to doubt his own beauty or appeal in his life."

Something bleak, almost…desolate flashed in his eyes before the thick fringes of his lashes lowered. What the hell? She reached for him, her fingers grazing the inside of his wrist, but he stepped back, scrubbing his hand over his head. It shouldn't have felt like rejection.

But it did.

"You dead set on this?" he demanded, voice hard, low.

A bolt of nerves attacked her, striking her and leaving her trembling. But it was that fear of change, of the unknown, that affirmed she was doing the right thing. She'd experienced this same feeling when she'd decided to secretly minor in fashion. And when she'd opened Intimate Curves. And, most recently, when she'd agreed to Kenan's proposal.

It hadn't served her wrong yet.

"Yes."

With one last, long stare, he pulled his cell out of his pocket and strode away from her. Curiosity and impatience warred for dominance within her, and she glanced down at the screen of her own phone. Her appointment was in fifteen minutes. She'd called him for moral support, but she wouldn't allow him to make her late.

A few minutes later, she took a step toward the shop when he turned and stalked back toward her.

"C'mon." He jerked his head, grasping her elbow.

"What?" Too shocked to disobey his command, she fell into step beside him, but then gathered the lady balls she'd temporarily misplaced. "Hold up." She abruptly skidded to a halt, jerking her arm free of his hold.

"At some point in the last five minutes you suddenly mistook me for a sheep. I don't know how that happened, but I'm going to offer you the benefit of the doubt since we're lifelong buddies. So let's try this again. What's going on and where are you trying to haul me off to?"

Kenan sighed. "If you're determined to go through with his crazy-ass idea, then I have a connection who hooked me up with a full-service salon in the Back Bay. Private, high-end, with a stylist and makeup artist. But we have to leave right now."

He shifted closer. Then closer still, completely invading her personal space with his scent, his body. All of *him*.

"But this needs to be said, Eve. You're perfect. Just as you are. I promised to help you get Gavin's attention by teaching you how to flirt with him, tease him. Not by changing yourself. You don't need to do that for him or any man. I know." He jerked up his chin when she parted her lips to object. "I heard you. This is for you. I'm just reiterating. There's no need for it. But this is your decision, and I'll support it. But, Eve, this…"

His hand thrust in her hair, his blunt nails scraping over her scalp before he fisted her curls. Her breath caught in her throat, and she barely jailed her whimper before it escaped. The needy sound that echoed in her head sent shock crackling within her like a live wire. Shock and something darker...hungrier... That *something* shivered through her, setting off tiny ripples that pooled low in her belly.

No. This is Kenan, she reminded herself. *My best friend.*

She blinked up at him, her hands coming to rest on his chest. Was she pushing him back or needing to feel his strength against her palms?

God. Why couldn't she answer that?

"This, Eve." He tugged on her hair, the pleasurable prickles dancing across her scalp—another sensory over-load adding to the confusion coalescing inside her. "This you're not changing." He lifted the strands still clutched in his fist to his nose, and in doing so, drew her forward until her forehead brushed his lips, and she had no choice but to inhale the sandalwood and citrus scent of him from the cradle of his throat. "This is mine."

This is mine.

Shit.

This was where she should open her mouth and pro-test. Tell him he was not her owner or her keeper. That she could make her own decisions about her hair, thank you very much. But she didn't. Not with that possessive declaration of "this is mine" echoing in her head—and between her legs—like a molten heartbeat.

"Where are we going again?" she whispered.

For a long moment, he didn't speak or release her. But then he shifted backward, his grip on her curls loosening.

"I told you, a place recommended by a friend. Now, where are you parked? I'll go get my car so you can follow me to my place. We'll drop your car off there, and you can ride to the salon with me."

"A friend?"

Like the friend he'd most likely left limp, tangled in sheets and smelling like him and the sex they'd had all night?

Okay, she really had to get a grip. From twelve to fourteen, she'd had a secret crush on Kenan. If these thoughts skidding through her head had happened then—well, obviously not the *sex*, but this inexplicable cattiness and... to hell with it, jealousy—that would make sense. But that was then, not now.

So yeah, she had to get it together. Because again, *best friend*.

"Yes, a friend. Mycah."

"Oh, right." Heat tinged her cheeks, as an image of Achilles's wife flickered in her head. She boasted gorgeous natural curls, just as Eve did. Dammit, she really needed to just shut up. "I'm parked down there." She pointed toward the other end of the street. "I'll just meet you at your house."

Without waiting for his agreement, she turned and strode off. Time by herself. That's what she needed. Time to calm her nerves, get centered. Cancel her original appointment and make Kenan paid the fee since, technically, he was responsible for the cancellation. And then, maybe she needed to examine the dregs of that morning coffee. Because there must've been something extremely funky in the cup she'd grabbed this morning. Nothing else explained her responses to Kenan in the last few minutes.

Or the tight ache pulsing deep inside her.

Good. God.

"I—I'm—" Eve stared at herself in the mounted, lighted mirror in the hair salon. She shook her head in disbelief, her newly winged eyes wide.

Her contemplation shifted to the smiling woman behind her.

"You're you." Jasmine, her stylist, fluffed Eve's curls, then settled her slender hands on Eve's shoulders. "Gorgeous. All we did was bring a little glamour to you. That's all."

"I think you're really underselling your skill, but okay," Eve drawled, still unable to stop staring at her reflection. At the woman with the flawless makeup and hair gazing back at her.

Jasmine chuckled, whipping the cape off her. "Trust me when I tell you I've worked with more…difficult clients. You, Eve, are not one of them. Come on to the front. I have a bag of products for you to take home with you."

"Do you have a three-page, single-space essay and video tutorial to go along with it? Because as gorgeous as you made me, I'm experiencing serious doubts if I can recreate this at home."

Laughing, Jasmine led her from her private room, which Eve had learned earlier she reserved for her VIP clients. Eve Burke. A VIP client. When did she step through the wardrobe and why did she have to go back to the real world?

In the three and a half hours she'd been at the exclusive Back Bay salon, Jasmine and her team had completely pampered her. Hair, a facial, makeup, manicure and pedicure. She'd never been so catered to and spoiled in her life. Growing up, extra splurging money had been a concept she'd heard of, not a real thing. And, as an adult, even though she held down a full-time job as a teacher and ran a successful company that turned a decent profit, she still wrestled with guilt.

Watching her mother squirrel away money to make sure Eve didn't go without necessities had branded an impression on her that Eve couldn't remove. Spending money on a new spring wardrobe when she could put aside extra money just in case her car broke down, or she lost her job, seemed selfish. Shelling out money on a spa day or a vacation when she could pour that back into her business was irresponsible.

Frivolous. The word whispered in her head, and it was her mother's no-nonsense voice. Yolanda had deemed several things frivolous. Eve's friendship with Kenan. Her wanting to try out for the school dance team. Her wanting the newest cell phone.

Her love of art and drawing...

God. Eve shook her head, focusing on Jasmine's retreating back. How had she gone down that morose rabbit hole? Nope. There was no room for glum thoughts today. Not when she'd taken the first concrete steps toward becoming her best self. The one she'd been scared of being for so long.

Because that meant putting herself out there. Being seen. Being potentially criticized. Being potentially rejected...

Okay, for the love of all that's holy, stop*!*

She stepped out into the waiting area, scanning the room decorated in black, white and chrome. Two couches, several chairs and tables filled the space, and gilded mirrors adorned the walls, along with several framed photographs of gorgeous women modeling different stunning hairstyles.

Kenan was perched on one of the armchairs, his phone in hand, attention centered on the screen. But, as if he sensed her, his head lifted, that focused, bright gaze finding her. His eyes flared wide then narrowed as he slowly rose to his feet.

Eve battled the impulse to touch her face, her hair, to fidget under that intense, hooded perusal. Its weight settled on her. But it wasn't suffocating. Oh, no, not that.

That gaze moved over her like a lover shifting between her legs, the solid bulk pressing into her body. Branding her. Heat, scalding and strong, like undistilled liquor, shot through her. Tingled in her breasts, beaded her nipples. Burned in her belly. Spasmed in her sex.

What. In the. *Hell?*

She stumbled, grasping the edge of the counter. This couldn't be—she didn't want Kenan. Not sexually. It'd always been Gavin. Maybe that's what…this was. The prospect of being on the precipice of having the chance to be with the man she'd desired for so long must be messing with her head…and other lady parts. Because, admittedly, it'd been a long while since a man had touched her. Covered her. Slid so deep inside her she couldn't breathe past that sense of fullness.

Yes, that had to be why one look from her best friend had her tangling with lust like a sordid game of Twister.

"Here you go, Eve." Jasmine handed her a black-and-white bag with pink accents. "Everything you need, and some extrafun things I threw in for you. And if you have any questions, please don't hesitate to call me. I included my card in here, as well."

"Thank you so much, Jasmine." Eve accepted the bag and, on impulse, hugged the other woman. "You have no idea how much I appreciate all you've done. How much do I owe you?"

"No worries." Jasmine waved off her question as Eve reached for the wallet in her purse. Eve paused, frowning at the stylist. "It's been taken care of."

Oh, she didn't need to ask by whom.

Saying goodbye one last time, Eve walked into the waiting area and approached a silent, frozen Kenan. He didn't blink, didn't budge, and that antsy, fidgety feeling returned.

"What?" She lifted a hand toward her hair but halted

at the last second. "I didn't change my hair. She just gave me highlights."

He still didn't say anything. Just stared. And, dammit, it was seriously starting to unnerve her.

She knew what he saw. Jasmine had washed, conditioned and moisturized her hair, and the curls, with their new red highlights, gleamed and framed her face, grazing her shoulders. The makeup artist had given her a full day look and her eyes had never appeared so wide, her cheekbones so high, her lips, painted a beautiful deep bronze, so full.

"Are you happy?"

She lifted her shoulder in a small, half shrug, accompanying the gesture with a slightly nervous laugh.

"Jasmine did a wonderful job."

"That doesn't answer my question. Are you happy?"

"Yes." This was what she wanted. A new look. A new beginning. A new *her* as she started this journey to putting aside fear, maybe becoming the face of her company and going after the man she'd desired for years. "Yes," she said again, firmer this time.

He studied her for a long moment, and for the second time in the history of their long friendship, she wanted to hide from that all-too-perceptive gaze.

"Okay." He nodded. "C'mon. We have another appointment."

Kenan turned, heading toward the salon's exit.

"Wait." She grabbed his arm, annoyance rippling through her. "What appointment? And that's it? That's all I get, is an 'are you happy?'"

"A clothing boutique. Someone is going to meet us there."

She shouldn't be offended. After all, this makeover had been her idea. But, damn, did he have to jump so fully on board?

"Look at me."

She jerked up her head, not realizing until then that she'd dropped her gaze and was scanning her completely fine but plain clothes.

"There's nothing wrong with the way you dress. The way you look. The way you fucking *breathe*, Eve. But if I'm going to hold up my end of the bargain, that means attending certain events where Gavin will be. And you need the wardrobe to attend them. No." He held up his hand, preventing the objection that she'd definitely been prepared to make. "This is my bargain. Consider it a business expense."

Once more, he pivoted on his heel and headed for the door. Just as his hand closed around the handle, he paused. "And you're stunning."

Eve stared. Even after he pushed through the door and it closed behind him, she remained rooted to the spot inside the salon.

There's nothing wrong with the way you dress. The way you look. The way you fucking breathe, *Eve.*

You're stunning.

His words played through her head in a continuous loop. Her breath shuddered out from between her lips, and she pressed a palm to her belly, as if the gesture could quell the quivering there.

It didn't.

Shaking her head, she exhaled a deep breath that ended on a dry, disbelieving chuckle.

She really needed to get her head on straight. Today might be like some reverse Cinderella story, but nowhere in that fairy tale did she fall in lust with her best friend.

This was not that kind of story.

Six

"**R**emind me why I'm here again? On a school night?" Eve muttered.

"I'm sorry. Did I miss the memo where you turn into a pumpkin at midnight? Or a lesson planner?"

Eve snorted. "Very funny. Ass."

Kenan smirked, murmuring a thank-you to the bottle-service waitress as she set vodka and Patrón tequila on the table in front of him and Eve, along with glasses, cranberry juice and a bucket of ice. She smiled at him, and he recognized and acknowledged the invitation in it with a dip of his chin. Not that he'd do anything about it.

Tonight wasn't about him.

It was about the woman sitting next to him on the dark red leather couch in the VIP section of The Trend, the new nightclub in the seaport district his brother had invested in. Gavin had invited Kenan to the opening, and he'd brought Eve along as his plus-one. Tonight he would start to uphold his end of the bargain.

Shit.

He might need to call back their waitress for more liquor if he was going to make it through this night. A night of not only having a ringside seat to Eve pursuing his brother, but Kenan also helping her to catch him.

Leaning forward, he grabbed the bottle of vodka and poured a healthy amount in a glass, forgoing the cranberry juice. He tilted the drink up to his mouth and shot it back. The burn razed a path down his throat, and he savored it. Concentrated on it. Because if he focused on that burn, then he could shift his attention away from the one that clawed at his gut and hardened his cock.

Jesus.

He moved his gaze away from her. The tangible, sexual *lure* of her.

He could take his eyes off her, but the picture of her was branded into his mind—that petite, curvy body poured into tight, black leather pants, a white, high-collared silk shirt with a feminine bow at the throat and ankle boots with "fuck me hard" stiletto heels.

She was sex and innocence. Sin and sweetness. A walking, breathing temptation in leather, silk and flesh.

Gavin wouldn't be able to resist her.

And Kenan had no one to blame but himself.

He poured another drink. Tequila this time.

"Whoa there. The evening is just getting started," Eve cautioned with an arched eyebrow. "Everything okay?"

"Fine." He poured her a vodka-and-cranberry and passed it to her. "Here. Catch up." He waited until she lifted the drink to her mouth and sipped, then clasped her hand in his and brought her to her feet. And turned away. Because, Jesus. Those hips and that ass. "Come on. Let's go do what we're here for."

The sooner he started this lesson in how to reel in his brother, the sooner he could start getting down to the serious business of drowning his brain in alcohol. He'd need it to stop seeing the images of Eve and Gavin twisted together, kissing and touching. Besides, if he was drunk, he wouldn't be sober enough to swing on his brother for taking what Kenan coveted.

"I can't believe your brother is an investor in this place." She held on to him, allowing him to guide her down the steps from the glass-enclosed VIP section to the bar and club section below. "It's amazing."

Kenan clenched his jaw at the awe and admiration coating her voice. All his life, he'd stared at the pedestal on which his parents had placed Gavin. Watching Eve worship at that same throne?

Alcohol.

Sooner rather than later.

He needed something to wash down the bitter flavor of envy.

As soon as the bouncer opened the door to the club, the muted, thumping bass and music that had vibrated off the glass of the VIP section bombarded them. Hundreds of people packed the grand nightclub that reminded him of a Vegas venue. Aside from the luxurious VIP lounges, a dual spiral staircase that wouldn't have been out of place in an English palace led to a second story, where a DJ spun her beats and more people danced on the landings and catwalks. Below, three bars, two huge dance floors and several scattered sitting areas filled with tables, chairs and booths encompassed the cavernous space. A lighting system flashed gold, green and white beams, while two LED walls played music videos.

If tonight's attendance was any indication, Gavin had made a sound investment. Kenan was happy for him.

Speaking of Gavin...

His brother stood at the end of the longest bar, surrounded by a group of men and women vying for his attention. Instead of heading over to him, Kenan steered Eve to the opposite end, sliding up to the bar top and shielding her with his body.

"Shouldn't we go talk to Gavin? Say hi?" Eve rose on her tiptoes, her lips brushing the rim of his ear. Even in those ridiculously high heels she remained several inches shorter than him. "He probably doesn't know we're here…"

"He knows we're here. It was his name and connections that granted us access to the VIP section."

Kenan slid an arm around her waist, his fingers splaying wide over the sexy, rounded curve of her hip. Her soft gasp puffed against his cheek as her chest met his, and he pulled her to stand closer between his legs. Cedarwood and roses greeted him, and he battled the urge to bury his face in the crook between her shoulder and neck, and inhale more of her delicious, skin-warmed scent.

"Kenan," she whispered, gripping his arms.

"Shh. Lesson number one, Eve." He pinched her chin, tilting her head back and to the side so that her breath ghosted across his mouth. Damn, he hungered to lick his lips, taste her in the only way he could. "You don't chase after anyone. Let them do the pursuing."

She scoffed, but he caught the slight tremble in her voice. The uncertainty. "Isn't that what I'm doing here? Pursuing?"

"No. I'm teaching you how to make the one you want work for you. Now…" He bowed his head, his lips skimming over her cheek, hovering just above her ear. Because he could, under the guise of pretense, he tangled the fingers of his free hand in her hair, fisting the curls. "Gavin is used to people—women—chasing him, currying favor with him, throwing themselves at him. And while he doesn't duck and dodge, he doesn't experience the thrill of the chase. Every man craves that thrill, the excitement of it. The challenge of it. The arousal of the takedown and the conquering."

"God, Kenan. You make him sound like an animal." She chuckled, and it sounded breathless. His grip on her hip tightened before he deliberately eased it. That wasn't for him; that telltale signal of excitement belonged to the idea of being captured and covered by his brother. *Don't get it fucking twisted.*

"That's what we are, sweetheart. At the core, we're beasts who convince ourselves we're predators. But the truth? The truth is—our secret—we're your prey all along, and we love every goddamn moment of being taken by you."

"Kenan." Her lashes fluttered, and her fingers flexed against his arms.

Suddenly, he knew with crystal clear certainty how she would cling to him during sex. Knew the exact pressure her nails would exert against his skin, his muscles. Lust beat at him with merciless fists, and he delighted in being its punching bag, even acknowledging he couldn't do a damn thing about it.

"Kenan." A new voice—deeper, lower and familiar—intruded, dousing Kenan with a brutal, icy dose of reality. Forcing a casual smile, he untangled his fingers from her hair, but kept his arm around her waist as he turned them to face his brother.

"Hey, man," Gavin said. "Thank you for coming out tonight."

Gavin pounded Kenan on the shoulder in greeting. His curious and, goddammit, admiring gaze slid to Eve and lingered on her. Roamed over her face, pausing on her lush mouth before dipping lower to her equally lush body. Anger, pain, jealousy—they all roared inside Kenan, pounded against his bones, rattling him from the inside out.

But he kept his mask in place. This time, it was one that showed him as the carefree, "rejection rolls right off my back" younger brother.

Fortunately, he was well versed in maintaining this facade.

"Of course. I wouldn't miss it," Kenan said with a wide grin, clapping his brother on the shoulder in return. "Since you said I could bring a guest, I convinced Eve to tag along."

"I'm glad you did." Gavin turned to Eve, and instead of the usual polite but distant smile, this one held an appreciative warmth that reflected in his dark eyes. "Eve, it's good to see you again. You look…stunning," he said, his voice lowering, deepening.

"Thank you, Gavin," she murmured, and even in the darkness of the club, Kenan glimpsed the flush across her cheekbones. Or maybe he just knew her so well, he could picture it there. "Congratulations, by the way. I was just telling Kenan how amazing the club is."

"I appreciate it. A lot of hard work went into renovating it." He cocked his head to the side, a corner of his mouth quirking. "How about you two join me? I was about to head up to our VIP section with my partners and a few guests. I'd love if you two—" he glanced at Kenan, then quickly returned his gaze to Eve "—would come with us."

Eve smiled. "I would—"

"Maybe a little later." Kenan slid his arm from around her and grasped her hand. "Eve promised me a dance first. We'll catch up with you, Gavin."

Tapping his fist to his brother's chest, he led Eve away from the bar and toward the crowded dance floor. Instead of pushing his way to the middle, he stopped on the edge and drew her close against him. Clasping her wrists, he wound her arms around his neck, then stroked his hands down to her shoulders, over the dip of her waist to rest on the flare of her hips. Her soft breasts were pressed to his chest, and as he slid a leg between her rounded, tight thighs, need, hungry and raw, clawed at him. It was impossible—his rational mind convinced him it definitely wasn't possible—but he swore the damp, feminine heat of her penetrated the layers of their clothes to sear him in the sweetest, dirtiest way.

"What are you doing?" Eve stiffened, leaning back to glare up at him. She shifted her hands from his nape to his chest, exerting pressure. "I may not be an expert in flirtation, but I can tell when a man is interested. And Gavin *was interested*. He asked us to join him, for God's sake. Why did you tell him no?"

"Don't push me away. Put your arms back around me."

Her immediate obedience triggered a primal response in him. A response that had him needing to praise her, touch her for that show of instinctive trust. In him. It stimulated his heart…and his dick.

He bowed his head over hers, and to anyone looking— to Gavin—he would appear to be on the verge of taking her mouth, a prelude to another kind of conquering.

"Lesson number two. A dog is man's best friend for a reason. Because we have a lot in common. For instance, a dog can ignore or play and be finished with a bone. But as soon as another dog comes sniffing around, suddenly that bone is the most desirable, delicious thing he's ever possessed, and he wants it with a single-minded focus that's scary."

"I don't know if I want to roll my eyes at the man-baby ridiculousness of that or deliver a stinging diatribe on the indignity of comparing women to bones," she drawled. Her nails scraped the nape of his neck, and he wrestled back a shiver at the whisper of pain under the wave of pleasure. "Personally, the way I'm leaning includes the words *junk* and *punch*."

He shook his head, giving her a small smile. "Please, sweetheart. Don't act like you haven't heard that before. I'm just giving you truth as it pertains to Gavin. He invited you to join him in that VIP room, and if I hadn't stepped in, you would've agreed so fast, there would be skid marks on that staircase right now."

Her lips parted to object, but when he arched an eyebrow, she narrowed her eyes on him.

And remained silent.

"That's right." He nodded. "He put forth the barest amount of effort, and you weren't going to require him to do more. Your mother's an elder in her church, and God knows you spent enough hours there growing up. What does Scripture say about a man who doesn't work?" He lowered his head until their foreheads nearly brushed. "He doesn't eat."

Her eyes briefly closed and a puff of sweet, vodka-and-cranberry-scented breath bathed his mouth. "I'm about ninety-eight-point-nine percent sure that's not how God intended that scripture to be used."

He chuckled, and yes, it was filthy even to his own ears. "The concept's the same. So here's what you're going to do. Dance with me. Flirt with me. Pretend you've forgotten Gavin even exists. And make him come for you. Fucking *earn you*, Eve."

She blinked. Stared at him. And he stared back, maintaining that visual contact as if his heart wasn't slamming against his chest because he'd said too much. Allowed too much passion into his voice, more than what belonged to someone who was only a friend.

After a long moment, she turned around, lifted her arms…and undulated her body against him. Like a match to dry kindling, he ignited in flames. He moved with her, losing himself in the pounding rhythm of the music, as it echoed the wild beat in his blood, his cock. It spoke of need, of greed. And he gave in to it.

Burying his face in her curls, he was no longer Kenan, and she ceased being Eve. They became two people, strangers, meeting, flirting with their bodies, letting a heat that had nothing to do with the crush of people rise between them. He became a man indulging in foreplay with a woman.

With each roll of her hips, she stroked her ass over his cock, and dammit, he should have shifted away, inserted space between their bodies. He should have. But he didn't. He clenched his jaw, entrapping the growl that rumbled in the back of his throat, and danced with her. Let her feel the effect she had on him. He'd find a way to explain it away later. Not that she seemed to mind. Maybe she was as caught up in this pretense as he was, because she didn't whirl around and accuse him with those beautiful eyes or tear into him with that sometimes sharp tongue. No. Instead, Eve rubbed over him again…and again. Teasing him, arousing him, tempting him.

Jesus, she was pure, condensed temptation.

A thick, erotic haze enshrouded his mind, settled in his limbs, weighing them down even as it buoyed him. This—her in his arms, inhaling her sweat-dampened cedarwood-and-roses scent, her small, thick body grinding against him—was his moment to let go.

And he did. He could give himself this. He *owed* himself this.

She spun around, wound her arms around his neck and pressed her breasts, hips and thighs to him. Her hooded gaze met his, and even in the dark, he glimpsed… God, the glint of desire there. For him? Yes, he convinced himself. *For him.* Desire wrapped its hot, sticky fingers around his throat and squeezed, cutting off all ability to think, to process his actions, to consider the consequences.

He slid a hand up her back and tunneled his fingers into her hair, cupping her head, tilting it. His breath punched out of his lungs, and his heart hurled itself against his rib cage. To get to her? To escape him and spare itself from this colossal mistake he was on the verge of making?

Didn't matter. Not when his dick was in full control at the moment.

He lowered his head, close enough that he tasted his error on her parted lips. Its flavor was regret and greed.

Fuck it.

He took her mouth.

Invaded it. Claimed it. Sexed it.

Eve stiffened, and her shock vibrated from her trembling frame right into his. He absorbed it, his arm around her waist, curling her into his body. A warning blared through the dense fog in his head, and he started to draw back. Kenan was not so far gone that he would force what wasn't willingly offered. But then, she softened, melted into him, her lips opening wider, granting him more access.

He groaned, closed his eyes. And fell.

Urgency and years of need didn't allow him to be gentle or tender. Didn't allow him to ease into this mating of mouths, or leisurely explore this territory that was both endearingly familiar and terrifyingly new.

Being denied this—being denied *her*—for so long stripped him of his famed charm, of his control. Ruled by lust, by a soul-deep yearning and the knowledge that this would be his one and only taste of her, he delved into her. Twisted his tongue around hers and sucked and licked. He demanded. Demanded that she give in return. That she devour him just as eagerly, as desperately as he feasted on her.

And she did.

God, did she.

Her nails bit into the skin on his neck as she tilted her head, met him thrust for thrust, chasing his tongue for more. She didn't need to pursue him for what he wanted, needed, to give her. What he would beg for her to take. He stroked inside her, harder, deeper. And when she tangled with him, he couldn't have stopped grinding his erection against her soft belly. Barely stifled the howling urge to hike her up in his arms, wind those legs around him and rock into that hot, soft place between her thighs. She emitted a whimper that echoed in his chest, his gut, his cock.

But it was her needy sound that snatched him back to the dance floor in his brother's club.

What the hell am I doing?

The question ricocheted off the walls of his skull. Jerking up his head, he broke off the kiss. He barely managed not to return for one last sample, but he licked his lips, savoring that last bit of her. Because it would have to sustain him.

"Kenan," Eve whispered, slowly lowering her arms, resting her palms on his chest. She stared up at him, eyes wide but still a little hazy, lips swollen and damp from their kiss.

Slowly, he untangled his fingers from her hair and released her waist, stepping back. Placing much-needed space between them. As if that would help. It hadn't in fifteen years.

"Is Gavin still standing at the bar watching us?" He clasped her hand in his and lifted it to his mouth, pausing just shy of brushing his lips over it. "Do we still have him as our captivated audience?"

The clouds in her gaze cleared, and her head jerked back in a slight flinch. She stared at him for a long, charged moment, then glanced over his shoulder.

"Yes, he's still there." She shifted her attention back to him, her bottom lip pulled between her teeth. "So that kiss... It was for Gavin's benefit?"

I don't give a fuck about Gavin. I've been hungry for the taste of you for over a decade. And now that I've had your addictive, delicious flavor on my tongue, you might have ruined me more than I already am.

The admission roared so loud in his head, he paused before replying, balancing himself, afraid he might have actually voiced it. When she continued to look at him instead of gaping in horror, relief poured through him.

He could do this. Pretend.

It was all a part of the show. And between trying to be the perfect son for his parents and the platonic best friend for her, he'd become one hell of an actor.

"Of course," he lied, tugging her close and bending his head over hers. "Remember what I said about him wanting what he believes another man desires? If that doesn't get his ass in gear, nothing will. And the fact that he's still standing there instead of heading to the VIP section means he either wants, or is interested in wanting."

"Jesus, Kenan." She touched a finger to her still-damp bottom lip.

And, dammit, he wanted to replace those fingers with his tongue.

He took another step away from her, but her hand clutched in his prevented him from moving far.

"It's just a kiss, Eve. A tool to get the job done. You want Gavin, and I want you for my Bromberg's project. I'm only holding up my end of the bargain."

Dammit. He was trying too hard to render that "hot as fuck" melding of mouths into something inconsequential. But it needed to be said. To ensure she didn't guess his secret and to remind himself that she wasn't his. That she was here in this club for his brother, the one she truly desired. Her response to his kiss could be chalked up to shock, to playing the game. He was the liar here; she'd never pretended to want anyone but Gavin.

Better he remember that and avoid any fanciful, foolish thoughts of "what if." He'd always come in second place with his parents, with his career and with her love.

But at least they had their friendship.

No way in hell would he fuck that up.

"Let's go see if it worked. You ready?" He arched an eyebrow.

Her intense scrutiny didn't waver from his face, and it unnerved him. Worried him.

Finally, she glanced away, and he almost groaned with relief.

"Actually, I'm going to head to the bathroom. I'll be back."

"I'll go with you—"

"No." She shook her head. "I'm okay, and I need a minute."

She didn't wait for his agreement, but walked away, leaving him to stare after her. After a few moments, he pivoted and strode back to the bar, where Gavin still waited.

"Hey, Kenan. Everything okay?" his brother asked, his gaze flicking in the direction Eve disappeared.

Okay? Hell no. Everything was most definitely not *okay*.

But Kenan smiled, hoping the darkness of the club hid how forced it felt. "Yeah, Eve just had to use the restroom."

"Good, just checking." Gavin nodded, then slid his hands into his pants pockets and leaned against the bar's edge. "It's not my business, so feel free to tell me to mind it, but—" he hiked his chin up "—I thought you and Eve were just friends."

"We are." He shrugged a shoulder and caught the bartender's eye. Only after he ordered a whiskey and felt the liquid burn as it slid over his tongue and down his throat did he continue answering his brother. "If you're referring to what you saw out there, that was nothing serious." And the lies kept coming. Right. It wasn't *nothing*. It was *everything*. "Eve and I are friends."

"If you're sure. It looked like…"

"I'm sure." He took another sip of his drink, his grip on the glass nearly threatening to shatter it. "Why are you asking?"

He knew damn well why Gavin was asking.

Gavin studied him, then shook his head, a smile quirking a corner of his mouth. "I just want to make sure I'm not stepping on any toes. She's…" Gavin blew out a breath. "Fuck, she's gorgeous. Why haven't I noticed before?"

Kenan knocked back the rest of the whiskey to prevent himself from answering that stupid-ass question.

"She's always been gorgeous," Kenan said, voice smooth, even. "But, no, you aren't stepping on any toes. Eve is single."

"You sure you don't mind?"

Bitterness tinged with sorrow bloomed in his chest.

"It's Eve's decision, not mine. But, no, I'm good."

Gavin's smile broadened, and he clapped Kenan on the shoulder. "That's great. Thanks, Kenan."

"No problem."

Right. No problem.

Eve would finally have the man she'd wanted for years.

And with the success of this project, he would finally have the recognition of being more than the "other Rhodes son" or a Farrell Bastard.

It was all he needed.

Seven

Lesson plans turned in. Check.

Grades updated. Check.

Netflix pulled up and *Bridgerton* loaded and ready to play...for the sixth viewing. Check.

Eve smiled as the doorbell rang, and she hopped off the couch, snatching up several dollar bills off the coffee table.

Large meat-lover's pizza with extra cheese and onions. Check and check.

The last three weeks had been filled with work—both at school and with Intimate Curves—and social events. Lord, so many social events. Kenan was taking his end of their bargain seriously. If a gallery opening, fundraiser or dinner party was happening and Gavin would be in attendance, Kenan escorted her there. And, damn, Gavin had an active social calendar. If she didn't know better, she'd suspect Kenan of feverishly trying to throw her at his brother…as if he was attempting to pawn her off on him.

It was ridiculous; they'd been friends for over two decades. Yet, that knowledge didn't stop her feelings from smarting like alcohol splashed on a scraped knee.

Before, she would've just asked him about it. Just demanded to know what the hell was up. But that pesky *before*…

Before that night in the club.

Before that dance.

Before that kiss.

Nope. Not going to think about it. Her first free Friday in weeks, and she intended to stay home, relax and not spend another second dwelling on that…

A shiver rippled through her, and she sank her teeth into her bottom lip, unwilling to free the moan climbing up her throat. Again. Friday. No date. No pretending she hadn't buried her tongue in her best friend's mouth. And liked it.

Hell.

Grimacing, she hurried to her front door like robed Dementors floated at her heels. Huh. Maybe she should indulge in a Harry Potter binge instead of sexy historical-romance shenanigans…

She opened the door, the delivery person's tip in hand, ready to exchange it for the pizza she'd paid for online.

"Hi… Kenan." She stared at her best friend, gripping the doorknob. Flutters that she decided to attribute to shock quivered in her stomach. "What're you doing here?"

"Better question. Why didn't you ask who it was before answering the door?"

"Look, *Dad*," she drawled. "Not that it's your business, but I was expecting a pizza delivery."

"Dad." The corner of his mouth twitched. "Kinky."

Laughter tickled her throat, but she crossed her arms over her chest, blocking the doorway. "What're you doing here? I thought we didn't have anything scheduled for tonight?" Leaning forward, she pinned him with a glare. "And if you say that we do, I can't promise you won't end up in a montage of pictures on ID Discovery as I talk fondly about you from my jail cell."

He snorted. Cradling her hips in his big, elegant hands, he shifted her backward as he moved forward until they were both standing in her apartment. He closed the door behind him, then turned to lock it, and she used that opportunity to assure herself her skin wasn't tingling from that tender but firm clasp.

That night in the club, he'd gripped her like that—gently, but with more than a hint of dominance. Then, electricity had crackled inside her, currents of heat moving through her. She'd flowed with it, letting go and losing herself for the first time in so long, confident and secure in the knowledge that Kenan would catch her, protect her. Even as he was the one sending her flying.

Even as the hot, thick weight of his cock grinding against her behind had kept her grounded.

And there went those flutters again.

Followed by a flood of "what the fuck?"

Kenan was her friend. Her *best* friend. And aside from that brief teenage phase, she didn't associate him in the same sentence with heat, flutters and cock.

She didn't…right?

Right, dammit.

And, yes, she was negotiating with herself.

"At the risk of repeating myself for a third time…" She headed to the kitchen and the bottle of wine she'd bought on the way home to drink with her pizza. Classy. That was her. "But, seriously, what are you doing here?"

"Where else would I be?" He followed her and leaned

a hip against the breakfast bar that separated the spacious living area from the kitchen.

"Let's see." She tapped a finger to her bottom lip, squinting at the ceiling. "Friday night. You're single. And you don't have to escort me anywhere. All that equals freedom." She smirked, opening the refrigerator and pulling out the wine. "So if you don't have to hang with me why are you here at my house?"

"First, let's make one thing clear. I've never had to hang with you. This might come as a surprise to you, given your often curmudgeonly demeanor, but I enjoy your company."

"Spell *curmudgeonly*," she muttered, then narrowed her gaze on him. "Isn't there a party you should be attending? Business associates to schmooze? Beautiful people to entertain?"

He studied her for a long moment, his bright gaze piercing but shuttered. "If I didn't know any better, I'd think you were trying to get rid of me, Eve," he murmured.

Guilt shimmered inside of her. How did she explain that for the first time in their long friendship, she needed a break from him, from the stunning vitality of him? The nearly visceral sexuality of him.

It was startling. Disconcerting.

Confusing.

And she'd wanted time to find her equilibrium and figure out how to return to the easy familiarity they shared. One not threaded and *alive* with this awareness.

Awareness? Why don't you call it what it is?

Nope.

Damn. More arguing with herself. She really should've bought another bottle of wine.

"That's ridiculous." She dismissed his very accurate conclusion with a wave of her hand, then popped the cork free of the wine bottle with a corkscrew. Scooting her glass closer, she focused all her attention on pouring the merlot as if scrying the deep red alcohol for the answers to the universe. "I just would've thought you'd want a night off from me."

"Eve." He flattened his palm on the counter near her drink. "Look at me."

Slowly, she set down the bottle and lifted her gaze to his.

"Are you having second thoughts?" he murmured.

She froze, her hand hovering near the glass stem. Second thoughts? Was she?

Their plan appeared to be working. Gavin flirted with her, not hiding his attraction or his desire to get closer to her. And she would be lying if she claimed not to be flattered by his attention. After craving it for so long, who wouldn't be thrilled? Gavin was handsome, smart, charming, successful...

And yet...

Her gaze dipped to Kenan's mouth. Yet, she couldn't exorcise that damn kiss from her mind. That wet, lush, raw tangling of lips, tongues and sighs that haunted her during the day and chased her into her dreams. It'd shocked her then, and now, how quickly she'd surrendered to that undertow of lust, letting it drag her under until she forgot all about clubs, people and thoughts of "what the hell am I doing?" That kiss had shamed the ones that had come before it and ruined the ones that would follow. Arousal slid through her like melted butter—warm, soft, utterly delicious...and so fucking bad for you.

But while her world had been rocked, apparently Kenan hadn't even suffered a 0.5 on the Richter scale. It shouldn't bother her; Kenan enjoyed a reputation as one of Boston's most eligible bachelors, a lovable but elusive playboy. He wasn't a stranger to kissing women. Still, maybe if she could erase from her head how she'd clung to him, whimpered into his mouth then walked away aching and wet while he stood there unmoved, maybe she could extinguish the humiliation in her belly.

Stop being silly. She shook her head, raising her glass for a deep, long sip. Of course, he'd been unaffected. Kenan had never exhibited any signs of desire for her, even as a teenager who probably got stiff with every passing breeze. She'd always been nothing but a friend to him.

Which was fine, because she wanted Gavin, not Kenan.

Are you su—

Oh, shut up.

Wine. Wine, wine, wine.

"No," she said, finally answering his question. "I'm not having second thoughts. Why would you think that?"

His blue-gray eyes roamed over her, and with liquid courage warming her veins, she met that intense scrutiny.

"Eve, I don't—"

The doorbell rang, and she swallowed her sigh of relief. "Pizza's here. Are you staying?"

"Have I ever turned down free pizza?" Before she could answer or head toward the front door, he held up a hand. "I got it. You want to get plates and pour me some of that wine? Especially since you're staring at that bottle like a lion about to chase down a gazelle."

Ass.

He wasn't wrong, though.

A few moments later, he returned with a large, grease-spotted pizza box, and the orgasmic scents of oregano, cheese and crisp dough stained the air. Her stomach growled, and Kenan, arching an eyebrow, didn't even have the grace to pretend he didn't catch it.

"Oh, shut up." She set plates and napkins on the coffee table. "Put it here, and I'll get the wine."

For the next forty minutes, they ate pizza, drank wine and watched the first episode of *Bridgerton*. That familiar, easy comfort they'd always shared returned, and by the time Simon and Daphne enacted their fake-relationship arrangement, she was glad Kenan had shown up at her door. She'd missed evenings like this with him.

"If Daphne hadn't taken the duke up on his offer, I would've," Kenan said with a shake of his head. "Simon is fine."

She snickered, then picked up the remains of their dinner and carried them into the kitchen. When she returned, Kenan had her sketch pad in his hands. That instinctive urge to snatch it away, flip the lid closed and hide away her drawings flared within her. She curled and straightened her fingers, reminding herself this was Kenan. Not a stranger. Or her mother.

Yolanda had never understood Eve's need to create, to lose herself in filling up page after page of her many sketch pads. Especially with things her mother had considered frivolous and useless, such as fashion. Eve had learned to be protective and secretive early, and some habits died a very slow death.

"You still draw in your pads first?" Kenan studied a page, and anticipation and nerves dueled it out inside her.

"Call me old-fashioned, but I initially like to get the vision out of my head on paper."

He finally lifted his gaze, and her breath jammed in her throat at the burning admiration that lit his eyes like a blue flame, nearly eclipsing the gray.

"You're so fucking gifted, Eve."

Pleasure suffused her. Kenan had never been stingy with compliments, but he'd really been the only one in her life who'd offered them to her. She'd never doubted her mother's pride in her or her love, but Yolanda wasn't an emotionally effusive person. Her mother exhibited love through her actions, such as providing for her, pushing her, motivating her. But Kenan, he'd given her the words, the praise, no matter how difficult a time she had accepting them.

"Thank you," she murmured. Clearing her throat, she approached the couch and removed her tablet from her laptop bag. "I'm not finished yet, but would you like to see a few of the designs I'm working on?"

Excitement brightened his eyes, reminding her of a child spying his gifts on Christmas morning.

"Absolutely."

She lowered to the couch, and he sank down next to her. His crisp and earthy scent teased her, and the heat from his thigh pressed alongside hers threatened to derail her concentration. Inhaling a low, deep breath, she tapped the tablet's screen, bringing up her program and the lingerie sketches she'd been working on.

"Here you go." She handed him the device and waited, stomach in knots.

This was the first time she'd designed pieces for another project other than her website and store. It didn't escape her that Kenan had hung the bulk of the success of his rebranding proposal on her designs. And she would do her very best to come through for him.

For the next several minutes, he studied the sketches, scrolling through from screen to screen. Objectively, she could admit that she'd done some of her best work. But would the butter-yellow demi bra created in the shape of a butterfly, with the wings forming the lace cups, and the matching boy shorts fulfill his expectations? Or maybe the mesh-and-lace lilac bustier with the ribbon lace-up detail in the front and the high-cut panties in the same material? She loved both pieces, but that didn't mean he would see and understand her vision...

"When I first thought of this project and asked for

your help, I had zero doubts you would come through for me." Kenan lifted his head, his bright gaze gleaming. "But, Jesus, Eve. You've exceeded what I hoped for and expected. Just when I think you can't surprise me…" He shook his head and his attention dipped back to the tablet. "These are fucking brilliant. Thank you."

Relief and delight fizzed and bubbled inside her like the most expensive champagne.

"You don't have to thank me." She waved her fingers. "It's not like I'm not getting exposure from this deal."

"No, I do have to thank you," he said, lowering the device to the coffee table.

For a moment, he trailed his fingertips over the screen and the black racerback with the rosebud appliqués and scalloped edges. When his gaze returned to hers, she fisted her hands at her sides. Either that or go to him, drag him down to the couch and hold him until that stark, almost haunted look disappeared from his eyes.

"Kenan," she whispered.

"You give me hope, do you know that?" he murmured, lifting his hand between them. It hovered over her cheek, but at the last moment, he lowered his arm and instead slid his hand into his pants pocket. "So many people believe you benefit from our friendship because of my last name and because your mother works for my father. But that's not the truth, is it?"

She didn't know how to answer that; she was one of the "many people." From the day he'd appeared in that break room, he'd become not just her friend but her protector, her comforter, her confidante. At times, her savior. So, no, she couldn't affirm his truth.

"When everyone else in my life doubted me, didn't see me as strong enough, smart enough or 'Rhodes' enough, you never did. You always accepted me, and I found a place to belong. You gave me that."

Sorrow, pain and love for him swirled inside her, a furious storm whipping at her, howling *for* him. She'd been a witness to his family dynamic for the past two decades. And it never ceased to infuriate her. Nathan Rhodes was a good man—a loyal husband, a dedicated father, a provider. And he'd never expressed that he favored Gavin… but his actions had declared his preference. Every time Nathan praised Gavin for his grades but criticized Kenan's one B in the midst of all A's… When he attended all of Gavin's football and basketball games but only made a few of Kenan's… When he carried both sons to his office but only spent time tutoring his oldest on the inner workings of the company…

When Nathan claimed that he desired both sons be enfolded in the family business, but trusted Gavin with the authority, titles and responsibility, he'd made it abundantly clear that his oldest received the lion's share of his respect, if not his love.

Eve resented Nathan for his constant dismissal of Kenan. And she couldn't understand how Dana could stand by and allow this treatment of the child she'd adopted and raised with the promise to love as much as her natural son.

Eve briefly closed her eyes, shoving down the anger. That wasn't what he needed from her right now.

"You gave me the same. And more, Kenan. You still do."

A dark emotion flashed through his gaze, but she didn't have time to decipher it before he bent his head and once more stared at the tablet with her designs.

"I feel useful at Farrell International in a way I never did at Rhodes Realty. I feel…wanted." He cleared his throat, then got off the couch, stepped back and picked up his glass of wine, taking a long sip. She didn't speak as he peered down into the ruby depths, but her palms itched to touch him, soothe him. "Cain welcomed me, trusted me with the company's marketing and PR. But this rebranding proposal? It's huge for me. This will prove to everyone that I deserve to be at Farrell. And not just because Barron fucked up and got a woman pregnant, leaving me with his DNA. It'll show that I earned my place there. Asking Cain for this opportunity was scary as hell. But as soon as you agreed to be on board, some of that fear disappeared. Because as long as I know that you have my back, I'm strong. I'm damn near indestructible."

God, what he did to her.

Break her. With his words, flashes of his unexpected vulnerability, he could just…break her.

Her feet moved before she gave them permission, and in just a few steps, she stood in front of him…then she wrapped him in her arms. She pressed against him, holding his tall, solid frame, relaying without words that she had him.

"You don't have to prove that you belong at Farrell. Or show anyone that you deserve to be there. There is no *deserving*. You are Barron's son as much as Cain. Being there is your right, and you bring your brilliance, your work ethic, your particular insight and talent to them. *They* should be thankful they have *you*. And just from the time I've spent around Cain and Achilles, they are. Those who can't see what you bring to the table, or refuse to acknowledge it for whatever reason, can go screw themselves."

He didn't reply, at least not vocally. But his arms tightened around her. But it wasn't enough. She needed him to confirm that he heard her. That he *believed* her.

She tipped back her head, but as her gaze met his, the gentle reprimand on her tongue died there. His blue-gray eyes burned as if lit with a flame, and the thought of being consumed by that bright fire flitted though her head.

He lifted a hand, and unlike before, this time he

touched her. Brushed his fingertips over her jaw, her temple, her cheek. Her pulse drummed in a frantic, primal beat, and its throb echoed in her head and her throat, and between her legs. Anticipation. It dripped into her like an IV, straight into her veins. Anticipation and... want. Pure *want*.

Move.

Step away.

End this.

All wonderful, wise advice that her mind hurled at her. But she ignored it all. Because something had taken ahold of her—something achy, hot and wholly inappropriate for a best friend.

"Kenan," she whispered.

Again, no answer, but his fingertips ghosted over the curve of her bottom lip. Nerve endings she hadn't known existed lit up and danced in glee. On a shuddering breath, she closed her eyes, tilted her head—

The sudden, shrill ring of her cell pierced the room. *Funny*, she mused, flinching. It hadn't seemed jarring until this moment. Until she'd been about to quietly beg her friend for his mouth.

Thrusting her fingers in her hair, she whipped around, searching for her phone. Or she used that as a handy excuse. Her heart pounded against her rib cage, but for a different reason now. Jesus, what had she been about to do? What was she thinking?

You weren't. That's the problem.

She didn't see any point in arguing with herself this time. Not when she happened to be right. She would've kissed Kenan. Again. And this time, she wouldn't have the excuse of a pretense.

Spying the bottom half of her cell peeking out from under a couch cushion, she skirted the coffee table—and

Kenan—and dove for it. Without bothering to glance at the caller ID, she swiped at the screen and answered.

"Hello." Dammit. She sounded breathless even to her own ears.

"Hey, Eve. This is Gavin."

Shock doused her in a frigid wave. And right underneath lurked guilt. Unbidden, her gaze shifted to Kenan.

"Hi, Gavin. How're you?"

A random person would've missed the subtle change in him. But, knowing him as well as she did, she caught the tension that stiffened his powerful body. Noted the slight flattening of his sensual mouth. Noticed the taut skin over his cheekbones, causing the dusting of cinnamon freckles to stand out in stark relief.

"I'm fine. Better now that I have you on the phone." His blatant flattery should've had warmth cascading through her, but instead she struggled to even concentrate on the conversation. All of her attention was laser-focused on the silent, brooding man several feet away from her. "Are you busy?"

She glanced away from Kenan. No way in hell she could look at him and continue to talk to his brother. Not when she could still feel the promise of his kiss on her lips. Taste it on her tongue.

"No, not really. I'm just relaxing at home for the night."

"That sounds like a perfect evening. Especially if I could spend it with you," Gavin said, his voice lowering, deepening.

Wisps of pleasure shivered inside her, and warmth flowed into her cheeks. She couldn't misread the flirtation in that statement. Flirtation, hell. Gavin Rhodes wanted to spend time with her. Part of her—the part that reverted back to a shy, crushing teenager—delighted in his words.

"I'm sure you have more exciting plans on a Friday night then spending it bingeing on Netflix," she murmured.

The nape of her neck prickled with awareness. She didn't need to peek over her shoulder to confirm that Kenan's stare would be pinned on her. It touched her. *Branded* her.

"You'd be surprised at how exciting that sounds." Gavin's chuckle resounded in her ear. "But, unfortunately, you're right about me having plans tonight that I can't get out of. Which is why I'm calling to see if I can claim your time for next Friday. I want to see you outside of a party or opening. I'd like to take you out, Eve."

"Oh, um…"

This was what she wanted, right? Gavin's interest. His attention. His desire. Years. She'd longed for all of this for years, and now, when she hovered on the verge of it being in her grasp, she hesitated.

She didn't bother asking herself why. The "why" stood behind her.

No. She pinched the bridge of her nose. Kenan didn't want her; other than that kiss, which he'd brushed off as part of their charade, he'd never given her any indication he felt the same inconvenient and inexplicable lust that had coursed through her just a few minutes ago. He'd always been affectionate, touching her, hugging her. It wasn't his fault that her hormones had decided to throw their panties at him.

God, this was wrong. On so many levels.

Kenan was her best friend. That's it. He had available women—plenty of them—who scratched his sexual itch. Who had permission to survey the landscape of his hard, perfect body. And she wasn't one of them. Would never be.

Which was fine because she wanted Gavin. He was

her unobtainable fantasy that was suddenly very obtainable. Now wasn't the time to be distracted from that goal.

Exhaling a long, silent breath, she nodded, even though Gavin couldn't see the gesture. "Yes, I'd love to go out with you."

"Wonderful." His satisfaction and delight reached out to her. She should be enjoying this moment. But the knots twisting her stomach wouldn't permit it. "I'll call you next week with details."

"Sounds good."

"Eve…" He paused, and she closed her eyes, as if that could somehow fill the emptiness that yawned inside her. "I'm already counting down the days until Friday. I'll talk to you later."

She murmured a goodbye and ended the call. A deep silence filled the room, and its heavy, icy weight pressed down on her chest. She'd done it; she'd grabbed Gavin's attention. She was going on a date with him.

The elation, the effervescent happiness that came from victory, would fill her at any moment. Yes, any moment it would replace the edginess. Scrub away the cloying, grimy sense of betrayal.

Tossing the phone to the couch, she turned around and forced herself to meet Kenan's gaze. What had she expected? Anger? Irritation? Satisfaction, even?

Anything but a cold blankness that completely blocked her out of his thoughts.

Shock and hurt punched her in the gut. He'd never looked at her like that before.

He'd never shut her out.

"Congratulations," he murmured. "This is what you wanted."

Yes, it was…wasn't it?

Confusion swirled within her. She should be celebrating. And yet all she wanted was…what? To return to that easy camaraderie they'd shared for decades? To thank him for helping her obtain her dream man?

To cross the space that separated them and return to his arms? Beg him to ease the ache, satisfy this nagging need…?

"Thank you for dinner. I'm about to head out." He pivoted and strode for her front door, snatching up his coat and shrugging into it.

"Kenan," she called out, unsure what else to say, just that she couldn't let him leave. Didn't want him to leave. Not like this.

But he didn't stop, didn't turn around. Instead, he paused, his hand on the doorknob.

"Enjoy yourself, Eve," he said. "You deserve it."

She stood, frozen, as he let himself out of her apartment. And she continued to stare at that door long moments after he closed it behind him.

Enjoy herself, he'd said.

Right.

Now she just had to find a way to accomplish that while worrying if she'd lost her best friend.

Eight

"I can't imagine losing a parent so young." Gavin shook his head, then lifted his glass and sipped his Macallan. "That poor girl. What she must be going through. Teaching isn't an easy job. Not only are you educators, but confidantes and part-time counselors…" He trailed off, eyes narrowing as Eve wrinkled her nose. "What was that look for? Did I say something wrong?"

Eve huffed out a short laugh. "No, you didn't. I would just hold up on the sympathy for my student. Especially considering not two weeks after telling me she'd been absent for three days and missed her midterm exam because her father died, I met said very alive father at a basketball game. Now either he's Jesus and resurrected, or he never died in the first place."

Gavin's loud crack of laughter echoed in the elegant private dining room he'd reserved for their dinner date. He propped his arms on the table, leaning forward. His eyes gleamed, the light from the candles dancing in their pretty brown depths. "Are you serious? Tell me you're not serious and this freshman didn't actually fake her father's death."

Eve grinned. "Oh, but she did. Even went so far as to create a funeral program, print it out and bring it in as proof. The girl was good. Or scary. Needless to say, the parent-teacher conference we had was very interesting."

Still laughing, Gavin fell back in his chair and rubbed a hand over his jaw. "What was her endgame? And did she at least explain why she went through all that?"

"I have no idea how she expected to keep that big of a secret. From what I understand, the father is a pilot and travels a lot, so maybe she thought her mother would be the one coming up to the school." She shrugged. "But she's fifteen and probably didn't think that far ahead. And I guess she believed missing school to travel to New York and see BTS was well worth the possible fallout from figuratively offing her father."

"Kids."

Their gazes met, and after a beat of silence, they dissolved into chuckles. When the hilarity ebbed, they continued to smile at one another across the table.

She'd had fun. So much fun.

Who would've thought she could be so at ease in the presence of her long-time crush and speak without her words tripping all over each other like a drunken frat boy? The hideously expensive Brazilian steakhouse, with its sumptuous decor, had only increased her nerves when she'd first arrived. Being led to a private room where Gavin waited with a heart-stoppingly romantic setting of candles, roses and soft music only heightened her anxiety. What if she spilled the wine? What if the dolman sleeve of her off-the-shoulder dress dipped into the olive oil when she reached for the bread? What if she accidentally choked and couldn't talk?

But she shouldn't have worried. Charming, funny and kind, Gavin had put her at ease. With a beautiful restaurant, exquisite cuisine and a handsome, amazing gentleman for company, the evening had been beyond what she'd imagined. Utterly perfect.

And she couldn't wait to leave.

Regret and guilt clogged her throat, and even a sip of freshly brewed, delicious coffee couldn't dislodge them. All through the evening of wonderful conversation and laughter, she should've been focused on the man across from her. But her mind kept drifting to his brother. What was Kenan doing? *How* was he doing? Was he mad at her? Was that why he'd been avoiding her this week?

The questions trampled through her head, loudly, rudely and with not one damn care when or where they did it. Like now.

And if that wasn't the definition of fucked up—that her thoughts were preoccupied with one man while she dated another—then *Webster's* needed to update their latest edition.

About twenty minutes later, she rose from the table, Gavin behind her, holding out her chair. She smiled up at him even as she swallowed a sigh. Because as much as she wished—longed for—her heart to race, it just went about its business behind her rib cage. Just pumping blood as if this was any old, ordinary day.

She'd dreamed about a night like this, with Gavin staring down at her with *that* particular light in his eyes, since she'd been a girl. And now that it was happening, she couldn't revel in it. Because something was missing.

No, not a vague "something."

Desire. Need. That belly-twisting, aching hunger that had her desperate to climb him like a rope ladder in a long-ago gym class.

Not like when…

Stop. Nope. Not going there.

Picking up her purse, she stepped away from the table and turned up the wattage on her smile. And, yes, she was overcompensating.

"Thank you for a wonderful evening, Gavin. I really enjoyed myself."

"So did I." He settled a hand low on her back as they walked toward the door of the private room. Then he paused, cupping her elbow, and turned her to face him. Tipping back her head, she looked up and her nerves returned with a solid, air-stealing blow. "Eve, I don't think I've been very subtle about how attracted I am to you. I'm just sorry it took me so long to do anything about it."

Because it took a makeover, new clothes and another man kissing me to make you notice me.

She shut down the uncharitable thought, but the faintly bitter dregs of it remained.

"Tell me we can do this again." His voice thickened, and he gently cupped her jaw. "I want to see you again."

Kenan's advice to make him work for her, to not give in so easily, whispered through her head. But she didn't need to call his words to mind. Didn't need to pretend to play coy. Her hesitation was real.

"Like I said, I had a great time tonight. And spending time with a friend over a wonderful meal is never a hardship." She smiled, and though it felt tight on her lips, she held it there. "School and my other responsibilities have kept me pretty busy, but call me next week? We can work out the details then."

And the time would grant her a reprieve to figure out what the hell was going on with her. Why the thought of another date left her cold…and guilty.

"Friends?" he repeated softly, brushing a thumb over her cheek. "Okay, I'll accept that for now. But know I'm not content with leaving it there." He lowered his head and brushed his mouth over the spot his thumb had just caressed.

A little later, she waved at him as the valet held open the door for her to duck into her car. Only once she'd pulled out of the parking lot and melded into the busy Friday-night traffic did she release her breath on a heavy sigh.

When she stopped at a light, she reached for her cell, scrolled to her favorites list and tapped Kenan's name. The peal of the phone ringing filled the car's interior. After the fourth ring, the automated voice clicked on, requesting she leave a message, but she pressed the screen on her dashboard and ended the call.

"Dammit, Kenan."

Irritation flickered in her chest, and her grasp on her steering wheel tightened. She glanced at her dash again—9:17 p.m. In the three times she'd managed to catch him on the phone this week, he hadn't mentioned plans. But then again, he probably wouldn't have. But whether he was at home or out painting the town a particularly lascivious shade of red, he could *answer his damn phone*.

The irritation flared into anger, and she narrowed her eyes on the road. For some reason, he'd been punishing her since last Friday, and screw it, she was through letting it go. He was going to talk to her. Because that's what friends did. It seemed he'd forgotten that.

Well, fuck it.

She was going to remind him.

Kenan peered at his laptop's screen, but the art concepts the marketing team had sent over for him to approve could've been hieroglyphics for all he comprehended them. The longer he stared, the more the visuals blurred, the more the notes his team added became a muddled mess.

"Shit." He shoved back from the desk, his chair rolling over the hardwood floor. Rubbing his palms down his face, he muttered, "Shit," again, and dragged his hands over his head.

Sitting here trying to work when his concentration had ceased to exist hours ago was a fool's errand. And if he spun around and gazed out the dark bay window of his home office, he'd catch a reflection of that fool.

He stood, then rounded the desk and stalked to the built-in bar on the far wall. He should've taken up Cain and Devon on their offer to have dinner with them. Even going to that mausoleum Barron Farrell had once called home and had left for Cain would've been better than holing up in his too silent, empty Back Bay brownstone. Or, since he didn't live far from the Back Bay Fens and Fenway-Kenmore hugged the other side, he could've gone to any number of the restaurants and bars that were always busy on a Friday night.

Instead, he poured his third Glenlivet and brooded. Yes, he'd become *that* guy. The brooder.

Sipping his whiskey, he retraced his steps. But instead of settling back at his desk, he moved to the window. The moon illuminated the private, walled-in garden behind his brownstone, transforming it into a nocturnal, mysterious enclave of hedges, stone benches and a dormant fountain. Yet he could appreciate none of it. Saw none of it.

Not when images of Eve smiling and laughing with Gavin occupied his brain like a squatter. Visions of her turning up her gorgeous face to him, accepting his touch, his kiss. Would she go home with him after dinner? Let him take her to bed, caress that sexy body…?

Fuck.

He was torturing himself. Had been all evening. Hell, all week. He'd vacillated between reminding himself that this was their bargain and dialing her to demand she cancel dinner with his brother. That she was his, had always been his.

Lies.

He'd become accustomed to spinning them in his life, but he tried never to deceive himself as he remained the only person he could truly be honest with. And that truth hadn't changed in fifteen years. She wasn't and never would be his—not in the way his body needed. Not in the way his soul craved.

Bowing his head, he stared into the golden brown depths of his glass. Exhaling, he knocked back the rest of the alcohol. At least he had it as a companion to get through the night. A few more shots and he wouldn't even remember his own name. Oblivion sounded real sweet right about now.

"Since you're here, not comatose and seem to have all of your body parts, I'm going to assume you're fine and just ignoring my calls on purpose."

His heart slammed against his sternum, and his body tightened, adrenaline pumping through him. But then the voice and words registered, and his shock at suddenly not being alone in his house released him.

He slowly turned, lowering his empty glass to his desk. And met Eve's furious glare.

As the surprise retreated, the familiar dueling emotions of delight, lust, pain and love surged in. Even though the distance of the room separated them, he swore her fresh, cedarwood-and-roses scent teased him, had his mouth watering for a taste.

His gaze lowered, and he felt a spasm in his gut. The walnut-brown skin of her shoulders, bared by the dark red dress that flowed over her body before molding to her thick, tight legs, gleamed in his office's light.

She'd worn this for Gavin. Gone to him looking like living, breathing sex.

He picked up his glass and strode over to the bar.

"Kenan."

"I gave you a key to my house for emergencies. Fire. Flood. My imminent death from a fall and crack on the head. Since neither flames nor water are destroying my crown molding, and I'm vertical, I'm assuming," he said, tossing her words back at her, "that this isn't a real emergency."

"Well, when you refuse to answer my calls and are suddenly too busy for even a lunch, I thought that fall scenario could've been possible and let myself in," she drawled.

Out of his peripheral vision, he watched her stride over to him. She snatched up the glass he'd just splashed alcohol into and threw it back. Reluctant admiration wavered inside him as she didn't even flinch from the strong hit of whiskey. She slammed down the tumbler on the bar top.

"Thirsty?" He arched an eyebrow.

"Pissed. I'm hoping the liquor will mellow me out long enough to listen to your explanation for why you're avoiding me."

Kenan refilled his drink and raised it to his mouth for a long sip. Stalling. He could admit it. But could he confess that, yes, he'd cut her off this week? It'd been painful but necessary. He'd needed distance to get his head together, so when he finally saw her again, he could maintain the facade of being happy for her and Gavin.

He wasn't there yet.

Especially with her standing so close that her body heat warmed him. If he inhaled, would he catch his brother's scent mingling with hers?

He stepped back. Another step. And another.

Giving her his back, he walked to the dark fireplace and paused in front of it, staring at the framed pictures on the mantel. Him with his parents and brother. Him and Gavin. Him, Cain and Achilles in the garden behind Achilles's home. Him and Eve. Several of them through the years.

His friend. His secret. His heartache.

Jesus, if he could, he'd exorcise his feelings for her. Purge them so they could both be free. Briefly closing his eyes, he took another sip of Glenlivet. It'd ceased to burn after about drink two, but when the warmth hit his stomach, he savored it. Welcomed anything that beat back the ice in his bones.

"Kenan."

"How did your date go? Was my brother a perfect gentleman?"

Masochist streak still going strong, I see.

But as much as he hated himself for asking, he didn't rescind the question. He waited for her answer, a vise squeezing the hell out of his ribs.

Her heels clicked over the floor as she approached him. But she didn't stop next to him. Instead, she slipped between him and the fireplace, giving him no choice but to look at her. Look at the face that followed him into his dreams and offered him no mercy.

"Are you drunk?" She frowned.

He snorted and sipped from the whiskey. "Unfortunately, no." *Not yet.*

"Kenan, what's going on? Talk to me."

The anger bled from her expression, replaced by a concern that had the hairs on his arms and neck standing up. It veered too close to pity. And he hungered for a lot of things from her, but pity was not one of them.

It sparked a fury in him. Fury at himself for foolishly yearning for the impossible for so long. Fury at her for tormenting him with her scent, her voice, her damn *existence*. Fury at Gavin for always possessing what Kenan desired most—their parents' love, their parents' fucking DNA.

Eve.

Stretching his arms out on either side of her head, he deliberately set down his glass on the mantel and gripped the edge of it with both hands, caging Eve in. He shouldn't have delighted in the slight widening of her eyes. But he did. A dark, twisted delight coiled and tightened within him. And when he bent his elbows, leaning forward, he felt her swift intake of breath whisper over his dick in a filthy, sweet caress.

Goddamn, he'd offer up his soul on a lit pyre for the real thing.

"Talk to you?" he murmured, cocking his head, leisurely studying the delicate arch of her eyebrows, the coffee brown of her eyes, the impudent flare of her nose, the flagrant sensuality of her beautiful mouth, the gleaming teak of her skin... Hunger to touch, to sample, clawed at him. Coupled with the jealousy burning in his gut along with a good amount of alcohol, his usual control unraveled. "What should I talk about, Eve? How this week has been hell? Or how I've tried but can't evict you from my head? Or how the thought of you with my brother tonight has me seeking oblivion at the bottom of a bottle? Which topic do you want to tackle first?"

Silence crackled between them. The vestiges of restraint cautioned him to move back, grant her space. Find some way to joke off those charged questions.

He ignored them.

"Why?" she breathed, her gaze dark with surprise, confusion and...

That last emotion stirred a low, rough growl in his chest.

"Why, what? The hellish week, the eviction or the attempt to get drunk off my ass?"

"Yes," she breathed.

Another plunge into taut silence. Self-preservation clawed its way to the surface, and he shuffled a mental step back on the shaky limb he'd crawled out on.

"You first." He straightened, levering himself away from her, although his arms still penned her in. "Why are you here instead of out with my brother?"

She blinked, and the tip of her tongue swept across her bottom lip. His fingers curled into the mantel behind her, and he locked his arms. His body damn near trembled with the control he exerted not to bend his head and retrace that damp path with his own tongue.

"The date's over. You didn't answer my call, and I was worried. So I came by to check on you."

Well, damn if that didn't cut deep. He didn't want her concern. He wanted—

Fuck.

This was pointless. He shifted his gaze from her to the whiskey on the mantel. He'd had enough alcohol for one night. Shoving away from her, he turned and headed toward the office door.

"Well, you can see for yourself that I'm fine. No need to worry." Scrubbing a hand down his face, he walked out into the hall and toward his bedroom. "Lock up behind yourself."

"Kenan." Her fingers wrapped around his arm, drawing him to a halt. Since he couldn't drag her with him, he stopped, but didn't turn around. "I lied." She circled him, coming to stand in front of him. Her throat worked as her lips parted, but no words emerged. Dropping her hand from his arm, she glanced away. "I…"

He didn't speak. Was frankly afraid to. Afraid of what would escape his mouth.

She skimmed her palms down the sides of her thighs,

and his own hands tingled with the need to trace that same path.

"Yes, I was worried about you, but that isn't why I came by." She paused, gave a minute shake of her head, and a curl clung to her dark red-painted lips before she brushed it away. Hell. How ridiculous did it make him that he wanted to throw down with that strand of hair for the privilege it just enjoyed? "The truth... The truth is the date went great. Wonderful, even. Gavin was perfect, so was the food and conversation. But—" she lifted her gaze back to his, and his chest rose on a harsh, deep inhalation "—the entire time, I couldn't shake the feeling of it being...wrong. Because I couldn't stop thinking about you. You're my friend—my best friend, Kenan. I shouldn't have been sitting there regretting answering the phone last week. Shouldn't have been wondering what would've happened if I'd ignored it. Shouldn't have..." Her voice trailed off, but her fingers lifted, trembled just over her lips. "Shouldn't have been wanting your mouth on mine. Feeling it there. Needing it there again," she whispered.

Kenan briefly closed his eyes. Lust howled and snapped inside him, and only the most threadbare of bindings kept him in place. Prevented him from charging forward and crowding her against the nearest wall. Stopped him from hauling her in his arms and giving her his mouth and his cock.

At his continued silence, she staggered back a step. "I'm sorry." She pressed her fingertips to her forehead, dipping her chin. "Shit." Wincing, she edged around him. "I'm sorry," she repeated. "I shouldn't have— I crossed a line, and... Dammit, we're friends..."

"Eve." Heart a primal drum in his chest, he shifted, blocking her path. Jesus, how could he speak, or fucking think, with so much need pumping through him? "Look at me."

"No, it's all right. I'm—"

"Don't make me beg." *That* had her gaze jerking up to his. He moved closer. And closer still until only a breath of space separated them. "Because I will. You have that much power over me." He bowed his head, whispered in her ear, "And I almost resent you for that."

Her soft, shaky gasp kissed his cheek, quivered over his dick.

"Kenan." Her fingers fumbled at his hips, then hooked into the waist of his pants, holding on to him.

"What, Eve?" He moved forward, ushering her backward until her back met the wall. Pressing his forearms on either side of her head, he surrounded her. And she besieged him—her scent, her warmth, the short, fast breaths on his skin. He was under her sensual assault, and fuck if he wasn't a willing prisoner of war. "Tell me what you want. Make it clear."

She didn't reply to his demand, but a hard shiver wracked her body, and it ricocheted through him even though the slimmest of spaces remained between them. He straightened his arms, levering back so he could peer down into her face. Glimpse the confusion and—*God*—desire that darkened her eyes to near black. Note her hesitation in the cinching of her eyebrows, the tightening of her lush mouth.

"You need me to say it?" he asked. When she tentatively nodded, he cupped her cheek then slid his hand into her curls, bunching the thick mass in his fist. "I can do that for you."

He surrendered to the driving urge to taste her. Just a little. He brushed his lips over her forehead. Over the bridge of her nose. At the corner of her mouth. He lifted his head, his pulse deafening in his head. Too far. He was pushing himself too far, too fast.

"You need me to take your mouth like I did in that club. Take it, bruise it, make you feel me long after the kiss is ended. But you don't want it to end, do you? You've been thinking about my hands on you." His voice deepened, roughened. Hunger twisted inside him, grabbing him, insisting he satiate it. "Wondering if I'd cup your breasts, mold them in my hands, or if I'd start with these pretty nipples." He dipped his head, taking in the hard tips clearly outlined beneath her dress. Beautiful. So damn beautiful and he needed them between his lips, on his tongue. He shook his head, raising his gaze back to hers. Jesus, what had he been saying? "You've been thinking about how I could give this petite, gorgeous body pleasure. How I'd push into you, filling you..." His mouth hovered just above hers, and he tasted each pant that painted her lips. "Fucking you."

She closed her eyes, that full, tempting mouth trembling. That wouldn't do.

He craved the weight of that gaze on him.

"Eyes on me," he softly ordered. Once she complied, he cocked his head. "How did I do, Eve? Did I get it right?"

"Yes." Her grip on his waist tightened, pulled harder. "God, *yes*."

That moaned word splintered the last of his control.

He captured her mouth, plunging his tongue between her lips in a swift, carnal attack. They were past shy, gentle introductions. No, he consumed her like a lover who'd been here often. And he had.

In his dreams, he'd conquered her sweet mouth many times before.

He was a fucking connoisseur of her mouth.

Did Gavin kiss her? Is she coming to me with my brother on her?

The image of the two of them together, like this, tried to shove its way into his head, and for a moment, he stuttered, paused. Did he care? Yes. And no. If Gavin had tasted her, then he would wipe the memory from her. Brand himself on her. Tomorrow, her lips would still throb with his possession.

Sliding his other hand into her hair, he held her still and set about his mission. Corrupting. Marking. Owning. At least for tonight.

Eve tugged him against her even as she rose on her toes and met him stroke for stroke, lick for lick. Nip for nip. Their tongues, lips and teeth melded, clashed, battled. This wasn't a leisurely kiss, or a tender one. It was hurried, messy, wet.

It was perfection.

Goddamn, the fresh yet earthy flavor of her. He could gulp it down like his favorite Scotch and let it set him aflame. Drown him in heat and pleasure until he was completely intoxicated. He could become a glutton with her and regret nothing.

Which was why he should halt this now before they went too far and couldn't cross back over that line. He should—

"More." Her whimper slid over his skin in a silken caress. "Give me more."

He should grant her everything she asked—pleaded—for. It would be his pleasure…his honor.

With a groan, he possessed her mouth again and gave his hands free rein. First, her bared, graceful shoulders received his adoration. Then the strong yet delicate line of her collarbone. The slim, elegant column of her throat. He touched. He indulged. And with one last hard kiss, he lowered his head to follow the path his hands had tread.

Right there. Right in the hollow where shoulder and neck met. That cedarwood-and-roses scent greeted him, so rich and heady. He nuzzled the nook, licked it. Sucked it. Damn. Would this fragrance be thicker, even more potent, between her beautiful thighs? Oh, he intended to find out.

He dragged his lips over the top of her chest and slid his palms to just under her breasts. The weight of them rested on the back of his hands, and he stopped. Waited.

"Yes?" he asked, his voice little more than a hoarse rasp, sandpapered by lust.

Eve covered his hands with hers and pushed them up until he cupped her firm breasts, a shade less than a handful. They both groaned, and she arched into his hold, her head pressing into the wall. Her lashes fluttered down, her teeth sinking into her bottom lip. She was erotic art come to beautiful, carnal life.

Inhaling a breath that seemed infused with need, he stared down at his hands squeezing her, at his thumbs rubbing small circles around the taut peaks that pushed against her dress. Wonder sighed through him. He was touching her; this wasn't one of those nights when he woke up, sweating, hurting, with his cock in his fist. Because he could, he grazed his teeth over a dress-covered nipple, and satisfaction roared loud and fierce within him when she jerked, a small cry piercing the air.

Her hands flew to his head, holding him to her, encouraging him without words to give her what she'd demanded—more.

Reaching behind her, he located the zipper and tugged it down. Impatience rode him, and in moments, he had the dress stripped down over her hips and legs and pooled around her stilettoes.

"Fuck, sweetheart," he breathed, reverence heavy in his voice, his chest. Standing in front of him in a sexy strapless black bra, matching panties and heels, she stole the air from his lungs. And had hunger pouring through him like gasoline just waiting for the match. "You're beautiful." He brushed the side of her breast with the back of a knuckle. "So goddamn beautiful. More than I—"

He cut himself off, trapping the rest of that too-revealing sentence between his teeth. This was about tonight, the here and now. Tomorrow, she might very well look at him with regret in her eyes, and damn if he would compound the pain of that with a revelation of how he'd dreamed about her stripped bare and trembling before him. Because the tiny part of his mind not clouded with lust acknowledged that she would hurt him. There was no avoiding it.

But at this moment, while unsnapping her bra and filling his hands with her perfect breasts, the dark brown beaded nipples stabbing his palms, he didn't give a fuck. This—he dipped his head, sucked a tip into his mouth— was worth that inevitable pain.

She hissed, her nails scraping his scalp as she clutched him to her. And when he switched to the other, neglected breast, she guided him, lowering a hand to her flesh, holding herself up to his greedy lips and tongue.

By the time he sank to his knees, bracketing her hips in his palms and trailing his mouth down her stomach, she twisted in his grasp, working those rounded hips in a sensual dance that enticed him to join her. And he did.

With his mouth.

"Kenan." She choked out his name, rocking against him. "Please…"

He didn't need her to finish that plea; he understood. And he answered by nipping at her folds through the insubstantial lace of her panties. Hooking a finger in the soaked panel, he tugged the material to the side and feasted on her. He sucked and nibbled. But soon that wasn't enough, either. He removed her heels and yanked her underwear down and off. Then he returned to her, licking up that drenched path until he nudged the engorged bundle of nerves at the top of her sex.

Her muted scream punched the air just as her hips bucked forward. Growling against her, he restrained her restless, wild movements with an arm low across her belly, holding her still for his greedy mouth. With every lap and caress, every stroke and swirl over her swollen, hot flesh, lust gripped his dick, pounded in it, squeezed it.

He'd never come from giving oral sex before, but he'd never had his mouth on Eve before. And there was a first time for everything.

"Your choice, sweetheart." He tipped back his head, met her passion-glazed eyes. Pride and satisfaction blazed as fierce and bright in him as the need howling in his blood. No matter what happened after tonight, he'd put that flush in her cheeks, that haze of pleasure in her eyes. He'd sent shudders rippling through her, had cries breaking on her pretty lips. Him. "Come first on my tongue or on my cock." He licked a slow, teasing path around her clit, and her nails grazed over his scalp, trailed down to bite into his shoulders. "Tell me what you want."

"You." She gasped then moaned long and sweet as he slid two fingers inside her tight sex. "Oh, God. You."

He hummed, thrusting lazily, twisting his wrist at the end of each stroke. "Those weren't your choices. Mouth or cock, Eve."

For several seconds, she didn't answer, too consumed with riding his hand. And he allowed it, enraptured by the sight of her. She whimpered, bending over him to cup his face, slide her thumb into mouth. He nipped it, soothing away the sting with his tongue.

"You. Inside me," she rasped. "I need that. I need you."

He froze, those words penetrating the thick fog of lust

to reach deeper inside him and fist his heart, brush his soul. Would he ever hear those words outside of this aberration of a moment?

Shoving aside the thought, he rose to his feet, fingers still pumping into her, still stroking her stiff nub of flesh. He crushed his mouth to hers, letting her taste herself on him. And she clung to him, driving her tongue between his lips, taking, taking…

"I want to give you gentle. You deserve it." He bent low enough to hike her into his arms. And when her strong legs wrapped around his waist and her hot, wet center ground against his abs, he didn't bother suppressing the rough sound of need that clawed its way up and out of his throat. "But I don't know if I can."

He'd wanted her too long. Even now, his body shook with that years-denied hunger.

"Don't be gentle. Don't handle me," she whispered against his neck.

Then she bit him. Lightly, but that soft sting arrowed straight to his dick, and he almost stumbled with her in his arms.

Steeling himself, he focused on stalking to his bedroom, entering and heading for the bed. Carefully, he laid her down on the mattress. And without removing his gaze from her gorgeous body of curves and dips and hollows, he removed his clothes in indecent haste. He'd become single-minded in his purpose.

Which was getting inside her.

He climbed on the bed, crawling over her body until he crouched over her.

"Kenan." She breathed his name, and the wonder that laced her tone as her gaze took in his bare shoulders, chest, thighs and his hard, erect dick. That visual caress had him throbbing, and he gripped himself, squeezing to try to alleviate that deep ache. He stroked himself, his fist sliding over his head, then sliding back down. Her lips parted and her heavy pants peppered the air. Pure hunger suffused her expression and his gut was hit with a spasm in response. She looked at him like she wanted to replace his hand with hers...or with her mouth.

Fuck. He might not survive this. But damn, if he didn't want to lay his life on the line to find out.

"You're stunning," she murmured, her scrutiny of him returning to his face. She cupped his cheek, levered up to brush a kiss over his mouth. Then dipped her tongue between his lips, tasting more of him. "God, you're stunning."

He buried his face in the crook of her neck, breathing her in. Hiding. Because he knew what his face would reveal.

A moment later, he shifted, reaching for the bedside dresser, and pulled open the drawer and removed a condom from it. Quickly, he opened the package and sheathed himself, then returned to her. Eve wound her arms around his shoulders, his neck, drawing him down to her. Damn, his heart. It thumped against his rib cage. Love, need and fear hurled through him at warp speed. Once he drove inside her, they couldn't go back. They couldn't undo this. Alarm sizzled down his spine, a warning.

"Is this what you want, Eve?" He threaded his fingers through her hair, gripping her head on both sides. "Be sure."

"I want this. I want *you*." Her hands slid under his arms and curled over his shoulders, tugging him close until his chest pressed against her full breasts. "Inside me, Kenan."

He closed his eyes and gave them both what they craved.

Heat. Pressure. Wet.

He locked down a hoarse shout as he pushed into her,

but it echoed in his head. Nothing had ever felt this good, this *vital*. And nothing mattered but being completely surrounded by her. Embraced by her tight, quivering flesh. Everything in him hissed that he should thrust hard, sink inside her. But a small part of him that retained a semblance of sanity slowed, halted. Allowed her clenching sex to become accustomed to him. They were the best of friends; he knew it'd been a while for her. And though it stretched his control so far that sweat dotted his face, back and chest, he waited. Because possibly hurting her killed him more than being tortured by the sweet and sinful clasp of her body.

"This is about you," he whispered, nuzzling her jaw and scattering kisses along the delicate line. "Let me know when you're ready."

She slipped her hands down his damp back, over his hips, not stopping until she grasped his ass.

"Move. Please, move."

"Jesus, Eve." He groaned, slowly withdrew and released another moan when her flesh sucked at him, as if bemoaning his leaving. When only the head of his cock remained notched inside her, he paused, then thrust back home.

Home.

Because he'd never truly belonged, never really experienced a place of utter safety and beauty until this moment. Inside her.

He pulled free and plunged back into her again, slowly, tenderly. Gritting his teeth, he fought against the urge, the need, to ride her hard and raw. Despite what she'd said earlier, what he claimed about not being able to go gentle, he could give her this. Even if it drove him insane.

"You promised." Her harsh breath brushed his cheek, then his mouth, as she grazed her teeth over his bottom lip, then nipped it. "Take me like you need. Don't handle me."

As if her permission was the shears that snipped his control, he let go. Wrapping his arms around her, he cuddled her close and fucked her. Hard. Wild. Like he needed.

Like *they* needed.

Their bodies crashed together in a carnal war—loud, sweaty, laying siege to one another. With each short, fast thrust or slow, grinding glide, she gave it back to him in equal measure. Her cries and his grunts punctuated the air. The slap of damp skin greeting damp skin, the sound of her sex releasing and receiving him, created an erotic soundtrack that was now his favorite album. One he would replay over and over.

This couldn't last. Already that record skipped as electric pulses rippled up and down his spine, sizzling in the soles of his feet. Pleasure stretched him tight, and one wrong move, one sudden twitch, and he would hurl over that ledge into oblivion. But not without her.

Reaching between them, he swept his thumb over the stiff button of flesh, murmuring to her when she jerked and bucked against his touch. Once more. And once again. That's all it took for her flesh to clamp down on him in an almost brutal grip, milking him, coaxing his orgasm from him even as she shook and screamed in her own.

Somehow, he held back, riveted by the sight of her lost in ecstasy. He pistoned between her thighs, burying himself over and over, determined to wring every ounce of pleasure for her. And only when her whimpers echoed between them and her body started to go lax, did he unleash the fury spiraling inside him.

Part of him fought going over. He needed just a little more time inside her. Just a little. But his cock wasn't hearing it. Pleasure plowed into him, and he followed Eve into that abyss.

Afraid that when he crawled out, he would be alone. Again.

Nine

Kenan stepped off the elevator onto the fifteenth floor of the downtown office building. Silence greeted him, as did the familiar offices of Rhodes Realty. On a Saturday morning, no employees sat at the desks, the phones didn't ring and the hum of voices didn't fill the air. He would've thought it odd to be summoned to his family's business by his brother on a weekend if Kenan wasn't aware that five-day workweeks didn't apply to his brother or parents. When a deal called, they answered. Kenan had adopted the same work ethic. Although his father might not believe that Kenan had actually inherited something from him.

Exhaling a breath that seemed to echo in the empty offices, he scrubbed a hand over his head. Not only did he have to face his brother possessing the knowledge that Gavin wanted the woman Kenan had just been balls-deep inside, but now he also had to face his ghosts.

It'd been months since he'd visited this place that used

to be his second home. Not because it contained painful memories. No, he didn't feel as if he would be welcomed. Not when he'd abandoned the company for Farrell. At least that's how his family defined it. Which only increased his curiosity over this mysterious request from Gavin. That curiosity hadn't been the only thing that had driven Kenan from his house, though.

Eve had.

Or, rather, thoughts of Eve. Because when he woke that morning after a night of the hottest sex he'd ever had, she'd disappeared. He'd reached for her again and touched cold, empty sheets. Any remnants of sleep had evaporated then, and in the hours since, he'd been vacillating between calling her and demanding to know why she'd crept out like a guilty thief, and avoiding his phone in case she did call. Hearing her voice and discovering she regretted the night before...

Yeah, ignorance was indeed bliss.

Giving his head a shake, he focused on his brother's closed office door. A vise tightened around his ribs as he glanced to his left and the door that once held his nameplate. It didn't any longer. That shouldn't have had pain spiking in her chest. But it did.

Hell, he'd been erased.

Clenching his jaw, he strode toward his brother's office. With a perfunctory knock, he opened the door.

"Hey, Gavin. What's all this—" He slammed to a halt, noting the other two people sitting in the chairs in front of his brother's desk. "Mom. Dad." He frowned as Gavin straightened from his perch on the furniture. "This is... unexpected. What's going on? Is something wrong?"

"No, nothing's wrong." Gavin waved him inside. "Come on in."

Then why all the secrecy? Why do I feel like I'm being ambushed? The demands burned his tongue, but he doused them as his parents stood. Wariness sidled through him, but so did a cautious joy. He loved his family, and this strain on their relationship, this separation of the last eight months, had been a punishment. A punishment for a crime he hadn't committed.

Tucking aside that old wound with new scars for the moment, he closed the door behind him and walked farther into the office.

"Kenan." His mother held her hands out to him, and he grasped them, dutifully bending down so she could kiss his cheek. "It's good to see you."

He didn't miss the light note of censure in her voice. Translation: you've been too busy for your family.

"You, too," he murmured. "Dad, how're you?"

His father nodded. "Fine, Kenan."

So formal. So reserved.

In other words, business as usual.

"While I'm glad to spend time with you, I'm assuming there's a reason for this meeting. And that it's not just a coincidence that we're all here." He arched an eyebrow at his brother, who at least had the grace to look sheepish. "So what's going on?"

"Dad, Mom and I wanted to talk with you about something. A proposal, if you will."

Unease curled into a tight ball inside him, lodging between his ribs.

"Okay." His gaze shifted from his brother to his parents' matching stoic expressions, then moved back to Gavin. "I'm listening."

"For the last few weeks, we've been negotiating a possible project in Suffolk Downs with Darren and Shawn Young of The Brower Group for a mixed-use development," his father said. "The deal is almost closed."

"That's wonderful. Congratulations. A project with

The Brower Group of that size means only good things for Rhodes Realty."

Nathan crossed his arms. "Exactly. I'm glad you understand that." He paused, and that unease in Kenan's chest expanded, sprouted roots that snaked down to his stomach. "Because Darren and Shawn have made it clear that they would prefer you to be a part of this deal. They like what you did with the marketing on the Allston Yards development last year and want you to replicate it for them."

Kenan frowned. "That's flattering. But they do know I'm not with the company any longer, right?"

His mother released a choked sound that could've been dismissive or signaled disgust. Probably somewhere in between, considering the topic. "Yes, they're very aware. Which is why they've issued this not-so-subtle condition as part of the deal. They want you involved."

Kenan's head jerked back. "Are you telling me that if I'm not included as part of the marketing team, then the deal doesn't happen?" What the hell was going on here?

Gavin stepped forward, sliding his hands into his pants pockets. "That's what was implied, but if push comes to shove, I don't know how serious they are about sticking to that stipulation." He glanced at his parents, his mouth firming before he shifted his attention to Kenan. "What Mom and Dad are trying to say—what *we* are trying to say—is that we'd like you to return to Rhodes Realty."

Kenan stared at his brother, any icy fist plowing into him. The cold crept inward to his veins, to his bones, until he couldn't move. A maelstrom of emotions swamped him. Yes, shock, but also anger because after all these months, they only wanted him back in the company when it might potentially cost them. Delight because, God, they needed him—his family wanted him. And pain because he was going to disappoint them; he had no choice.

"You know I'd love to help you in any way I could—" he held his hands out, palms up "—but I can't leave Farrell right now. I explained the stipulation of the will to you. For one year, I have to stay with the company or we lose everything—not just me, but Cain and Achilles, too. I've made a commitment, and I can't renege on that."

"So you would just let our company, our family company, suffer because you've defected to another business? For men you've known a matter of months, while you've been a part of us for thirty years?" his mother snapped. She laughed, but it contained no humor, only a scalpel sharp edge. "Does what we've built together mean so little to you now?"

What they'd built together? Bitterness coated his tongue. He'd never felt as if he truly belonged here. Only his last name had afforded him an office, because it damn sure hadn't given him respect. That had been offered unconditionally to Gavin, not him. Not even Kenan's talent as a businessman had been appreciated or acknowledged, especially not by Nathan.

But he swallowed down those bitter words. Dana didn't want to hear it, and Kenan recognized the futility of trying to make them understand. Frustration surged hot and bright, mating with a helpless anger that, for a brief moment, stole his power. Left him standing there as the boy who always felt like the orphan with grubby fingers staring into a window at the happy, *complete* family that he'd never be a part of.

Inhaling a deliberate breath, he shut down his feelings, boarded up his heart with a No Trespassing sign. If he didn't allow them entrance, they couldn't hurt him.

At least that was his theory.

"I don't believe I have to dignify that question with a response, because you already know the answer," Kenan quietly said. "You know I love you and would help you if I could. But you're asking me to break my word. And you and Dad have always taught me that a man's word is his bond. And if I go back on mine, it doesn't affect just me or Cain and Achilles. It harms employees, investors and countless others. I won't do that."

"What about a commitment to us?" his father demanded, voice as hard and unflinching as stone. It matched the gaze that narrowed on Kenan. "You made promises to us first that come with being family. None should take precedence over that."

"They're family, too, Dad," Kenan murmured. "As much as you hate to recognize them or their existence, they're my brothers."

"This is *bullshit*," his mother hissed, slashing a hand through the air. "Utter bullshit!"

Silence, quivering with shock and tension, descended on the office. Gavin and Kenan stared at Dana, stunned into speechlessness. Kenan could count on one hand the number of times he'd heard his mother curse, and he might have a couple of fingers left over. And while he'd witnessed her anger, she'd never trembled with it, red streaking her cheekbones. At her sides, her fingers curled and straightened.

Kenan glanced at his father, who studied his wife, his expression inscrutable.

"Mom," Gavin said, moving toward her. "It's okay. I—"

"No, Gavin, it's not. There's nothing about this that's *okay*," she snarled, then whipped around to Kenan. "*We're* your family, Kenan. We've been there for you all your life, and *we* deserve your undivided loyalty. Somehow, you've forgotten that, and I'm ashamed of you for it."

He flinched, a hole ripping open in his chest.

"For the last few months, you've lorded Barron Farrell over our heads as if he's some great savior because he gave you a company to run. As if that makes you better than us."

"That's not true," he murmured thickly.

But she didn't seem to hear him, she was so caught up in a vitriolic diatribe, one that she must've been holding in for a while. She stabbed a finger toward him, and continued, voice shaking with her fury.

"Well, let me enlighten you, Kenan. Regardless of his money, status and influence, Barron Farrell was a bastard, and you shouldn't be proud to claim him as your father or his sons as your brothers. There's nothing honorable in that last name. We raised you, loved you. But you're so caught up in their spell, you've forgotten that. Forgotten us."

With one last, long glare, she stalked out of the office.

Pain pulsed through him, pumped with each heartbeat. It stole his breath, his voice. How was he standing when every bit of him *hurt*?

"Kenan." Gavin took a step toward him, arm outstretched. Sadness weighed down his brown gaze. "She didn't mean that…"

Kenan looked at his father. "Didn't she?" he murmured, replying to his brother but maintaining visual contact with—issuing that demand to—his father.

Not waiting for an answer, he turned and left the office the same way he'd entered.

Alone.

Ten

Eve laid down her stylus pen, stared at her tablet and slowly smiled.

Oh, yes, she'd knocked this out the park.

Rising from the couch, she stretched, but her gaze remained on the screen with her latest design for Kenan's proposal. A complex but sexy crisscross of straps comprised the black bra-and-panty set, offering a peekaboo of skin while also providing adequate coverage. The design was a flat-out tease, and she adored it. Kenan would, too...

She frowned, slowly lowering her arms.

Kenan.

It'd been a little over twelve hours since she'd sneaked out of his bed as if performing a walk of shame. In hindsight, she should've just woken him up and told him she was leaving. Or...

She could've stayed.

Closing her eyes, she pinched the bridge of her nose.

Regret swarmed inside her, stinging. Not remorse over having sex with Kenan. God, how could a person bemoan multiple, reality-bending orgasms? She was no hypocrite.

No, she regretted the aftermath. Her uncertainty. The silence. The worry that they'd blown up a decades-long friendship.

The confusion, because God help her, but she didn't think she cared...

Groaning, she bowed her head, more than a little disgusted with herself. Had Kenan mesmerized her with his dick? That had to be the only explanation for why she was willing to risk their long relationship to have more of what he'd given her last night.

She was officially dick-matized.

She huffed out a ragged chuckle.

She was in so much trouble.

Even now, as memories from the night before filled her head, heat licked at her and she shifted, squeezing her thighs together at the ache tightening her nipples and blooming between her thighs. Kenan possessing her mouth like she was oxygen and he'd been deprived for years. Kenan kneeling before her, head tipped back, bright eyes burning up at her, lips swollen and damp with her. Kenan crouched over her, hard, beautiful cock notched in her sex, ready to push into her...

A breath shuddered out of her. That ache intensified and she pressed a hand low to her belly. She wanted more—more pleasure, more orgasms, more of *him*. She was honest enough with herself to admit that. But the consequences of that "more" scared her. Her body might be willing to risk her friendship with Kenan, but her heart? Her mind? They weren't on board. Yet, with Kenan's silence all day, the damage might have already been done.

The doorbell rang, dragging her from the morose road her thoughts had traveled.

Thank God.

Striding to the door, her pulse sped. And, grimacing, she hated herself a little for it. She'd gotten over her pre-teen crush on Kenan eons ago. Reverting to that time of sweaty palms and eternal blushing didn't appeal to her.

Oh, oops. Too late.

Dammit.

Running her hand over her bound curls, she peeked through the peephole. Astonishment rippled through her, and she quickly twisted the lock and pulled open her front door.

"Hey, Mom. This is a surprise."

Yolanda Burke smiled at her, leaning in to kiss Eve's cheek.

"A good one, I hope. I haven't talked to you in a couple of days." Her mother moved forward, and Eve shifted backward, allowing her entrance. "I was out having dinner with some friends and decided to stop by and see how you were doing."

"You're right, then." Eve returned her mother's smile. "This is a good surprise. Would you like something to drink? Coffee? Water? I was about to grab a glass of wine."

"I already had two glasses at dinner." Yolanda laughed. "I think I better take you up on that coffee."

"Look at you being a lush out in public." Eve grinned at her mother's snort.

She headed into the kitchen to prepare the coffee and her wine.

"What've you been up to? Work's been keeping you busy?" Yolanda asked a couple of moments later.

"Definitely. And it's starting to get warmer, so you know what that means." She chuckled, pouring the wine as the coffee maker brewed behind her. "Spring-itis. I'm fighting to keep their attention from the window, the girl or boy next to them, their phones. Everything but the lesson."

When her mother didn't answer, Eve frowned but continued preparing their drinks. Grabbing the coffee cup and her wineglass, she exited the kitchen and entered her living room. And drew up short.

Yolanda was standing in front of the couch, Eve's tablet in her hands.

The tablet that held Eve's latest designs for Intimate Curves.

Fear flooded her, filling her mouth until she almost choked on its briny taste. Her grip on the cup and glass tightened. She parted her lips to say…what? *Put that down. It's nothing. I've just been sketching again. It's not what you think.*

How about the truth?

She shook her head at that last suggestion. Keeping her secret from her mother had become such a habit that revealing it now wasn't even an option.

"What's this, Eve?" Yolanda finally lifted her head, flipping over the tablet and holding it up. As if Eve wouldn't recognize the sexy lingerie design. "Did you do this?"

Hypersensitive to her mother, she listened, ears straining, for any disappointment, any anger…or disgust. But she didn't catch anything. Nothing colored her voice. No, that wasn't true, either. Maybe curiosity? But how could that be true?

Eve was perched at a crossroads.

Continue to conceal the truth about her lingerie company from her mother and not risk upsetting and failing her.

Or finally confess and trust that their relationship would survive Eve's fear of not being the daughter Yolanda wanted…and, frankly, deserved.

Oh, God, she was scared.

Swallowing hard, she silently weighed her options over the symphony of her pounding heart. Fingers growing numb around the drinks in her hands, she forced her feet forward, fully entered the living room and set the cup and glass down on the table. Then she gently took the tablet from her mother and stared down at the design she'd been so proud of only minutes ago.

Scratch that. That she was still damn proud of.

And that thought made her decide which road to take.

"Yes," Eve said. "I designed this. It's one of many I've done."

Whew. Funny, she'd expected a weight to have lifted off her chest with that admission, but it still pressed on her rib cage. And when her mother tilted her head, pinning her with that unwavering gaze she'd employed since Eve's childhood, it became a little more difficult for her to breathe.

"One of many," Yolanda repeated. "I didn't know you were still drawing. I thought you'd stopped doing that in high school."

Here. This could be her out. Claim that, yes, this was just a hobby. But she was so tired of hiding this part of herself from one of the most important people in her life. So she inhaled and leaped.

"No, Mom, I never stopped. I couldn't if I wanted to, and believe me, I tried all those years ago. But sketching, art, designing—I love it too much." She paused, fear bottoming out her stomach, but she pushed on. "I adore teaching and it's been a great career. But… But it's not my only career. For the past four years I've run Intimate Curves, an online lingerie company catering to plus-size women. I own it and am the designer. This—" she tapped the tablet's screen "—is one of the designs that will be featured in my first brick-and-mortar store in the Bromberg's renovation."

Her mother stared at her, brown eyes almost black with shock. After several moments, Yolanda turned her head to the side, as if she couldn't stand the sight of Eve. That pit in Eve's stomach filled with pain, grief and anger. Was the thought of her designing underwear so salacious that her mother couldn't even look at her? Just because Eve didn't walk the path Yolanda believed she should, had Eve so horribly disappointed her?

I'm a successful businesswoman of an award-winning company. I earn a living doing what I love most. My business will be in a nationally recognized chain of department stores. You should be proud of me.

The rant reverberated in her head, and she strangled the tablet, her fingers aching in protest.

"Mom—" she rasped.

"For four years you've had a whole part of your life that you've kept hidden from me?" her mother interrupted, facing her again. Her eyes, which had been dark before, nearly smoldered with heat now. They narrowed on Eve even as her chin jerked high. "I'm your mother and until this moment I believed we were close, that we had the kind of relationship where you could tell me anything, but obviously I was wrong."

Wait. *What?* She was angry because she hadn't told her about the business? "Mom, I didn't think—"

"That's right. You didn't. Not about how it would feel to find out *years later* that my daughter thinks so little of me, of our relationship, that she would hide something as important to her as a business, a career. And for what? What have I done to you, Eve, that you would hurt me like this?"

Voice cracking on "this," her mother rushed around the table and toward the front door.

Panic attacked Eve and she charged after Yolanda.

"Mom, I'm sorry," she whispered. "I didn't mean to hurt you. This is on me."

"You're right this is on you." Yolanda grabbed the doorknob and yanked it open, then paused in the doorway. Her shoulders straightened even though Eve caught the catch in her mother's breath. "We're going to talk about this, Eve. But I need space. I'll call you."

She stepped outside and quietly pulled the door closed behind her. Eve stared at it and part of her wished that her mother had slammed it shut. That soft snick somehow seemed more accusatory, more condemning.

More final.

What had she done?

Minutes, or what seemed like hours or, God, *days* later, the doorbell rang while she was still standing there, and Eve lunged for the knob, twisting it and yanking the door open, her heart lodged in her throat.

Please, let me just have the chance to apologize. I'm so sorry. I swear, I didn't know—

"Kenan." She blinked, trying to adjust to seeing her friend on her welcome mat instead of her mother. "What are you doing here?"

"I came by to see you." He cocked his head, and his blue-gray gaze seemed brighter in her small, shadowed porch as he studied her with an intensity that she longed to hide from. "What's wrong?"

"What? Nothing." The automatic denial leaped from her, and she waved a hand. "Nothing," she repeated.

"Right." He stepped forward, and by habit, her feet moved backward, letting him inside her ground-level apartment. "And nothing is why you're standing there looking shell-shocked."

He closed the door behind him, locking it. Then pulled her into his arms. And the familiarity of his embrace, of his scent, of *him*, enveloped her, and the ice that had encased her since her mother left cracked. And she did, too, right down the middle.

Standing there in the foyer, she told him about her mother's visit and the resulting blowup. He listened, his hold on her never faltering even as her voice thickened with the admission that she'd hurt her mother and potentially damaged their relationship.

"I'm sorry, sweetheart," he murmured, his big hands rubbing up and down her spine. She burrowed closer into his tall, powerful frame, seeking his strength, leaning into it. "I know how much you love her and the courage it took for you to tell her the truth. I hate it for both of you that the conversation ended that way."

"You should've seen her face, Kenan." An image of her mother's expression flashed on the back of her eyelids and Eve flinched. "I've always been so afraid of disappointing her. That's what I was hoping to avoid by not telling her about Intimate Curves. And it's what I ended up doing, anyway. She might have been angry, but underneath, she was so hurt. I did that to her."

She eased out of his embrace and scrubbed both hands down her face. Pacing away from him, she let loose a small, humorless chuckle.

"All my life I've tried to be the perfect daughter for her. To compensate for being a burden—for being the replica of a man who didn't have the guts or the integrity to stick around. Can you imagine how painful it is to have a constant reminder of the man who abandoned you? So to make up for that, I've tried to never cause her worry or trouble or pain. Even if that meant giving up certain activities she didn't approve of. Even if it meant obtaining a degree and job in a field that didn't fulfill me, but it made her proud. It meant she didn't have to worry about me. She deserves that peace, that security. If the price was hiding a part of myself, then it was a small cost and one I was willing to pay. For her, I would do anything."

"But, sweetheart, did she ever ask you to?"

She paused midstride, whirling around to face him. "She didn't have to." She thrust out her hands, palms up. "Don't you see? She sacrificed for me all those years— it's my privilege to do the same for her. It's not something people who love each other should have to ask for."

Kenan slowly approached her as one might with an injured animal. And as offensive as that thought struck her, the sentiment wasn't that far off. The ache in her chest throbbed like an open wound.

"Eve." He swept a hand over her hair, his fingers curling into the bun on top of her head before continuing down, where he cupped the back of her neck. "We've been friends for a long time, and that affords me some leeway that others don't have, to be honest."

He lifted his other hand to her cheek and skated his thumb over her it. For a long moment, he peered down at her, those startlingly beautiful eyes too knowing.

"You are not, nor have you ever been, a burden. And it pisses me off to hear you refer to yourself like that. Almost as long as we've been in each other's lives, I've seen you try to reach this unobtainable standard and expectation of perfection that no one set—not your mother, not an absentee father—except you. You have been too damn hard on yourself, have driven yourself...have punished yourself. And for what reason? For being born to a single mother? Hell, Eve, you didn't ask to be here. That was your parents' decision, your mother's choice, not yours. And I can say with an absolute certainty that she's never regretted her choice. She loves you. Would do anything for you. *Has* done everything for you. And I think you underestimate that love she has for you and yours for her when you deny your dreams and passion. She wouldn't want you to sacrifice either for her like some penance. That's an insult to her. To both of you."

He pressed his lips to her forehead, and Eve closed her eyes, savoring that caress as much as she soaked up his words. She didn't know if she believed them, but dammit, she grasped hold of them like a lifeline. Because, God, she wanted to believe him. She was desperate to believe him.

"You are a gift to her, Eve. And to me, too. And gifts are given without strings or expectations."

He was going to break her. Without even trying, he was going to break her open, and all the need, confusion and snarled feelings of fear and love were going to spill out all over both of them. And she couldn't have that. Not now. Not when she was so raw and uncertain about where they stood in this no-man's-land between friendship and...other.

Nodding, she stepped back, forcing his hands to drop away. Good. She could think clearer when those big, mind-muddling hands weren't touching her.

"Your turn." She strode into the living room, making a beeline for her neglected wineglass. She needed it more than ever now. "What're you doing here? And don't try to tell me you were in the neighborhood because Back Bay is twenty minutes away."

With the question out there, a dense tension, fraught with sex, filled the room. At least on her part. Because images from the night before bombarded her—the two of them twisted, tangled and naked.

Snatching up her glass, she downed half in several gulps before turning to look at him. And from the gleam brightening that gaze until it damn near glowed, she guessed his thoughts had ventured in the same direction. But then he shook his head, glancing away. When he returned his scrutiny to her several moments later, that heat was banked, and frustration and disappointment comingled inside her.

Fine. They were going to ignore the topic of cataclysmic sex. Duly noted.

"Honestly, I don't know." He lifted a shoulder, a wry smile quirking the corners of his mouth. "I was sitting at home and had no plans for the evening, but then I'm in my car and sitting outside your house. I think I couldn't stand my own company."

"I understand that. I haven't been able to stand your company before." She smiled around the rim of her glass, taking another sip as he snorted. "There's something you're not telling me. Might as well spill, because if you drove all the way over here, I'm not letting it go." When he didn't immediately reply, she exhaled. "Oh, shit. Is this going to require more wine?"

"Probably. Definitely. If you have anything harder, get it."

Minutes later, she had another bottle of merlot on the coffee table and passed him a glass filled to the brim.

"Sorry. Nothing stronger. Now tell me. Let me make it better."

He stared at her, and her breath caught at the flash of desire in his gaze. Yeah, her word choice could've been different. Damn if she'd take it back, though. If he needed her body again she'd willingly give it to him.

Lowering his thick fringe of lashes, he accepted the glass, their fingertips grazing and sending an electrified current snapping up her arm and tingling in her breasts. Silently, she ordered her nipples not to harden beneath her thin hoodie.

"It seems today is the day for family issues." He gave a low laugh that had her stomach tightening...and not in a good way. "Gavin called me this morning and asked me to come down to the office. When I arrived, my parents were there, too."

She frowned. "He didn't say anything about them being there? That's weird." And shady.

"No, and I soon found out why. They have a deal on the table, and one of the conditions of it is my participation as head of marketing. They want me to leave Farrell and return to Rhodes Realty." His lips twisted into a dark caricature of a smile. "Of course, Gavin had to say that part—my parents couldn't. Or wouldn't."

"Are you serious?" She set down her wineglass on the table and leaned forward. "They just want you to quit a company you're part owner of and return to the fold. Just like that?"

He huffed out another of those humorless chuckles that pained her to hear.

"Just like that. Although, that's not how they view it. According to my parents, my loyalty belongs with them, not Farrell, or Cain and Achilles. There shouldn't be a choice. I believe my mother's words were they 'deserved my undivided loyalty and she's ashamed of me for forgetting it."

He delivered that news with a flippancy that didn't match up with the shadows swirling in his eyes or the death grip on his glass. Fury blasted through Eve, incinerating all thoughts but marching over to the Rhodeses's Back Bay brownstone and laying into their self-righteous asses for daring to question the fidelity and adoration of this son who'd always been so desperate for their acceptance and affirmation. Screw. Them.

But her anger wasn't what Kenan needed from her at this moment; he needed his best friend's listening ear.

"You know that's bullshit, right?"

He snorted. "That's exactly what my mother said when I told her I couldn't return to the company." Sighing, he set his glass on the coffee table next to hers and rubbed a hand over his mouth and chin, the scrape of his thick five-o'clock shadow against his palm a rasp in the room. "I haven't been able to escape that conversation all day. Thinking maybe they're right. I've known Cain and Achilles for months. *Months*. And my parents, Gavin—they're my family. If they need me, I owe them my allegiance."

"Okay, wasn't it you who just talked to me about not owing our parents? I called bullshit before, and I'm still calling it." She jabbed a finger toward him. "Let's just put aside the whole loyalty thing for a moment. Because time doesn't determine love or affection. Yes, you've known Cain and Achilles for a few months, but you've bonded with them. The three of you didn't come to know each other and work together under ordinary circumstances, and what you've been through since the reading of that will would unite anyone fast. But that's neither here nor there, because that's not the only thing at issue here, is it?"

She didn't wait for him to reply, but reached for his hand, taking it in hers. Stroking her thumb over the back of his knuckles, she met his unwavering gaze. She knew this man better than herself, and she ached for him.

"This is about making your own way. Standing on your own, apart from Rhodes Realty, from your family, and being your own person, forging your own path. Not as Nathan Rhodes's son or Gavin Rhodes's brother. Right or wrong, whether I agree with your reasoning or not, this is about you proving to yourself that you can make it on your own. And here's another thing to consider. You're happy at Farrell. Working with your brothers, who appreciate you, who listen to you. Do I believe you're putting undue pressure on yourself? Putting those same expectations and standards on yourself that you lectured me about? Yes. But you're challenged at Farrell, and you enjoy it. Why would you walk away from that? This idea of owing unconditional loyalty is your parents' hang-up, not yours. Loyalty is *not* unconditional. It's not blind. That's a fucking myth. It's earned. And while they have yours as the people who raised you, you don't owe them your life."

His gaze dipped from hers to their clasped hands, and he flipped his over so his fingers wrapped around hers and squeezed.

"We're a pair. Each giving advice but finding it difficult to take." A ghost of a smile flirted with his full lips. "Thank you, Eve."

"You don't believe me, though, do you?"

His stare lifted to meet hers. "Did you believe me?"

"Yes."

"Liar."

She narrowed her eyes on him, then shook her head and laughed softly. "Fine. I swear, I'm going to try, though." Pausing, she sobered and studied him, emotion that had too many names to parse lodged in her throat. "If you don't accept anything else, Kenan, receive this. You're the best man I know. Brilliant, generous, kind and, yes, loyal. You said I'm a gift to you? I'm the one who's been blessed to have you as my friend."

He lifted their hands and brushed his lips across her knuckles. There was a spasm inside her belly so hard, her breath caught, and she clenched her teeth around a soft whimper. Just this light touch already had her damp and pulsing with need.

"There's another reason I came over here," he said in a low voice that stroked over her skin in a silken caress. Her nipples didn't stand a chance against that voice. And her sex just gave up the fight. "Because I'm weak. I've tried to give you space today, but I wanted to see you.

Inhale that scent directly from the source that's embedded in my sheets. Touch this body that I can still feel on my hands. I needed to look in your eyes and see if you regretted taking me inside you."

Taking me inside you.

Oh, how her core clenched around those words as if they were his cock. Regrets? Not that. Not when he'd filled her so completely that even now, she felt him. Even now, she wanted more.

"Talk to me." He flipped over her hand, grazed those wicked lips over her palm and, damn, who knew that nerve in the center had a direct line to her sex? "What are you thinking, Eve?"

"No." She cleared her throat. "I don't regret last night. But I would be lying if I didn't say I was worried."

He lifted his head, and his gaze grew hooded, shuttered. She'd known him long enough to recognize when Kenan was hiding something. Disquiet bloomed in her belly.

"Worried? About what?"

"What it means for us." As hard as it was to maintain visual contact with him, she did it. Because she needed to glimpse the truth in his eyes. "Where do we go from here? Are we just fuck buddies? What does this do to our friendship?" She whispered the last question, part of her afraid to hear his answer.

If he said he wanted a "friends with benefits" relationship, that might crush her because she couldn't stand to be treated like one of his other women. They meant more to each other than that—were more to each other than that. But what if they tried for more and it didn't work out? What if they didn't survive adding sex to their relationship? Where would that leave them? Losing Kenan... That would break her.

Her phone vibrated on the coffee table, preventing

Kenan from answering and disrupting her spiral of thoughts. Tendrils of relief and frustration whirled within her as she reached for the cell. But one glimpse at the caller ID on the screen and dread replaced it. Her gaze shifted to Kenan, who stared at her with a calm, cool expression. That demeanor didn't fool her, though. He'd seen the name on the phone.

Gavin.

The phone continued to vibrate on her palm as they stared at one another. Kenan obviously expected her to answer it, and it startled her a little that she had no desire to pick it up. As a matter of fact, the only thing she felt was annoyance at the bad timing. Which was even more surprising given Gavin had been her crush since a teenager. But she sent the call to voice mail and set the phone back on the table, never removing her focus from Kenan.

So she didn't miss the flare of astonishment in his eyes.

Followed by heat so bright, so intense, she swore it seared her skin. And she glorified in the burn.

Using the grip he still retained on her hand, he reeled her closer, and she willingly went to him. Perched on her knees, she hovered over him, straddling his thigh. Releasing her hand, he cupped her face, bringing it down to his, allowing her the opportunity to pull away. As if she would deny either of them the pleasure that awaited them.

He took her mouth. Tenderly. Softly.

And it brought tears to her eyes, so she closed them. But she didn't stop him. Didn't demand he take her harder, wilder.

This. After everything they'd both gone through today, they needed this with each other. *From* each other.

Kenan didn't hurry, although under Eve's palm, his heart thundered. He loved her mouth. That was the only description she could apply. He made love to her mouth, sexing it so thoroughly, her hips twisted and bucked in a restless pattern. She ground her sex against his thigh, seeking relief from the lust coursing through her like a swollen spring flood. Her fingers clawed at his shoulders, and she pressed her chest to his, not caring if he felt the diamond stiffness of her nipples. She had zero shame. Want had taken full control, and modesty had left the building.

Covering his hands with hers, she lowered them from her face and, leaning backward, trailed them down to her aching breasts. Their twin moans inundated the room as his palms molded her, shaped her, relearned her. And when his strong fingers plucked at her nipples, she tossed her head back on her shoulders, arching tighter into his caress.

But, God, it wasn't enough. She grabbed the bottom of her hoodie and whipped it up and over her head. His growl did things to her, nasty things right between her legs. He cupped her braless breasts again and captured a beaded tip between his lips, his tongue circling her, tugging, sucking. And every stroke and pull echoed over the pulsing button of flesh at the top of her sex.

Oh, God, she could come from this. Just explode from his mouth on her nipple and his thick erection on her core.

When Kenan switched to the neglected mound, his fingers teasing the wet peak, she fluttered her fingers over the smattering of freckles decorating the crests of his cheeks. Then lowered her hands to grip his cock through his pants. The almost feral rumble in his chest ratcheted up her hunger to feed on him as he did her.

Urgency rippled through her, and she scrambled off him, ducking his grasping hands. But when she slid to the floor, kneeling between his legs, his complaint snapped off, his thighs going rigid.

"Sweetheart." He thrust his fingers through her hair,

dislodging the bun on top of her head. Blunt nails scraped over her scalp, and she shivered, her own nails biting into the dense muscles of his legs. "This what you want?"

She worked the closure open and the zipper down, then dipped her hand into his black boxer briefs, closing her fist around his hard, hot dick. They both shook and moaned. Damn, he filled her palm to overflowing. Thick. Long. Beautiful. And hers.

Only once she'd pulled him free and stroked her hand down to the base of him, then back up, swallowing the plum-shaped tip in her tight fist, did she glance up and meet his glazed, burning stare.

"You have no idea," she whispered, bending her head and swiping her tongue over the head, tasting his salty, delicious flavor. His hips bucked, sliding a bit more of his length into her mouth, and she took him, sucking gently before sliding him free. "I want all of you."

Let him read whatever he wanted into that. Not like she knew for certain, either.

Closing her eyes, she set about driving them both wild.

Over and over, she swallowed him down. Licking, sucking, teasing, she worshipped him, accepting each grunt and groan and hoarse word of praise as her due. And when he grasped her head, holding her still as he drove into her mouth, using her for his pleasure, she exulted in it. Opening herself wide for him, glorying in each thrust, each plunge, each nudge to the back of her throat.

"Fuck," he snarled, his hands gripping her hair as he breached her throat, slipping into the narrow channel. "Not here. But, goddammit, I will."

He curled his fingers under her shoulders and yanked her back onto the couch, slamming his mouth onto hers. With hurried movements, he stripped her lounge pants from her, leaving her naked and shivering. In the next several moments, he had his shirt over his head, his pants and shoes off and a condom rolled down his dick. Sitting back on the sofa, he cradled her hip and guided her over him. As soon as her thighs bracketed his, he gripped his erect flesh and pressed it to her folds.

Their harsh, fast pants punched the air as she slowly sank down on him.

A keening, sharp cry climbed the back of her throat, but she clenched her teeth, trapping it. In this position, he seemed bigger, thicker. And she breathed through her nose, inhaling deeply and pausing to grant her sex time to accommodate him.

She was stretched so far, packed so full, she could feel him everywhere.

Bowing her head, she pressed her mouth to his forehead, her arms encircling his shoulders, and she clung to him.

"You're so tight, sweetheart. So wet, hot and perfect for me." He pressed a kiss to the hollow of her throat, his arms banded around her waist. "Utterly perfect."

A whimper escaped her, and she circled her hips, pulsing them to claim more of him. With each inch she took, a fierce joy pierced her, along with a wild, raw pleasure. Oh, damn, she didn't know if she could survive this. And when the length of him finally, finally filled her, she admitted to herself that while physically she would come out on the other side of this, emotionally…?

No. She was a goner.

"There you go," he soothed, rubbing his big palms up and down her back, praising her, his ragged chuckle another caress on her cheek. "Look at you, sweetheart, taking all of me. So fucking beautiful and sweet."

She was. For him, she was. And as she rose up, up, up his cock and plunged back down, tearing a gasp out of both of them, she was also fierce and powerful, too.

She rode him hard, giving him no quarter and offering

none to herself. In the furious pace, pleasure careened through her, transforming her into a carnal creature that in parts thrilled and terrified her. She could forget that Kenan hadn't answered the question about where they went from here, about what they were to each other.

She could forget everything but the ecstasy threatening to implode and leave her in so many pieces, she might never be the same.

And yet, she didn't care. She fucked him, racing for that ending, dragging him along with her. She didn't wait for him to take them there. Crushing her mouth to his, she plunged her tongue between his lips, claiming his kiss. Then she reached between them and circled the stiff nub of nerve-packed flesh. Once, twice.

That was all it required to soar over the edge, taking him with her.

Her core clamped down on him, milking, rippling. She flung back her head, crying out his name. Dimly, she heard him shout hers, felt the hard, almost brutal strokes inside her before his arms clinched her to him.

Together, they fell.

And whatever else might happen, they'd catch each other.

Eleven

Kenan studied his computer monitor and the email that filled it.

It was Monday afternoon, almost two days since Gavin had called him to that meeting with him and his parents, and Kenan hadn't reached out to them. Even though his talk with Eve had soothed some of the rawer edges, the pain hadn't disappeared.

I'm ashamed of you.

No matter how hard he tried, he couldn't evict those four words from his head. They taunted him, berated him. And call him a coward, but he hadn't contacted his parents because hearing more of their disappointment, or their rejection, would devastate him.

Yet Gavin, ever the peacemaker, had already done what Kenan and his parents couldn't. Because Kenan hadn't answered his brother's texts or calls, Gavin had emailed, apologizing for setting him up and for what their mother had said. There'd been no way Gavin could've known the meeting would go so left, but Kenan would be lying if he didn't admit he felt a little betrayed that Gavin hadn't given him a heads-up about the subject of the conversation. About them wanting him to return to the company. At least Kenan could've been prepared.

No... Closing out the email, Kenan sighed and reclined back in his chair. He wasn't ready to tackle that yet.

And then there existed the lingering remnants of guilt and jealousy toward Gavin over Eve. Guilt because Kenan was sleeping with the woman Gavin was interested in. Hell, Gavin had called Eve just before they'd had sex Saturday night. That had been awkward as fuck.

But not as awkward as Kenan's reaction to her picking up that phone and waiting to see if she would answer it. Or Kenan on the verge of demanding she not answer it. Begging her not to answer it.

Disgusted with himself, he rubbed his eyes hard with his thumb and forefinger.

Since Saturday, he'd been in Eve's bed, or she'd been in his. Regardless, he'd been inside her. But neither of them had broached the conversation she'd attempted about the status of their relationship. Maybe because she didn't want to know. He couldn't speak for her.

But in the last couple of months, he must've developed a latent cowardice gene because he damn sure didn't want to touch the subject.

Shit, who was he kidding? When it came to Eve, he'd always been a coward.

And though she'd let him have her body, entrusted her pleasure into his hands, nothing had changed. He was still too scared to admit his feelings for her. Even though she'd appeared to choose him over Gavin on Saturday, he was still too insecure over whether he was just a stand-in for his brother. He couldn't forget how many years she'd pined for Gavin. Those feelings didn't just evaporate in days. What would happen when she saw Gavin in person again? Would the love, the need, return? Leaving Kenan where?

Broken.

He didn't trust this…whatever he and Eve had. Especially with it being so new. Not even a week old. How the hell could he trust it, believe it would last, when it was up against a love she'd possessed for years. And with his family already slipping away from him, he couldn't lose Eve, too. So, yeah, he'd gladly be that coward and avoid the "what are we?" conversation. If it allowed him more time with her—touching her, kissing her, going to sleep buried inside her—then he'd duck it like a game of dodgeball. Because that was the selfish bastard he was.

Maybe he'd inherited something from Barron Farrell after all, besides his eyes.

A knock on his door interrupted his thoughts, and he glanced up from blindly staring at his computer screen to see Achilles enter his office.

"Hey," Achilles said. "Bad time?"

"No, not at all. Great timing actually. You can save me from myself."

His brother emitted a low grunt in response, stepping inside and closing the door behind him.

"Anything I can help with?"

A smile tugged at Kenan's mouth in spite of the circumstances. Only months ago, his older brother by months would've never issued that offer. A closed-off, broody giant, the man had had one aim—finish his time at Farrell and get the hell out of Boston. But he'd ended up falling in love with Mycah and bonding with Cain and Kenan, and though Achilles would never be warm and cuddly, he'd definitely come a long way. As evidenced by his question of concern.

Damn. This might mean Kenan couldn't tease him anymore about suffering from middle-child syndrome.

Nah. Where would be the fun in that?

"No, I'm good." When Achilles arched an eyebrow, Kenan grinned. "Wow. Has Mycah been taking you to those childbirth classes again? I'm getting daddy vibes right now."

Achilles pinned him with a grim stare that promised all kinds of bodily injury.

"Fine, fine. I take it back. No daddy vibes." Kenan snickered, holding up his hands. "But if you ask me about my feelings or try to pat me on the back, you're getting side-eye."

"And here I am, sorry for even asking the question."

Kenan laughed. "I'm kidding." But he didn't even attempt to tone down his grin. "What's going on?"

Achilles held up a manila folder. "I have some information on your adoption."

That took care of his amusement. His smile ebbed, falling away completely. And though excitement should've surged inside him, instead a dark sense of foreboding eddied in his chest. He couldn't tear his eyes from that folder, even as he rose from his chair and rounded the desk.

"Kenan?"

"Yes, I'm okay," he murmured, then shifted his gaze to his brother. "Tell me."

Achilles nodded. "I tracked down the lawyer that supposedly handled your adoption. I say supposedly because, Kenan…" He paused, an emotion that deepened the fear in his stomach flashing in Achilles's eyes. "Without betraying confidential information, he revealed that he didn't handle the adoption for your parents. The papers they allowed you to see were falsified."

Falsified.

The word boomed in his head over and over, growing louder and louder. What did that mean?

"Kenan, are you with me?" Achilles moved closer, his hand outstretched toward him.

"I'm good." He nodded. "What else?"

Achilles studied him then jerked his chin. "I kept digging, thinking maybe an attorney with a similar first or last name or maybe a different spelling could've handled the adoption. Maybe it was a mistake on the paperwork. But I couldn't find anything. And that's the issue. There was nothing to find. No filings for Nathan and Dana Rhodes adopting a newborn baby boy. And I've spent months on this, Kenan, but nothing."

Kenan shook his head, frowning. Achilles had been his last hope. His brother was a tech genius. If he couldn't unearth any information, then Kenan didn't have any hope left of finding out the identity of his birth mother.

"Don't worry about it, Achilles," Kenan said, fighting past his disappointment. "You did your best, and I appreciate it. I guess I'll need to find a way to let this go now."

There was a twinge of sadness across Achilles's face, and he closed the distance separating them, gripping Kenan's shoulder.

"No, you don't need to let it go." Achilles stared into his eyes, holding his gaze before he handed him the folder. But he didn't drop his hand from his shoulder. "I promised you I would give you answers. And I wasn't stopping until I could."

Don't take it. Walk away and don't take it.

A voice yelled the warning in his head, and his heart hurled itself against his rib cage. The violent beat echoed in his head, deafening him even as it pumped adrenaline through his body. An acrid taste coated his tongue and bile roiled in his gut. Yet, he still reached for the folder, accepted it.

He flipped it open and scanned the lone document within. A birth certificate. *His* birth certificate.

"How did you...?" He glanced up at his brother, confusion swirling in his head. "My parents told me this had been sealed with the adoption."

Achilles shook his head, and Kenan dropped his gaze back to the printout, studying it with eager, greedy eyes.

Child.

Kenan Anthony Rhodes.

He frowned. Rhodes? Why would his adoptive last name be on his birth certificate?

Father.

Blank.

Not a shock there. Barron Farrell wouldn't have agreed to have his name recorded.

Mother.

Dana Rhodes.

"Dana..." He choked. Stumbled backward. Or he would've if Achilles's hold on his shoulder hadn't prevented him from falling. All the while, his grip on the folder and the printout didn't ease up. "Dana," he rasped again. "What...?"

It couldn't be. This had to be a lie.

Pain blasted him, stealing his air, his strength, his ability to think.

"I'm sorry, Kenan," Achilles whispered.

The pain in his brother's voice, the grief in his eyes. They confirmed what his numb mind couldn't grasp.

His adopted mother was his birth mother.

Twelve

Eve stood outside the break room at Rhodes Realty, twisting her fingers in front of her.

"Really?" she muttered, forcing her hands to her sides.

This was her mother. She'd never been scared to talk to her mother before. Nervous maybe, but not scared.

But you've never insulted and hurt her so deeply before, either.

Dammit. She really had to find a muzzle for her subconscious.

Yolanda had asked for time, and since Eve had been the one to inflict the harm, she should really allow her mother to determine the length of that time and space. But it was late Monday afternoon, and Yolanda had yet to reach out to her. Eve couldn't allow this wound to fester; she needed to try to heal this rift.

And approaching her mother at her job lessened the chances of her mother going off on her.

Inhaling a deep breath, Eve pushed open the glass

door, silently thanking God for her mother's predictability with her late-afternoon cup of coffee.

"Hey, Mom."

Yolanda glanced up from the coffee maker, and though Eve expected to see surprise in her expression, it didn't appear. A faint, wry smile twisted her mouth.

"You don't seem shocked to see me here," Eve said.

Her mother arched an eyebrow, hitting a button and filling the room with the scent of fresh, brewing coffee.

"You're my daughter. I wouldn't have given you more than a few days before I sought you out, either, if there was discord between us. And—" she shrugged a shoulder "—Mr. Leonard called and let me know you were on your way up."

Eve smothered a snort. Right.

A tense silence fell that carried a hint of awkwardness. God, she detested it. This wasn't them. They'd never been uneasy with each other. Since this was her fuckup, it fell on her to fix it. In any way she could.

It helped that her mother didn't seem as angry as she'd been Saturday. But that hurt... The hurt still lingered in her eyes, and Eve would do anything to erase it.

"Mom, I'm sorry I lied to you. Because I can call it keeping a secret or just not telling you, but it comes down to that one thing—I lied to you. For four years. And I'm so sorry."

"*Why*, Eve?" Yolanda leaned a hip against the counter, rubbing her hands together then crossing her arms. For a woman who was the epitome of composure, the fidgety movements screamed volumes. Guilt swam in Eve's chest. "I've gone over and over the other night. And all I can come up with is, for some reason, you were afraid to tell me. And if that's true, then I'm to blame. I've done something that prohibited you—"

"No, Mom." Eve rushed forward, cupping her

mother's upper arms. "No. This is on me. All on me." Releasing her mother, she pressed her fingertips to her mouth, searching for the words to explain a mindset that she'd battled with her entire life. "All my life I've watched you work hard, often struggle, to provide for us. For me. And I never wanted to do anything to render that struggle a wasted effort. So I put my everything into school, into a career that would make you proud. My one fear in this world is disappointing you...or shaming you. Teaching was something you could tell your friends, coworkers and pastor about. Your daughter designing underwear and selling it? That's not something you could proudly share."

"And why not?" her mother scoffed, slicing a hand through the air. "What? I don't wear underwear?"

"Mom. You've never approved of me taking art. Then there's the instability of it as a job. And your being an elder in the church. What would your members say if they knew your daughter sold lingerie?"

"Oh, I suppose because we worship Jesus, we don't like sexy panties?"

"Mom, I'm being serious!"

"So am I." Yolanda threw up her hands, heaving a loud sigh that reeked of her exasperation. And possibly love. "Baby, let me explain why I was so angry. I'm your mother first before anything else. And as your mother, you didn't allow me the opportunity to brag about you, to celebrate milestones with you. To comfort and be there for you during setbacks. That's my job as a mom. I felt like I failed you in some way, when all I've ever wanted to be is your cheerleader and your safe place."

"You have been," Eve whispered.

"No, I haven't been," she disagreed just as softly. "And regardless of what you're saying, that's on me. Somewhere, somehow, I gave you the impression that you had to prove yourself to me. That my love was based on works instead of you being you. And that's just not true. I love you. I'm proud of you. Did I worry that if you chose a difficult career that you'd struggle? Yes. I didn't want that for you. I wanted more. But, baby, that's what parents do. We want better for our children than we had. But even worrying, I would've supported you with your lingerie company. Shoot, I would've given you money, been support staff, anything you needed, because I want you to succeed in all you do. You, Eve, are my greatest joy and accomplishment. And if you're happy—whether that's teaching, operating a lingerie company or picking up garbage off the side of the highway—then that's all that matters. I'm going to be there for you, in your corner. Although, we're going to have a long conversation about the garbage picking and the career trajectory in that."

Laughter burst from Eve, along with tears. Unable to hold back any longer, she threw her arms around her mother. Yolanda's arms closed around her, and they held one another tight. Saturday night, that weight hadn't disappeared from her chest. But today, it did. She could breathe. Her heart was lighter.

She was…free.

Laughing again, she squeezed her mother, then leaned back. Tears glistened in Yolanda's eyes, too, as she smiled at Eve.

"So-o-o… Does this mean you want free samples?"

Yolanda arched an eyebrow. "Of course. What's the point of having a daughter who's a businesswoman if I don't get free stuff?"

Their snickers filled the breakroom.

Twenty minutes later, Eve pushed out of the office building onto the sidewalk. Smiling, she turned her face up into the late-afternoon sun, embracing the last of its rays.

"Oof."

She jerked up her hands, bracing herself as she

slammed into a hard surface. Or a hard chest, she realized, when strong hands clasped her arms, steadying her.

"Hey, stranger."

Glancing up, she met Gavin's dark brown gaze and beautiful smile. She stilled, waiting for that familiar warm, melting desire that the sight of him brought. For years, it'd encompassed her, but now, standing in his embrace...

Nothing.

Nothing except for a twinge of guilt for leading him on and perhaps a little sadness because Gavin was such a good man. And, dammit, it would've been less complicated for her to love him instead of her best friend.

"Hi, Gavin." She smiled, stepping back out of his hold. "It's good to see you."

"You, too."

His gaze dropped down over her, and in spite of her newfound revelation regarding her lack of feelings toward him, she still blushed. Because, well, a handsome man had just checked her out. She was in love with another man, not dead—

Holy shit. She was in love with Kenan.

She'd loved him for years. But *in* love with him?

Terror streaked through her, screaming like a freight train on greased wheels and no breaks.

This wasn't good. Oh, God, this *so* wasn't good.

For her, the transition wasn't shocking. She'd meant it when she'd told him he was the best man she knew. No man had ever understood her, supported her, believed in her...loved her like him. And since she'd never been one to indulge in casual sex, she couldn't have separated her feelings when they became lovers. That couldn't be said of Kenan, though. Yes, they were intimately involved, but he'd never expressed wanting anything more than friendship. Unlike her, he was the king of casual sex, and just because he'd been inside her—repeatedly—didn't mean he'd suddenly developed deeper feelings for her.

Her stomach bottomed out, her heart thudding.

What did this mean for them? Because if he rejected her... Would she survive that? Would their friendship survive that? She didn't know if she could be around him, loving him, when he didn't feel the same way. It would hurt too much.

"Eve?" Gavin cupped her elbow, and she jerked her gaze back to him from over his shoulder, where it'd wandered. "Are you okay?"

"Yes." She exhaled a trembling breath, shaken by her self-revelation. "I'm fine. I'm sorry, what were you saying?"

He cocked his head, studying her. "I was saying, I called the other night to see if you were free this weekend. I'd love to take you out on another date."

Regret tightened her stomach. Considering what she'd just admitted to herself, she hated having to reject someone.

"Gavin, you're incredibly kind and sweet, and I really enjoyed our date, but I'm sorry. I have to say no. I can't this weekend. Or any other weekend. I—"

He squeezed her elbow, cutting off her explanation. "Let me guess," he said, a wry smile curving his mouth. "Kenan."

Her lips parted on a soft gasp. Was she so transparent? Damn, how pathetic.

"How did you...?"

"How did I know? I might be a little slow on the uptake but looking back on it, you two have always been very close."

"We've been friends for a long time."

"Okay, but the way my brother has looked at you is not very...friendly." He shook his head. "And neither was that kiss at the club, regardless of the story he spun for me. If I hadn't wanted to get to know you so badly, I would've dug deeper into that explanation instead of just accepting it on its face, but…" He shrugged. "The signs have been there. Kenan's been in love with you for a very long time. So while I'm disappointed, I'm not shocked."

"You're wrong about that." Oh, how she wished he wasn't, but he couldn't be more wrong. "That really was an act that night just to get your attention." She winced. "This *thing* between your brother and me—it's new."

His mouth tightened, and she had the impression he was fighting back a smile.

"Okay."

She narrowed her eyes on him, but after a moment, huffed out a chuckle. Then, sobering, she said, "Gavin, I'm sorry. I didn't mean to—"

"No apologies necessary, Eve." He pulled her into his arms, hugging her. "If anyone deserves happiness, it's my brother. And he deserves you." He brushed a kissed over her cheek.

"Well, this is sweet."

Eve jerked out of Gavin's arms, whirling around to face Kenan. His beautiful, frigid gaze roamed over her before shifting over her shoulder to Gavin. The stern, forbidding lines of his face didn't soften as he smiled. If anything, his expression hardened.

"Please, don't let me interrupt," he said in that same, pleasant voice that carried a bitter undertone.

"Kenan, this isn't…" She trailed off. Jesus, she couldn't utter that cliché.

But he didn't have a problem finishing it.

Arching an eyebrow, he drawled, "It isn't what it looks like? Really? C'mon, Eve, you can do better than that."

"Kenan," Gavin murmured. "Take advice from your

brother. The brother you've been avoiding. Don't fuck this up." Squeezing her shoulder, he said, "Goodbye, Eve."

Gavin walked off, entering the office building and leaving her and Kenan alone. Well, as alone as they could be on a busy sidewalk.

"Kenan," she began, "I know how that looked, but honestly, there's nothing going on between me and Gavin. Actually, we were talking about—"

"Let me guess. This is a case of believing you or my lying eyes, right?" He let loose a harsh chuckle that abraded her skin. "Sorry, sweetheart. I'm not that gullible. Or rather, I'm through being that naive."

Confused, she frowned. What did that even mean? Taking a step toward him, she ignored the people teeming around them, focusing only on the man—her best friend, the man she loved with her whole heart—before her. The man who currently looked at her as if he didn't know her…and didn't care to.

"Kenan, if you'd only listen to me. I just happened to bump into Gavin. I was here to see my mom, and I ended up talking to him. Nothing other than that happened between us."

"Other than a kiss, Eve."

He glanced away from her, but not before she glimpsed the slip of his hard mask and the tortured expression that replaced it. Her hands jerked to her chest, pressed there over her aching heart. What the hell was going on? There was more here than him being angry about what he *thought* he'd witnessed.

"Kenan—" she whispered.

"No," he interrupted, voice as cold as a winter wind sweeping over Boston Harbor. "I'm through blindly accepting lies. I'm done being someone's secret and their Plan B. Never again."

"I don't know what the hell that's supposed to mean,"

she said, her hands fisting over her chest, desperation and anger curdling inside her. Deliberately, she stretched out her fingers and stared down at them, as if she could literally see her future with this man slipping through them. Yet, she tried. She *fought*. For him. For them. "I've never lied to you, and you've never been a secret for me. I've never been ashamed of you, never hid you. And I don't even understand what a Plan B means. Kenan, you've been my best friend and—and…" She swallowed, shifted closer to him, slid her hands up his abdomen to his chest until her palms covered his heart. Hope crashed inside her at the heavy, wild beat under her hand. "And I love you, Kenan. Yes, as my friend, but also as more. As the man who makes me whole, gives me joy, is the other half of my heart. I love you."

The air stalled in her lungs, and her pulse echoed in her ears, that hope, so fragile yet strong in its will to grow, beating, waiting. But as she stared at his shuttered, aloof face, it died a slow, excruciating death.

The pain in her chest expanded, though, threatening to explode until she sucked in a breath. She stumbled backward, and Kenan reached for her, but she batted away his hands, not able to bear his touch. His rejection.

"You don't believe me," she rasped.

"Maybe the kiss was platonic." His eyes dipped to her mouth, and for a moment, she caught a flicker of heat in the bright depths, igniting that traitorous hope again. But when he returned his gaze to hers, the emptiness there gutted her. "But in love with me? No. How could you be when not just weeks ago, I was helping you try to win my brother because you were in love with him? He's had your heart for years, Eve. Years. Now suddenly I'm supposed to believe it's mine?" His mouth twisted into a hard—cruel—caricature of a smile. "No, I'm not that lucky. Not that willing to believe in fairy tales anymore."

She shouldn't be able to still stand on her feet. Still breathe. Shouldn't be able to exist under so much pain. Part of her needed to pound on his chest, demand he fight along with her for not just who they were but who they could be. But the other half? That half had perhaps seen this coming, and she protected herself. Wrapped herself in the remnants of pride she had left that she refused to sacrifice at his feet.

Yes, she loved him, but she also loved herself.

More importantly, she *valued* herself.

"I can't make you believe me, and I can't force you to accept a love I'd freely give you without any strings attached. But if there's one thing that you, yourself, taught me, it's that love is a gift. Loyalty is earned. My love for you is yours because it's mine to give, not for you to determine who it belongs to. And despite what you think, you've more than earned my loyalty, which means I'd never lie to you, never betray you. So for you to believe differently is on you, not me."

She inhaled a shuddering breath, unable to believe after all these years, this was how their friendship would end. On a busy street. Because he couldn't get past his own issues to see her. To love her.

"In spite of us introducing sex into our relationship, I thought we were close enough that you could come to me with whatever is going on with you. Maybe we were wrong to go there with each other because I've lost you to whatever demons have always chased you."

"I don't know what you're talking about."

She shook her head, smiling, having no doubt it reflected the soul-deep sadness that hollowed her out. Because try as she might, she couldn't conjure up anger toward him. Not when she understood him more than he understood himself. Not when she loved him so much.

"It all comes down to fear, Kenan. You're afraid to

trust that I could possibly love you. That I could prefer you over Gavin. How could I when you've always believed your parents never have? You can't accept that you're so special, so beautiful, that loving you is as easy as breathing. So you're pushing me away out of fear." She spread her hands wide, palms up. "I can't make you believe that I love you, that I want only you, because that would require you believing in yourself. That would mean you'd have to extend a trust to me that's beyond you. As a friend? Yes. But with your heart? With the possibility of perhaps hurting you? No. And that saddens me, Kenan. Because you deserve more than that. But when it comes down to it, your fear and your insecurities broke us. And that's something you'll have to live with."

Not giving him a chance to reply—a chance to utter one more word that might score another hit that could devastate her further—she turned and walked away.

Walked away from him, but toward herself.

Thirteen

Kenan stared out the window of his home study, not really seeing the private, walled-in garden in the back of his home. He fisted his fingers inside his pants pockets, his hands feeling a little empty without the ever-present glass tumblers that had been in them since Achilles's bomb and the later sidewalk confrontation with Eve. He'd spent all that Monday evening and Tuesday drunk. Wednesday, he'd crawled out of the bottle, but he hadn't returned to the office, calling in ill. Not that it was a lie. He was sick.

Heartsick.

Soul sick.

If that wasn't a thing, it should be.

Sighing, he rubbed a hand over his head, dragging it down his face and chin. Scruff from the last couple of days scraped his palm, and it reminded him that he needed to shave before he returned to the office tomorrow. Because he had to return. He couldn't hide out in his home nursing his open wounds forever. No matter how much he longed to. The thought of facing anyone right now had him longing to open another bottle of Scotch.

Facing anyone?

More specifically, Eve. Every time he closed his eyes, an image of her on that sidewalk saying she loved him wavered on his eyelids. Her voice rang in his head, and he couldn't escape himself. Couldn't escape her.

I love you, Kenan. Yes, as my friend, but also as more. As the man who makes me whole, gives me joy, is the other half of my heart.

When it comes down to it, your fear and your insecurities broke us. And that's something you'll have to live with.

No amount of alcohol could shut out those words. Words that followed him into sleep, so he didn't. They tortured him, condemned him. Because she'd spoken truth. He couldn't believe she loved him, chose him over Gavin. And, yes, it did come down to his own fears and insecurities. Yet, he couldn't shake them. But, God, he wanted to. Didn't she know he yearned to believe her? To be able to claim her as his, and to be claimed by her in return?

But like he'd told her, he'd ceased to be a dreamer, a believer in fairy tales, in happily-ever-afters. As soon as he'd read the birth certificate in that folder, it'd been drilled home for him that this world was hard, cold and a place of lies.

So he'd rather let her go than risk her brutalizing his heart when she walked away later.

If that made him a coward, then so be it.

His doorbell echoed through his house, and he closed his eyes. He could ignore it and maybe whoever it was, who'd shown up uninvited, would go away. Several seconds passed, and the tension eased from his body.

The doorbell rang again. And again.

"Shit."

Sighing, he exited the study. Only three people wou be so bold to lean on his doorbell and refuse to leav One of them had walked away from him a few days ag cutting him out of her life. The other two were bound show up at some point. He was actually surprised i taken either of them this long.

Opening the front door, he met Achilles's famili patient gaze.

Without a word, Kenan shifted backward, allowi his brother to enter.

"Beer? Water? Whiskey?" Kenan offered, walki into the kitchen.

"Beer's good." Achilles leaned back against the cou ter, crossing his arms as if there for a casual visit inste of an intervention.

After pulling open the refrigerator door and remo ing one for himself, as well, Kenan passed his brothe brown bottle. They twisted off the caps and drank in lence, facing each other across the kitchen.

Lowering the beer after a long pull, Kenan cocked head, peering at his brother.

"Go on and say it. Get it over with."

Achilles nodded but didn't immediately reply. He til the bottle, downed another gulp. "Have you talked your mother yet?"

Kenan barked out a sharp laugh. "Jumping right ir it, are we?" He shook his head, setting the bottle behi him on the counter. "No, I haven't talked to her yet."

"Why not?"

"Because I don't trust myself. I'm too fucking ang And she's still my mother, and I won't disrespect her.

Achilles nodded again. "I understand that. When I fi went to jail, I was so angry with my mother. Because i been her boyfriend. Because she'd brought him home. I cause it hadn't been the first shithead she'd dated. A then I felt so much guilt because I was blaming the victim. And she was my mother. I loved her. The only person I had. But I realized I could be both. Mad and still adore her. The important thing is love always wins out."

A ball of emotions—the very emotions Achilles spoke of—lodged in Kenan's throat, rendering it impossible for him to speak. He picked up his bottle again and tried to drink the blockage down.

"But there's something else, isn't there?" Achilles asked quietly. "Something else that has you upset. And—" he arched an eyebrow "—rough?"

Kenan snorted. "If by 'rough' you mean 'look like shit,' then thank you for being diplomatic."

He stared down at the floor. Did he really want to go into it? Not really. But then Achilles had gone through hell with Mycah. If anyone would understand, he would. And, well… Achilles was his brother. Not long ago, Kenan had willingly been there for Achilles. Obviously, Achilles wanted to do the same for him. So Kenan would let him.

"Yeah. Yeah, there is something else," Kenan admitted.

Then he spilled everything.

About approaching Eve about the Bromberg's proposal.

Their deal regarding Gavin.

The turn in their relationship.

Finding her and Gavin together, and her declaration of love.

His rejection.

He even confessed about how this proposal was his way of proving himself at Farrell. Proving himself worthy to be there.

Achilles shoved off the counter, slowly straightening to his full height, which topped Kenan by a couple of inches. "We'll get to Eve in a minute, but let's tackle the Farrell thing first. Are you fucking with me?" he demanded. "That was my hang-up, not yours. If anyone belongs there, besides Cain, it's you. And you are more than worthy to be there, just like Cain, just like me. This proposal doesn't determine that. These next few months don't. You are enough. And fuck those who don't know it."

Kenan blinked. Cleared his throat.

"You must be taking pep-talk lessons from Cain," he rasped.

"I took notes." Achilles's grin flashed in his thick beard before he dipped his chin, studying him. "You know what I went through with Mycah. How I almost allowed my past to dictate my future with her. I let it color how I saw myself and my own worth. And I nearly lost Mycah. I nearly lost you and Cain."

Achilles cupped Kenan's shoulder, squeezing it.

"If you don't talk with your parents and deal with this fear that's eating away at you, you'll lose Eve. I grew up in a house that didn't have much, but I never doubted how much I was loved. I don't have that burden, Kenan. And I'm so sorry you do. No child should ever feel second in their parents' love. But one thing I can guarantee you, because I've been around you and Eve, you have never been second with her. Your welfare, your happiness. *You*. Accept that, Kenan. Because she's right. You need to be brave enough to risk your heart. And there's no safer bet than her."

The cold of the beer bottle numbed Kenan's palms and fingers.

They were the only things numb on him. Everything else—his chest, his stomach, his head, hell, even his legs—hurt, throbbed. Almost as if all his limbs had been deadened, and all of him had come back online at once. He tingled, his skin prickled.

Because he was alive.

All his life, he hadn't felt like he'd belonged in his family. He had the last name, but not the acceptance. Now he understood why. And that wasn't on him. It'd never been on him. And yet, it'd ruled him.

It'd even prevented him from telling Eve he loved her all these years. Because he feared her rejection. Feared she couldn't possibly see him as more than a friend, see more in him to love because his mother and father didn't.

Because he didn't.

Yet, Eve had been the one person in his life who'd unconditionally offered him acceptance, affirmation, forgiveness…love. She'd always given him love.

I love you, Kenan. Yes, as my friend, but also as more. As the man who makes me whole, gives me joy, is the other half of my heart.

When he'd replayed that in his head earlier, it'd brought him pain.

Now it brought him a cautious joy.

It brought him hope.

Could he reach for that future with her? Grab hold of the happiness that could be theirs?

He wanted to be brave enough to. He wanted to be the man she needed. Whom she deserved. Was that man him? He didn't know. But she'd chosen him, and he damn sure would never make her regret it.

That is if he could convince her to forgive him for hurting her and give him another chance.

Damn.

He was going to need a miracle.

Or maybe… He lifted his head and met Achilles's steady gaze.

Just maybe a little help from family.

Fourteen

The early afternoon sun beamed down on Kenan's head and shoulders, and he basked in it as he stared out over the pond in Boston Public Garden. With the warmer weather, the ducks and a couple of swans had returned. Tourists, as well as some locals, pedaled swan boats around the water, while a guide regaled them with facts about the city and the park that sat right in the middle of it. This had been one of his favorite places when he'd been a kid. His mother had brought him here often, and they'd feed the ducks, he'd hang off the statues and they'd just spend time together. Those were some of his happiest memories.

It's why he'd asked her to meet him here.

Nerves played a brutal game of kickball with his stomach. Since calling his mother the evening before, after his talk with Achilles, he'd been going over and over in his head what he intended to say to her. How to broach the subject of being lied to about his very identity for his entire life. How to ask why his own mother didn't want to claim him as her own...

He still didn't know.

Part of him would have preferred to avoid this and her. But he couldn't go to Eve, have a healthy future with her, if he didn't confront his past.

For her, he'd do anything.

"Kenan."

He turned to face his mother, his hands sliding into his pants pockets. An ache caused twinges and spasms in his chest. She looked the same—beautifully dressed, carefully composed, a professional, older, wealthy woman. But he looked at her with new eyes. He saw the shape of her mouth and cheekbones, which they shared. He might have Barron's eye color, but the shape of those eyes belonged to her. Why hadn't he noticed all of this before?

Because he hadn't been looking. He hadn't been seeking himself in the face of his adoptive mother. But now, with newfound knowledge, he spied himself in his birth mother.

"Mom."

She didn't come closer to kiss him on his cheek, and he didn't move near to offer. Instead, they stood, facing each other like long-ago gunslingers. Instead of guns, though, they wielded lies and truth.

"We haven't been here together in a long time," she murmured. "I see Romeo and Juliet have returned." She hiked her chin toward the two swans in the pond named after the Shakespearean couple. "Somehow, though, I don't think you asked me here to visit Boston's favorite couple and a trip down memory lane."

"No, I didn't." A jumble of frustration, anger, love and pain rolled inside of him. He couldn't begin to untangle them, so he embraced them, as Achilles had suggested. Trusting that love would win out. "I needed to talk to you, and this place that holds good memories for both of us seemed like a safe place."

"We need a safe place?" She laughed, and he caught the jangle of nerves underneath. "That certainly sounds ominous."

"Mom, you and Dad didn't want me to dig into my adoption, but I did." He didn't reveal Achilles's involvement since she already resented his brother because of his relation to Barron. "I found my birth certificate."

He didn't elaborate—didn't need to. Her face blanked in shock before it crumpled, and tears glistened in her eyes. Her fingers fluttered to the base of her throat, and though her lips moved, no words emerged.

"You're my birth mother," he stated, and she didn't deny it. Amazed that his voice remained calm and steady, when inside he yelled until his throat was raw, he continued, "Let me tell you how it was, growing up in our house believing I was adopted and abandoned by a biological mother who didn't want me. I should've felt blessed because I was chosen by our family. Instead, I was an outsider, an interloper. Raised by a father who never could quite successfully pretend to want me as his son. I grew up needing to prove myself worthy of the Rhodes last name, of earning my place in my home because I should be grateful to you and Dad for giving it to me. But no matter what I did, I never could achieve that gold standard. I was never enough simply because of my birth. And all that time—*all that time*—you knew I was yours. And you let me believe otherwise. You refused to claim me. I need to know why."

The tears that had glinted in her eyes streamed down her face. Trembling, she reached into her purse and removed a handkerchief, then blotted at her tears and pressed the cloth to her face, hiding behind it. Kenan didn't rush her, but gave her time to gather herself.

Finally, his mother lifted her head, her mouth trembling.

"I'm sorry, Kenan. I'm so sorry. I didn't mean—" She shuddered out a breath, her shoulders drooping. "No, I won't make excuses. You deserve more than that from me. I owe you the truth." She paused and her gaze shifted to the pond. "Years ago, your father and I... Our marriage was in a bad place. All we did was argue. I felt unloved, he felt unappreciated. It was...rough. During that time, I met Barron Farrell at a dinner party. We were seated next to one another, and he could be very charming. That would've ended there, but a couple of weeks later, we bumped into one another again at a gala. I'm not proud to admit it, but we started a brief affair."

The honking of ducks pockmarked the silence between them as she fell quiet and Kenan studied her stoic expression. Stoic except for the sadness in her gaze. And the shame. His fingers curled into his palms to prevent him from wrapping his arms around her. But he couldn't give that to her right now. Not when a chaotic storm raged inside him.

"I became pregnant, and I swear to you, Kenan—" she jerked her head to him, and her voice lowered, harshened "—I never once considered not having you, regardless of the circumstances of your conception."

"I was a mistake," he said, the words barreling out of him on a bitter wave.

"No." She grabbed his arm, shook it. "No. My affair was a mistake, a betrayal of my vows. But you were not a mistake. You were *mine*. Are mine. You always have been."

You just didn't claim me.

The accusation burned on his tongue, but he doused it, the ashes acrid in his mouth. With a heavy sigh, she dropped her grip on him and wrapped her arms around herself.

"I know my actions contradicted—contradict—my words. I'm not making excuses for myself, but back then, I was so scared. Scared of having another baby by a man who wasn't my husband. Scared to lose my husband and marriage, my family. Barron didn't want anything to do with you. We all know he's good for walking away from his responsibilities with no consequences," she said, anger flickering in her tone. "I had to tell your father the truth, and he was furious, of course. Not only had I cheated on him, but I was pregnant. Still… He wanted to save our marriage. To protect my reputation, he insisted we pretend that we adopted you. That way, I could keep you, raise you and everyone could avoid the pain and damage of a scandal."

"You sacrificed me on the altar of your marriage."

She sucked in a sharp breath, pressing her hands to her chest, but again she didn't deny his statement.

"You sacrificed my identity, my sense of security, my authentic, honest relationships so you and Dad could keep your ideal of a marriage and family. And the sad part? We were never perfect. I grew up with an emotionally distant father, who even as a child I sensed resented me, but I could never pinpoint why. Now I know. Because I was a constant reminder of his wife's affair. He would never appoint me to replace him when he retired because I'm not his son. And he made that abundantly clear without saying the words. And all along you knew why, but let me believe it was in my head. I needed you," he whispered.

"I'm so sorry, Kenan." She lifted her hand and it hovered above his face. When he didn't dodge it, she cradled his cheek. Love and so much pain shone in her eyes that it almost hurt him to meet her damp gaze. "God, you have no idea how many regrets I have. Thirty years' worth. Every day I've woken up deciding to lie to you, to not tell you who I am, has been hell. You're my son, not just by love and choice but by birth and I'm so damn proud of you. I love you." She cupped his other cheek. "Tell me what to do. What you need from me. Admit the truth to everyone? I will. Whatever you need because for the first time this is about you."

He covered her hands with his, bowing his head, tears stinging his eyes. Jesus. The anger flickering inside him demanded she submit a press release in every news-media outlet and expose the truth. But the sadness, the love, the…acceptance and need to just move on didn't require the penance of her blowing up her life, reputation and marriage just to appease his hurt heart.

Where did they go from here? He didn't know. They— him, her, his father—had a lot of healing to do individually and, one day, as a family. And maybe he and Nathan would never be close, but for the first time, the weight of that didn't constrict his chest. Because finally, Kenan understood, it wasn't his burden to bear.

He inhaled a deep, cleansing breath. A lighter breath. They had time to figure it out. And while he couldn't do anything about the pain, disillusionment and anger that still swam inside him, he could offer the one thing he needed in his life—forgiveness.

Drawing her into his arms, he held her. And she clung to him, her sob vibrating through him.

"I forgive you, Mom. I love you."

Fifteen

"This way, Ms. Burke." The older woman who'd introduced herself as Charlene led Eve through the executive offices of Farrell International.

Eve recognized her as Cain Farrell's assistant, although they'd never been formally introduced. Which only deepened Eve's curiosity about why the company CEO's personal assistant was leading her to a mysterious room for a mysterious meeting after an equally mysterious summons downtown.

She'd almost told Cain to forget it. Who cared if he helmed one of the wealthiest, most powerful conglomerates in the world? Her heart littered her chest in itty-bitty pieces. Besides, she'd overnighted the final designs and samples for the proposal to Kenan days ago. She had no more business with him or Farrell. But that rebellion had lasted about ten seconds before she'd conceded and agreed to show up.

As long as she didn't have to meet with Kenan. Cain

wouldn't be that cruel...would he? No, she refused to believe that. It'd been a little over a week since she'd last seen Kenan on that sidewalk, and she wasn't ready to change that. Not yet. Eventually, she'd have to face him, but...

She gave her head a small shake, focusing on the arrow-straight spine of the woman in front of her. Curiosity drove her here, but already she itched to leave for her heart and sanity's sake.

"Right in here." She paused before a glass door where closed blinds prevented her from glimpsing inside. "Go on in. They're expecting you." Charlene smiled and cracked open the door.

They? Who in the world was *they*?

Stomach dipping in trepidation, she gave the assistant a tremulous smile in return and slid through the opening. She entered a packed conference room, and a sweep revealed an empty black, leather chair at the very end of the long wood table. She quickly sank into it, her gaze centered on the man standing next to a screen at the front of the room.

Kenan.

Their gazes locked, and a current of electricity pulsed through her, sizzling in her veins. Lust and need had no care for a broken heart and injured pride. All her body and sex knew was that the man who delivered orgasms like he'd invented them stood mere feet from her.

Traitors.

But... Oh, God, she'd missed him.

Everything about him. It was a physical ache, and not all of it sexual. That part of who they were was so new, it didn't encompass even half of what she longed for. She hungered to hear his deep, whiskey smooth voice, breathe in his comforting, earthy scent and feel the security of his tall, powerful body. The security of his arms.

And, yes, she yearned for the devastating pleasure only he could bring her.

Thank God a room full of people separated them. Or else she might do something she'd promised herself she wouldn't—throw herself at him.

Averting her gaze, she scanned the room again, noting Cain, Achilles and his wife toward the head of the table. The other men and women she didn't recognize, but Eve could guess the purpose of this meeting. Kenan's proposal.

Anxiety pooled in her belly again, but this time for him.

Please, God, let him nail it. He deserves this.

"A major component of the rebranding of the Bromberg's chain is modernizing its stores and businesses while still maintaining the class, fashion and lavishness that the department stores are nationally recognized for. We're seeking a fusion of classic and contemporary, while retaining our established customer base and inviting a younger clientele. And, of course, a wider profit margin. Here is just one example of how we plan to accomplish it."

He shifted to the side, and the slide on the screen displayed her pink-and-black logo. Her heart pounded, pride straightening her shoulders even as tension and tendrils of nervousness curled inside her.

"Intimate Curves is an online lingerie boutique that caters exclusively to plus-size women. It also sells lotions, jewelry and other merchandise from local artisans and entrepreneurs. The business has been in operation for four years and has been hugely successful. I've included numbers for the last two years in your file so you can see for yourself. Intimate Curves has not only enjoyed a very healthy profit, but its reputation is also exemplary both regionally and nationally. As a matter of fact, the company was recently the recipient of this year's Small

Business Award from the National Association of Women Entrepreneurs."

Warmth flooded her, and under the table she tightly clasped her hands together. She didn't know if anyone else in the conference room could detect the pride in his voice, but she did. God, she did.

"If we go forward with this rebranding, the very talented and gifted owner and designer agreed to provide us with six exclusive designs that won't be for sale anywhere except for the Intimate Curves flagship store. Imagine that. Bromberg's having the only brick-and-mortar boutique with designs that aren't even available online. That kind of exclusivity is guaranteed sales."

"And the owner is fully on board with this?" an older man in a suit that probably cost more than her condo asked, his eyebrow arched.

Kenan's gaze briefly rested on her but shifted away. "Yes, she is."

"Is she going to be the face of the boutique?" the man pressed.

Kenan hesitated. "That hasn't been deter—"

"I will be."

The words escaped Eve before she acknowledged her intention to speak. Or her full decision to reveal her identity. Since the inception of Intimate Curves, she'd hidden behind a logo and a brand out of concern for backlash from her mother, her job. The truth was, she'd used that as an excuse to not fully step out on faith and claim her dream of being a full-time businesswoman.

Staring into Kenan's gleaming eyes, she wasn't afraid anymore.

"I'm sorry to interrupt," she said, glancing around the table before meeting the curious scrutiny of the gentleman who'd first spoken. "My name is Eve Burke, owner and head designer of Intimate Curves. If the rebranding goes through, I will be fully involved with the flagship store, and will continue to provide exclusive designs for the boutique as well as operate my online company."

"Thank you, Eve," Kenan murmured. "As you can see, Intimate Curves is just one example of how we will cultivate new business partnerships while still maintaining established relationships. The plan isn't to alienate our current client base, but to retain them and attract more. And with this marketing plan in place, I believe the chain will be more successful and profitable than ever before."

Kenan continued with his presentation for another fifteen minutes, and when he finished, she barely managed not to break out in spontaneous applause. Barely. Regardless of how things had ended between them romantically, he was first and foremost her best friend, and she, more than anyone, understood what this proposal meant to him.

As the vote on it went forward, she held her breath.

And when the majority of people voted for the rebranding, approving the proposal, the air released from her lungs on a delighted sigh.

Her heart pressed against her sternum, seeming to expand until her chest couldn't contain it. She glanced at Kenan, and as if he'd been waiting on her, his bright gaze captured hers. A slow smile curved his sensual mouth, and she returned it.

Shortly after, the meeting adjourned, and she waited at the back of the room. Congratulate him and leave— that was the plan.

"I believe congratulations are in order to you, too, Ms. Burke," a tall, olive-skinned man said, stopping in front of Eve. Thick, dark hair tumbled over his forehead and framed an indecently lush mouth and solid jaw. Glittering black eyes stared down at her with an intensity that verged on unnerving. "The product, artistry and numbers from your company are impressive."

"Thank you, Mr...."

He extended a hand toward her, dipping his chin. "Nico Morgan. Minor shareholder in Farrell and future investor in the Bromberg's project." A faint smile flirted with his mouth, but it didn't reach those onyx eyes. And as she shook his hand, a shiver tripped down her spine. "I look forward to a great partnership, Ms. Burke."

Nodding again, he released her and exited the office. She stared after him for a moment, then shook her head. He was *intense*.

"Eve? Can we talk for a minute?" A warm, big hand wrapped around hers, and the crackle that rippled up her arm and sizzled across her breasts telegraphed who touched her before she turned around.

Briefly closing her eyes, she pivoted and offered Kenan a polite smile. "Congratulations," she said. "You did a great job, and everyone recognized all your hard work, like I knew they would. You were brilliant, Kenan."

"Thank you. But you helped sell it. If not for you on board, the proposal might not have been approved. You had my back—you've always had my back, Eve," he murmured, an urgency entering his voice, his hold tightening on her hand. "Give me five minutes. I don't deserve it, but I'm asking for it, anyway. Please."

It was the "please" that did it for her. Not that he'd never said that word to her before, but it wasn't often. And for him to use it now... Well, she didn't have the armor to resist it.

"Fine. Five minutes. I have to get back to work." Not true. She'd taken the day off when Cain called and asked her to come by the office, but Kenan didn't know that. And besides, she did have something work-related to do— write a resignation letter.

"Thanks, sweetheart."

Still grasping her hand, he led her out of the conference room and down the hall to his office. She should remove her hand. Should insist he not touch her. Should do a lot of things. But, dammit, she couldn't. She *wanted* his touch. Missed it.

As soon as they entered his office, she summoned up the strength to withdraw from him. Rubbing her thumb into her palm, she tried to erase the brand of his hand on hers. The craving it stirred for more.

"Thank you, Eve," he murmured, and she tried not to get lost in his blue-gray eyes. "Thank you for coming here, first of all. I didn't think you'd come if I invited you, so I apologize for the subterfuge of putting Cain and Achilles up to it. But I wanted you there for the presentation. First, so you could see the excitement for Intimate Curves and your designs for yourself. Second, for more selfish reasons, I needed you there. I'm at my best with you, and I couldn't have done any of this without you. I didn't expect you to reveal yourself as the owner, but damn, Eve, I've never been so proud. So happy for you."

"I'm proud of myself."

A smile flirted with his mouth and, unlike Nico Morgan, Kenan's pleasure reached his eyes.

"You should be." He held out his hands, studied the palms, then lowered them. And when he lifted his head, she stifled a gasp at the pain in his eyes. "Eve, I don't have the words to express how much I hate that I hurt you. That *I* was the one who caused you pain, who rejected you. Since we were children in that break room, it's been my job to be your soft place to land just as you've been mine. And I tore that safety net out from under you, and I will never forgive myself for that. But I'm not above asking for *your* forgiveness."

He clenched his jaw, the muscle there working.

"Kenan," she whispered, unsure what to say, but he shook his head, cutting her off.

"I haven't been honest with you, Eve. You know I've been searching for information on my birth mother." He paused, and she nodded, frowning. What did that have to do with them? "I recently found out her identity. She's my mother."

"What? I don't... What?"

He nodded. "My adoptive mother is actually my birth mother. She had an affair with Barron Farrell all those years ago and got pregnant. To avoid anyone finding out, my parents decided to pretend I was adopted. And they've lied to me all these years."

"Jesus, Kenan." She went to him, grabbing his hands, clasping them between hers. "I can't... When did you find this out?"

"Last Monday."

I'm through blindly accepting lies just because someone tells me their truths. I'm done being someone's secret and their Plan B. Never again.

Oh, God. She hadn't known what he'd meant by those words at the time. But now she did. He'd just discovered his parents had lied to him for thirty years and then walked up on her and Gavin, thinking she'd betrayed him. No wonder he'd been so hurt and acted so coldly. The knowledge didn't lessen the pain, but she did understand.

"Kenan, I'm sorry. I can't imagine. Are you okay?"

"Yes." He flipped their hands so he held hers in his. "I've talked to my mother, and she and Dad are going to tell Gavin the truth, but there's no point in letting it go past the family. It's going to take some time, but..." He shrugged a shoulder. "I love her, even if I don't know what the future holds. What I do know is I can't see one without you." He stroked his hands up her arms, over her shoulders and neck until he cradled her jaw. "I have another confession. I love you. I've been in love with you for fifteen years. There's never been anyone else who has owned my heart.

And when you accused me of being scared, you had no idea how right you were. I've been terrified for half my life of telling you how much I love you. Afraid you could never see me as more than a friend. Afraid of losing you. Afraid I would always be second to Gavin. Rather than take a risk and tell you the truth, I hid the truth. But I'm tired of hiding. I want to live free. With you."

He pressed his forehead to hers, his breath mingling with the soft pants that broke on her lips. Joy, hope and disbelief warred for dominance inside her. He'd been in love with her for years. *Years.* Damn, he was a fantastic actor, because she'd never guessed, never known. So much wasted time. She wanted to kiss the life out of him and smack him in the back of the head.

"Please, sweetheart, don't take your heart from me. Just when I finally had your love, I threw it back at you, and I'm begging you for another chance. You can trust me. I'll spend the rest of my life showing you, proving you can trust me with the most precious thing in this world—your heart."

"No more secrets," she said, circling his wrists. "Complete honesty between us from now on. And I'll start right here…" She tipped back her head farther, met his bright, piercing gaze and basked in the love there as if it was the sun, warming her. "My heart and my trust are yours and only yours. First as my friend and now as the love of my life. I love you, Kenan Rhodes."

Murmuring her name, he bowed his head and kissed her, taking her mouth in a hungry, furious kiss that weakened her knees and sent love and lust spiraling through her.

This man. He did it for her.

And she was claiming him as hers.

Forever.

* * * * *

THE BAD BOY
EXPERIMENT

REESE RYAN

One

Cole Abbott stepped down out of his crew cab truck, which towered over the other vehicles in the small parking lot of the Magnolia Lake General Store, and went inside.

He scrolled through a text message from his mother, Iris. Then he got a shopping cart and made his way through the store, picking up last-minute items for his family's weekly Sunday dinner.

Cole grabbed a few tubs of Häagen-Dazs vanilla ice cream, then went to find whipped topping. He dumped two cans into his cart, thought about it, then added another.

"I don't even want to know what you plan to do with those."

Cole turned toward the warm voice coming from behind him. A voice that had always managed to be both teasing and reprimanding in a way that left him unsure of whether he was being teased or reprimanded. He blinked, barely able to believe his eyes.

"Renee? What are you...? I mean...*wow*. You look...

amazing. Good to see you," Cole stammered. They share
an awkward hug that she leaned into, but extricated he
self from just as quickly.

Renee Lockwood was both a ghost from his past an
an enchanting vision in the present. He'd always like
Renee. A lot. But he hadn't ever dated her. She'd been h
high school math tutor, a fellow member of his graduatin
class and the granddaughter of his mentor. They'd becon
friends. But he hadn't been a very good friend to her
the end. Something that often haunted him.

"Thank you." Renee spared him a faint half smile an
raked her fingers through her glossy, dark hair, settling t
strands over one shoulder. "Good to see you again, too

Cole honestly might've walked right past Renee, n
recognizing that she was the awkward, shy, geeky girl he
once adored. In fact, not much about the woman standi
before him resembled his old friend and tutor.

The Coke-bottle glasses and braces were gone. An
Renee's boyish figure had been replaced by full breas
and curvy hips, her dark brown skin smooth and clea
Her inherent shyness seemed to be a thing of the past. I
stead, she held her head high and her shoulders back. B
her eyes still didn't quite meet his. Those almond-shap
eyes, shielded behind dark, thick lashes, had always fa
cinated him.

In school, to fit in she'd downplayed her excitement ov
math and science. But at her grandparents' kitchen tab
she'd beamed as she waxed poetic about hypotenuse, int
gers and the periodic table. That year he'd even purchas
a T-shirt for her birthday that bore the periodic table a
the words, "I wear this shirt periodically. But only wh
I'm in my element." Ren had loved it, and Cole had lov
seeing the way her eyes lit up whenever she wore it.

That shirt had kicked off his own obsession with sma

ass T-shirts, like the one he was wearing now beneath his button-down shirt.

"Family dinner," Cole finally blurted, in response to Ren's initial comment about the whipped cream. Though, now that he'd encountered her, he had some very different ideas about how to use it. When Renee raised an eyebrow in disbelief, Cole held up his phone, showing her the list. "My mother asked me to buy it."

"Hmm…" One side of Renee's mouth lifted in a reluctant smile. The kind he'd frequently teased out of her when she was trying to be serious and keep them on track so he'd graduate from high school on time, despite his academic struggles. "Ms. Iris asked for *two* cans of whipped cream." She held up two fingers. "That leaves one can unaccounted for."

Shit. She was right. He'd planned to take that last can home for… Well…you never knew when you might find yourself in need of a pressurized can of lickable sweets.

How the hell was Renee able to walk in here after more than sixteen years and still read him like one of the algebraic equations she'd been able to solve without breaking a sweat?

"Relax, Cole. I'm kidding." Renee smiled, then leaned in and whispered, "No, I'm not."

It had been a running joke between them. Something he would often say because he couldn't help flirting with her, though he knew he shouldn't. They both laughed, and a little of the uneasiness between them seemed to dissipate.

"I saw your grandad the other day," Cole said, once the laughter between them had faded. "He didn't mention you were in town."

Renee lowered her gaze. "It was an unplanned visit. I arrived yesterday."

The Renee Lockwood he'd known hadn't done *anything*

unplanned. She'd planned her life, her career and her day with precision.

Cole's gaze went immediately to her left hand and bare ring finger. "Sorry to hear about you and…"

"Dennis," Ren said the name as if it left a bitter taste in her mouth. "It's been over for a while. We made it formal a year ago. It was the best thing for everyone."

"Right." Cole hadn't met the man. But from what Ren's grandfather Milo had told him, Renee's ex was a golden boy. The only male heir of a wealthy family who'd made their money in pharmaceuticals. He hadn't much liked the man when his granddaughter had married him. Now Milo hated him.

Cole wanted to ask about her kid. Because it seemed like the polite thing to do. But before he could ask, Renee changed the subject.

"Your family still does Sunday dinners, huh?" Ren smiled faintly. The sadness in her dark eyes made his chest ache. "It's sweet you all still get together for dinner once a week. Are all of your brothers and your sister still here in Magnolia Lake?"

"Yes. Blake is married with two kids. Parker is engaged to Kayleigh Jemison."

"I thought they hated each other."

"So did they." Cole chuckled.

"What about Max and Zora?"

"Max is seriously involved with Quinn Bazemore," Cole said.

Cole and Quinn had been close friends. He'd thought they might eventually end up together. But he hadn't known that his brother and Quinn had been involved the summer Max had been an intern at her grandfather's orchard. It had taken thirteen years, but Max and Quinn reconnected when their families collaborated to add fruit brandies to the King's Finest product line. Cole hadn't been thrilled when Quinn and Max started dating again. But the two were madly in love. He was happy for them.

"Quinn Bazemore...as in Bazemore Orchards?" Renee asked.

"Dixon's granddaughter," he confirmed. "And as for my baby sis...she and her best friend, Dallas Hamilton, got married in Vegas a few months ago. This is our first dinner since they got back from a four-month stint in Iceland for his work."

"That's wonderful." Renee's smile was reserved. Like she was happy for his siblings but maybe sad about the end of her own marriage. "And let me guess. You're the Abbott family's eternal bachelor."

Much to the chagrin of his mother and sister, *eternal bachelor* was a title Cole wore proudly. But something about hearing Ren say it made him uneasy.

"Clearly." He winked. "Gotta spread the love."

Renee rolled her eyes. "How selfless of you."

"You know me." Cole shrugged.

"I do." Ren studied him, her head tilted.

Translation: *I haven't forgotten what a jackass you were to me back then.*

Cole swallowed hard, his mouth falling open. He wanted to tell Renee he was sorry. To explain himself. But the words wouldn't come. He snapped his mouth shut, and she smirked. Probably because he was standing in the middle of the general store looking like a damn guppy.

"You must be eager to see Zora and her husband. I won't keep you." Ren shifted her purse to the other shoulder. "Guess I'll see you around." She turned and walked away.

Cole stopped himself from inviting Ren to dinner with his family. Because as much as he'd like to see more of Renee, he didn't want to give her or his family the wrong impression.

He liked Renee. Missed having her as a friend. Regret-

ted that their friendship had ended the way it did. But
wasn't looking to get seriously involved with anyone. Le:
of all someone with wealthy, asshole ex drama and a ki
No, sir.

Maybe the rest of his siblings had fallen victim to t
love bug. But Cole was perfectly content with his life j
as it was. Renee Lockwood's return wouldn't change th:

Cole bit his lip and sighed. He hated to see her leav
but as he watched the sway of Ren's full hips in her se:
little skirt, he definitely enjoyed watching her go.

Two

Renee stood in line at the general store, waiting to check out. But she couldn't help staring out the window at Cole loading his oversize pickup truck with its fancy wheels.

Boys and their toys.

Her ex had a stable of expensive classic cars he'd restored. He'd kept his favorites in the six-car garage of their home, built on his family's secluded estate. A light blue 1964 Aston Martin discovered in an old, run-down barn in Spain; a red 1968 Chevy Camaro; and a gorgeous blue 1965 Ford Mustang Shelby Cobra. All of which he adored far more than he'd ever really cared for her or their son.

Dennis's obsession with cars was his way of overcompensating for the fact that he was a real-life Tin Man with no heart or soul, who was less than adequate in bed. What was Cole overcompensating for with his oversize truck? It didn't matter, because Cole Abbott was no concern of hers.

"Ma'am?"

The cashier's soft plea, accompanied by a big, friendly

smile and a deep Central Tennessee twang, roused her from her thoughts. Renee's cheeks burned beneath the stare of the teenage cashier and the other shoppers in line

"Sorry." Renee returned the girl's smile and set her basket on the counter so the cashier could ring her up. There was a tug on her skirt. Her little boy, Mercer.

"What is it, sweetheart?" She studied his handsome face, which bore features of both her and her ex. Yet, somehow, the boy was the spitting image of her grandfather Something which had annoyed her ex to no end.

Four-year-old Mercer pointed out the window at the large black truck Cole was climbing into. "Vroom!"

Ren lifted her son, whose long legs dangled to her knees, so he could get a better view of the truck before Cole pulled off. "Truck," she said. "The big truck goes *vroom*."

The boy nodded, leaning his head against hers.

Ren kissed his temple before setting him back on the ground.

"Sorry, Renee. He got away from me. Took off the moment he saw you." Her grandmother hurried toward them out of breath.

"It's okay, Gran. I should've warned you that Mercer is a little speed demon. Once he gets loose, he's off to the races."

The little boy looked up at his great-grandmother with an apologetic smile. He reached a hand out to her as a peace offering.

Renee tried to hold back a smile as she passed him over to her grandmother so she could pay for her groceries.

Her four-year-old son was autistic and mostly nonverbal. But he was a charmer who'd learned to communicate his desires clearly without saying a word.

"That's Cole Abbott's truck." Her grandmother nodded toward the truck pulling out of the lot.

"I know." Renee thanked the cashier and gathered her bags. "I saw him in the store earlier. He was picking up a few things for dinner with his family."

"How nice," Gran said, following her out of the store as they headed toward Ren's Midnight Silver Tesla 3. "We really should invite Cole over to—"

"*No*, Gran." Ren turned to her grandmother.

"No?" Her grandmother frowned.

"It's your house, so of course you can invite over whomever you want. But *please* don't try to set me up with Cole or anyone else. That's not why I'm here. Mercer is my focus. Everything I do in my life…it's only about what's best for him."

"The boy needs a father," Gran argued as they continued their trek toward the car.

"He *has* a father," Ren noted. "He just happens to be a shitty one," she added under her breath so neither her grandmother nor Mercer could hear.

Ren put the groceries on the back seat, then strapped Mercer in.

"I meant a *real* father." Her grandmother lowered her voice as they both slipped into their seats. "And you deserve a *real* husband. A man who is going to cherish you. Take care of you. Be a partner to you in raising your son."

Ren's chest ached as she considered all the ways her ex had been lacking in that regard. To say she'd chosen her mate poorly would be the understatement of the century. But she'd had an entire year to contemplate her failings. She'd come here, to the little town where she'd spent her teenage years, to escape her mistakes. She had zero interest in revisiting them with her grandmother now.

"I know you love us, Gran, and I appreciate that you want what's best for Mercer and me." Ren put a gentle hand on her grandmother's forearm. "But the last thing I need is the distraction of a relationship, especially with

someone like Cole Abbott, who probably doesn't do rela
tionships anyway."

"Yet." Gran held up a finger. "But when the righ
woman comes along, his skirt-chasing days will be ove
You'll see." She chuckled. "So if you have any interes
in—"

"I don't," Ren said quickly.

"But you did," her grandmother countered.

"I also once thought I could pull off a bra top and bagg
jeans look, like Aaliyah. I was wrong about that, too."

"You wore what, now?" Her grandmother frowned.

"The point is…my crush on Cole was a lifetime ago
Gran. We're both different people now." Renee settled bac
against the black, vegan leather seat. "Scratch that… *I'm* a
different person. I have serious responsibilities and ambi
tious goals. He's pretty much who he's always been. Play
ing the role of the carefree bad boy and loving it."

"That isn't fair, sweetheart." Gran buckled her seat bel
"I know the boy had his faults, but he's a good and kin
man. Always has been. And he's got quite a bit of ambi
tion of his own. He could've just taken some cushy job a
his family's distillery. Instead, he built his own construc
tion and development company."

"Because he bought Gramps's construction compan
and because Grandpa mentored him." Renee put on he
seat belt and started the car.

"Cole's company had outgrown your grandfather's lon
before he purchased it. He didn't need your grandfather'
business or his run-down equipment. Cole offered to bu
the business as a courtesy to your grandfather. He eve
insisted on paying more than the business was worth. H
wanted to ensure that we lived a comfortable life in retire
ment. And he's been there whenever we've needed him."

Her grandmother's mention of Cole being there wa
a silent reminder that she hadn't been. During her seven

years of marriage to Dennis, she'd been notably absent from the lives of her own family.

Dennis hadn't liked coming to Tennessee to visit. Nor had he and his family been particularly delighted when her family had come to visit them. And if she was being honest with herself, she'd refrained from visiting her parents and grandparents alone because she hadn't wanted them to see the truth. That she was miserable because marrying into the Chandler family had been the biggest mistake of her life.

"Gran, I'm sorry I haven't been around more. But I'm here now and—"

"No need to apologize, sweetheart. I realize how difficult it must've been for you. I'm sorry your marriage didn't work out—I really am. But I'm glad to have you back here, where you and Mercer belong."

Renee blinked back tears. She glanced back at her son, who happily sucked his thumb. The corners of his mouth lifted in a little smile and he pointed forward.

Her son had a language all his own, and the gesture was Mercer for *Mommy, let's go already.*

"Gotcha, big guy." She checked the rearview mirror. "We're headed home to Grandpa."

Mercer's smile deepened and he kicked his feet happily.

Renee headed back to her grandparents' home, where she would make them a big, fancy gourmet meal, put Mercer to bed for the night, then try to convince her grandparents to let her revive their family farm.

Ren had spent her entire career as a pharmaceutical scientist researching and developing therapeutics for Alzheimer's disease while in pursuit of a cure. She'd made substantial contributions, of which she was proud. But with her son's autism diagnosis at the age of two, her focus had shifted. Her primary concern was Mercer and his future.

She had big plans for the property where generations

of the Lockwood family had raised cattle and grown corn and soybeans. Resuscitating the farm would be a huge task. Especially since she'd be managing the project alone with the help of a few hired hands.

Between raising Mercer and managing the farm, there'd be no time for romance. So she'd dismiss her less-than-pure thoughts about how good Cole's rather impressive ass looked in those jeans. And how his button-down shirt had been just tight enough to accentuate his strong biceps and broad chest. She'd forget how handsome he'd looked with his trim beard and cinnamon-brown skin. But she'd remind herself of just how dangerous that devilish smile could be.

She was here to start a new life for herself and her son. Not to revisit old wounds or set herself up for new ones. That meant putting Cole in her rearview mirror and never looking back.

Three

"Hey, baby sis." Cole grinned as he opened his arms to his younger sister.

"Cole!" Zora leaped into his arms and gave him a bear hug. "I missed you, knucklehead." She grinned. "I worry about you when I'm not around. We both know you need constant supervision."

Cole chuckled. She wasn't wrong.

His younger sister was more of a hawk over him and his brothers than their parents were. Sometimes, he swore Zora thought *she* was their mother.

"What about those three?" Cole indicated his three brothers as they entered the den. Blake sat in a wingback chair with his infant daughter, Remi, on his lap and his son, Davis, on the floor nearby playing with his toy cars and trucks. Max and Parker were seated on the sofa having a debate about something related to the distillery. Their grandfather occupied the other wingback chair. And their father, Duke, stretched out in his favorite recliner. "Why aren't you worried about them?"

Zora propped a hand on her hip and cocked her head with a dramatic eyebrow raise. A silent *What do you think.*

Cole and Zora burst into laughter. Their older brother were already low-key. But now that they were in committed relationships, they were total bores.

"Point made," Cole said.

"Okay, what does today's T-shirt say?" Zora asked impatiently.

Cole unbuttoned his shirt enough to permit his sister to see the words imprinted on the T-shirt he wore beneath it

If you met my family, you'd understand.

Zora burst out laughing. She waved a hand. "No, sir. You will *not* blame your nonsense on us."

"Hey, babe. Your mom needs you in the kitchen." Dallas entered the room and slipped his arms around Zora's waist from behind. He kissed her neck. "What's up, Cole?"

Dallas extended a closed fist to Cole and he bumped it Things were good between them again. But Cole and his brothers had initially been angry when their sister had returned home from spending her birthday weekend in Vegas suddenly married to her longtime best friend.

"Nuthin' much." Cole shrugged. "Also, I know she's your wife, but that happens to be my baby sister. So maybe a little less of the PDA."

"Hush!" Zora giggled as Dallas nuzzled her neck.

"Don't be a jealous hater, bruh," Max said on his way out of the room.

"I am not—"

Max was already gone before Cole could argue.

"Don't worry, Cole. Your day is coming. Promise." Zora's warm smile radiated love and maybe a tiny bit of pity. "I'm gonna go see what Mama wants."

Cole didn't bother to respond. Growing the town one

little person at a time had apparently become the mission of his siblings. He'd leave that to them. He was expanding the town in his own way. One home, one building, one community at a time.

And if things went his way, he'd leave behind an even greater legacy in the town of Magnolia Lake.

Cole helped his mother and Kayleigh clear the dishes from the table while Quinn and Blake's wife, Savannah, brought out two pans of peach cobbler, dessert plates, the tubs of ice cream and the whipped topping.

"Everything okay, son?" his mother asked as she rinsed the dishes, then handed them to him so he could put them in the dishwasher.

"Everything is good." Why were the women in his life so good at getting into his head?

"But there is *something* on your mind," she pressed.

"I ran into Renee Lockwood at the general store." He put another dish in the rack.

"I didn't know Ren was back in town," Iris said. "What a sweet girl. I was sorry to hear things didn't work out with her husband. But I'm glad she's come to spend some time with Milo and Janice. They could use the company." She turned off the water and looked over at him. "That must be the first time you've seen Renee in seventeen or eighteen years." She cocked her head. "You all right?"

"Why wouldn't I be?" Cole reached for another plate.

"You were quite fond of her in high school. I thought seeing her again might've brought up some…feelings for you."

"We were friends. That's all," Cole reminded her, his tone sharper than he'd intended. "After all, you thought I was wrong for her," Cole said bitterly. "And you were probably right."

"I *never* said that." His mother's voice was tight. "I said

you shouldn't play with her emotions. Renee was obviousl
head over heels for you. But she was so bright and—"

"I wasn't." It pained Cole to say the words.

All the memories of his school struggles and the fight
it had caused with his parents hit him squarely in the ches
Growing up, he'd been the Abbott family disappointmen
He was the youngest boy and clearly hadn't lived up t
the expectations his academically gifted brothers had es
tablished.

He didn't resent that his siblings were scholastic star:
But he'd been bitter no one seemed to understand tha
his underperformance wasn't because he was a slacker
He'd honestly been doing his best. But his family an
teachers had all felt that if his brothers had excelled
why couldn't he?

Eventually, he'd leaned into the role of slacker. Becaus
it was easier to pretend he didn't care than to admit he wa
struggling and needed help. He'd only accepted tutorin
from Renee because Milo had insisted that he'd be helpin
her as much as she'd be helping him. Being a tutor looke
good on her academic résumé.

"We pushed so hard because we knew how bright yo
were. We just wanted you to live up to your potential." Hi
mother's eyes shone.

"You wanted me to live up to your expectations." Col
hated seeing the pain in his mother's eyes. But he'd trie
hiding his feelings on the subject. It only led to resentmen
Especially between him and his father. It'd taken years fo
their relationship to recover. He wouldn't go there again

"You're right, sweetheart," she said. "You were mean
for a different path, and we're proud of everything you'v
achieved." Iris handed him another dish. "And for the re
cord, I never thought you weren't good enough for Renee
Cole. But you were both so young, and she was a brillian

young woman at an important crossroads in her life. I didn't want to see her get sidetracked."

The entire town had pinned their hopes and dreams on Renee, who was Ivy League bound. Just as they'd cheered on every other native who'd gone on to do great things. That kind of support and camaraderie was why, though he traveled the world and owned rental property in South Carolina, he would always call Magnolia Lake home.

"Did Renee say how long she's staying?"

"Didn't ask." Cole put the last of the dishes into the dishwasher and shut the door. But he'd wanted to.

"Just remember, son, Renee has been through a rough divorce, and she's raising a child on her own. She's not your usual conquest."

Before he could object to having a conversation about his sex life with his mother, Zora called them.

"Will you two hurry up? We're waiting for you."

"Would've gone faster if your impatient tail had helped us," his mother responded.

That shut his sister up.

His mother slipped her arm through his. "I was by no means a perfect mother, but I tried very hard to be the best mother I could be."

"And I'm lucky to have you and Dad as parents. I know you've made a lot of sacrifices to ensure that we had a better life." Cole kissed his mother's temple. "I'm glad you're finally fulfilling one of your dreams."

"Seeing all my babies happily married?"

"Real subtle hint, Ma." Cole chuckled. "I meant opening a restaurant like you've always wanted."

"Opening a restaurant in the same building where my dad once ran our little family café... It still feels like a dream. And to have your company renovating the space... It just doesn't get any better." She sighed happily.

Cole couldn't help grinning as they returned to t seats at the table, where everyone was waiting.

"We have *huge* news." Zora gripped her husband's h and leaned into him. "We're pregnant."

"Oh my God, Zora!" Iris was on her feet in an inst wrapping her daughter and son-in-law in a tight hug. D las's mother, Tish, hugged them next.

The family made the rounds congratulating the tw Zora informed them that her baby was due in about months.

"I swear we aren't trying to steal your thunder h Brat," Max said. "But Quinn and I have news of our ow He glanced over at Quinn with a dreamy look in his ey "I proposed last night, and Quinn accepted. We're gaged."

Quinn held up her hand and wiggled her fingers, playing the ring. Evidently she'd just slipped it on, or Co mother and sister would've noticed it sooner.

"You two are getting married?" Zora practic squealed. "I'm so excited for you."

"Have you set a date?" Grandpa Joe asked as every gathered around to look at Quinn's ring.

"We'd like to get married around the anniversary when we first reconnected," Quinn said.

"But that's in a few months," his mother noted. " barn is booked every Saturday for the rest of the year.

"I know." Quinn slipped a hand into Max's. "And I alize how much the barn means to you. That it's where eryone else in the family has been married. But Max I plan to get married at my grandfather's orchard, wh this all began for us."

Quinn seemed to hold her breath as she awaited Ir response.

"How romantic." Iris's eyes were wet with tears. " us know how we can help."

Quinn nodded, seemingly relieved.

"You're going to need a new plus-one," Zora said, so only he could hear her. Quinn had been his plus-one for both his cousin Benji's wedding and his parents' fortieth anniversary. "And Dallas's cousin Vanessa has been asking about you since she met you at our wedding here."

"I'm good, Zo. Thanks," Cole said.

Maybe now that Zora had her own bun in the oven, she could play mama bear to her own little cub and stop worrying over him all the time.

Cole ate his peach cobbler, piled high with whipped topping, in silence as his family chatted about another upcoming wedding and the impending arrival of Zora's baby.

It was official. With Parker and Kayleigh and Max and Quinn getting married in a few months, and Blake and Zora already married, he was the last lone wolf in the family.

Fine by him. He was content to be the best damn uncle that ever lived.

Four

"Dinner was delicious, sweetheart." Renee's grandmother stood to gather the dishes.

"Thank you, but you just relax, Gran." Ren stood. "I'll clear the table."

"I'd rather you have a seat and tell us what's on your mind." Her grandfather steepled his hands over his belly.

"How'd you—"

"When you were a teenager, you'd clean the house inside and out whenever you wanted to ask for something and you thought I was gonna tell you no." He chuckled. "I'll let you in on a little secret. Most of the time, I would've said yes anyway. Even without all of them extra chores."

Ren sank onto one of the wooden chairs her grandparents had owned for as long as she could remember. "I thought I'd wait until after I gave Mercer a bath and put him to bed."

They all looked at the little boy, who plucked a blueberry from the bowl in front of him and carefully examined it before popping it into his mouth. Mercer was a picky eater, but blueberries were his favorite.

"Is it something he shouldn't hear?" her grandmother asked. "Like something about his father?" She whispered the last word.

"This isn't about Dennis."

"Then no time like the present," her grandfather said.

All right. Here goes.

"I wanted to talk to you about the farm." She met her grandfather's stern gaze.

"What about it?" He sat up, giving her his full attention.

"I'd like to buy it."

Her grandparents exchanged a look of concern, then looked back at her.

"You'd like to buy the farm?" He repeated her words. "What on earth do you plan to do with it?"

"Restore it to a working farm again," she said matter-of-factly. "Only better."

"Better *how*?" Gran asked.

"I'll employ science and technology to make it a sustainable organic farm. One that will provide employment for neurodiverse men and women." She nodded toward her son.

Her grandparents' frowns eased and their eyes flickered with understanding.

"An admirable ambition, sweetheart." Milo's voice had softened. "And I can certainly understand why it would be so important to you." He glanced at Mercer, who contentedly picked through his blueberries without a care in the world. "But I don't think you realize what a monumental task it is to run a farm."

"Alone," Gran added. "We did it together for years, honey. It's an awful lot of backbreaking work."

"I know it won't be easy," Ren said. "But recent scien-

tific breakthroughs and the latest technology will exped
things. And I'd hire knowledgeable, experienced help.

"Renee, sweetheart…" Gran was saying.

"Your grandmother says you ran into Cole earlier tod
Did you two discuss the farm?" Milo rubbed his chin.

"Why would I discuss this with Cole?"

"Because he's been badgering me about buying th
plot of land for the past two years." He folded his arms

"Cole wants to buy *our* family farm? Why? Don't t
Abbotts have enough land of their own?"

"He wants to turn it into a new community of luxu
homes. Keeps going up on the offer every few month
he said.

"Do you plan to sell to him?" Ren asked.

"It's a tempting offer. But it don't sit quite right, selli
the land that's been in our family for generations." M
dragged a hand over his head. His gaze settled on h
"Don't seem right saddling you with it, neither. I kn
you're brilliant and determined, Renee. But it's a lot
work for a single—"

"Woman?" She narrowed her gaze at her grandfath

"A single *parent*," he finished. "It's a much bigger u
dertaking than you seem to realize."

"I know it won't be easy, but I have a plan. I won't try
take on the entire thing at once. I would start with one
the smaller tracts of land your sisters lived on," Ren sa

Her great-aunts had owned two tracts of land sitti
side by side, their homes fairly close. One great-aunt gr
strawberries and blueberries, which local folks would off
stop and pick for themselves. The other grew flowers, su
plying florists in the region. They had a little stand o
front where they'd often sit and chat while they waited
customers to stop by.

Her great-aunts, Wilhelmina and Beatrice, had been t
last of her grandfather's siblings. They'd been gone for fi

years now, dying within months of each other. Her grandfather was now the sole owner of the entire parcel of connected farmland. He'd given up farming for construction many years ago and moved off his tract, so the land was in disuse and overgrown.

Milo's eyes were glossy at the mention of his sisters. "Hard to believe I'm the last man standing. All my brothers and sisters are long gone."

"I miss them, too. And I'd like to continue their legacy by growing fruits and vegetables like Aunt Willie and flowers like Aunt Bea."

"What you want to do is a nice tribute to your great-aunts and a wonderful thing to do for Mercer and other children and adults on the spectrum." Gran gripped her husband's free hand, recognizing he was too choked up to speak. "But honey, you already have your hands full with Mercer. How do you expect to—"

"I appreciate your concern, Gran and Gramps. But it's no different than if I had a demanding full-time job. Which I did when Mercer was a baby. This way, even if I hire a nanny, I'll just be steps away if Mercer needs me."

Her grandfather sighed. "This plan you say you've got. Give me the quick and dirty version."

Renee folded her hands on the table in front of her. "I'd start with growing organic carrots, tomatoes, cucumbers and berries along with companion flowers like marigolds and lilacs and herbs like basil and thyme. The companion plants will safely deter garden pests and can also be sold locally."

"Any animals?" He rubbed his grizzled chin.

"I'd probably get a few chickens. For organic eggs, not for food," she clarified.

"Free-range, I'd imagine." The term was clearly suspect to Milo Lockwood.

"Supervised free-range, but yes. That's the plan," she confirmed.

"Nothing like how my parents did things or their parents before them. Why does everyone always want to change things?" he grumbled.

"So we don't have to wash our clothes on a rock in a stream and dial rotary telephones on a short cord attached to the wall," Ren teased.

"Now that's *definitely* the kind of smartass answer I'd get from Cole." The old man chuckled, as did her grandmother. Mercer, not wanting to be left out of the fun, laughed, too.

Renee ruffled her son's tight curls. "So what do you think, Grandpa?"

"You've given me a lot to consider. But I'll need some time to think on it, all right?"

Ren tried not to sound as defeated as she felt. "Yes, sir. Of course. I realize I sprung this on you seemingly out of nowhere. But I've been thinking about this for at least a year."

"Since the divorce." Her grandfather nodded. "Well, I promise to give your proposal fair consideration." He patted her hand, then stood and rubbed his rotund belly. "Gonna walk off some of that fine meal you made. Why don't I take Mercer?"

"He'd like that."

Her grandfather lifted Mercer from his booster seat and took his hand. "Coming, Janice?"

Gran looked to her. "You're sure you don't mind cleaning up by yourself?"

"Not at all. Enjoy your walk."

She grabbed a jacket for Mercer, who bounced up and down on his toes, excited about going for a walk. Then she slipped his little Skip Hop backpack over his arms and strapped the belt that spanned his chest before handing the attached tether to her grandfather.

"He's fast," she explained, when her grandfather looked puzzled. "That's so he doesn't get away from you."

"I don't need—"

"Trust me, we do." Gran took his free hand. "Now come on. It'll be dark soon."

"Have fun," Ren called after them. "Don't get into any trouble."

"Not making no promises." Her grandfather winked, slipping on his own jacket.

Renee gathered the dishes and took them to the kitchen. She rinsed them and loaded the dishwasher.

Why did her grandparents keep bringing up Cole Abbott? And there were countless plots of land in this county that Cole could build on. Why was he set on buying her family's land?

It didn't matter, because she was back in Magnolia Lake to stay, ready to put down roots. Her family was here. Though her dad and older brother, both still serving in the army, were stationed overseas, she had her grandparents, and her mother was just an hour away in Knoxville.

People in town had been nothing but kind to her and Mercer. They'd shown her son more consideration than his own father or paternal grandparents had. Mercer seemed happier and more relaxed, and so was she. The knot in her gut had loosened. Her shoulders and back didn't feel so tight. And she stood a little taller than when she'd first arrived, feeling worn-out and broken.

Here, in Magnolia Lake, was *exactly* where she and Mercer needed to be. Whether it took two days, two months or two years, she was determined to turn her dream of revitalizing the family farm into a reality.

Cole Abbott could go and turn someone else's family legacy into luxury villas.

Five

Cole made his way inside the Magnolia Lake Bakery a
waved to the owner, Amina Lassiter.

"Your usual?" Amina asked.

"Please."

"I'll bring it to you, sugar. Grab a seat," Amina s
before returning her attention to the customer she w
waiting on.

Cole looked around and quickly spotted the man wh
summoned him here, the man to whom he owed his car
and in some ways, his life: Milo Lockwood. He was sitt
in one of the booths near the back, but he wasn't alone

He was with his granddaughter, Renee.

It'd been two weeks since they'd encountered each ot
in the general store. Cole hadn't realized Ren was stil
town.

He walked back to where they were seated and sto
in front of their table.

"Good afternoon, Milo, Renee. If you need some ti

I can grab something to eat first." Cole glanced at his watch. The Breitling Navitimer was a birthday gift from his brother Parker, who was obsessed with acquiring expensive watches from government auctions. "Or I can check on my crew's progress over at the restaurant and come back in an hour."

"No, son. You're right on time." Milo stood, gesturing to the other side of the booth where his granddaughter was seated. "Please, have a seat."

Renee gave her grandfather a pointed look and pressed her pouty lips into a hard line as she scooted over. She turned toward him.

"What brings you here this afternoon, Cole?"

"I was summoned." He nodded toward Milo.

"What a coincidence." Renee eyed the older man. "So was I."

Milo, who looked like he'd pulled a big joke on them, tried and failed to contain his grin.

"Well, now I'm really intrigued. He was pretty vague when he asked me to meet him here. I figured he just wanted to catch up," Cole said.

"And I assumed that this was about my proposal to buy the farm." Renee folded her arms on the table, still staring at her grandfather, who seemed endlessly amused.

Some things about Renee had changed. Being remarkably adorable, even when she was annoyed, apparently wasn't one of them.

"Wait…you offered to buy the Lockwood family farm holdings?" Cole's brain—distracted by Ren's enticing scent and how damn good the woman looked in her tortoiseshell cat-eye glasses—finally caught up. He turned toward her, and his knee brushed against hers beneath the table.

A jolt of electricity traveled up his thigh and settled into places it was best he didn't think about at the moment.

Renee reacted as if she'd felt it, too. She scooted toward the wall.

"Yes. It is *my* family's farm." She slapped an open palm to her chest. His gaze dropped to the hint of her full breasts revealed by a deep V-neck T-shirt.

He cleared his throat and forced himself to meet those mesmerizing, coffee-brown eyes.

"I've offered to buy the farm. Repeatedly," Cole informed her.

"I'm aware. Gramps told me two weeks ago when I made my offer." Renee sat taller in her seat and they both turned to her grandfather. "Which is why I'm surprised he invited us *both* here."

The old man shoveled the last spoonful of his baked-potato soup into his mouth, then took his time dabbing his lips with a napkin.

"I invited you both here because I've made a decision about how to handle you both wanting that land. I'm not a man who enjoys repeating himself unnecessarily," Milo said. "So I thought I'd tell you both at once."

"All right." Cole braced himself for the older man's decision. "Let's hear it."

"Both of your plans could be beneficial for Magnolia Lake. But I don't have enough evidence to determine which would be better."

Renee and Cole started speaking simultaneously, but Milo held up a hand, silencing them.

"I've come up with a plan to make a fair, well-informed decision," he said. "Just hear me out."

Shit. Cole definitely didn't like where this was going.

Milo had been a farmer for years, but he'd quit the farm and had been working in construction for well over a decade by the time Cole had begun working for him. The old man had generously taught Cole everything he knew about building and construction. He'd shown Cole how to be a good businessman and an upstanding individual through object lessons. Cole had a strong sense he was in store for yet another.

"Okay, Grandad." Renee leaned back against the booth and sighed. "We're listening."

A wide smile spread across the man's face and his gold tooth sparkled in the sunlight streaming from the window. He clapped his hands together, then leaned forward, studying each of their faces.

"There's an awful lot of land. I could divide the plot, giving you each half of it to develop your chosen project," Milo said.

So he was going King Solomon on them. Under different circumstances that might've been okay. But not for what Cole had in mind.

"That won't give me enough land for this project. I'm building an entire community of luxury homes about the size of my parents' house," Cole said.

"That would certainly bring in a lot more revenue around here. Maybe help the town finally get that new bridge, so we won't have to worry about the old one washing out whenever the river floods." Milo nodded thoughtfully.

"My plans are just as beneficial for the town," Renee piped up. "The wealthy can take care of themselves, believe me," she added bitterly. "My plan is better for the environment and it's an opportunity to improve the lives of those who actually could use our assistance." Her eyes gleamed with what looked like tears.

Cole fought back the urge to squeeze her hand. For all he knew, Renee was playing them both. Though that didn't track with the girl he'd once known.

Still, this was a business deal, pure and simple. And he was prepared to pay Milo Lockwood handsomely for the prime location.

"If it's a matter of the price—"

"It isn't." Milo seemed insulted by the insinuation th money alone would sway his decision. "It's about wha best for the community."

Cole nodded. "Of course."

"I don't want to split the property, either," Renee cc curred. "I'd start slowly with the organic farm. But I pl to use the entire plot. Besides, I doubt Cole's wealthy re dents would want to live next door to my berry bushes a free-range chickens."

"You want to turn the land back into a working far *Alone?*" Cole eyed her.

"Yes, I plan to revive the family farm," Her tone v indignant and there was fire in her dark eyes. "And do y build your houses alone?"

"Fair," Cole said. "But managing a farm is a lot of we for a—"

"If you say a single mother, I swear to God…"

Milo chuckled. "My granddaughter is a bit sensiti about this. You don't want to challenge her on it, belie me. Janice and I learned that the hard way."

"Fine." Cole threw his hands up. "Farming is a lot work. *Period.* Whether you're doing the work yourself not. I'd hate to see you get in over your head with th Renee."

"And I'd hate to see you turn my family's legacy ir a bunch of in-ground pools and tennis courts for tr fund babies and socialites, *Cole.*" She folded her ar over her chest.

Cole returned his attention to Milo and tried not to thi about how gorgeous Ren looked in the simple long-slee T-shirt and pair of jeans. Or how amazing she smell Or how much he'd like to hear her say his name, just li that, but in a very different setting.

Mind out of the gutter, man. Mind out of the gutter.

"It was a fair idea, Milo. But splitting the land doesn't seem to work for either of us." Cole stated the obvious.

"Thought you two might say that."

"So how can I convince you that reviving the family farm is the better option?" Renee asked her grandfather.

"Or that turning that land into high-end residential homes will significantly increase the per capita income of Magnolia Lake so we can improve the town's infrastructure?" Cole interjected.

"King's Finest Distillery is the largest employer in town. One would think that KFD would contribute to building up the infrastructure." Renee leaned back against the booth, her arms still folded.

Cole was the only member of his family who didn't work for their world-renowned distillery. However, it was a universally acknowledged rule that you got to talk shit about your family but other people didn't.

"They do. In addition to being the largest employer—which pays its workers quite generously, by the way—my family has done *a lot* for this town. Always has. Always will." He turned to her again, folding his arms, too.

"Many of the businesses in town have been recipients of grants, loans and business mentoring sponsored by King's Finest. My business included," Milo acknowledged. "That's how I was able to get started in construction when I was drowning in debt from the farm."

Renee's eyes widened. "I never knew that, Gramps."

"I never wanted you to." Milo sighed heavily. "Things were rough in those days. You were just a little girl then. I'd never have started my construction business without KFD's helping hand. That's why your grandfather felt betrayed when I gave you an option for building yourself a career outside of the distillery." He nodded toward Cole.

"I know." Cole sighed.

When he was a teenager, there was a point at which

his grandfather and Milo had nearly come to blows. Milo and Grandpa Joe's relationship was cordial now. But it had been hell being caught up in the animosity between two men he greatly admired.

"Here's what I plan to do." Milo reached into his jacket and pulled out a piece of paper. He unfolded it and pointed to one of two homes he'd sketched. "This here is Wilhelmina's old house. Right next door is Beatrice's old place. The rest of this sheet represents the remaining property.

"Renee, you say you'd like to continue the legacy of your great-aunts. Fine. Move into Willie's old place and prove that you can turn that overgrown jungle of hers into a viable organic farm."

Renee nodded thoughtfully. "I'd planned to start with a section about that size anyway. So that'd work for me."

"I can't very well take the other plot and build on it without knowing *exactly* what your plans are for the remaining land," Cole said.

He'd expected Renee to have the edge, but this was ridiculous. Why present it as a fair challenge when he didn't have a shot in hell of winning this thing?

"No, but you can renovate and restore that property any way you choose," Milo said.

"I'd end up tearing down the place if I wanted to build on the land later," Cole argued, annoyed that Renee was grinning, as if she'd already won.

"Those two houses *must* stand," Milo said, his voice filled with emotion. "My sisters would've wanted that. They loved that land. Devoted their entire lives to it. I can't let anyone tear down their homes. It's all I have left of them." Milo cleared his throat. "But whichever one of you impresses me most, that's who I'll sell the remaining property to."

Cole frowned. The old man had just gotten choked up

about losing his sisters and being the last living member of his family. He could hardly pummel him with a barrage of questions or complain that this wasn't a fair fight.

Renee was swimming across the river in a tiny bathing suit and he was forced to wear a pair of lead shoes.

Bad choice of metaphor. Now he couldn't stop imagining Renee with all those delicious curves wearing a little bikini.

Cole squeezed his eyes shut and dragged his fingers back and forth across his forehead a few times as he considered his response.

"I was hoping to buy the entire block of properties, Milo. Including the plots these two houses occupy." Cole indicated the houses sketched on the sheet.

"I know, but I just can't bear to see those homes destroyed." He shrugged. "Still leaves plenty of land, though."

True.

"I think it's a brilliant idea, Gramps. Mercer and I can move into Aunt Willie's old place. Make it a home again."

"I'm banking on that." Her grandfather winked. "In fact, you would both need to live in your respective houses for six months, then I'll decide."

"What?" they asked simultaneously.

"I already have a place," Cole said.

"Which you've put up for sale." Milo grinned at him like the Cheshire cat. "You've been moving from one long-term flip to another for the past five or six years. Think of Bea's old place along the same lines. Keep the same footprint, add to it, whatever you want. Just...*don't* tear the old place down."

Cole's hands clenched into fists on his lap beneath the table. He wanted the land; he *really* did. He'd been practically stalking Milo for the past couple of years, hoping to acquire it.

He'd completed some breathtaking projects: his p
ents' home, his cousin Benji's multimillion dollar ma
sion, two new multiuse shopping centers that includ
both storefronts and condos. He had the restaurant re
ovation for his family, just across the street. Howev
with this project he hoped to leave his mark on the tov
and create a legacy of his own. The way his family h
with King's Finest.

But maybe it just wasn't worth all this. After all, if h
liked being told what to do and how he had to do it, he'd
working for his family at KFD. But his grandfather's a
father's "my way or the highway" stance had prompted h
to forge his own path. He had great respect for Milo, l
bristled at the idea of being forced to play by the old ma
rules. Particularly when Milo wasn't showing his hand

"Grandad, Cole and I both think the world of you, a
we appreciate your wisdom." Renee glanced at Cole. "E
we aren't teenagers anymore. We're busy current and f
ture business owners. So could we cut to the part whe
you explain the point of this little next-door neighbor e
periment?"

Renee spoke calmly, but Cole could feel the tensi
rolling off her. She was as frustrated as he was.

"If the town of Magnolia Lake is going to continue
grow and thrive, we need plans like Cole's to make it ha
pen. I love the prospect of a shiny new bridge that wo
flood out and a fancy new shopping center. But I'm *
willing to lose our precious way of life to make it happe
Milo huffed. "The sense of community and family we g
in this town… Ain't no amount of growth and new inf
structure in the world worth sacrificing that."

The old man shifted his gaze between them. Both kn
better than to interrupt during his long pause.

"I've seen what rapid growth can do to small tow
like ours, and I don't want that. What we have here

worth fighting for. But we have to be smart about how we wage this battle." Milo tapped his temple with two fingers. "Gotta accept that change is inevitable, even necessary. But we must grab it by the reins and direct it carefully. That way, we keep what's best about this town and who we are while embracing the future."

"I agree with all of that, Gramps," Renee said. "But why does that require Cole and I to jump through these elaborate hoops?"

Milo shook his head, as if disappointed they didn't get it. "You two represent the future of this town. And if I can drill that lesson into the two of you…then maybe other folks will get it, too. We can expand the town while saving it from any negative impacts of that growth."

Cole pushed to his feet and checked his watch. He needed to do a walk-through over at the restaurant to make sure things were on track for the grand opening in the fall, then he needed to do a final inspection of Benji and Sloane's home since they'd be returning from Japan in just a few days. Not to mention the three other projects he was currently managing. He didn't have time for…whatever this was.

"Look, Milo, I appreciate how much you care about this town. I do, too. I would never do anything to hurt it or the people here. But what you're asking… It's a lot. I don't know if I'm prepared to…"

"Giving up already, Cole?" Milo asked with a chuckle. "Thought you were tougher than that. Afraid you'll have to go a few weeks without your fancy spa tub and *bidet*?"

Cole frowned, one eye twitching as Milo and Renee chuckled at his inference that Cole had somehow gone soft. That he was a pretty boy who couldn't rough it for a few weeks in the old house in dire need of renovations.

He was not amused.

"My resiliency isn't the issue here," Cole said. "You

know how much I love and respect you. But like you always taught me…this is business and time is money. There has to be a more efficient way to resolve this issue."

"Nope." The stubborn old coot leaned back in the booth and folded his arms, like Cole's four-year-old nephew, Davis, when instructed to eat his brussels sprouts. "If you feel like my request is somehow beneath you…well, I guess you've proved my point. That maybe you aren't in touch with who we are and what we need in this town. Which makes me worry about that project you got planned."

Cole narrowed his gaze at Milo.

He had to admit, that shit hurt. Like his mentor had just plunged that fork on the table in his gut. Still, he wouldn't allow the old man to manipulate him.

"I'll think about it," Cole said.

"Give you a week to decide." A sly smile lifted one corner of Milo's mouth.

Cole slid on his shades and said his goodbyes to Milo and his granddaughter before grabbing his order to go. The one thing that gave him a perverse sense of satisfaction was the fact that Renee looked like she was fit to be tied.

Damn.

The visual of Renee tied up in his bed would definitely be stuck in his head.

Six

Cole stood in front of the abandoned home that had once belonged to Renee's great-aunt Ms. Bea. He vaguely remembered the older woman as being a little eccentric and always smelling like lavender.

He'd come here with his mother a few times. Beatrice grew the most beautiful flowers, which his mother had always adored. Right next door, her sister, Ms. Willie, grew some of the sweetest, most delicious berries he'd ever tasted.

The remnants of their little stand still stood out by the road on the property Milo had given his granddaughter.

Cole glanced over at Ms. Willie's place, less than a stone's throw from where he stood. The houses were surprisingly close together, given that each property was nearly two acres. He was torn about this idea of living so close to Ren for the next six months.

"You've changed your mind." Renee was standing in the yard of the house next door.

How had he not noticed her?

"Haven't decided." He shrugged. "But I promised you grandad I'd at least take a look at the place."

"So what's the verdict?"

"Too early to say." Cole shifted his gaze to the over grown yard and then to the old farmhouse with its peelin paint and missing porch boards.

He'd expected to look at the place and immediatel deem it worthy of a wrecking ball. But there was som thing about it he found intriguing. Or maybe it was th nostalgia of coming here as a kid.

"I'm surveying the property first. Then I'll take a loo inside."

"I'd like to see the place, too, if you don't mind," sh said.

"Afraid I got the better plot?" He raised a brow.

"She was my great-aunt, and I haven't seen the plac since…" Her words trailed off.

"Of course." Cole cursed himself silently for being insensitive jerk. "Take your time. I'll wait for you befo I go inside."

Ren thanked him but she'd already walked toward h property before he could reply.

He'd told himself that he'd hoped to avoid Ren, but th truth was that a part of him was anxious to see her agai The part of him that missed the hours spent at her gran parents' kitchen table talking comic books and sci-fi shov and debating the superiority of the Marvel versus the D universe. How she'd made learning fun for him by inco porating the things he enjoyed, like badass superhero and sports, into their lessons.

But if starting something with Ren had been a bad id then, it was a horrible idea now. Ren was still his mento granddaughter. Plus, she was a single mom divorced for year. Not the kind of woman he normally hooked up wit

So he'd keep things casual and hope they could eventually reestablish the friendship that had once meant so much to him.

Cole walked around the building, assessing the property and its overgrown acreage. When he returned to the front of the house, Renee was seated on the front steps clutching her hands, one knee bouncing. Her worn jeans were smudged with dirt, as was her oversize navy T-shirt. She stood, her shoulders stiffening and her expression suddenly grim.

"Maybe we should do this some other time." Cole tilted the heavy planter on the front porch and retrieved the spare key Milo had left him. "And if you don't want me to go in without you, I'll put the key back and we can try this another day."

Her expression of distress morphed into one of shock. "You'd put off checking out the house just because…" Renee dropped her gaze from his for a moment. "No, I need to do this. But thank you."

"All right." Cole unlocked the front door and pushed it open.

The house was musty and stale, like every other old house he'd acquired. Particles of dust floated on the air, disturbed by the gentle gust that blew in through the open door.

The place was neat and orderly, but it looked as if it'd been frozen in time.

Renee's soft gasp drew his attention. One hand covered her mouth, and her eyes were misty.

Of course, it was an emotional moment for her. Ren had always spoken so fondly of her eccentric great-aunts. Neither of them had children of their own, so Renee had been their grandchild by proxy. They'd doted on her and had been there to celebrate every single success in her life.

"It seems so surreal," she whispered, venturing deeper

inside the house with small steps. Her lips curved into
small smile as she ran her hand over the old-fashioned r
tary telephone on the hall table. "Still in perfect shape
she marveled, then laughed. "My parents bought them bo
cordless phones for Christmas one year. They're probab
still in the boxes somewhere."

"I never got to tell you how sorry I was about yo
great-aunts," he said softly. "I saw you at the funeral wi
your husband. But—"

"We didn't stay long," she said abruptly, her eyes we
ing with fresh tears. "Dennis didn't do well outside of h
own element. And *this*—" she held up her open palms "
definitely wasn't his element. We were back on his family
private plane not long after the service ended. So if y
think I intentionally slighted you, you're wrong. I didn't

That was exactly what he'd thought. But there was
need to say as much.

"I assume your family wants all the furniture. The
are some valuable antique pieces here. Is Ms. Wilhelm
na's house like this, too, with all of the furniture still
place?"

Renee lowered her gaze and shrugged. "I'm not sure
haven't been able to bring myself to go inside." She seem
embarrassed by the admission. "I've been here three tim
in the past week. I walk the property and look at the o
outhouses. Make my plan for what I'll plant and whe
But the one thing I can't seem to do is—"

"Go inside." Now he understood why she'd been
eager to enter the house with him. "Look, I know you lc
your aunts a long time ago, but in some ways, this mu
all still seem fresh to you."

She dabbed at her eyes with the back of her hand.

"It's like I'm just processing their loss. My grandpa
ents offered to come to the house with me, but they alrea

think I can't handle this. Admitting I couldn't even bring myself to go inside wouldn't inspire much confidence."

"I get it." Cole checked his watch, then glanced around. "I'll tell you what. We'll take a basic inventory of Bea's place. You tell me what your family would like to keep and what we can donate, sell or give away. Then we'll do the same thing over at Ms. Wilhelmina's."

"You realize that'll take hours," Ren said.

"I know." It wasn't how he'd intended to spend the rest of his afternoon. But he wasn't about to leave Ren out here wandering the property alone. "Why? Did you have to get back to your kids?"

"Kid," she corrected him. "I have one son. But I would assume you have some work project or maybe a hot date."

"I did."

"A business project or a hot date?"

"Both." He gave Ren a knowing smile. She was fishing. Trying to find out whether he was involved with someone. "Nothing that can't be rescheduled. Give me a minute to—"

"You don't need to do that, Cole. I'm being a baby about this. Now that I've been inside Aunt Bea's place, I know what to expect. It'll be fine."

"I know I don't have to. I want to. You helped me out of a tough jam. I wouldn't have graduated on time if it weren't for you. This is the least I can do."

"You realize your parents paid me to tutor you in math and science, right?"

"Of course." He chuckled. "But I'd like to think that we're friends, too." He shrugged. "What kind of friend would I be if I wasn't willing to help you out of a jam?"

"Thanks, Cole. That means a lot. But if I accept your offer, there's one thing you need to understand."

"Okay." He folded his arms, his feet planted wide as he

prepared himself for the imminent *there is nothing h pening between us* speech.

"This farm is just as important to me as this lux development is to you. So don't think you can be all and charming and helpful or whatever and I'll fall on fainting couch and concede."

"First, what the hell is a fainting couch?" He furro his brows as he considered the possibilities. "Second, just called me cute *and* charming, so I'm pretty sure winning."

"Oh my God. Seriously? *That's* what you got ou what I just said?" Renee propped a fist on one hip. shook her head and sighed. "And *that's* a fainting cou She pointed to what looked like a burgundy loveseat her gaze softened. "It was Aunt Bea's favorite piec furniture."

"So a chaise, then?"

"More of a daybed in the Victorian era," she said. ' totally beside the point. The point is, we're still on op site sides of this thing, and only one of us can walk a the winner. I fully intend for that to be me. So maybe call a little truce right now to help each other get set into our places. But then it's game on."

"Fine." Cole tried to hold back his smirk. Renee apparently just as competitive now as she had been b then. "But you said that we're helping each other out. V exactly is it that you plan to do for me?"

She turned her back to him as she glanced around house. "Since you were willing to rearrange your scl ule today to help me out... I'll help you sort through stuff and clean up the place so you can move in. Tha if you've decided to move in."

Cole stared at Renee. He almost had the feeling *wanted* him to say yes. Maybe he was making one of a mistake.

"Looks like I am, neighbor." Cole smiled. "I've got a notebook and pen out in the truck. Why don't I grab it? Then we can start tagging everything."

Renee nodded, her sensual lips curving in a grateful smile.

And just like that, Cole knew he was already in way over his head.

Seven

Ren sat on the dated shag carpet covering the floor of her Aunt Willie's old bedroom with her legs folded. She carefully sorted through a box of photos she'd found in the closet.

"Those photos are fascinating. Are they all family members?"

Ren was startled by Cole's voice. He leaned against the door frame holding two paper cups.

How did the man manage to look so incredibly delicious in a pair of distressed jeans, a pair of old Timbs and a white T-shirt that read "I'm not lazy. I just entered energy-saving mode"?

Seriously, it was criminal. Or maybe her own personal sex drought had her hallucinating, like a parched woman wandering the desert.

Yes, Cole was hot. That was an indisputable fact. But he was also trouble. She was thirty-four years old and she'd never dated a single bad boy in her entire life. Her high school crush on Cole had been her first and last foray into the world of bad boys. It had reminded her that she wasn't the kind of girl that guys like Cole Abbott went for. They'd flirt a little to get her to help them with their homework, but there would be no dates to prom or home-coming weekends.

"Yes," Ren said finally, when Cole started to look wor-ried by how long it had taken her to respond. She pushed up her glasses, which she'd worn because she'd forgotten to order a new supply of contacts. "Aunt Willie was ap-parently the Lockwood family historian. I'm going to take these to Gramps and see what he wants to do with them."

Cole ventured inside the room. He handed her one of the paper cups from Magnolia Lake Bakery, where he'd stopped to get them coffee each of the past three morn-ings they'd worked together to clear out Aunt Bea's place and the sheds on her farm. All of which would soon be-long to Cole.

They were done at Aunt Bea's. The furniture had either been donated or stored in a shed on Ren's property; she'd decide whether to sell it or keep it later.

"Thank you." Ren accepted the cup, the scent of hazel-nut rising with the steam as soon as she flipped open the lid. "But we're finished with your place. Didn't expect to see you this morning."

She blew into the cup of hot coffee, and she could swear that Cole's already dark eyes went darker.

He got down on the floor and sat beside her. Close enough that his clean, fresh scent tickled her nostrils, but not close enough that his legs touched hers. "You spent three days helping me clean up my place. You didn't think I'd just abandon you to do all this on your own, did you?"

"You're a busy CEO," she said.

"And you're a busy mom in the midst of starting her own company." He sipped his coffee.

Her heart fluttered a little in response to the acknowledgment. She felt seen in a way she hadn't in so long. Especially since she'd taken a leave at the lab to care for her son full-time soon after he was formally diagnosed as being on the autism spectrum.

Taking time off was a luxury most families didn't have. Dennis and his family hadn't appreciated her taking it. They'd urged her to let the nanny care for Mercer, so she could continue to head up their lab. But after her son had gotten burned and neither the nanny nor Dennis, who'd also been home at the time, knew how it had happened, she hadn't trusted anyone else to take care of her child.

It had even been hard for her to leave Mercer with her grandparents while she worked on getting Aunt Wilhelmina's house ready.

"I was surprised you did the cleaning and sorting yourself." She nodded toward the house just across the way. "Don't you have a crew to do that kind of thing?"

"On my commercial projects, yes. But this project is personal." He glanced over at her and her skin warmed.

"Why?" Ren couldn't help asking. "I know you have to live here for six months. But you're only doing it to acquire the land, which makes it business."

"I didn't think you'd want a crew of burly guys trampling through your aunt's home and manhandling her things." Cole sipped more of his coffee.

There was that damn fluttering in her chest again. Because what an incredibly sweet thing for him to have done. He'd given up three days' worth of his valuable time and had rescheduled several work meetings and at least one date to make her more comfortable during this process. His thoughtfulness meant more to her than words could say.

"Thank you for taking my feelings into consideration, Cole. But you know I would never have expected you to do this."

"I know." There was something so warm and sweet in his dark gaze. Now there was a fluttering in her tummy, too. "But I wanted to. Or maybe I was just looking for an excuse to spend more time with you." He gave her shoulder a teasing nudge.

"Why?" Maybe it was a stupid question. But she needed to know why Cole Casanova Abbott would want to spend his Saturday morning navigating old photos and chasing dust bunnies with her. After all, he'd probably just tumbled out of the bed of some trust fund heiress and social media influencer who modeled in her spare time.

He smirked and for the first time in her life, Ren truly understood the term *devilishly handsome*.

"You're gonna make me say it, huh?" He chuckled softly. "Okay, here goes. I miss those afternoons hanging out with you. That's when I first learned to get comfortable with just being myself. Accepting every part of who I am."

"A rebel with a cause who loved the *Godfather* movies and gangsta rap but also geeked out on all things superhero and sci-fi." Ren smiled as she put the lid on the box of photos and set down her coffee. "I appreciate the credit, but I'm not sure I understand how I helped."

"By accepting me for who I was. By never looking down on me because I learned differently. By gassing me up whenever I was down on myself." Cole set down his cup and turned to her. "My mother taught us to always be kind to people because you never knew the impact even the smallest act of kindness could have on a person. Our short-lived friendship had a huge impact on me. On how I saw myself. On what I believed I could achieve."

She was incredibly moved by his words. "I had no idea."

"By the time I was able to pinpoint exactly why my life got better…you were already long gone. So I never got a chance to thank you for everything you did for me." Cole ran a hand through his mass of dark curls, which he'd always worn a bit longer on top than his brothers.

Ren's mouth was dry. Her heart thudded as her gaze was drawn to Cole's full lips.

Over the past few days, she'd been reminded of how desperately she'd wanted to know what it would be like to kiss Cole. This moment between them felt like the perfect time to find out.

Renee's eyes drifted shut as she pressed her mouth to his in a tentative kiss. She drew back, her eyes fluttering open when Cole didn't react. He stared at her, his chest quietly heaving.

Her face warmed and her stomach churned. Ren pressed another kiss to Cole's lush lips.

He leaned in closer and her glasses shifted, sitting askew on the bridge of her nose. His mouth curved in a half grin. He removed her glasses, then cradled her face in his hands as he kissed her again.

Cole was now clearly the one in control. With his fingers on the back of her neck and his thumbs against her cheekbones, he gently tilted her head. His lips, firm and lush, glided against hers.

It was all lips, no tongue. And yet her skin felt like it was on fire. Her nipples tightened and the space between her thighs grew damp.

Cole was an exceptionally good kisser. Even better than she had imagined all those nights she'd lain in her bed staring at the ceiling as a teenager. Regretting that she hadn't been brave enough to do just this.

Now that she had, she wanted more.

Ren parted her lips on a soft gasp and pressed a hand to Cole's chest. He sucked her lower lip between his, then gently sank his teeth into it, just shy of breaking the skin. He tightened his grip on the back of her neck and ran his tongue along the seam of her lips in a delicious, torturously slow movement that was driving her insane with want.

She parted her lips farther, making it clear she wanted him to deepen their kiss.

Suddenly, the wooden back screen door slammed, followed by her grandmother's distinct voice. "Renee, sweetheart, we're here. Mercer wanted to bring Mommy lunch."

Renee groaned quietly, pulling away.

She was thirty-four years old, and her grandparents still had an uncanny knack for ensuring she wouldn't get beyond first base.

Or maybe they had saved her from making a huge mistake. She was a single mom with responsibilities and a to-do list as long as her arm. She barely had the time and energy to deal with everything currently on her plate. She didn't have room in her life or time in her day for whatever she was doing now.

"Coming, Gran!" She called downstairs, then sighed softly as she turned back to Cole. She lowered her voice. "I'm sorry. I shouldn't have… I'm sorry," she said again.

Cole stood, then pulled Ren to her feet. "We were reminiscing about the past and got caught up in the moment." He shrugged.

"Right." She nodded. Maybe randomly kissing people was a regular thing for him. For her it was an anomaly. "We should probably head downstairs."

"You should probably go first. And take the photos. They'll be too distracted to worry about what we were doing up here." Cole handed her the box and her glasses.

Clearly, he'd done this before.

Ren made her way down the stairs with Cole lagging behind.

"Hi there, sweetheart." Her grandmother grinned broadly as she wiped down the kitchen table with a sponge. "Cole?" Her grandmother dropped the sponge in a bowl of hot, soapy water in the sink, then dried her hand on a dish towel. "Didn't realize you were here. In fact, Milo saw your truck and assumed you were next door. He took Mercer over to check on you."

"Mercer? Is that your little boy?" Cole asked.

"Yes." Ren's mouth curved in an involuntary smile whenever she thought of Mercer's wide eyes and contagious grin. "He's four."

"If you hurry, you can catch up with him," her grandmother said, lifting a picnic basket from the counter and setting it on the table. "Then you're welcome to come back here and join us for an early lunch. I brought plenty. Leftovers from last night. Smothered pork chops, loaded mashed potatoes and butter beans."

"Yes, ma'am." Cole grinned, leaning in to kiss the older woman on the cheek. "You know how much I love your cooking. You don't have to ask me twice."

Her grandmother giggled, then shooed Cole away. Evidently, she wasn't the only woman in the Lockwood family who'd been charmed by Cole Abbott.

"Are you blushing, Gran?" Renee grinned once the screen door slammed behind Cole.

"Don't try to change the subject." Her grandmother narrowed her gaze at her as she pulled items from the basket and laid them out on the table. "It took you two an awful long time to come down those stairs."

"Cole is helping me get the house ready. Since I helped him, he wanted to return the favor."

"But—"

"And look what I found." Renee held up the large wooden photo keepsake box engraved with the words Lockwood Family.

"Oh my gosh." Gran placed a hand over her mouth. "Your grandfather and I bought that for Wilhelmina one Christmas, ages ago. I didn't realize she still had it."

"Well, she did. And look what she kept inside." Renee slid the engraved lid from the box, revealing the treasure trove of photos inside.

"I knew she'd been collecting family photos, but my goodness. Wait until your grandfather sees them."

"I know. I can't wait to show him." Renee beamed. "But in the meantime, I'll help you get lunch ready."

Renee washed her hands at the old farmhouse sink. She gazed at the two acres of farmland behind the house, wondering what her great-aunts would think of her plan to revive the farm.

It was better than reliving her ill-advised kiss with Cole. A mistake she knew she shouldn't repeat.

Eight

Cole stepped onto the back porch of Renee's house and dragged a hand across his lips.

That had been…*unexpected*. Since her return, Renee had been cold and distant. Not surprising, given how their friendship had ended. But over the past week, tension between them had eased and Ren had warmed up to him. Cole was grateful for that. Still, he hadn't expected Renee to kiss him. He sure as hell hadn't intended to kiss her back.

Since their encounter at the general store, Cole had been reminding himself of all the reasons Renee was off limits. Two of them stood a few yards away.

Cole jogged over to his Dodge Ram 1500 TRX Crew Cab 4x4, which sported twenty-inch rims with candy-apple-red accents. Milo was standing beside the truck, holding the little boy's hand. *Renee's* little boy. The kid had his mother's almond-shaped eyes and her heart-stopping smile. He bounced up and down excitedly on his toes as he pointed to Cole's truck.

"Vroom!" the little boy said.

"Hey there, Milo." Cole shook the older man's hand, then turned his attention to the child, whose gaze was still on the truck. "Hey there, little guy. You must be Mercer."

When he didn't respond, Cole turned back to Milo. "I'm not quite as interesting as the truck." Cole grinned. "I guess if I was four, I'd feel the same way."

"Don't take it personally, son." Milo chuckled. "Mercer here don't speak much. Nonverbal, they call it. But he does say a few things, like—"

"Vroom!" Mercer said again. Only this time, he wasn't pointing at the truck. He was pointing at Cole.

Cole smiled. "Hey there, Mercer. It's good to meet you. I'm Cole."

"Vroom!" Mercer said, then pointed to the truck.

"I think he's asking you to fire up that oversize machine of yours," Milo explained.

"Oh, so you're a car man." Cole nodded. "I can respect that. Would you like to climb inside with me?" Cole reached out a hand, but Mercer stepped back, wrapping an arm around his great-grandfather's leg.

The boy peeked at Cole, just one eye visible from behind the old man's leg. Mercer pointed at the truck again and repeated his request.

"You've got it, little man." Cole winked. The truck was a favorite of his nephew, Davis—his brother Blake's four-year-old son. Cole climbed into the truck and turned it on, the engine roaring.

The little boy giggled as he jumped up and down, bouncing on his toes as Milo held on to his hand.

Cole pulled the truck forward and back a few times there in the driveway before killing the engine and climbing out of the cab.

Mercer clapped and cheered.

"Gran sent me out here to collect the three of you for lunch," Renee said. "What's Mercer so excited about?"

"Cole here gave the little guy a show, at Mercer's request." Milo chuckled.

"Your son has a thing for my truck." Cole folded his arms. "Adorable kid. Looks a lot like his mom."

"Thanks." Renee took her son's free hand, and her grandfather released the other one. A smile lit her lovely brown eyes. "Mercer is my everything." She bent down to kiss her son's temple. "We'd better get inside before Gran comes looking for us."

"I'd hoped to get a look at Bea's house," Milo said.

"Why don't we tour the house after lunch?" Cole suggested. "I'm helping Ren with her place today, so I'll be around."

"Mighty generous of you to stick around to help, son." Milo clamped a hand on Cole's shoulder. "This independent granddaughter of mine won't let Janice and me help her. I'm glad she's allowing you to give her a hand."

"You and Gran *are* helping me." Renee slipped an arm through her grandfather's. "There aren't many people in the world I'd trust with my baby. I appreciate knowing he's safe with you while I get everything prepared for us here."

Cole hung back, feeling like an intruder on their family moment.

He owed Milo and Renee more than he could ever articulate. So he wasn't about to do *anything* that might threaten his relationship with either of them. Kissing Renee was a huge mistake.

He was glad Renee was back. Glad they were slowly rebuilding their friendship. But flirting with Ren and leading her on—even though that hadn't been his intention—had blown up their friendship back then. He was supposed to be older and wiser this time around, so he needed to act like it and not screw things up again. Besides, this was business. They were barely a week into this, and already he'd allowed things to get too personal.

Don't forget why you're doing this.

Renee wanted to continue her family's legacy. But his legacy was at stake, too. And no matter what, Ren would have her Aunt Wilhelmina's house and farm. If he was awarded the rest of the Lockwood property, he'd sell her Bea's house and land, too.

She'd have plenty of space for her organic farm.

Cole's phone buzzed with a text message from his foreman on the restaurant project. The man's question could probably be resolved with a quick phone call. But after their kiss and all of the unsettling thoughts turning over in Cole's head, it felt like a good time to create some distance and get his mind right.

"Everything okay, son?" Milo asked.

"Yes, but there's something I need to handle." Cole hated being less than honest with the old man.

"But Janice prepared lunch. You know how much you love her smothered pork chops." The old man chuckled.

Milo wasn't wrong. Cole's mouth watered just thinking of Ms. Janice's delicious smothered pork chops.

"I'll be back in a couple of hours. Save me a plate?"

Milo's frown indicated that he wasn't buying his story. But he didn't challenge him. "All right, son. If you just have to go right now, we won't keep you."

"I realize how busy you are, Cole. So if you can't come back—" Renee was saying.

"I promised to help, and I will. Just as soon as I handle this."

Cole said his goodbyes and got into his truck. He needed a little distance and to put things into perspective. Then he'd return and help Renee, like he'd promised. And he'd keep in mind that they were friends and nothing more.

Nine

Renee loaded more of the books in her aunt's library into boxes, sorting them based on whether she wanted to keep them, donate them or sell them. She picked up an e-reader she'd gifted her great-aunt nearly a decade before. Like the cordless telephone, it was still in the box, unopened. She wiped the dust off, dropped it in the donate box and sneezed.

"Bless you," Cole said, startling her.

She nearly stumbled over the boxes stacked on the floor. "Cole, what are you doing here?"

"I told you I was coming back. You didn't believe me?"

"Let's just say I figured you had something…or *someone*," she murmured under her breath, "to do."

"I did have something to do. And no, it wasn't a date—" He made it clear he'd heard her snide remark. "But I said I'd be back, and I'm a man of my word. So I'm here."

Maybe he was a man of his word now, but he hadn't been back then. Cole had made her believe he was going to ask her out in high school, by dropping lines like, *Maybe we should go to prom together.* He'd carefully avoided making a commitment while keeping her hopeful and anticipating his invitation.

Cole hadn't been the first jock or rich kid she'd tutored. So she'd been foolish to take those musings seriously. It was Manipulative Hot Boy Tactics 101. Dangle the carrot of a relationship in front of the lonely, undatable girl and watch her twist like a pretzel and run herself ragged trying to catch up to it.

Spoiler alert: it *never* happened.

No matter how fast you ran, no matter how thin you got. Even if you got the expensive makeover—a new hairstyle, all new clothing, contacts, expensive skin care and expert makeup tips—as she had at her former mother-in-law's behest. In the end, she was still that same geeky girl inside. It had taken some time, but she was okay with that. She was proud of who she was and what she'd accomplished in her career.

"I appreciate you honoring your word, Cole, but I'll be fine. I'm sure you have better ways to spend your Saturday afternoon." Renee returned to the shelf and grabbed a handful of books.

"Hey, is something wrong?" Cole put his large hand on her shoulder. "Before I left, we were cool. And now—"

"I shouldn't have kissed you, and I'm sorry. Things have been really good between us the past week, and then I ruined it." Ren sighed. "I apologize for that."

"Things still are really good between us," Cole insisted.

"You couldn't get out of here fast enough," Ren noted. "Seriously, you skipped out on my grandmother's pork chops—your favorite meal of hers. The Cole Abbott I remember wouldn't have done that, even if his ass was on fire."

"I had some business to take care of at the restaurant

my family is opening in the fall." Cole rubbed the back of his neck. "But trust and believe that if I didn't want to be here, Renee, I wouldn't be. You should know enough about me to realize that. Now, how can I help?"

Renee studied Cole's dark eyes, framed by neat brows. He seemed sincere, but she'd fallen for Cole Abbott's charm before.

And look how well that worked out for you.

Ren sighed quietly. She'd had a momentary lapse in judgment. She needed to put her mistake out of her head. Start with a clean slate.

"For starters, let's close these windows." Ren rubbed her arms.

"I've got it." Cole closed the windows that offered a view into his house next door. He frowned. "You're shivering. Here…"

Cole tugged off his Abbott Construction & Development sweatshirt and offered it to her. Beneath it, he wore a blue T-shirt with a picture of a huge muffin on it and the words STUD MUFFIN printed underneath.

Can't accuse the man of false advertising. He does look good enough to eat.

"Take it." His no-nonsense tone sent a chill down her spine and warmed a few other places. "Can't have you getting sick. I plan to win this thing fair and square."

"Thank you." She slipped the sweatshirt over her head. *Great.* Now she'd have to spend the next few hours surrounded by Cole's enticing scent with his company's name splashed across her chest while she tried *not* to think about their kiss.

"Are we boxing up all the books?" Cole turned to study the shelves, but Renee couldn't help studying him. Her gaze was glued to Cole's firm bottom.

Now that's an ass worthy of being chiseled in marble for all eternity.

She sighed quietly. That ass had done its fair share of squats. And she, for one, appreciated it.

"Ren?" Cole glanced over his shoulder at her.

"I…uh…no," she stammered. She stood beside him and studied the bookshelves, too. "I'm deciding which ones to keep, which should be donated and which ones might be worth something. The keepers stay on the shelf. Donations go there. This small stack on the desk I'll have evaluated."

After they created a system, the two of them sorted through the books, mostly in silence.

"Look at this, Ren." Cole set what looked like a stack of books on the table. When he turned it around, she saw that the covers had been hollowed out and attached to a wooden frame.

"Is that a secret compartment?"

"Exactly."

"What was in it?" Ren asked.

Cole climbed the ladder again. He grabbed an armful of leather-bound journals and set them on the coffee table. "These. I think they're your aunt's personal diaries."

"You're kidding." Ren sat on the floor in front of the coffee table and picked up one of the soft, worn journals. She ran her fingers over the faded gold lettering on the front cover. Then she opened the book and traced her fingers across the blue ink and smoothed the pages, yellowed with age and curled at the edges.

It was her aunt's distinct handwriting.

Ren flipped through the pages of the book, reading bits and pieces. But one entry grabbed her attention.

Today, I begin what I'm calling the Bad Boy Experiment. A secret relationship with Eduardo Cordeiro. I'm not seeking love or marriage. My sole interest in Eduardo is lust—plain and simple. During my summer stay here in Maine, while I'm house-sitting for Aunt Elizabeth, it feels like the right time. Eduardo is a charming ladies' man, but also sweet and kind. He seems like the right man.

When I proposed the idea, Eduardo thought I was joking. Then he was worried about my reputation or that I'd be hurt when things ended. But I've wanted this for a while. I just hadn't met the right man. Until now.

He said he needed to think about it. But yesterday, he was waiting on me when I walked into the village to get supplies. We've made arrangements for him to come here late tonight, after the rest of the village is sleeping.

Renee slammed the book shut, her cheeks warm and her heart racing.

"What's wrong?" Cole asked.

"Nothing." She set the journal back on top of the pile. "It just feels wrong, you know. Reading my aunt's most private thoughts. I have no idea what to do with these." She glanced up at Cole. "Do I keep them, or should I burn them?"

"I don't know. But there's something else you should see."

Cole sat on the edge of the coffee table and handed her a large reference book. It was clearly hollow. When she shook it, she could hear the contents of the faux book shifting around inside.

"Is this a book safe?" she asked, suddenly aware of how close Cole was. His scent—the same scent that surrounded her in his soft, warm sweatshirt—teased her senses. She was nearly eye level with his…

"That's what I'm thinking," Cole agreed, clasping his hands between his knees.

Ren's cheeks flamed. Cole had probably seen her

checking him out. Not that she'd intended to. But it was *right there*.

Who could blame her?

Ren shifted her attention to the black book in her lap. She examined it closely. There was a three-digit number lock.

"Please, please, please," she whispered, then tried to open the book. She sighed. "It's locked."

"Wouldn't be much of a safe if it wasn't." Cole winked. "Fortunately, I have about six different tools in my truck that could make quick work of that lock."

Ren pressed her lips together as she turned the idea over in her head. There were literally a thousand possible safe combinations. But wouldn't figuring out the combination be far more satisfying than ripping into this lovely faux book and destroying it with a drill or hacksaw? Besides, if she was meant to see the contents, she'd figure out the combination. If not, she wouldn't. And her aunt's lifetime of secrets would remain safe.

Ren hugged the book to her chest, as if it needed protection from Cole and his power tools. "Thanks for the offer, but I'd prefer to try and figure out the combination."

"It's like a mystery your great-aunt left for you to solve." A soft smile lit Cole's dark eyes. "You always did enjoy a good puzzle."

There was a small fluttering in her chest as she met his gaze. A tiny piece of her heart melted knowing Cole remembered that small detail about her.

"True." She placed the safe in the box with the journals. All of it felt like precious found treasure. "You've been great, Cole. I don't know how I would've gotten through all of this without you."

Cole stared at her without speaking, making Ren feel self-conscious.

She was unsettled. Both by the discovery of her aunt's

secret and by the nearness of the man who still managed to turn her knees to jelly and make her heart flutter after all this time.

Maybe I should conduct a bad boy experiment of my own.

It was a ridiculous thought. A recipe for disaster on more levels than she could enumerate.

So why couldn't she stop staring at those full, sensuous, incredibly kissable lips?

Ten

A wave of warmth traveled down Cole's spine as Ren's gaze raked over him, as if she was seeing him for the first time, her eyes filled with heat. It had him feeling things he shouldn't and reliving every moment of their kiss.

"I can transport these books, if you'd like." Cole gestured toward the stacks of boxes.

"Would you, please?" Ren sounded reluctant to ask but he honestly didn't mind. It would take countless trips for her to transport those boxes in her Tesla.

"For you, Ren? Absolutely. I'll start hauling them out to the truck."

Renee thanked him, then scrambled to her feet before he could offer her a hand. She lifted one of the boxes, despite his objections, and quickly dropped it, nearly smashing her foot. "My God, that's—"

"Heavy?" Cole shoved his hands in his pockets. "That's what I was trying to tell you. I've got a dolly out in the truck. No point in us throwing out our backs for no good reason."

"Is there ever a good reason to throw out your back?" she asked, then cringed. "Never mind. I stepped right into that one."

"You kind of did." He chuckled. "Which means you already know the answer."

"Have you ever actually…?" She held up a hand. "No, I definitely don't need to know."

Cole broke into laughter as he headed toward his truck. "Be back in a flash."

He returned with a black hand truck and stacked three boxes onto it. It took several trips, but they managed to get all the boxes loaded into his truck without destroying the farmhouse's rickety back stairs.

"Thanks, Cole. Good night," Renee said once he'd returned the dolly to his truck.

"You done for the night?" he asked.

"Now that all the books are down and sorted, I'm going to clean and dust the shelves and decide which pieces of furniture to keep. I need to feel like I've completed something tonight. It's just the way my mind works." She shrugged. "I know you don't get it, but—"

"I do get it." He folded his arms. It was her coping mechanism. Ren dealt with the factors in her life she couldn't control—like her parents being deployed overseas—by controlling the hell out of the things she could. It was one of the many things about Ren that had been burned into his memory. "Well, let's get to it."

"I've got this." Ren walked toward the house.

He trotted to catch up with her. "Did you honestly think I'd leave you here to finish up on your own?"

"If how frequently your phone keeps buzzing is any indication, someone is looking for you," she said.

She wasn't wrong, There were two missed calls from

a casual hookup and text messages from both his mother and sister—each of them trying to set him up with a date for his brothers' upcoming weddings. But he chose not to acknowledge her observation.

"These properties have been abandoned for five years. I'm not leaving you out here all alone at night." He glanced around at the overgrown farmland surrounding them. "Someone could be hiding in those thickets, watching the house."

"You're more worried about this than my grandfather is, Abbott," she noted.

"Don't bet on it."

Milo had asked him to keep an eye on Ren and Mercer once they were all moved in. But he'd asked Cole not to mention it to Ren, who'd already accused him of being overprotective.

"Which reminds me, you should keep this locked when you're here." Cole closed and locked the door behind them.

"Like you said, this place has been sealed up for five years. It needs a good airing out. And before you know it, the days will be getting hotter. I'll have to open the front and back door to get a good cross breeze. I just need to get better screen doors so Mercer doesn't get out. He's obsessed with doors and locks these days."

"I'll have my guys install security screen doors and central air when you're ready." He folded his arms.

"Why do you care so much, Cole?" Renee folded her arms, too.

"Because I do." His face was suddenly warm. He walked past her toward the library. His phone buzzed with another text message from his mother.

Have you considered one of those dating websites, son? Marilyn Diaz's son met a nice girl on one, and now they're getting married.

Cole groaned. His mother and sister were driving him up a wall about who he was going to bring to these weddings. And the first was still several months away.

"And you just assumed I'd hire your company to do the work?" Ren's words brought him back to his current dilemma: trying to get this stubborn woman to accept his help.

"I'm the only person who'd be willing to do the work at cost *and* pass on my bulk discounts. So yeah, I kind of did," he said.

"You're willing to do the work without making a profit, even though we're competing to impress my grandfather?"

"Yes."

"Why?"

Cole narrowed his gaze. "You're familiar with the phrase *don't look a gift horse in the mouth*, right?"

Renee picked up one of the books from the keep pile and fanned through it.

"I guess I'm just not accustomed to someone going the extra mile without there being some ulterior motive."

That was it.

Cole rubbed his chin. If Ren needed to believe that he had to have some selfish motive, he'd give her one. They could make a trade, just as they'd done by helping each other clean out the houses.

She propped a hand on her hip. "You *do* have an ulterior motive."

Cole laughed in response to the shift in Renee's expression. It reminded him of Arnold from the old sitcom *Diff'rent Strokes*, when he'd ask his older brother *What chu talkin' 'bout, Willis?*

"I prefer to think of it as bartering," he said. "Your aunts were farmers. They must've bartered with neighboring farms and other vendors all the time."

"They did. But something tells me this won't just be an innocent, neighborly barter." She eyed him suspiciously.

Did she actually think he needed to trade sex for discount services? *Damn.* He was more than a little insulted by that.

"I need a date. Three, actually. One for Parker and Kayleigh's wedding, one for Max and Quinn's wedding and one for the opening of my family's restaurant later this fall." He ticked each event off on his fingers.

"And you want me to be…what? Your fake girlfriend or something?" she asked. "I'm a little too busy to be battling clingy exes in the street."

Cole burst into laughter at the image of Ren removing her earrings and greasing her face in preparation for a street fight. Ren laughed, too.

"I'm not asking you to be my fake girlfriend, and there are no clingy exes in my past," he assured her. "So you won't need to fight anyone in the street over me. Though I'm pretty flattered that the only thing holding you back is that you're busy."

"That's *not* what I meant, and you know it." Ren shoved Cole's shoulder playfully.

A wave of warmth settled over him. He'd missed the easy, teasing friendship he and Ren once had. He couldn't help wondering if she missed it, too.

Ren raked her fingers through her messy hair. "So what are you proposing?"

"I'm asking you to be my plus-one for these family events. We'd be going as friends—that's all." He shrugged.

"Don't you have a *friend*—" Ren used air quotes "—for this sort of thing?"

"I did. But since she's marrying my brother in a few months, I'm pretty sure she already has a date to all this stuff—including her own wedding." Cole forced a smile.

"Oh… I see."

Cole didn't miss the pity in Ren's voice. A knot tightened in his gut. He wanted to tell her that he was happy for them. *Really*.

But even in his head, it made him sound pitiful.

Maybe the twinge of envy he felt was less about Max marrying Quinn and more about the fact that he would be the last unmarried Abbott standing. Which was fine, because he wasn't looking for a serious relationship. But still, seeing all his siblings happy and in love, starting families and building futures with their significant others, it had made him think about his own future in ways he hadn't before.

"And you don't want to take any of your other women *friends* because…?"

"I think it's better if I don't… I mean… I…"

"Ahh…" Ren nodded, knowingly. "You don't want to take someone you're involved with to a wedding, lest she get wild ideas about marriage and kids…with you."

Cole prided himself on being open and genuine. But maybe he needed to be a little more mysterious. Then again, his transparency had always been part of his charm. What you saw was what you got. No cat-and-mouse games. No bullshit. Just a little fun and a whole lot of—

"I'll take your silence as confirmation." Renee interrupted his thoughts.

"You haven't answered my question." Cole didn't want to delve any deeper into his commitment issues. They were there. He was aware of them. They'd become old friends.

Renee frowned. "And these dates would be strictly platonic?"

"Absolutely." Cole didn't wait for a response. He climbed the ladder with the furniture spray and a cloth and started dusting.

If he was being honest, his ego was taking a hit. Renee

had kissed him. He would've expected her to readily agree to his proposal.

They worked together another hour to dust the shelves and organize the furniture. Finally, Ren locked up the house. Cole walked her to her Tesla. He opened the driver's door and gestured for her to get inside.

Ren tossed her small purse into the passenger seat, then pushed the sleeves of his sweatshirt up her arms. "I'll wash your shirt and return it."

"Keep it." The thing practically swallowed her. But there was something about seeing Ren in his oversize shirt that warmed his chest. "Got plenty."

"Thank you again, Cole." Ren propped her folded arms on top of the door. "For everything you've done tonight and for your generous offer." Ren glanced back at the old house fondly, then gazed up at him. "I accept the proposal to be your plus-one."

"Great." He responded a little too quickly, his voice a little too high.

Ren giggled. "It'll be nice to see your family again. Your mom was always so sweet."

"That reminds me..." Cole snapped his fingers. "My mother asked me to invite you and Mercer to the birthday party for my nephew, Davis, and Benji and Sloane's twins. The kids would love to meet Mercer."

"Thank you." Ren tucked her hair behind her ear. "But I don't know if we should. Mercer doesn't take well to everyone."

"He took to me." Cole studied Ren's face. There was something else she wasn't saying.

"He did," Ren agreed, seemingly surprised. "But the truth is I don't want him to feel...out of place." Ren shifted her gaze from his and wrapped her arms around herself.

"Because he's nonverbal?" The pained look on Re
face made his chest ache. He wanted to punch her ex
the face for leaving her and Mercer to fend for themselv

"That and his stimming. The constant little soun
he makes and how he runs in circles sometimes. They
self-soothing behaviors some autistic children use
manage their emotions or cope with anxiety," she cla
fied in response to his look of confusion. "And no, I'm
embarrassed by any of it. But it sometimes makes peop
uncomfortable. And *that* makes Mercer uncomfortabl
Ren sighed heavily. "We went through that with my e:
family. I won't put my son through that again."

"It won't be like that, Ren. I promise." Cole put a ha
on her shoulder, his heart breaking for Ren and Merc
How could her ex and her in-laws have acted like that?
know it feels easier to just avoid people rather than givi
them a chance. But you came back here for a new sta
You and Mercer should meet people. Become part of t
community. After all, everyone in town is a potential cu
tomer for the farm. And my family is opening a new farr
to-table restaurant. Quinn—my future sister-in-law—
working with my mom to ensure all of the food is loca
sourced. It wouldn't hurt to start building a relationsh
with both of them."

"And they'll both be there," Ren said more to herse
than him. She sighed. "Okay. We'll come. And now th
my social calendar is full, I'd like to go back to my gran
parents' place, take a hot shower, then snuggle up to n
kid and go to sleep for the night. Thanks, Cole." She lift
onto her toes and kissed his cheek. Then she got into h
Tesla and pulled onto the unlit, rural road.

Cole climbed into his TRX and started it. His han
drifted to the cheek Ren had just kissed.

He heaved a sigh and shifted the truck into Drive.

Cole still had a gooey, soft center when it came to Renee Lockwood. But regardless of how good Renee looked, smelled, tasted…his focus was on his next building project. And he wouldn't let anyone—not even Ren—get in the way of that.

Eleven

Renee collapsed onto the sofa in her aunt's old library, which she'd converted into her office. She propped her feet on the arm of the couch, draped an arm over her face and tried to catch her breath.

Aunt Wilhelmina's old house now officially belonged to her, and she and Mercer had moved in a little more than a week ago. But the sudden change in their daily routine had been a difficult adjustment for her son. He'd been cranky and miserable all day, and Renee had spent the past hour on the verge of tears, trying to decipher exactly what it was her frustrated little boy wanted. Now that he was finally down for his nap, she could use a power nap of her own to recover.

Renee was exhausted, her head was throbbing and she was pretty sure there were bits of banana in her hair. All she'd eaten was a handful of Mercer's Cheerios earlier that morning in an attempt to get him to eat them.

She reveled in the stillness of the room and the absolute

silence throughout the house. For the first time today, she could hear herself think. More importantly, she needed this space of solitude to work on her plans for the farm and make phone calls to potential vendors.

Ren glanced around the room. The place was slowly coming along. Her office, painted sea-foam green, felt brighter but also warm and cozy now. On an accent wall painted a bolder, deeper shade of green, she'd hung an array of family photos, many of which she'd retrieved from her aunt's collection.

She'd gotten rid of a lot of the oversize furniture but kept the antique wooden desk—the piece she most associated with her aunt. The room flowed better now and appealed to her minimalist aesthetic. But it was also safer for Mercer. The more spacious layout would permit him to make a circuit around the coffee table or sofa without hurting himself.

Renee rolled onto her side with her arm folded beneath her head. She set a ten-minute timer and shut her eyes. She was close to drifting asleep when she heard a faint rumbling sound. Was that thunder or a truck rumbling down her street?

She rolled onto her back, her eyes open, and listened carefully. Everything was quiet. Perhaps she'd imagined it. She closed her eyes again. But then she heard what was definitely the rumbling of a vehicle engine, and the low thump of bass from Bob Marley's "Could You Be Loved."

Renee rose from the couch and walked over to the window. A white moving truck was slowly backing into Cole's driveway, making a beeping sound. When the truck came to a halt, three men hopped out, laughing and joking. Moments later, Cole's truck pulled into her driveway.

Renee ducked away from the window, hoping Cole hadn't seen her. There was the slam of his truck door, and then a knock at her kitchen door.

She froze and considered not answering. It'd been
month since she had kissed Cole. Ren cringed reme
bering it. She'd always been low-key and reserved. A
she'd never, *ever* made the first move on a guy. So w
had possessed her to kiss him?

Ren hadn't spoken to Cole since their encounter. H
sent her a text with the info on the events she'd comm
ted to attending. And they'd waved to each other in pa
ing. But that was it.

Why did he have to show up at her door today when s
looked an absolute mess? She was wearing her old, be
up glasses, a cruddy pair of gray sweatpants permanen
stained with finger paints and food and, to top it all o
the sweatshirt Cole had loaned her.

Cole knocked again.

Shit.

If he kept knocking, he'd wake Mercer from his nap.
much as she adored her little boy, she valued her two fi
hours in the middle of the day. Besides, if Merce did
get his nap, he'd be even crankier the rest of the day, a
no one wanted that.

Ren considered taking off Cole's sweatshirt but s
wore only a bra beneath it. She groaned quietly. She wor
choose today, of all days, to look like a raging dumps
fire and to be wearing Cole's sweatshirt while doing it

She huffed, then hurried to the door before Cole cou
knock again.

Renee swept back the loose hair that had escaped h
half-ass ponytail. She opened the door just enough to sho
her face.

While she looked like a hot mess, Cole looked…rid
ulously handsome. How did the man manage to do th
in a simple pocketed T-shirt bearing his company's lo
and a pair of broken-in but expensive jeans? Maybe it w

the dark shades. They lent an air of mystery, since she couldn't see his eyes.

"Hey," she finally said.

"Hey." Cole's mouth curved in a slow smirk and one brow shifted upward.

Was he amused because she looked like a disaster? Or because she was peering out of a small crack in the door with one eye, in an effort to hide the fact that she looked like a disaster?

"Not sure if you just don't want to be bothered right now or if I should ask you to blink twice if you're being held hostage." Cole peered over her head into the kitchen.

"I'm fine." Ren sighed, opening the door wider. She tried to ignore the flames licking the sides of her face as she died a slow death of embarrassment. "I laid Mercer down a few minutes ago, and I'm trying desperately to make sure he stays asleep. As you can see, it's been a rough day." She indicated her stained and wrinkled outfit. "Let's just say this nap is essential to his sanity and mine."

"Sorry, I didn't consider that Little Man might be taking a nap." Cole rubbed the back of his head. "I came to ask if it'd be okay for me to park in your driveway while the guys are moving my stuff in. I'm expecting a few deliveries today, so I wanted to leave room for the drivers to go in and out."

"Yeah…sure. I'm not going anywhere or expecting anyone, so help yourself."

Cole thanked her but didn't move. "Told you that sweatshirt looked good on you."

"Uh…thanks?" Ren self-consciously pushed up the too-long sleeves. "Is there anything else?"

"No, but I definitely don't want to wake your son." Cole rubbed his beard. "So why don't I give the guys a break? I'll treat them to a long lunch. Then we can start moving once Mercer is up from his nap."

"You're going to halt work for two hours to accommodate my son's nap?" Ren asked in disbelief.

"My sister-in-law, Savannah, adores my niece and nephew, and she's an amazing mom. But she looks forward to those daily naps. You're raising Mercer alone. I'd imagine that's especially true for you."

"Yes." Ren wrapped her arms around herself and nodded. "It's been more challenging than I expected to get work done when it's just the two of us here." She hated admitting that her plan already had a fatal flaw. She expected Cole to gloat, but he didn't.

"Then I'll let the fellas know before they get started. Text me when the little guy is up."

It seemed like a small thing, Cole adjusting his day for the sake of her and her son. He was just being a decent neighbor, after all. So why were her eyes stinging with tears of gratitude?

Perhaps because he'd offered the concession without her asking for it. Such thoughtful consideration had come to mean the world to her.

Ren stepped onto the back porch and called quietly to Cole, who'd trotted down the stairs.

"Yes?"

"Thank you. I didn't mean to come off as…" She sighed, running her fingers through her messy hair. "I'm sleep-deprived and a little hangry."

His mouth curved in a soft smile that made Ren's heart melt. He nodded, then jogged over to deliver the news to the movers.

Renee returned to the sofa in her office because she really did need that nap. But as she lay there staring at the ceiling, she couldn't fall asleep. Every time she closed her eyes, all she could see was that damn smile of Cole's.

Twelve

Cole tapped quietly on the window of Ren's office. There was no answer, so he tried again.

Ren came to the window, her beautiful face twisted in a frown as she pushed her glasses up her adorable nose. She obviously didn't appreciate the additional interruption. But even annoyed and completely disheveled, Ren was gorgeous.

He held up a box of pizza and pointed to it.

Ren twisted her mouth before nodding and gesturing for him to go to the back door.

Cole trotted to the back porch, where she was waiting with the door open. She held a finger to her mouth, indicating he should be quiet, and for some reason he couldn't help focusing on her full lips or get the visual of Ren as a stern schoolteacher out of his head.

Get it together, man. Ren is off-limits.

A fresh, lemony scent filled the room. The kitchen floor shone, as if recently mopped.

"Hold this." Cole handed her the pizza, then loosen
the laces on his Timbs and toed them off.

"You brought us pizza?" Ren held up the box.

"And a lunch date." Cole grinned, stepping inside. '
you don't mind some company."

Her deadpan expression indicated she had zero inte
est in entertaining anyone. But she forced a smile anyw

"Sure. Company would be nice. That is if you do
mind eating with someone who looks like they've be
dragged through hell." She glanced down at her sweats-
including the sweatshirt he'd loaned her, which was cu
rently dotted with various stains and little handprints.

Why did that make her even more adorable?

This woman was seriously messing with his hea
Making him feel all warm and fuzzy when warm a
fuzzy definitely wasn't his thing. He preferred to fe
hot and bothered. Then again, Ren managed to ma
him feel that, too.

"You look like a busy mom." Cole shrugged. "But you
look good wearing a paper bag, Ren. So don't sweat
Tell you what. You've had a rough day. Why don't you
me serve you?"

Ren raked her fingers through her hair. "You want
serve me lunch?"

"It's pizza, Ren. Minimal effort required." He smirke
"But yeah. Where can I wash my hands?"

She blinked, her mouth opening, then snapping sh
again. "This way," she said finally as she led him down
narrow hallway.

"Ren...you have... I mean there's—"

"What?" Ren stopped in front of the door of the ha
bathroom and turned to face him.

Cole turned her back around and carefully peeled a ha
eaten pink Starburst off her perfectly round and excee
ingly plump ass. He handed the candy to her.

Ren's eyes widened. "That little boy. I swear. He must've found my candy stash. *That's* why he was so hyper and irritable today. Sugar, especially large amounts, throws him off." She stepped inside the bathroom and tossed the partially eaten candy into the toilet and flushed. "You've just solved the mystery of my awful morning."

She washed and dried her hands, then gestured that the sink was all his before disappearing down the hall.

When he returned to the kitchen, she was sliding slices of pizza onto their plates.

"I'm supposed to be serving you, remember?" Cole raised an eyebrow. "I see you're still not great at following instructions."

"Actually, I'm excellent at following instructions." She shoved her lopsided glasses up the bridge of her nose. "It's direction I don't take very well. As in when two men—you being one of them—tell me I can't and shouldn't do this on my own." She gestured around them.

"Never said you couldn't. And neither of us doubt your ability." He accepted a plate from her and set it on the table. "Milo and I just want to make sure you know exactly what you've signed up for here. Honestly? Your grandfather is a genius," Cole declared. "Plenty of folks move here from the city with aspirations of starting a little organic farm or raising free-range chickens. It's not nearly as glamorous as reality TV makes it seem when you're standing ankle deep in cow manure."

"Dude!" Renee cringed with a mouth full of pizza. "I'm trying to eat here."

"My bad." He chuckled. "My point is that most people don't stick with it, and they often come out of their little fantasy experiment with substantial losses. You gotta admit, making you invest six months into converting this smaller plot to a working farm first is a great way to prove to him and to yourself that you're in this for the long haul.

And if you decide this isn't what you want...there's no shame in that, Ren."

"I have no intention of changing my mind." Renee regarded him suspiciously. She wiped her hands. "I don't make snap decisions. I've been thinking about and planning this for a year. So if this impromptu luncheon was designed to convince me to give up—"

"That isn't why I came." He set his pizza down, wishing he'd kept his mouth shut. "You hadn't eaten, and you've had a tough day. I wanted to feed you and maybe make your day a little better, like you did so many times for me when I had a shitty day in high school. That's all."

Ren's gaze softened. "I didn't think you remembered any of that."

"Did you really think I'd forget you making my favorite cookies in geometric shapes and only letting me have one when I got a problem right?" Cole chuckled, his chest warming at the memory of those afternoons they spent together in winter and spring of senior year. "Despite the fact that there was math involved—which I actually do use on jobs, just like you said I would—those were some of my most cherished high school memories." He placed a hand on his chest.

"If doing math with me at my grandparents' kitchen table was one of your best high school memories, your high school experience was even sadder than mine." She nibbled on her pizza. "So forgive me if I have a hard time believing that."

"It's true. Scout's honor." Cole raised his hand in a three-fingered salute.

"Weren't you tossed out of the Scouts?" Renee raised a brow.

"I quit, actually. Too many rules. But completely irrelevant."

Ren rolled her eyes.

"You still don't believe me." Cole took another bite of his pizza. He'd gotten one half wall-to-wall meat, the other side plain cheese. Just in case Mercer was as picky about what he wanted on his pizza as Blake's and Benji's kids were. "Why?"

Ren frowned, shifting her gaze from his.

"Go ahead." He already knew what she was going to say. But she needed to say the words to him aloud and he deserved to hear them. No matter how blistering they might be.

"What do you want me to say, Cole?" She walked over to the cabinet and grabbed two glasses, filling them with filtered water from a pitcher in the fridge.

"Say whatever is on your mind and be honest."

"You're reminiscing over the past like we were the best of friends. And for a time, I was foolish enough to believe maybe we were. But then you were flirting, and I flirted back." Her eyes filled with fresh pain. "You *implied* we should go to prom together. I turned down other offers because I was so sure you were going to ask me. But you didn't. I felt like such a fool for believing someone like you would want to go to prom with someone like me."

Ren's voice trailed off. She leaned against the wall in the archway between the kitchen and dining room.

Cole came to stand in front of her, shoving his hands in his pockets. His chest ached with guilt and regret.

"I'm sorry if I hurt you, Ren. I genuinely intended to ask you to the prom but—" Cole had wanted to apologize to Ren for so long. Yet he hadn't been prepared to revisit the insecurity and self-doubt he'd felt back then.

"But *what*, Cole?"

Her dark eyes demanded an answer, and he wouldn't deny her the satisfaction of finally knowing the truth.

He could still hear the words of his buddy when he'd told him that he'd planned to ask Ren to the prom.

Your math tutor? Seriously, man? No way that girl [is]
into you. She's a fucking genius. Meanwhile, your fam[ily]
won't even give you a job sweeping at the distillery 'ca[use]
you refuse to go to college. What would you two even t[alk]
about? Look, every girl loves a bad boy, especially a r[ich]
one. That's what she's interested in.

"Cole?" Ren said again.

"I…uh…" He rubbed the scruff on his jaw.

"You were the popular, ever-cool Cole Abbott, and y[ou]
were embarrassed to be seen at the prom with the ner[dy,]
sci-fi-obsessed bookworm whose wardrobe was a dis[as]-
ter." Ren shrugged. "I get it. It was snobbish and rude, [but]
we were just kids. You obviously aren't that guy anymo[re.]
So let's just forget about it."

None of that was true. It was Ren who was too go[od]
for him. He opened his mouth to tell her as much, but [the]
words seemed to get stuck in his throat.

"Maybe you're right," Ren continued. "I was still ho[ld]-
ing a grudge over the entire thing. That was silly after [all]
this time. I accept your apology. Truce?" Ren opened [her]
arms for a hug.

Cole nodded, angry with himself for not leveling w[ith]
her. He wrapped his arms around Renee, resting his c[hin]
atop her head. "I hope we can be friends again. Becaus[e I]
honestly do miss those days at your grandparents' kitc[hen]
table."

"Me, too." Ren stepped out of his embrace and swi[ped]
the back of her finger beneath her eyes. There was a pai[ned]
smile on her sweet face. "Of all the places I've lived, M[ag]-
nolia Lake is the only one that's ever really felt like hom[e.]
And you are the closest friend I had here." She wiped [the]
damp corners of her eyes and gave a nervous laugh. [" It]
would be nice if we could salvage that friendship."

"Regardless of your grandfather's final decision?"

hated to break the hazy bubble of nostalgia and friendship, but he needed to know.

"Regardless of what Grandad decides." Ren extended her hand.

Cole accepted it, holding it a beat longer than he probably should've. Electricity sparked in his palm and seemed to travel up his arm.

Had she felt it, too? Or was it all in his head?

"Ma, ma, ma!" Mercer's voice was accompanied by the sound of his bare feet slapping against the wooden stairs and the thump of a toy he was dragging down one step at a time.

"Hey there, sweetheart. You're up from your nap already." Ren slipped her hand from Cole's, then opened her arms to her son as she stooped to hug him.

Mercer wrapped one of his wiry little arms around her neck. Then he gazed up at Cole, his smile widening. "Vroom!"

Cole pointed a thumb to his chest. "Me?"

"Vroom," Mercer said again, clutching the toy truck he'd dragged down the stairs.

"He loves trucks, and apparently he remembers yours." Ren stood behind her son with her hands on his little shoulders. "Say hello to Mr. Cole, sweetie."

"Mr. Cole? God, that makes me sound old," he groused.

"Vroom!" Mercer's smile was big enough to light up an entire city.

"I much prefer that." Cole chuckled. He squatted so he was eye level with Mercer. "Hey there, little guy. It's good to see you again. I brought pizza."

"Eat!" Mercer dropped his truck and headed for the kitchen.

Cole laughed as he watched the little boy climb into his booster seat at the kitchen table.

Ren followed her son to the kitchen and pulled out colorful plates and cups. She put a slice of cheese pizza on Mercer's plate and cut it into smaller pieces. "You should probably let the movers know they can get started." Ren poured water into a blue kiddie cup.

"Oh, yeah. I should." Cole went toward the door, then stopped and turned back to Renee and Mercer. "Actually, I could just call them and let them know, if you wouldn't mind me hanging out here to finish lunch with you two."

Ren smiled. "That would be nice."

Something about Ren's smile had always done things to him, but never more than right now. If he'd been smart, he would've taken it as a warning to turn and run.

But instead, he sank back onto his chair, made a quick call to the movers and spent the next hour enjoying his time with Renee and Mercer.

Thirteen

"Nervous about your date with Cole?" Renee's mother, Evelyn, glanced up from buttoning Mercer's purple plaid shirt. She'd come to spend the week with them and help with the house.

"It's not a date, Mama." Ren fussed with her hair in the mirror of the front hall.

"You're going to tell me that a children's birthday party typically calls for this much primping?"

"What?" Ren tugged her hair over one shoulder and met her mother's teasing grin. "You're the one who said I should make self-care a priority."

"I was thinking a hot-stone massage and a facial or something." Her mother laughed. "But a little bad boy experiment of your own…that sounds even better."

"A—I told you, there is nothing going on between me and Cole. B—don't make me sorry I told you about Aunt Wilhelmina's diary." Ren pointed a finger at her mother, then smoothed down her skirt, hoping she wasn't over-dressed.

"You can keep telling yourself there's nothing going on. But I've seen the way you two look at each other. And that giddy laugh of yours whenever Cole is around… Seriously, sweetheart, the only person you're fooling here is yourself." Her mother clucked her tongue. "And if there isn't anything going on between you two…maybe there should be."

"Mom, what on earth has gotten into you?" Ren brushed past her mother in search of Mercer's shoes. "I'm not interested in getting involved again. I was married to the rogue son from the wealthy family, remember? It's completely overrated. Besides, what happened to the woman who always lectured me about not letting some knucklehead boy sidetrack me from my goals and aspirations? In case you've forgotten, I'm starting a new business here. Between Mercer and the farm, I'm too busy for a relationship."

"Well, you've certainly made time to rekindle your friendship with Cole. And he's made it his business to help you get the farm started—even though it isn't in his best interest to do so." Her mother retrieved Mercer's shoes from beneath the sofa and held them up. She chased him down and sat on the sofa with Mercer on her lap.

Ren sank onto the sofa beside her mother and put on Mercer's shoes. When she was done, Mercer ran off. She could only hope he kept his shoes on. Her son hated footwear.

"Of course, I haven't forgotten what you're doing here, and I admire you for it, sweetheart." Her mother squeezed her hand. "It's a worthwhile ambition, but it's going to be tough. Tougher than you seem to realize. You're a selfless, dedicated mother. I applaud the sacrifices you're making to give Mercer the best life possible. All I'm saying is that maybe Aunt Willie was on to something with this idea of having a temporary fling."

"Mom!" Renee honestly couldn't believe her mother was saying this. Since her parents' divorce, her dad had remarried and seemed reasonably content. But her mother was living her best, sexually liberated single life.

"Fine. We won't talk about it." Her mother collected some of Mercer's toys and dropped them into the toy chest in Ren's office. "Have you considered my offer to keep Mercer for a few weeks? It'd give you a chance to get some things done around here. You're on the clock, and there's still so much to do."

"It's a generous offer. But I don't know. Merce has never been away from me for that long."

"You don't know if he can handle the separation?"

"I'm not sure *I* can handle it." Ren sighed.

"You'll both be fine." Her mother draped an arm over her shoulder. "We'll only be an hour away in Knoxville. If Mercer doesn't adapt well, I promise to bring him back. But you could use the break. You have lots to do, and I know it isn't easy when Mercer is underfoot."

Her mother wasn't wrong, but she wasn't about to admit it.

"Vroom! Vroom! Vroom!" Mercer ran out of her office and toward the back door; his shoes and socks had been discarded.

"Mercer!" His grandmother went hunting for his socks and shoes. Ren couldn't help laughing.

The distinctive knock at her back door instantly elicited a deep smile.

Cole.

Mercer must've seen him walking along the path toward their house from her office window. The window where he often stood waving to Cole when he returned home each evening.

Ren stood, smoothing down her skirt. She sucked in a deep breath and headed for the back door.

"Definitely a date," her mother called after her in a loud whisper.

Maybe her mother was right, but it seemed best to ignore her mom and the little voice in her head that agreed that this was totally a date.

Cole watched Ren as she chatted with his mother, Savannah and his sister, Zora, who seemed more pregnant every time he saw her again.

Honestly, it was still weird to realize that his baby sister was married—to her lifetime best friend, no less—and that she would be a mother in a few short months. During which, two of his four brothers would be getting married. Thank God for the grandkids, or all of Iris Abbott's effort and energy would be devoted to marrying him off, too.

"So I hear you have a new bestie." Quinn handed him a beer from the cooler and stood beside him.

"Why, you jealous?" He smirked, accepting the beer and twisting off the top.

"Only the tiniest bit." Quinn peered between her thumb and forefinger and laughed. "Because though I lost a close friend, I gained a brother." She nudged him with her elbow. "By the way, when your new bestie isn't watching her adorable little boy, she's got her eyes on you. Is there something you need to tell us?"

"Not you, too." Cole frowned, then sipped his beer. "Ren and I are friends. That's all."

"Does she know that?" Quinn sipped her peach brandy. It was the product line his family's distillery had collaborated on with Bazemore Orchards—owned by Quinn's grandfather, one of Grandpa Joe's closest friends.

"Yes, *Peaches*, she does." Cole emphasized Quinn's

childhood nickname, which she only let her grandfather and fiancé get away with using.

Quinn elbowed him in the side and pointed a finger. "Don't make me jump you."

"All right, all right." He held up his hands in surrender.

"But seriously, Cole," Quinn said once their laughter had died down. "Maybe it isn't more than just friends for you. But the way the two of them look at you... There's definitely something more there for them. I'd hate to see anyone get hurt."

"Why does everyone assume I'm going to hurt Ren?" He'd already gotten versions of this speech from his mother and Zora. It was disappointing to hear it from Quinn, too.

"Actually, it's *you* I'm worried about." Quinn gave him a warm smile. "You're a good guy, Cole. And you're softer in the center than you like to think you are. That little boy adores you." She nodded to where Mercer was bouncing on his toes while Kayleigh's dog, Cricket, danced on her paws, seemingly in sync with him.

"Because I'm a big kid, too." Cole shrugged as if it were no big deal and sipped more of his beer. "I'm the fun uncle, and I take my job seriously."

"Maybe." Quinn sipped her drink. "Or maybe it's because you get each other and you really care about him and his mom, and Mercer is perceptive enough to recognize that."

Cole swallowed hard, her words running through his head. But he couldn't form a response.

Quinn smiled softly. "I'd better go. Looks like Sloane could use help with the cake."

Cole drained the rest of his beer, unable to shake off Quinn's observation. He did feel a kinship with Mercer. He'd struggled with a language-based learning disability, while Mercer's was a developmental one. Still, he did understand that struggle. And maybe the reason he'd fallen so hard for the kid so quickly was because he understood a little of what he must be going through. Seeing how damn hard his mother fought for him made him respect and adore her, too.

But respect, adoration and even friendship did not necessarily equate to a relationship. So yes, they were just friends. He was a friend who also just happened to admire her perfect bottom and the full breasts having a child had evidently gifted Ren.

"See that? That was definitely not a friendly look." Zora poked Cole in the arm, her other hand resting on her ever-growing belly.

"Are y'all tag teaming me?" He tossed his beer bottle in a nearby can.

"Someone has to." Zora shrugged. "But what I wanted to ask is—are you absolutely certain you're bringing Renee to Parker and Kayleigh's wedding?"

"Yes, why?"

"Savannah and I want to invite her to Kayleigh's wedding shower in a couple of weeks. But if we invite her and then you decide to bring someone else...*awkward*."

Okay, so maybe that had happened that one time. His bad. But at least he'd learned his lesson. That was exactly why he didn't bring people he was involved with to family functions anymore.

"You're good," Cole insisted. "Ask her. She'll try to wiggle out of it. Not because she doesn't want to attend, but because she's a little shy and afraid she's intruding somehow. Let her know you really want her to be there, and she won't say no."

"You know her pretty well." Zora's voice had softened, as had her expression. "Whatever this is, bro..." She waved a hand in his direction and smiled. "It looks good on you."

"Don't start again, Zo."

"I know you love playing the role of the family badass—" she indicated his Badass Mama's Boy T-shirt visible beneath his open button-down "—but we both know you're probably the most sensitive out of all of us."

"I am *not* fucking sensitive." Cole pointed a finger, which only made Zora laugh.

"Okay. Bighearted. That better?" Zora slipped her arm through his. "There's nothing wrong with that, Cole. I happen to adore bighearted men. Got one of my own." She smiled at Dallas, who was holding his niece, Remi. "Seems Renee appreciates a bighearted man, too."

When Cole glanced over at Ren, she was staring at him. She tucked her hair behind her ear and leaned down to say something to Mercer, who was chasing bubbles across the yard.

Why was it that every time he met that gaze and soft smile, his heart felt like it was growing in his chest? Like he was tumbling in a dream? Maybe Zora was right. He was sensitive as fuck. Which was why he normally avoided this kind of entanglement. But he was already in too deep.

"You're the only one who seems to think I have a big heart." Cole nodded toward where Max stood with his arm looped around Quinn's waist.

"Max treats you like the family asshole because that's what you want him to think." Zora glanced up at him, sadness in her eyes. "Because that's easier than being vulnerable and telling him or Dad the truth."

"And what is the truth, Zo?" He frowned.

"That how they treated you wasn't fair. That it didn't take into account who you are. Your sensibilities. The learning differences you struggled with." His sister's eyes were filled with compassion. "You have a unique way of seeing the world, and working at King's Finest wasn't the best use for it."

"I don't need validation from Max," Cole said. "Or Dad or Gramps, for that matter."

"Then why are you always trying to prove something that no one but you gives a damn about?" Zora slipped her arm from his and rubbed her back. "From where I'm standing, you care an awful lot about proving them wrong. But you don't have to. Dad and Grandad are immensely proud of you, Cole. We all are."

"Then why does Max bring up me not working for KFD every chance he gets?"

"Maybe Max still doesn't understand why you didn't want to work for the family. But he does admire what you've accomplished." Zora ran her fingers through her shoulder-length two-strand twists and tugged them over one shoulder. "So instead of always trying to piss him off, why don't you try talking to him for a change?"

"So this thing with me and Max is all my fault?"

"There's enough blame to go around, believe me," Zora acknowledged. "But someone needs to make the first step. All I'm saying is…why can't that be you?"

Cole groaned and looked over at Max begrudgingly. "Fine. I'll talk to him."

"When?"

His sister was relentless. "We just had a moment here. Can't we just celebrate that for a minute?"

She pursed her lips and cocked her head. "I'm glad you had your little epiphany. Knowledge is power. But knowledge not acted upon—"

"Amounts to a whole lot of nothin'," Cole interrupted, completing their late grandmother's frequent advice. He sighed. "Dad and Grandad, I've made peace with." Cole shrugged. "But I'll talk to Max. Not today. But I will talk to him. Promise."

"Good." Zora wrapped one arm around his waist and leaned into him. "Because you deserve to be happy, Cole."

"What makes you think I'm not?" He shoved a hand into his pocket.

A soft smile curved his sister's mouth as she glanced over at Renee blowing bubbles from a wand and Mercer bouncing on his toes happily as Cole's niece and nephews chased the bubbles around the yard.

"I'm not saying you weren't happy before." Zo glanced up at him. "But you're so much happier now, and we both know why."

God, he hated it when Zo was right.

Fourteen

Ren pressed a hand to Cole's back to steady him as he toed off his Timbs and carried her sleeping son into her house.

"Well, the party must've gone better than you expected. I thought you two would be home a few hours ago." The lights went on in the living room and her mother descended the stairs in her robe. She seemed startled to see Cole carrying Mercer, and straightened the bonnet covering her hair curlers. "Sorry, I didn't realize we had company."

"Na, Na, Na." Mercer rubbed his eyes and lifted his little head. Her mother's voice had awakened him.

"Here, let me." Her mother took Mercer from Cole, lifting the sleepyhead boy onto her shoulder.

"Would you mind giving him a bath? I'll be up to read him a story shortly," Ren said.

"Leave story time to me." Her mother grinned, glancing between the two of them. "It'll give us a chance to practice for when he stays with me."

They watched as her mother ascended the stairs with Mercer on her shoulder.

"It's great your mother was able to come and help out. How long is she staying?"

"Another few days. But she'd like to keep Mercer in Knoxville for a week once or twice a month so I can get some things done around here."

"You okay letting Little Man go away for an entire week?" Cole asked.

It tugged at her chest that Cole understood her anxiety about being separated from her son. It wasn't that she didn't trust her mother to keep Mercer. She had difficulty trusting *anyone* with watching her fearless little daredevil.

"Not really, but it would help me get back on schedule."

"Then you should do it." Cole gave her a reassuring smile. "Evelyn will take good care of him."

Before she could respond, her mother hurried down the steps, clutching her robe. "I don't want you to panic, but I can't find Mercer."

"He was with you a few minutes ago, and he hasn't come downstairs. He has to be up there." Renee did her best not to freak out. It wasn't as if Mercer was wandering the overgrown fields. "He's probably fallen asleep under his bed or mine."

"I checked under his bed. He's not there. And he can't be in your room. Your door is locked," Evelyn said, panicked.

"I didn't lock my door. I didn't even realize that the lock on that door worked." *Now* she was panicking. Mercer had accidentally locked himself in her room. She bounded up the stairs two at a time, with her mother on her heels.

Ren got on her knees and peeked through the skeleton keyhole of the old door. The room was dark, so she couldn't tell for sure whether Mercer was in there or not. He'd probably crawled into her bed and fallen asleep, so she didn't want to bang on the door and startle him.

"I swear, sweetheart, I turned my back for one minute to run his bathwater and find him some pajamas. When I went to put him in the tub—"

"It's okay." Ren squeezed her mother's arms. "I'm not blaming you. Mercer is an active, curious kid. He's here, and we'll find him. But not if the two of us stand here panicking, all right?"

Ren could see the moment her mom shifted from a concerned grandmother to a retired army officer. She held back her shoulders and tipped her chin.

"We need to pick the lock," her mother said.

"Can you pick this old lock?" Ren asked. "Because I can't."

"Then we need to break the door down."

"This door is solid pine. It'll take a lot more strength than either of us can muster."

"I beg your pardon." Her mother put a hand on her hip. "I might be retired, but I still work out. I'm stronger than I look."

"Yeah, and the last time you went all G.I. Jane, you threw out your back. We can't afford to have that happen again," Ren reminded her.

"Fine. Cole should be able to handle it." Her mother turned around.

It was the first they'd noticed that Cole hadn't followed them up the stairs.

"Cole?" Ren walked toward the stairs. Her son wasn't Cole's responsibility. But as fond as he and Mercer were of each other, she couldn't believe he'd just walk away without trying to help.

"He probably went to his truck to get a tool. I'll check."

Her mother hurried down the stairs.

Suddenly, the light in her bedroom shone from beneath the door, and there was the sound of the door being unlocked.

"Mercer?" Ren's heart was racing.

The doorknob slowly turned, and the door creaked open.

"Cole?" There were half a dozen questions in her head. "Did you find Mercer?"

"He's not in the bed or in the closet. I've already checked." His brows were furrowed with worry. "But we'll find him. Like you said, he has to be up here some—"

"Wait." Ren covered Cole's mouth with her hand. "Listen."

"Is that snoring?" Cole asked.

She nodded. "He's definitely here. You're sure you checked the closet?"

"Positive. There's no way he's in there." Cole stooped, then got on his hands and knees. He lifted the bed skirt and peeked underneath. Cole reached beneath the bed, and when he climbed to his feet, he was holding Mercer in his arms, sound asleep.

"Thank you, Cole." Tears blurred her vision. She stroked her son's cheek with the backs of her fingers. "How'd you get in here?"

"Climbed the trellis, hopped onto the balcony, then entered through the window."

"You climbed that rickety old trellis?" Ren stared at him. "Do you have any idea how dangerous that was?"

"It was the quickest and easiest way to get in here," Cole said. "I did it once when I was in middle school. Your great-aunt was babysitting someone's kid and he locked himself in here."

"You're a lot taller and heavier than you were then. You could've gotten hurt," Ren pressed. Yes, she'd been terrified about Mercer being locked in here. But she'd never have forgiven herself if Cole had been seriously hurt while trying to rescue him.

"You found him!" Her mother appeared in the doorw a hand pressed to her chest. "Where was he?"

"Under the bed, asleep," Ren whispered. "I'm going put him to bed. I'll bathe him in the morning."

"I'm sorry, sweetheart." Her mother's face was wrack with guilt. "You probably think you can't trust me w Mercer, but—"

"It's okay, Mom. Just go back to bed." Ren squeez her mother's hand. "It's been a long night for all of us.

"I don't know how you got in there, but we can't tha you enough." Her mother squeezed Cole's arm. "Go night, you two."

Cole carried Mercer toward his room, where he'd b a makeshift tent over Mercer's bed a few weeks ago. laid him down.

His phone rang, signaling a video call. When he pull the phone from his pocket, Ren could see the face of stunning woman who was trying to reach Cole.

Cole's expression was neutral as he rejected the cal

Ren couldn't help wondering who the woman was a what her relationship with Cole was. But it was none of business. Despite the fact that tonight might've felt da gerously close to being a date—it wasn't. She and C were just friends.

"Thanks for everything, Cole," Ren said. "Mercer a I enjoyed spending the day with your family."

"Does that mean you're kicking me out?" Cole ask "Because I swiped a couple bottles of that peach bran your mother said she likes. After the excitement of tonig I thought we could all use a drink. Maybe watch a movi

"You want to stay and watch a movie?" Ren ran fingers through her hair. "That'd be nice. But if you ha somewhere else to be—"

"Then I'd be there," he said.

Her heart danced and her belly fluttered. "I'll me

you downstairs as soon as I get Mercer out of these sticky clothes and into his pajamas."

Cole nodded, then left the room.

She closed her eyes, trying to slow her racing heart and remind herself that no matter what her body and heart might be feeling, she and Cole were just friends.

Fifteen

Renee tiptoed up her back steps and unlocked the door. She'd stayed at Kayleigh's wedding shower much longer than the obligatory hour or two she'd intended.

When her mother had been struck with a migraine, Cole had generously offered to babysit Mercer. Even though he and her son had become inseparable over the past few weeks, Ren hadn't wanted to impose. But Cole had convinced her that it wasn't an imposition.

Still, Cole's family had made her feel so welcome at the shower. She'd had a great time. And since Cole had insisted he and Mercer were fine when she called to check on them, she'd stayed until the party ended.

Renee went inside, toed off her shoes, then padded toward her office. The television was playing softly. Cole was asleep on the sofa, and Mercer was tucked beneath his arm, asleep too.

The two of them were adorable. She almost hated to disturb them.

The house was still intact, and her son was in one piece. No evidence of bumps, cuts or bruises. Which was more than she could usually say on any given day. Mercer was a little daredevil with no sense of fear.

Renee lifted the arm Cole had draped over Mercer's shoulders. After carrying Mercer, already in his jammies, up to bed, she returned to her office, where Cole was still sleeping.

She muted the television and eased onto the couch beside Cole, not wanting to startle him. He looked so peaceful, but she couldn't leave Cole asleep on her sofa. He'd be much happier in his own bed.

And you'd be much happier with him in yours.

That was a horrible idea for more reasons than she was currently prepared to enumerate. Still, she was grateful to Cole. And not just for tonight. For being there whenever she'd needed him, even though the two of them were vying for the same land. Even though helping her succeed could directly impact his chances of acquiring her grandfather's property.

Ren kissed Cole's cheek. It startled him and he jumped. He patted the space beside him in a panic. "Mercer—"

"Is fine," she assured him with a soft smile. "I put him to bed. He seems well-fed and in one piece. And so do you." She placed a gentle hand on his cheek. "Did my little guy give you any trouble?"

"None." Cole's eyes seemed to linger on her lips. "We had a great time."

"Good." Ren reluctantly dropped her hand from his face. "I brought you a plate."

"Thanks." Cole spiked a hand through his short curls. "Those little chicken nuggets Merce likes are fine. But a brother could use some adult food right about now."

She stood and extended a hand. "Need help, old man?"

"You're older than me," he reminded her.

"So we're both getting old. Do you want a hand or not?"

Cole gave her his hand. But when she tried to tug him up, he wouldn't budge, and she stumbled forward onto his lap.

"No fair." She poked his hard chest and laughed.

"*That* was for calling me old." Cole studied her with his dark, penetrating gaze.

Ren swallowed hard, her cheeks flaming with heat. She made no effort to rise from his lap, though she knew she should. Being this close to Cole, wrapped in his delicious scent with his body heat surrounding her, felt too good. She wasn't ready for this small moment between them to end.

"I had no idea you were so sensitive about your—"

Before she could finish the words, Cole cupped her cheek with his large hand and tugged her forward, his firm lips crashing into hers.

The kiss took her by surprise, but she didn't object. Instead, her eyes drifted closed and she leaned into it, enjoying the firm pressure of his lips against hers.

Cole placed a hand on Renee's back, pressing his fingertips to her soft, bare skin. He shouldn't be kissing Ren. He'd promised himself he wouldn't. Yet it had been all he could think of in the weeks since she'd first kissed him. Now that he held Ren in his arms, his lips gliding over hers, his only thought was that he wanted…*needed*…more.

Everything about this woman was profoundly sexy. The gentle sway of her hips. Her voice, as warm, sweet and soothing as honey. Her single-minded determination. Her brilliant, intricate mind. Even that damn stubborn streak he'd found himself on the wrong side of more than once. The way Ren could walk into a room, draw every man's attention and be completely oblivious to the fact.

He'd seen her sweaty and speckled with mud as she wrangled a four-year-old whose speed rivaled that of Usain

Bolt. Yet all he'd been able to think of was how much he'd like to toss her over his shoulder, hop in the shower with her and lather up every inch of her gleaming brown skin.

Ren braced her hand on his shoulders, then shifted to her knees, straddling him, grinding the warm space between her luscious thighs against his growing length. Cole groaned against her lips in response, and Ren reciprocated with a breathy gasp.

Cole seized the moment, sweeping his tongue between her lips and exploring the sweet taste of her mouth. He palmed the full bottom he'd been admiring for weeks, pulling her tight against him. Intensifying the delicious sensation that made him painfully hard.

Their kiss escalated, Ren's eagerness seeming to match his ravenous desire. He ached to touch her, to taste her, to be buried deep inside her. To act on all the fantasies that had run through his mind as he'd lain in bed at night, his body aching and his brain replaying every damn word she'd uttered. Cataloging the moments that had stoked the fire in his gut and made his chest feel like it was about to explode.

Ren circled her hips, gliding up and down the ridge beneath his zipper. He swallowed her soft whimpers and matched them with his own groans, his body aching with need. He wanted to strip Ren out of that sexy little dress. Glide his hands over her soft skin. Plot the path his lips would soon take.

Cole slid the zipper down her back slowly, half-expecting Ren to object. She didn't. And when he unfastened the clasps on her bra, Ren slipped the garment off as if it was an unwelcome restraint. She slid the thin straps from her shoulder, allowing the top of her dress to fall.

Cole splayed one palm on her back possessively, reveling in the sensation of her bare skin beneath his and her bare breasts smushed against his hard chest through his shirt. Ren gripped the bottom of his black Darth Vader T-shirt and tore her mouth from his just long enough to help him pull the garment over his head. She tossed it onto the floor. But when she leaned in to kiss him again, he pressed a gentle hand to her shoulder, halting her.

He sank his teeth into his lower lip as he surveyed her bare torso in the glow cast from the television. Her full breasts were perfect, the tight brown nipples standing erect, begging for his attention. He palmed one of the heavy globes, then dipped his head, capturing its beaded tip with his mouth. Cole swirled his tongue over it.

Ren shuddered, sighing softly as he licked and sucked one nipple and grazed the other with his calloused thumb. She braced her hands on his shoulders, tilted her head back and swiveled her hips.

"Fuck," he whispered against her skin. He sucked in a deep breath, trying to regain his sense of control, which Ren seemed determined to wrestle away.

Renee whimpered softly and arched her back. The sound unleashed something in him. Broke through any remaining restraint he might've had. He wanted to touch Ren. Taste her. Be buried deep inside her. As he had countless times in his imagination.

He shifted Ren onto the sofa so she was on her back, then claimed her mouth with a greedy kiss that betrayed his growing hunger for her. Ren and Mercer had become an integral part of his life these past few weeks. But the line between their friendship and whatever this was had become increasingly hazy. And now he was ready to obliterate it. To stop fighting this and let it become whatever it was.

Cole glided a hand up the soft skin of Ren's inner thigh as he continued their kiss. He cupped her sex through her lacy panties. Ren moaned softly, her legs falling open to give his hand more space. Cole slipped the damp fabric aside, gliding his fingers over her wet heat. Ren gasped, her breath coming in short, quick bursts. Her chest heaved and her whimpers grew louder as he moved his hand over her slick, hot flesh. Slowly at first. Then more quickly, matching the increasing intensity of their kiss.

"Oh!" Ren clutched his bare shoulders, her short fingernails digging into his skin when he slipped two fingers inside of her.

Yep. He'd definitely found her spot.

God, Ren was beautiful. So incredibly sensual, but in the least obvious of ways. She was his personal kryptonite now, just as she had been back then. Like she had a string wrapped around her finger that was tethered to his heart and all the messy emotions he tried so hard to avoid.

When she whimpered his name, her voice breathy and tense, it was one of the sweetest sounds he'd ever heard.

Cole kissed Ren harder as he teased her sensitive spot with his fingertips and massaged the taut bundle of nerves with his thumb.

Ren cursed and called his name, her body stiffening and her sex pulsing as he took her over the edge.

Cole nestled into the warm space between her thighs, luxuriating in Ren's warmth and the scent of her arousal. He pressed a kiss to her lips.

A slow smile lit Ren's eyes. She gripped the back of his neck, pulling him forward into another kiss, their lips crashing and their tongues tangling in a sensual dance that made him hard as steel.

Ren pushed against his shoulders, suddenly halting their kiss.

"What's wrong?" Cole's chest heaved as he studied her face. "If this is too much—"

Renee pressed a finger to his lips and cocked her head as if listening for something.

"Ma… Ma… Ma…"

Ren sighed softly. "Cole, I'm sorry. I—"

"No need to apologize." He climbed to his feet, then pulled her up. "Go, or I can go while you…" He indicated her disheveled clothing as she tried to gather herself.

"I've got it. But could you…" Ren held up the front of her dress and turned her back to him, lifting her hair.

Cole had become an expert at removing a woman's bra with one hand. Fastening it was a totally different skill set, but he managed. "There. Good as new."

"Thanks." Ren turned around. "Did you remember to give Mercer his melatonin?"

Cole cringed as he tugged his T-shirt over his head. "I didn't. I'm sorry. We were watching TV on the couch, and I totally forgot to—"

"It's okay." Ren easily slipped back into mommy mode. "I'll give it to him now and read him a story. Hopefully that'll do it. I'll put your plate in the microwave before I go up."

"Don't worry about it. I'll just take it back to my place."

"Oh…" Renee tucked loose strands of hair behind one ear. "Well…good night, then."

"Good night, and say good-night to Little Man for me."

"I will." Ren gave him a pained smile on her way toward the kitchen.

Cole ducked into the little bathroom tucked beneath the staircase. The steps creaked above him as Renee went up to Mercer's room. He stared at himself in the mirror as he washed his hands.

What the fuck did you just do?

Cole heaved a sigh, his heart racing. Ren was a divorcee

mom who was trying to build this business on her own. She was stressed-out, overwhelmed and maybe a little lonely.

Had he taken advantage of that?

Cole scrubbed a hand down his face. He'd fucked up. *Again*.

Why couldn't he ever seem to get it right where Renee was concerned?

Sixteen

Any disappointment Ren felt was allayed the moment she saw her little boy's face. When she opened his bedroom door, he sat up and grinned.

"Ma… Ma… Ma…"

"Mama missed you, too, sweetheart." She sat on the edge of Mercer's bed and hugged him tight.

Ren extended her hand and Mercer gladly swiped the fruit-flavored gummy supplement. Then he hopped down from his bed, grabbed a book of nursery rhymes and handed it to her before climbing back into bed.

Renee slipped an arm around Mercer and read him a bedtime story. Then another and another. By the end of the third story, Mercer was sound asleep again. She clicked off the light and slipped out of his room.

She went to her room and got ready for bed, putting on an old T-shirt and sleep shorts. She wrapped her hair, tied it up with her satin scarf, then put on her glasses. Ren crawled into her bed—the same bed she might've been sharing with Cole right now if Mercer hadn't awakened.

Ren sighed. Everything that had just happened between her and Cole replayed in her head. The feel of his strong hands on her skin. The taste of his mouth. The weight of his body on hers. The shudder that rippled through her when Cole had taken her over the edge.

She really needed to pull it together. She also needed to lock up after Cole.

Ren went downstairs to turn off the lights in the kitchen and nearly screamed. Cole was sitting at the table with the empty food container in front of him and a half-eaten slice of cake.

"I thought you left." Ren pressed a hand to her chest.

"I thought we should talk." Cole moved the container aside.

The hint of joy she'd felt at seeing Cole quickly faded. Cole didn't need to say the words. They were written all over his face.

This was a mistake. It can never happen again.

And maybe he was right. Trying to figure out how to navigate whatever was happening between them was a lot to ask on top of everything else going on in her life.

So she would save him the trouble.

"No need. We got caught up in the moment." Ren shrugged. "We're both adults. Stuff happens. It's forgotten."

Cole stared at her, blinking.

Is he surprised or relieved?

It didn't matter. Now that she'd said the words, he wouldn't have to. That somehow seemed better.

"Ren," Cole said, "I don't want to hurt you again." The pained look on his face seemed genuine. But still, it was another rejection.

"I'm not the lonely teenage girl desperately hoping

you'll ask her to prom anymore, Cole. And I'm not lookin'
for a relationship any more than you are." Ren stood taller

Why did he look...*gutted*? Wasn't this the part where h
breathed a sigh of relief and then got the hell out of Dodg
before she could change her mind?

"I just wanted to say I'm sorry, Ren. I crossed a line
shouldn't have. I should know better than—"

"If there had been a line I hadn't wanted you to cross,
would've made that crystal clear without hesitation. Wha
happened...it was just two consenting adults having a li
tle fun." Ren sighed. "I know my grandfather probabl
asked you to watch out for us, and I appreciate everythin
you've done, but you are *not* responsible for me, Cole. An
you don't get to dictate my choices. So stop behaving as
you're Darth Vader and you pulled me onto the dark sid
or something. All right?" She indicated his T-shirt.

"All right." Cole stood, picking up the empty containe
and discarded napkins.

"Leave it. I'll take care of this." Ren forced a smile, n
wanting Cole to think she was angry. "I appreciate every
thing you've done tonight. Now, go home and get som
sleep. You've earned it." She walked to the back door an
opened it. "Good night, Cole."

"And we're still good?"

"Good night, Ren." Cole dropped a friendly kiss on h
cheek. Then he stepped out onto the porch, stuffed his fe
into his boots and took the path back to his own house.

Later, when Ren lay on her side in bed, her knees pulle
into a fetal position, she could see the light on in Cole
bedroom through the slit in her curtains.

Was he still thinking of their kiss, too?

She doubted that Cole Abbott would lay in bed and r
live their trip to third base when women who looked li
supermodels kept calling his phone. Women who probab
didn't have an adorable kid with a horrible sense of timin

It was just as well. She didn't need the distraction. Mercer was her focus, and she was creating a legacy for him and for their family. Cole was the one person standing between her and her dream of resuscitating her family's farm. She needed to remember that—no matter how amazing the man's kiss was.

Ren reached under her bed and rummaged through the small container where she'd stored her great-aunt's journals and the book safe she still hadn't managed to crack. She hadn't dared to read any more since the night Cole had discovered them. She'd felt badly about invading her aunt's privacy. But there was a part of her that needed to know if her aunt's little experiment had turned out as she'd hoped it would.

She clicked on the little bedside lamp, propped her pillows against the headboard and started to read.

Cole counted aloud as he did Spider-Man push-ups, alternately drawing each knee to his elbow as he lowered himself to the floor.

He needed to focus on the effort required and the tension in his shaking muscles. On anything other than the way it had felt to hold Renee's soft, lush body against his or the sweet taste of her warm mouth.

Cole squeezed his eyes shut against the memories of that kiss that flooded his brain, even as his triceps burned and his abdominal muscles and obliques begged for mercy. He cursed, shaking his head. He'd lost count again.

No matter how many push-ups he did, he couldn't stop thinking of what had happened between them or how it had made him feel.

It had been more than *just* a kiss. And Ren had become more than just a friend.

Cole lowered himself to the floor and rolled onto his

back, his chest heaving. He couldn't help glancing toward the window that faced her bedroom. The lights were out.

He draped an arm over his face and took slow, deep breaths as his heart rate slowed. On a typical Saturday night, he'd be out either in Gatlinburg or an hour away in Knoxville. But there had been nothing typical about his life in the weeks since he'd moved into Ms. Bea's old house and become Ren and Mercer's next-door neighbor.

The two of them had slowly become a central part of his life. He couldn't make a trip past the general store or local farm supply without phoning Ren to see if she needed something. He thought of them often. Worried about them constantly. As he glanced over at the darkened house, he was deciding which floodlights to install to ensure the two of them stayed safe.

When the hell had he become that guy? The old guy who worried over everyone, imagining the worst possible scenarios and what he needed to do to protect them.

Cole got up and gathered the T-shirt and jeans he'd stripped off earlier. There was a blueberry-stained handprint on his jeans.

Mercer.

Cole had no idea how it had happened, but the kid had him wrapped around his little finger. So did his mother, for that matter. Because he'd do just about anything for either of them. Anything except walk away from his plans for the old Lockwood family farm that lay beyond their two houses. That was the only part of his plan he'd managed to stick to.

Cole liked to think of himself as a compassionate person. One who gave a hand up to struggling entrepreneurs—as Milo had once done for him. But he hadn't gotten where he was in business by being a pushover who bent over backward for the competition. And yet, with Ren, that was exactly what he was doing.

He'd lost his edge; lost his focus. He needed to finalize his plans to remodel this old house. Show Milo exactly why his proposal was the better one. And stop being so damn eager to help Ren execute her plan.

Cole turned on the shower, stripped naked and dropped his clothing into the hamper.

His phone signaled an incoming video call. And though it was late, it wasn't an unusual occurrence. He checked the name on the screen. *Lisa.* The phys ed teacher in Knoxville he'd had an off-and-on friends-with-benefits relationship with the past couple of years. A call at this time of night meant one of two things: phone sex or an invitation to spend the weekend in Knoxville for the real thing.

Cole picked up the phone, pushed the message icon and chose Currently Not Available. It was their signal indicating that they were involved with someone else.

He set the phone down and stepped into the shower.

His relationship with Ren was definitely fucking with his head and throwing him off his game, so she was already winning. Because he couldn't stop thinking of her, wishing they'd been able to finish what they'd started.

Seventeen

Renee nearly jumped out of her skin in response to Col[e]'s distinctive knock. She hurried to the mirror by the fr[ont] door and checked her hair and makeup, then fiddled w[ith] the cowl neckline and thin shoulder straps of her peac[h] gold satin dress.

The dress, strappy gold heels and expensive jewelry [felt] like a costume. She was playing the role of someone s[exx]ier and more sophisticated than she could ever hope to [be.]

Cole knocked again, and Ren glanced toward the ba[ck] door.

She and Cole hadn't been in the same room since t[he] night they'd scandalized her poor sofa. Cole had wav[ed] from across the way. He'd even dropped off thought[ful] gifts for her and Mercer, sending a text to notify her h[e'd] left them on the back porch. But he'd clearly been avo[id]ing her. It was just as well. She hadn't known quite wh[at] to say to him, either.

Thanks for the finger bang, pal. But you're right. [I]

probably shouldn't do that again. Still, I'd really, really
like to.

But she'd committed to being Cole's plus-one at Parker
and Kayleigh's wedding, so they were in for an awkward
evening. Ren sucked in a deep breath, then opened the
newly installed screen door with a broad smile. "Come
on in. I just need to grab my purse."

"Wow." Cole's dark eyes were filled with heat as he
scanned her from head to toe. He dragged a hand down
his neatly trimmed beard. "You look...incredible."

"Thank you. You don't look bad yourself." Ren straightened the collar of his crisp white shirt, worn without a tie.
An indigo-blue dinner jacket, belted white pants and expensive leather boots completed his look. "There. Perfect."

Cole's nostrils flared slightly as he flashed her a devilish half smile that warmed her all over. They hadn't left
the house yet, and the man already had her all hot and
bothered.

Ren retrieved her sparkly clutch from her office and
returned to the kitchen with a flourish. "Plus-one, report-
ing for duty."

Cole shoved his hands in his pockets and frowned.
"Ren, about the other night—"

"Unless you have something new to offer on the subject, I didn't get all fancied up tonight to be rejected again."
Ren forced a smile. "Now, are we going to this wedding
or what?"

"I didn't reject you, Renee, I..." Cole dragged a hand
through his hair and sighed. "After you." He gestured toward the door, then he escorted her to his Jaguar F-Type,
parked in her driveway.

"Nice." Ren gestured toward the sexy all-black luxury
sports car. "New ride?"

"No, I keep it parked in a garage on the company lot
until I can build a garage here. But I couldn't have you

climbing in and out of the truck in that dress." Cole's gaze lingered on her thigh, exposed by the side split as she lowered into the passenger seat.

"Thoughtful." Ren smiled sweetly. "Now, if you could stop staring at my thigh for a moment…we have a wedding to get to. Wouldn't look good for the brother of the groom to be late."

"I was just…" Cole cleared his throat, quickly abandoning whatever excuse he was about to offer. "Right. We'd better go."

Cole got inside and pushed the black start button. The engine roared to life. After a few minutes of riding in silence, he asked, "Did Little Man get settled at your mom's all right?"

"He did." It was the first time she'd let Mercer spend the entire weekend with her mother in Knoxville. She'd video called them three times already in the twenty-four hours since she'd left him in her mother's care. "He's handling it like a champ. Me? Not so much."

Cole chuckled. "I miss the little guy."

"He misses you, too," Ren said. "But for the record, you're the one who's been avoiding me."

"I know," he admitted after a long pause. "I lost control with you that night, and I shouldn't have."

"Why not?" Ren was horrified that she'd asked. But now that it was out there, she needed an answer to the question that'd been dancing in her head for the past two weeks. "If you're not really attracted to me…fine. I get that."

"Of course, I'm attracted to you, Ren. Are you kidding me? Just look at you." He gestured toward her. "A lack of attraction isn't the issue, and it never has been."

"Then what is the issue?" She turned toward him. "Is it because of your relationship with my grandfather?"

"Not exactly."

Ren folded her arms like a pouty toddler. "Why don't you just say what you mean, Cole?"

He tightened his grip on the gear shifter. "I promised myself if I ever got a shot at fixing our friendship, I wouldn't fuck it up this time. That I'd keep things strictly platonic. I value our relationship, Ren. I don't want to hurt you again."

"Oh." Ren's chest tightened and her belly fluttered. She studied the profile of the handsome man who'd become her closest friend, despite being on opposite sides of the decision about the fate of her family's land. Despite the awkwardness of the past two weeks.

"Our friendship is important to me, too. But I'd be lying if I said I didn't think about this being *more*. Not a relationship," she clarified, in response to his panicked expression. "Neither of us is looking for that."

"You mean just sex?" Cole glanced at her quickly, then returned his attention to the road.

"I…um…" In her head, it had sounded scientific, almost clinical. She'd propose her own bad boy experiment. A basic, mutualistic relationship. Like the oxpecker and zebra or a bee and a flower. Each had something to offer that the other wanted or needed. She'd been prepared to eloquently lay out the terms. But in real time she'd been reduced to babbling like an idiot. "Yes?" *Shit.* That sounded like a question. "I mean, *yes*. Why not? Isn't that your usual MO?"

"I've had my share of no-strings relationships," Cole admitted as he entered the lot of the wedding venue and bypassed the valet stand. He parked the Jag in a space reserved for the family. Cole unbuckled his seat belt and turned toward her. "This is going to make me sound like an arrogant dick, but you insisted on honesty."

A knot tightened in her stomach. "Let's hear it."

"No-strings sex isn't hard to come by. It's the boonies.

There's not a hell of a lot to do around here." Cole leaned in, as if he was about to tell her the secret of the universe. "What we have is hard to come by. At least, it has been for me. So even if I do want this…" He lifted her chin. "And make no mistake, Ren. I really, *really* want you." Cole sighed and dropped his hand from her face. "But I won't ruin a potentially lifelong friendship for a short-term fling."

"Okay." Ren reached for the door, but Cole held her arm.

He hopped out of the Jaguar and opened the door for her, escorting her toward the front entrance of the elegantly remodeled barn—another renovation project he was tremendously proud of.

"I hope you understand." Cole turned to her, just before they entered the barn door.

"I do, and I appreciate your honesty." Ren smiled sweetly. "We should remain strictly friends, and I'll find someone else to have a no-strings fling with. Shouldn't be hard. Like you said, there's not much else to do around here."

"Wait… I…you…"

Ren stood tall and posed for the photographer taking photos of arriving guests. But she was pretty sure the photo had captured Cole with his eyes wide and his bearded jaw on the floor.

"You're not serious." Cole caught up with Ren, who'd walked…no, *strutted*…her fine ass away after the photo was taken. He pulled her off to the side and whispered loud enough to be heard over the din of the small crowd and the harpist playing what he was pretty sure was a Marvin Gaye song. "You're just saying that to fuck with me, *right*?"

"Cole, you're a phenomenal friend. I adore you, and I respect your decision." Ren glanced around and lowered her voice. "But did you think because you said no I was going to lock myself in some metaphorical tower while you sleep with half the single women in the county?"

Maybe. "Of course not," he said.

She waved and flashed a smile at Jeb Dawson's son, Leonard, whom Cole had asked to fix one of Ren's tractors. The man was staring at Ren like she was barbecue chicken and he hadn't eaten in a week.

Cole's jaw clenched and his blood boiled at the thought of Len laying one of his grimy fingers on Ren.

His heart beat furiously. His neck and chest were hot. Ren was right; he was being unfair and maybe a bit sexist. But knowing that didn't make it any easier to swallow the thought of Ren being with someone else.

Cole held his hands up in surrender. "I'm sorry. It was a knee-jerk reaction. But hooking up with some random just doesn't feel like you."

"I'm here because I wanted a new start." Ren's tone softened. "Part of that new start for me is spreading my wings and trying new experiences."

"And taking risks?" Cole frowned.

"Calculated ones, like starting the farm. Yes." Ren folded her arms.

Lawd...have...mercy.

The movement accentuated the cleavage exposed by the flirty neckline of Ren's dress. It was a common gesture. One Ren made frequently. And maybe she'd done it inadvertently. But right now, it felt like she was definitely fucking with his head.

Pull it together, man.

"And you consider this bad boy experiment thing a calculated risk?"

So much for keeping cool about it.

"Yes. Now, I think we should take our seats." Ren glanced over at where Zora was gesturing for them to come and sit with her and Dallas.

Cole extended his arm and Ren took it.

They greeted Dallas and Zora—who rubbed her growing belly. Cole tweaked the chubby cheek of his niece Remi, whom Zora balanced on her lap. Seated in front of them were Max and Quinn, Sloane and the twins—Beau and Bailey—and Grandpa Joe, whose shoulder Cole squeezed. After a few minutes of chatting with his family, the harpist started to play "Lovin' You" by Minnie Ripperton. Cole glanced up to see Parker escorting their mother down the aisle in a floor-length mauve dress. There was an effervescent grin on her face. Iris Abbott was on cloud nine, watching another one of her children walk down the aisle.

Parker kissed their mother's cheek and joined their brother Blake and cousin Benji, who were already standing up front.

Parker's placid expression revealed only a hint of his underlying terror. There was a good chance his brother would either lose his lunch or bolt like a rabbit.

Next, his sister-in-law Savannah floated down the aisle in a beige one-shoulder gown, followed by Kayleigh's sister, Evelisse.

Evvy's eyes filled with unshed tears as she carried both her bouquet and a framed photograph of her and Kayleigh's parents, who'd passed years earlier.

Next came his nephew, Davis, in his little beige suit—to match that of the groom and his groomsmen—and a tiny bow tie. In one hand, he held a small satin pillow with both rings. In the other, he held a leash wrapped with vines and flowers. On the other end of the leash was Kayleigh's golden retriever, Cricket: the flower dog. She tugged Davis down the aisle, garnering chuckles from the crowd.

The harpist shifted to another song Cole recognized: "A Thousand Years," by Christina Perri. Everyone turned toward the back, where Kayleigh stood looking ethereal in a bohemian, all-lace wedding gown. Her wild red curls were crowned with a jeweled vine halo sparkling with pale pink crystals and pearls.

Kayleigh clutched Duke's arm. He patted her hand reassuringly and whispered something to her. The bride nodded and seemed to relax. Kayleigh broadened her smile, her eyes focused on her husband-to-be standing at the head of the aisle.

His typically stoic brother's eyes were filled with emotion as he eagerly awaited his bride.

Duke kissed Kayleigh's cheek, then handed her off to Parker before taking his seat beside their mother.

Parker looked nervous as he extended his arm to Kayleigh, whispering loudly that she looked beautiful.

The expression on his brother's face could only be described as...*love*.

For the first time in his memory, Cole truly envied Parker.

The ceremony was simple but beautiful. When the couple was declared husband and wife, the barn erupted with applause.

Afterward, when the crowd began mingling, Cole's mother, who was still beaming, slipped her arm through his and whispered, "And then there was one."

She glanced over at Renee, who held Remi as she chatted with Quinn. His mother's smile widened. "But maybe not for long."

A few hours later, Cole stood at the old wooden bar with his brothers and cousin Benji. They'd had dinner, the toasts and the couple's first dance. Now he sipped his beer, oblivious to their conversation as he scanned the crowd.

"Looking for Renee again?" Blake sipped his bourbon, barely able to contain an amused grin.

"You know he is," Max said, chuckling. "For you two

not to be involved, you're doing a convincing imitation of a jealous lover, Cole."

Cole turned up the bottle and drained it. Prompted by his friendship with Quinn and his promise to Zora, he and Max had hashed things out and *finally* called a truce. So calling Max a meddling dickhead, while accurate, wouldn't be conducive to their new brotherly vibe.

"Leave Cole alone. Maybe he's just not ready to admit that he wants to be more than friends with Renee." Parker looked happy but mentally exhausted.

The day had required a lot of face time for Parker, who was admittedly far better at non-peopley things: like spreadsheets and data.

"Another beer for me and another old-fashioned for my wise older brother," Cole called to the bartender before turning to his brothers again. He lowered his voice. "So maybe I am into her. But I want the best for Ren and Mercer. And we all know I'm not it."

"That's bullshit," Max said. "You're making excuses because you're scared of commitment."

Cole clenched his jaw, hating that his brothers could see right through him.

"Commitment can be intimidating," Blake said quickly. "But I think we'd all agree that what we've gained is well worth any sacrifices we had to make."

Parker, Max and Benji all nodded in agreement.

"I'm glad you guys are so happy. I'm happy for you," Cole said. "But marriage isn't for everyone."

"True, and we all probably felt that way at some point. But when the right woman comes along…everything feels *different*." Parker nodded toward the dance floor, where Kayleigh was dancing with Grandpa Joe to Nat King Cole's "L-O-V-E"—a favorite song of their grandfather's.

A few feet away, his parents swayed together on the floor and Savannah danced with Davis.

"You had a thing for Renee back in high school, right?" Max asked. He didn't wait for an answer. "Then this is a second chance for you two. Take it from me, bruh. If you're as into her as it seems, you do *not* want to throw away a second shot."

"What if neither of us is looking for anything serious?" Cole asked, his gaze landing on Renee, who was chatting with Zora and Dallas.

Blake, Parker, Benji and Max all broke out into raucous laughter.

"I'm pretty sure that's what we all told ourselves in the beginning," Blake finally said.

"But if that's truly the case, neither of you have anything to lose." Parker sipped his old-fashioned.

Cole shifted his gaze to where Len approached Renee and asked her to dance—for the second time that night. He gripped his beer bottle tightly, his jaw clenched.

Maybe Parker was right. He and Renee were sensible adults. They could certainly navigate sex while keeping their friendship intact, couldn't they?

Or maybe he was just setting himself up for a fall.

"Thank you for a lovely evening, Cole. The wedding was beautiful. I'm glad I was there for it." Renee turned to Cole after he'd insisted on walking her to her door.

"It was a pretty amazing day." Cole rubbed his chin absently, seemingly distracted.

"Good night." Ren turned to go inside.

"Wait, Ren." Cole grasped her hand. "This…no-strings thing you want… I'll do it."

Renee spun around and stared at Cole, her heart beating faster. This was what she'd wanted, wasn't it? So why did she suddenly feel like she was in the midst of a panic attack?

"I thought you were worried it would ruin our friendship," she stammered.

"I am, but no matter how much I try to convince myself this is a bad idea... I can't stop thinking of you, Ren, and wanting you."

"Are you sure that—"

He cradled her face in his hands, and captured her mouth in a kiss that made her heart beat double time and filled her body with heat.

Cole glided his tongue between her lips, which eagerly parted. He dropped his large hands to her waist and pinned her between his muscled body and the wall behind her, his hardened length pressed to her belly. He kissed Ren until her legs were weak and the space between her thighs pulsed and ached. Until the intense beating of her heart rumbled through her chest like peals of thunder in a good old-fashioned Southern storm.

Finally, he pulled his mouth from hers, leaving her breathless and wanting. Desperate for the heat of his body. Cole propped a hand on the wall above her, his chest rising and falling, his face a few inches from hers.

"You still think I'm not sure?" Cole's voice was raw and husky as his lips brushed the outer shell of her ear. "Or is that the kiss of a man who's been dreaming about all of the ways I can make you scream my name?"

Ren swallowed hard, her hands trembling as she recalled that night on the sofa in her office. Even the memory of that night made her body react.

After all this time, Cole Abbott still had the ability to leave her babbling and tongue-tied. But here he was, offering exactly what she'd wanted...even before she'd been inspired by her aunt's journals to conduct a bad boy experiment of her own.

"Why don't you think about it and get back to me?"

Cole's eyes glinted and that sexy mouth of his pulled to one side in an impish smirk.

"That won't be necessary." Ren swallowed hard, her head light and her chest heaving after the dreamy kiss that had left her breathless. "Your place in an hour?"

Cole's dark eyes glimmered, and his nostrils flared. "Hydrate, sweetheart." He winked. "It's gonna be one hell of a night."

Eighteen

An hour after Cole had kissed her senseless on her back porch, Renee made the trek between her house and his, the gravel path crunching beneath her feet. It was a short distance. But every single step required all her effort.

Ren was terrified and thrilled and completely unsure about this. But she'd been thinking about it for the past two months, inspired by her aunt's bold proposal more than fifty years ago. And by her mother's fear that she would never experience that one great affair that curled her toes and left her with a lifetime of fond memories.

Ren wanted that.

She'd spent her entire life being the good girl. Doing all the things she was *supposed* to do. What she'd been left with was a decade of faked orgasms and a broken marriage. Nothing close to the experience her great-aunt had written about.

Despite what she'd said to Cole earlier, Renee couldn't possibly imagine doing this with someone she didn't know and trust. And despite her initial misgivings, which had proved wrong, she did trust Cole. She'd entrusted him with her son—the most precious thing in the world to her. She could trust him with this, too.

Ren climbed the stairs to Cole's back porch. She lifted a quivering hand and knocked on the newly installed screen door, which matched her own. The lights were on inside and there was music playing, but there was no answer. Ren knocked again.

Still no answer.

Evidently, the universe was trying to prevent her from making a colossal mistake. Or maybe Cole had changed his mind. Either way, she should heed the warning and walk away now. Pretend none of this had ever happened.

Renee turned and started down the stairs. Suddenly, the door swung open, taking her by surprise. She missed a step, tripping but catching herself on the banister before she face-planted in the gravel.

Graceful, Renee. You're a regular Misty Copeland.

"Ren?" Cole hurried down the stairs. "Are you okay?"

"Yeah, I'm fine. I thought maybe you'd… I don't know." She shrugged. "Changed your mind."

She was flustered and rambling like a fool. Yep, this was definitely a bad idea.

Stop talking and make a graceful exit, if that's even possible at this point.

"Not a chance, sweetheart." Cole extended a hand. "C'mon inside."

Renee swallowed hard, her hand trembling as she placed it inside his.

Don't chicken out now.

Cole led her into the kitchen. Like hers, it was outdated. It reminded her of her Aunt Bea standing at the old stove making fried corn or her famous chicken and dumplings— the first thing Ren had ever learned to cook.

"Still feels weird being here, huh?" Cole's voice shook her from her temporary daze.

"Very."

They entered the living room where an exercise mat and weights were on the floor.

"You were working out. I'm sorry. I shouldn't have disturbed you." Ren glanced at the equipment. "I know it's really late and—"

"Renee..." Cole drew her closer, pulling her attention back to him. His gaze was soft and warm as he stroked her cheek. "It's okay. We both know why you came here." He managed to say the words without sounding cocky. "But I need to hear it from you. Tell me exactly what you want from me."

Ren's head was spinning. No one had ever asked her that. Not in a relationship or her career. And now that he had, she wasn't quite sure what to say.

So instead, she clutched Cole's white Abbott Construction & Development T-shirt, pulled him closer and pressed her lips to his. Cole splayed one large hand on her back. The other arm snaked around her waist, tugging her lower body tight against his.

He kissed her as if he was a starving man, and she was the only sustenance he'd ever need.

This was why she'd come here.

She needed to get over her fear. Be clear about what she wanted, as she'd learned to do working in labs filled with men who didn't think she could possibly have the answers.

Ren slid a trembling hand down Cole's chest and over his taut abs. She cupped him as they continued their heated kiss, then glided her hand up and down his length through the thin fabric of his basketball shorts. She was delighted by Cole's tortured groan in response to her touch. He intensified their kiss, his tongue searching hers and his strong hands gripping her bottom.

His eager response emboldened her. She glided her fingertips beneath the waistband of his shorts and wrapped her fingers around the width of his heated flesh. She spread the silky drops of fluid at its tip with her thumb.

Ren swallowed Cole's soft gasp. Felt his back stiffen beneath her fingertips. She closed her fist around the velvety skin, pumping him slowly at first, then harder and faster.

Cole broke their kiss, lightly grasping her wrist. His chest heaved as he gently tugged her hand from his shorts. He stared at her, his dark eyes filled with need.

"Ren, I'm trying to be good here. But I swear, baby girl, you are fucking killing me right now," Cole whispered roughly, his breathing heavy. "I need you to say the words."

"If you already know why I'm here, why do I need to say it?" She shrugged innocently.

Ren tugged her hand from his grip and slowly slid down the zipper of her short denim dress. She shrugged off the dress, revealing a sheer bra and panties with strategic bits of lace.

Cole's eyes widened, and his Adam's apple bobbed when he swallowed.

"You look…*incredible*," Cole stammered. He took her hand. "But I still need you to be clear about what you want."

"I'd think this is pretty clear." Ren gestured toward her barely clad body. "Do you really need more than that?"

"Yes," he said emphatically. "We need to be clear about what this is, Ren. If you're really looking for a friends-with-benefits situation, I'm your man. But if you're looking for more…" Cole rubbed the back of his neck. "I can't give you that."

"You think I'm shopping for a husband and a father for my son?" Ren pulled her hand from his and folded her arms over her chest.

"Not consciously." Cole shoved his hands in his pockets, which made his hard-on more evident. "But the stakes are higher for you. You have your future and Mercer's to think about."

"Mercer is my life, and I'd do anything for him. But I can take care of us. I don't need you for that. Tonight is about what *I* want. And what I want is simple, Cole. Sex with no strings, no commitments and no expectations."

"Come here." Cole's voice was gruff. His dark eyes were filled with heat. When she stepped closer, he looped his arms around her waist.

Renee shuddered at the feel of him pressed to her belly.

"I'm no fairy-tale prince, Ren. I'm not sweet or gentle. And I'm no one's knight in shining armor. I'm not the man you deserve."

"But you're the man I want." Renee shivered beneath his intense stare as she lightly gripped his strong biceps.

She was nervous and quivering. Maybe even a little nauseous. She'd never done anything like this before. But she was sure—*damn sure*—she wanted this. That she wanted him.

Ren pressed a kiss to his chest. Then another to his shoulder. Then another to his neck.

Cole hauled her closer and captured her mouth in a greedy, demanding kiss. His fingers bit into the flesh exposed by the barely-there panties as he gripped her bottom. She'd probably have bruises in the shape of his handprints tomorrow. But it would be worth it. The sensation, which danced along the razor's edge between pleasure and pain, stoked the growing heat between her thighs and made her wet for him. Her already sensitive nipples grew taut as they brushed against his rock-hard chest.

Cole was leaving a mark on her skin and staking his claim on her body. Something deep inside her chest reveled at the thought of being claimed by this man whom she'd come to adore in so many ways. This was why she'd come here: a bad boy experiment of her own. One she'd never forget.

Cole stood in his bedroom staring at Ren, his chest heaving and his pulse racing.

He stripped off his T-shirt and tossed it to the floor, loving the feel of Renee's bare skin against his as he resumed their heated kiss. Cole had one clear thought in his head. He needed Ren in his bed this instant. But behind that thought was a much fuzzier one.

What will happen to our friendship after this?

Cole pushed the question aside, determined to focus on the hunger in Ren's kiss, the sweet taste of her warm mouth and the sensation of her soft curves cradled against him.

He'd often imagined this moment as a high school senior. It was a fantasy that had infiltrated his brain again when Renee had returned to Magnolia Lake. He was eager to make up for lost time.

His hands explored Ren's lush curves. His body ached with his need for this incredible woman. But his chest expanded with the feelings he had for Renee.

It's just sex. Don't be weird about it.

Only, it didn't feel like just sex. Because it was Ren.

Cole lifted her onto the bed; the covers were already pulled back. He trailed kisses along Ren's neck and shoulder, then pulled down the front of the sheer bra so the fabric framed her perfect breasts—round and firm. Her taut nipples, hidden by small patches of lace, had teased him from the moment Ren had stripped out of that minidress.

He dipped his head, covering one beaded tip with his mouth, loving the way Ren arched her back in response. Cole teased and sucked her hardened nipple as Ren squirmed and whimpered. Her dewy, freshly showered skin tasted sweet, like the pomegranate-scented body wash she used.

Cole kissed his way down her belly and over the sheer fabric. He roughly pulled aside the panel of fabric that shielded her sex. Inhaled the dizzying scent of her arousal as he studied her glistening pink flesh. Cole's eyes drifted shut as he swiped his tongue over her engorged flesh.

Ren shuddered and gasped. Cole couldn't help smiling up at her. She was so wet for him, her body so responsive. Just one taste of her salty but sweet essence and he was addicted.

He shifted the fabric further, resisting the urge to tear it. Then he licked and sucked, teasing her with his tongue and his fingers, taking Ren higher and higher.

She dug her heels into the mattress and tangled her fingers in his short curls, her touch tentative.

Cole glanced up at Ren, who seemed embarrassed that he'd caught her watching him as he tongued her. A deep smile spread across his face.

"Show me *exactly* where you want my mouth," he said between kisses to her slick flesh.

"Wh-what?" she stammered. "I don't want to—"

"Do it. *Now.*"

Ren gently repositioned his head. When his tongue ran over her clit, she gasped, then her eyes drifted closed.

"I need to see those beautiful brown eyes." Cole glided his tongue over her firm clit, and she shuddered. "I want you to watch me taste every last drop."

Ren's eyes widened and she swallowed hard. But she kept her eyes open, as he'd demanded. She swiveled her hips and rode his tongue like she was the registered owner who held the title and keys to it. Like he belonged to her.

As she guided his head, her touch was tentative at first. But as he took her higher, she directed his head more deliberately, grinding her sex against his eager mouth.

Finally, her legs shook, and her muscles tensed, her head lolling backward as she called his name again and again.

Cole pressed feathery kisses to her quivering flesh. Trailed them up her inner thigh, over her belly and between the valley of her full breasts as her chest rose and fell.

He was hard as steel, aching to finally be inside her. Cole climbed off the bed and stripped naked.

Ren's gaze dropped to his painfully hard shaft. She watched the sway of it as he moved about the room. He retrieved the box of condoms he'd yet to unpack since his move and grabbed a strip of them. He ripped one packet off and opened it, dropping the rest on the small table beside his bed.

"Bra and panties off," he practically growled as he rolled the condom on.

Ren complied without complaint, and he crawled beneath the covers, hovering over her. He kissed Ren's shoulder, then her neck, before kissing her lush lips again.

Cole wrapped his arms around Ren as he kissed her, then grabbed his length, pumping it before he pressed it to her slick entrance. He slowly glided inside her wet heat, allowing her body to adjust to his width while they continued their passionate kiss. When he was fully seated, he cursed beneath his breath, an involuntary groan of pleasure escaping his mouth.

Being with Ren, filling her with every inch of him, felt incredible. Sent an intense wave of pleasure rolling up his spine.

Cole planted a hand on either side of Ren as he slowly rocked his hips. His gaze was locked with hers as he moved inside her, his pelvis grinding against her clit. He watched as Ren's pleasure spiraled, their movements bringing them both closer to the edge.

Ren moaned softly. She clenched his biceps, her fingernails digging into his skin as she cried out again. Her sex pulsed around his heated flesh, until finally he too had tumbled over the edge, his body stiffening as he arched his back, cursing and calling her name.

Cole dropped to the mattress beside Renee. He wrapped her in his arms, pulling her to him. Then he kissed her damp forehead, both of them trying to catch their breath. Ren pressed her cheek to his chest, then lifted her head and smiled. She pressed a soft kiss to his mouth. "That was amazing."

Cole cradled Ren's cheek and kissed her again. "Yes, it was."

What was it about Ren that made everything feel...new and different? More consequential?

Cole remembered what Parker had said earlier that night.

When the right woman comes along...everything feels different.

He pushed his brother's words out of his head, then kissed her again before going to the bathroom. When he'd returned, Ren had drifted off to sleep.

His mouth curved in a soft smile.

So much for round two.

He turned off the light, slipped under the covers and cradled Ren's naked body against his. But he couldn't fall asleep. Parker's words kept filtering through his brain.

They'd spent one night together. So why did it feel like he was already addicted to Renee? Instinctively, he knew one time with her would never be enough.

Nineteen

Ren awoke wrapped in the warmth of Cole's embrace as he snored softly, both of them naked.

She was pretty sure it was a violation of the friends-with-benefits code to fall asleep in said friend's bed. And a general rookie mistake to fall asleep with her contact lenses still in.

Ren blinked repeatedly, trying to loosen the lenses, which had cemented themselves to her eyeballs over the course of the night. Her vision was blurry and sensitive to the light spilling into the room.

She needed to get dressed and get back home. Preferably before Cole woke up.

Renee carefully lifted Cole's heavy arm and slipped from beneath it, falling onto the floor in the process. Luckily, she caught her balance, bracing her hands on the floor.

"Not a good look, Renee. Especially naked," Ren whispered to herself as she stood up straight.

"I kind of liked it." Cole's gravelly morning voice startled her. He grinned. "You didn't quite stick the landing, but the part where your ass was in the air was spectacular."

Ren snatched the duvet up over her body, shielding her essential parts. Only the thin sheet was left on the bed, making Cole's early morning erection rather apparent.

"I…um…good morning?" Ren glanced around the room for something else to cover herself with.

"T-shirts are in those two bottom drawers." Cole indicated his dresser. "Take whatever you want."

Ren dropped the cover and ducked over to the dresser. She fished out a shirt with Cookie Monster on it that read 'Bout That Street Life and put it on. She couldn't help laughing, and it alleviated some of the awkwardness.

"Good choice." Cole shrugged on his boxer briefs and yawned. "Breakfast?"

"No, thank you. I should go." She slipped on her underwear, which she found kicked beneath the bed.

"Why?" Cole asked.

"Because I shouldn't have spent the night here."

"Why not?" He sank onto the bed and yawned again.

"Because you didn't invite me to." Ren slipped her arms out of the T-shirt long enough to put her bra on underneath it. "And since I've never seen a woman leave your place during the day, I'm assuming they don't usually spend the night."

"You've been staking out the house every morning?" Cole rubbed his neck.

"No, of course not." Ren's face went hot. "But I can see your house and driveway from my bedroom." She slipped her arms back through the sleeves. "I figured if there was no car in your drive and you didn't take anyone home the next day on your way to work—"

"Maybe we need to clarify the meaning of the words *staking out my house*." Cole chuckled dryly. He stood, rubbing one eye as he lumbered in her direction, clearly still half-asleep. "And you're right, I don't normally have overnight guests. But with us, it just kind of felt natural." He shrugged.

"Also, I fell asleep before you could send me home." Ren smirked.

"There's that, too." Cole held up a finger, then laughed when she rolled her eyes. "I'm kidding. Seriously, I'm glad you stayed." He slipped his arms around her waist and nuzzled her neck. "Otherwise, I'd have to eat breakfast all alone, and I wouldn't have a shower buddy." Cole grinned.

"You want to shower...*together*?"

"You're the one starting an eco-friendly farm. And you did say conserving water was high on the priority list," he hedged. His erection pressed against her back as he tightened his arms around her.

She should really say no. But taking a shower together sounded...nice. And wasn't the point of the bad boy experiment to try new things?

"Okay, yes to the shower. But I've been thinking..." Ren slipped out of his arms, turning to face him.

"All right." Cole folded his arms, his legs spread wide. "What is it?"

God, this man is handsome. Even when half-dressed and at half-mast.

"Last night was amazing, and I'd really like to do this again."

Cole's mouth curved in a half smile. "I'm one hundred percent with you on that."

"Good." The tension in Ren's shoulders eased a bit. "But this can only happen when Mercer is away."

"Agreed." He studied her face, one eyebrow shifting upward. "There's something else."

It hadn't been a question.

"I'd like to keep this between us."

"Whatever you want, sweetheart," Cole agreed. "But

my entire family already thinks there's something happening between us. We're fighting an uphill battle on that one."

Ren nodded and sighed. She'd figured as much. "Okay. Still, I'd really rather my grandparents not know that we're—"

"Fuck buddies?" One of his thick eyebrows lifted as he rubbed his beard.

"I prefer Friends U Can Keep," she said.

"Good song." Cole smirked. "Deal. Now, I have a request."

"Let me guess... No spending the night?" Ren asked.

"You can spend the night anytime you'd like." Cole tugged her closer by his T-shirt, then looped his arms around her waist as she gazed up at him. "But this can't make things weird between us. This friendship is too important to me."

Ren smiled, her eyes pricking and her heart expanding with affection. She nodded. "Promise."

"Then we're good." Cole wrapped Ren in a hug that lifted her off her feet.

She squealed with surprise and smacked his hard abs playfully once he'd set her down. "I need to brush my teeth and do something with my hair."

Cole squatted beside one of the moving boxes along the wall and rummaged inside. He produced a sealed box and handed it to her. "That's the extra head that came with my electric toothbrush."

"Thank you." She held the box to her chest. "Got a comb in that box?"

"I'm kind of digging the raised-by-wolves look," Cole teased. "But there is one more thing... I thought maybe you'd like to come to brunch at my parents' house this afternoon. It's a send-off for Parker and Kayleigh before their honeymoon on her friend's island in the Caribbean."

"Isn't this kind of a family thing?" A knot tightened in her stomach.

"You and Merce have kind of become family." Cole shrugged nonchalantly.

Ren's brain was screaming that it was a mistake. But she liked being with Cole and his family. The trick was not to make more out of this than it was. They were friends, and she'd be hanging out with her friend's family. Nothing unusual about that.

"Then thank you, I'd love to come."

Cole's eyes darkened and he sank his teeth into his lower lip. He tugged her forward, slipping his arms around her waist.

"Say that again." His voice was a husky whisper.

"Thank you?"

He shook his head and licked his lower lip. "The other part."

"I'd love to come?" She looked at him quizzically.

A devilish grin spanned the width of his handsome face. "And I'd love to make you come…again and again and again."

"Ahh…" Her nipples tightened and the space between her thighs pulsed at the prospect of a repeat performance. "I'd really, *really* like that, too."

Twenty

Ren hummed to herself as she stood in the full-length mirror of her hotel room and pulled her dress up over her hips. She and Cole had grown close in the months since they'd become neighbors. But the feelings of friendship and affection had grown exponentially in the weeks since she and Cole had become lovers, too. Now, she was preparing for her second Abbott wedding in just three weeks.

Max and Quinn were getting married at Bazemore Orchards, owned by Quinn's grandfather, Dixon Bazemore. And by a twist of fate, Ren got to be a part of their love story.

Quinn's best friend from college was supposed to be her matron of honor, but Naomi had gotten into an accident and was unable to attend the wedding. By the end of Parker and Kayleigh's honeymoon send-off brunch, Quinn and Zora had hatched a plan for Zora to replace Naomi as the matron of honor while Ren took Zora's place as a bridesmaid, who would be coupled with Cole as groomsman.

Renee declined at first. Mainly because she assumed it would be weird for Cole. But when he'd reminded her that she was his date for the night anyway and suggested it would be fun. She couldn't say no with the entire Abbott family imploring her to say yes.

At first, she felt as if she was crashing the intimate prewedding festivities. But after spending the past two days at a luxury boutique hotel in downtown Knoxville eating, primping and celebrating the impending nuptials with Quinn, her family and the Abbotts, Renee felt more at ease. They clearly wanted her there, and she felt as if she belonged. Something she hadn't ever really felt at her ex's family events.

Ren slipped the one-shoulder, floor-length, peach-colored gown up over her strapless bra and reached behind her to zip it.

"Let me get that, beautiful." Cole entered through the connected door between their hotel rooms. He zipped the back of her dress, then looped his arms around her waist from behind. His beard scraped her skin when he dropped a kiss on her bare shoulder. As he slowly kissed his way up her neck, her nipples beaded, and she could feel him growing hard against her back. "You look…stunning."

Ren wriggled out of Cole's grasp.

"Oh no, you don't." Ren smoothed down her dress. "You are *not* wrinkling this dress or messing up the expensive hair and makeup your future sister-in-law's family sprung for. Besides, we need to be downstairs for the limo bus in twenty minutes. And we have to be on time, so your brother won't see Quinn when she and her parents take their limo to the venue."

"Right." Cole shoved a hand in his pocket. "Knowing my sister, she'll be calling us if we aren't downstairs in ten minutes. She's taking her promotion to matron-of-honor *very* seriously."

"She is, but it's kind of adorable." Renee smiled. "Quinn and Zora have become good friends. Zora just wants to make sure Max and Quinn's day is perfect. Can you blame her?"

"No, I guess not." Cole straightened his peach-colored tie and smoothed down the collar of his white shirt. Both colors looked fresh and crisp against his blue grooms-man suit.

Cole seemed to get a little more handsome every day. More so in the weeks since they'd been together. Or maybe it was just her perception of him that continued to deepen as they had lain in bed at night sharing their lives and catching up on each other's pasts.

"Perfect. Ready to go?" She smoothed down her high topknot, then picked up the little sequined purse with her lipstick and cell phone.

"I'll go back through my room and meet you down-stairs, like last night." Cole inched toward the door to his room.

Ren grabbed his wrist and tugged him forward. She smiled broadly, her heart full.

"That isn't necessary. I'm not saying we advertise that you spent last night in my bed. But since Quinn requested that we have adjoining rooms away from all the other guests… I have the feeling that particular cat is out of the bag and strutting down Main Street by now."

Cole laughed. He threaded his fingers through hers and dropped a kiss on her temple. "Let's go."

Cole took his place on one side of the wedding arbor constructed of long, thin, entwined branches and deco-rated with sheer white panels of fabric, greenery and the most beautiful array of flowers in white, peach and orange.

He was standing farthest away from the groom. Parker, Quinn's youngest brother, Marcus, Blake and Dallas filled in the spaces between them. Dixon escorted Quinn's mother to her seat. Then Cole's parents made their way down the aisle to their seats. The music started and everyone looked up the aisle where Renee stood in her peach gown. She was gorgeous, but he could sense the sheer terror she seemed to feel.

Cole gave her a broad smile and placed a hand over his heart, signaling that she took his breath away. Ren's smile deepened and she stood taller. Her chin tipped upward as she moved down the aisle toward him.

Ren gave him a grateful smile, then took her place at the opposite end of the other side of the arbor.

Once the rest of the bridal party filed in, the music switched to Pachelbel's "Canon in D."

The bride looked beautiful in her off-white lace gown as she clutched her father's arm. They moved slowly down the white runner strewn with peach-and-orange flower petals. Her hair was up and twisted in a vine of peach, white and orange flowers.

Quinn's father kissed her cheek and handed her off to Max, who was overcome with emotion at the sight of his bride. Max took Quinn's hand, mouthing the words, *You look incredible*, as he escorted her beneath the arbor to join the officiant.

Cole was surprisingly touched by the scene. He was truly happy for his brother and Quinn. Despite his differences with Max, he was glad that he and Quinn had found their way back to each other and were starting a new life together.

During the ceremony, Quinn read the poem "In and Out of Time" by Maya Angelou, which she said was a favorite of Max's. The final verse was tattooed in script on her back, visible through the sheer back of her dress.

Then Max told the story of his own tattoo: Quinn's initials and lines from her favorite poem by Robert Frost. He read the poem, "Stopping by Woods on a Snowy Evening" and explained that it reminded Quinn of one of her favorite memories of her grandmother, whose wedding ring was now part of Quinn's engagement ring.

Cole honestly hadn't given much thought to the weddings he'd attended. He'd only cared about how everyone had looked and whether the food was good, the alcohol was flowing, and the music kept him on the dance floor. But he'd been moved by Parker's wedding a few weeks ago and by Max and Quinn's highly emotional ceremony.

By the time Max and Quinn had been declared man and wife, there were few dry eyes in the house. Cole glanced over at Renee. Quinn was a beautiful bride. But though it was his new sister-in-law's day, Renee was the only woman in the room he had eyes for. When her gaze met his, she smiled at him and gave him a discreet wave.

His heart clenched and it felt harder to breathe. It wasn't a feeling Cole was accustomed to. One that nearly knocked him off his feet.

Was he falling for Renee? And did she feel the same?

Twenty-One

Renee dried her hair after her shower with Cole. The reception had gone on late into the night and they were getting ready for bed. She wore a borrowed T-shirt of his that said, "I'm not weird, I'm limited edition," and a pair of lacy bikini panties.

Cole returned to the room with a fresh bucket of ice. He set the bottle of peach brandy Quinn and Max had gifted the members of the wedding party in the bucket and agitated it between his palms. Then he slipped his arms around her waist and kissed her.

"I'm glad you're here. I wouldn't have wanted to do this with anyone else." Cole cupped her cheek. A soft smile turned up the edges of his mouth.

Renee gazed into Cole's dark eyes. Her heart swelled with all the things she felt for this handsome, generous, sweet man she'd come to care for and rely on so much these past few months.

It was something she couldn't have imagined when

she'd first encountered Cole again at the general store. But now…it was heartbreaking to imagine her and Mercer's life without Cole in it.

Her son loved Cole. It was written all over Mercer's little face. And she understood exactly how her son felt. Because her own heart was bursting with her growing love and admiration for Cole.

Their relationship was a complicated dance. Friends. Next-door neighbors. Competitors. *Lovers.*

Growing up, Renee had become exceptionally good at compartmentalizing her feelings, something she'd watched her parents—who were both military officers—do. She'd convinced herself she could handle her unconventional relationship with Cole with the same logical approach. That she could simply enjoy their tryst and growing friendship with the same detachment.

That ship had sailed, because she was in deep. Sucked into a swirling tsunami of emotions that tugged her deeper still.

"Baby, what's wrong?" Cole brushed her cheek with his calloused thumb.

Renee struggled to hold back the unshed tears that made his handsome face a blur. "Make love to me, Cole. Like I'm yours. Like this thing we have is real."

His eyes widened momentarily as he studied her face. Cole's pained expression reminded her that she wasn't his. That she never would be.

Ren's forehead and cheeks stung with embarrassment. She pulled away from him, but Cole pinned her in place.

His only response was a slow, sweet kiss. The taste of his mouth was a mélange of smooth, rich King's Finest bourbon, tart apple crumb pie and sweet vanilla ice cream. Her body instantly reacted.

And that was what she needed to focus on. The physicality of their coupling. The passion Cole ignited in her.

A feeling she'd thought herself incapable of during seven long years of marriage in which faked orgasms were the norm and her desire for the man she shared a bed with had waned through the years.

She'd begun to wonder if Dennis was right. That she was cold and clinical. Incapable of this sort of fiery passion. Evidently, they'd both been wrong. Because Cole had stirred those feelings in her and so much more. Made her see herself in an entirely new light.

Cole hadn't changed her. He'd simply provided a space where she was comfortable being herself. Discovering what she liked in bed and out. She couldn't thank him enough for that.

But as he swept her in his arms and carried her to his bed, Ren tried to quiet the growing chorus of voices in her brain that whispered *Why can't this be real?*

She'd fallen hard for Cole, despite their agreement to keep things casual. Despite his insistence he wasn't interested in a serious relationship.

Cole obviously didn't feel the same, so she needed to pull it together. Compartmentalize. Enjoy this bad boy experiment for what it was and not ruin the moment.

He laid her in his bed and stripped off the shorts he'd been wearing commando. Cole opened the side table drawer and sheathed himself, then stalked toward her.

She slipped his borrowed T-shirt over her head and wiggled out of her underwear, tossing both onto the pile of clothing on the floor.

Cole climbed into bed and kissed her again. He kissed down her neck and shoulders. Over her breasts, teasing the hardened tips. He trailed slow, deliberate kisses down her belly. Finally, he gazed up at her with a glint in his dark eyes. He spread her with his thumbs and tasted her.

Renee shuddered as much from the intense pleasure that rippled up her spine as from the anticipation of the next stroke of his skilled tongue. Cole took another swipe at her engorged flesh, then another. She writhed, her hips squirming as she gripped the sheets.

She shut her eyes, lost in the delicious sensations, as she tried not to scream his name at the top of her lungs.

Cole stopped, and Ren opened her eyes.

"You know I love it when you watch me." Cole's voice was low and husky. "I love seeing your reaction to every single stroke." He swiped his tongue over her slick flesh, and she trembled.

She liked watching him, too. More than she would've ever imagined.

"Don't ever hold back with me, Ren," Cole whispered between lazy licks of her flesh. His cool breath ghosted over her heated skin. "Whatever you want, whatever you need...*that's* why I'm here, sweetheart. I want to give you everything you've ever desired. Everything you've been afraid to ask for."

Renee's eyes stung with tears. But she couldn't form the words. Couldn't tell him how much she wanted him. How much she needed him in her and her son's life. That she'd been happier these past few months than she'd ever been before. The joy she felt waking up with Cole's arms wrapped around her, clutching her to him as if she were his security blanket.

She was terrified of losing all of that once their little experiment ended.

Because Cole *would* eventually walk away. He'd assured her of that from the very beginning. Warned her that she shouldn't get too attached. And she'd run full steam through both of those warnings and opened her heart to him. But it honestly hadn't felt like a choice. She'd fallen for Cole *despite* her determination not to.

Cole slipped two fingers inside her, teasing that hidden

place that sent her hurtling toward the clouds, as he intensified the speed and pressure of his tongue.

Ren cursed, her heels digging into the mattress as she slid her fingers into Cole's soft curls and rode his talented tongue.

Her abdominal muscles tensed, and her entire body stiffened as she cried out his name, over and over, until her throat felt raw and she shattered into tiny, glittering pieces. Renee's chest heaved as Cole finally lifted his head, his lips and chin shiny with the evidence of her pleasure.

He pressed kisses to her inner thigh, then to her belly. And before she could catch her breath, Cole slid inside her. The sound of his skin slapping against hers and his low, determined grunts filled the space around them.

Ren gazed up at the gorgeous man hovering over her. He was focused. Beads of sweat formed on his forehead. His quiet moans of pleasure grew more intense, as did her soft murmurs. Cole rolled his hips, seemingly determined to make her feel him from every single angle. She'd hardly had a chance to come down from the intense high of the orgasm he'd given her. Yet he was taking her there again.

When Cole's gaze met hers, there was something in his eyes. Something he wanted to say but wouldn't allow himself to. He threaded his fingers through hers, lifting their joined hands above her head. His kiss was deep and passionate. His mouth was salty with the taste of her.

The friction of his pelvis moving against hers intensified the ecstasy building low in her belly.

An overwhelming sensation began building deep in her core, radiated up her spine and catapulted her into bliss, his name on her lips. She held onto him, as if he'd float away if she didn't anchor his solid body to hers.

Suddenly, Cole's muscles tensed and his back stiffened as he reached his own pinnacle. He whispered her name in a breathy moan again and again.

Cole kissed her, then collapsed onto the bed beside her. He gathered her to his heaving chest, folding one arm behind his head as he stared up at the ceiling.

There was an awkwardness they hadn't experienced before. Now things were weird between them because she'd broken the rules they'd established.

Ren traced the fine hair that trailed down his belly with light fingertips and frowned, her face buried in his chest. "What I said earlier... I shouldn't have said that. It's not what we agreed to."

"Don't apologize for asking for what you want, sweetheart." Cole lifted her chin, so their eyes met. "And don't think I don't have feelings for you, Ren. I do. I just... I'm not..."

"I know." She pressed her cheek to his chest again. "It was such a beautiful, emotional ceremony. I just got caught up in the moment. Please, let's not talk about it anymore."

Ren squeezed her eyes shut, hoping Cole wouldn't notice her silent tears.

Cole wrapped his arms around Ren and dropped a soft kiss on top of her head before lying back against the pillow. He stared at the ceiling again, his pulse racing as Ren's words replayed in his head.

Make love to me, Cole. Like I'm yours. Like this thing we have is real.

Cole rubbed a hand up and down the soft, dewy skin on her arm. His heart ached as he recalled Ren's pained smile. Her lips had said it was no big deal but the disappointment in her eyes nearly broke him.

He never wanted to hurt Ren. But she obviously wanted more from this relationship.

There was no denying that he'd gotten caught up in his feelings for Ren and Mercer. But a serious, long-term relationship wasn't what they'd agreed to. It wasn't what he'd been looking for. Because he enjoyed the freedom of being the eternal bachelor.

Or maybe you're just scared.

Cole tried to shake off the thought, but he could feel wetness on his skin.

Ren *was* crying silent tears, which meant she didn't want him to know.

Cole wanted to give her anything she desired to make those tears stop. But he cared too much for Ren to mislead her.

Yes, he had feelings for her. And yes, he believed he could be happy with Ren. Yet, there was some part of him that was terrified of the prospect and worried that he wasn't good enough for Ren and Mercer. Because they deserved the world.

"I adore you, Ren. You know that, right?" Cole kissed her forehead.

"Yes." Ren nodded, her cheek slipping against the wetness on his chest. She swiped her eyes and cleared her throat. "I feel the same."

Cole sighed, then rubbed her arm. "I'd better take care of this."

He went to the bathroom, but when he returned, Ren was gone. As were her clothes that had been piled on the chair.

"Ren?" He walked through the door to her hotel room.

"I'm here." Ren emerged from her bathroom dressed in a pair of leggings, a racing top and sneakers. She ran her fingers through her hair. Reminding him of how he'd sifted her strands through his fingers as she lay in his arms the night before.

"You're leaving?"

"I'm too amped to go to sleep. I'm going to run on the treadmill in the gym."

"We should talk, Ren," he said. "I'll go with you."

"Thank you, but I think I need a little time alone. Besides, I think maybe I'm becoming a little too reliant on you, you know?"

Cole frowned, his chest tightening. "I like doing things for you and Mercer."

"I know." She gave him a soft smile. "It's one of the many things I love about you. But right now, I just need a little space."

"If that's what you want." He pulled her into a hug. "But I'm here whenever you need me."

Ren pulled out of his embrace. "Don't wait up for me. I'm not sure how long I'll be, and I'll probably just crash in my bed tonight."

"Ren." Cole caught her hand and she turned to face him. "We're good, right?"

"Of course." She smiled, but there was pain in her eyes. She lifted onto her toes and gave him a quick kiss. "See you in the morning." She gave him a little wave, then left.

Cole returned to his room and shut the connecting door. Maybe he'd fucked up by agreeing to this experiment with Renee. Maybe it would've been better for all of them if he'd said no and meant it. But having Ren and Mercer in his life had brought him a happiness he hadn't realized he'd been missing.

So he couldn't regret the past few months they'd spent together. And he'd do whatever it took to salvage their relationship. Because going back to life without Ren and Mercer just wasn't an option.

Twenty-Two

Breakfast the next morning was quiet and uneventful. Ren and Cole shared warm, cordial conversation about the wedding, the hotel and about a sensory toy she wanted to get for Mercer. They talked about anything but what had happened last night.

It was a mistake. And it wasn't fair to Cole. She realized that, but she couldn't help the way she felt about him, either. She didn't just love Cole as a friend; she was in love with him. If she was being really honest with herself, she'd fallen in love with Cole long before she'd asked him to agree to their experiment.

When she returned home, Mercer was down for a nap. Her mom took one look at her and knew something was wrong. She had one question: had Cole done anything to hurt her? When Renee said no, her mother opened her arms and she fell into them, crying like a baby. Her mother was kind enough not to press her for details. She appreciated that.

The next day, her mom hung around to keep an eye on

Mercer while Ren went out into the field with a master gardener she'd hired as a consultant. They were making the rounds and checking on all the crops: blueberries and strawberries; shallots, tomatoes, cucumbers, beans and carrots; Swiss chard, several varieties of lettuce and kale.

Everything looked lovely, and the beans, lettuce and a few other plants were already starting to produce. Next, she would be meeting with Jeb and Leonard Dawson about building a chicken pen and roost.

But first, she needed to make lunch for her picky little eater. Today she was making one of his favorite meals: homemade chicken and dumplings. The house smelled heavenly.

"Merce?" Ren stayed calm as she looked all over for Mercer, despite the slight panic building in her chest. She tried her best to watch him like a hawk but it only took a moment for her curious little boy to get into something.

She found him lying underneath her desk. He sucked his thumb as he stared up.

"There you are." Ren got on her knees and tickled Mercer's belly, making him laugh. "What is it that you find so fascinating underneath my desk?"

Mercer pointed up, so Ren lay on her back underneath the desk beside him. He was pointing at an engraved silver plate Ren hadn't even known was there.

"That's why Aunt Willie always dusted underneath the desk, too," Ren muttered quietly to herself. She lifted onto her elbows so she could read the words engraved on the plate.

To my lovely Wilhelmina. A gift for our wedding day.

A date was inscribed beneath the words: September 16, 1972.

Wedding date?

Her Aunt Wilhelmina had never married. Had she planned to wed Eduardo, the man she'd had her bad boy experiment with? If so, what had gone wrong?

"C'mon, Bug." Ren scooted from beneath the desk and climbed to her feet. "I made your favorite—chicken and dumplings." A wide smile spread on the little boy's face, as he grabbed her hand.

They washed their hands, then Mercer climbed into his booster seat. His bowl was filled with the tender, juicy strips of chicken and the cooled dumplings, which he could eat with his favorite fork. He didn't care for the broth.

Ren sat beside him with her bowl, but she wasn't hungry. She couldn't help wondering what had happened between Aunt Wilhelmina and Eduardo. Had he changed his mind? Had she? Or had they come to realize their relationship was better off as it was?

She couldn't help thinking of Cole. Ren hadn't seen him since they'd returned from Max and Quinn's wedding. He'd sent her sweet little text messages to check on her and Mercer and see if they needed anything. Her reply was always gracious and warm. And she ended by typing: Talk soon. Because eventually they would. She just wasn't ready to talk now.

Cole hadn't done anything wrong. He'd simply kept to their agreement. She was the one who'd broken the rules by falling in love with him. Ren wanted Cole in her life, even if all he was offering was friendship. But she'd been devastated by the realization that she loved him as more than a friend, but he didn't love her back. It would take some time to come to terms with that.

Mercer reached out and touched her face. It was only then she realized tears were sliding down her cheeks.

"It's okay, sweetie." Ren wiped the tears away and forced a big smile. She kissed the little boy's forehead. "Mommy's fine. I promise."

But they both knew the truth. Mommy wasn't fine.

That night, after her mother had left for Knoxville, Ren put Mercer to bed, beneath the little tent Cole had created for him. He was clutching the sensory teddy bear Cole had bought him a few weeks ago.

Ren returned to her bedroom after her shower. She glanced at the spot on the floor where she was sitting when she'd first kissed Cole a few months ago and sighed. It felt like there wasn't a single place in this house that didn't remind her of Cole. As she put on her pajamas and prepared to get into bed, she noticed the box beneath her bed sticking out.

Mercer had evidently been under her bed again.

Ren reached for the box, to shove it back beneath the bed, but she couldn't help noticing the book safe. Over the past few months, she'd tried street addresses, family members' birthdates and every important date she could think of as the combination. Nothing had worked.

But now she had a new date to try. The date Aunt Wilhelmina had planned to get married.

Ren sat on the floor with her legs folded and tried to remember the date inscribed beneath the desk. September 16, 1972. She pulled out the little safe and carefully dialed each number: nine, one, six. When she lifted the lid, the book safe creaked open.

Ren set it on the floor and scanned the contents. It contained two stacks of letters tied with ribbon, addressed to Aunt Wilhelmina from Eduardo Cordeiro. The box also contained two more journals. The first picked up from where the last journal she'd read had left off. Ren opened the leatherbound book and started to read.

She read late into the night until she'd finished the first journal, in which she discovered that, like her, her great-aunt had fallen in love with the subject of her experiment. But Eduardo had fallen in love with Wilhelmina, too. They'd planned to secretly get married and tell their families—whom they feared wouldn't have approved—later.

In the second journal, she discovered that Eduardo had

wanted to save a little nest egg before they married. He didn't want Aunt Willie's family, which owned lots of land and was doing well financially at the time, to think he was marrying Wilhelmina for her money. He took a job as the captain of a tuna fishing boat. It was dangerous work, but he was well paid. But two weeks before they were to be married, Eduardo's boat sank in a huge storm off the New England coast, killing him and everyone on board.

Her great-aunt had been devastated. Not only because of losing the man she loved, but because she was pregnant with their child. She'd wanted to raise the child on her own, but when she'd finally confessed everything to Aunt Bea, her sister had convinced her it would be best if she gave the child up. Her great-aunt's journal entries ended soon after she'd left for California, where she would have her child and give it up for adoption. Ren shut the journal, devastated by Aunt Wilhelmina's tragic love story. Eduardo had reciprocated her aunt's feelings, and still their story hadn't had a happy ending.

Ren carefully replaced the items in the book safe. Then she set it on top of her dresser. A daily, visible reminder that, with the exception of her grandparents, the Lockwood family history was filled with failed relationships and tragic love stories.

She cared deeply for Cole. But he'd been right about not risking their friendship for a fling. She needed to cut her romantic ties to Cole and salvage their friendship.

Because bad boy experiments never ended well.

Twenty-Three

Cole pulled the Ram TRX into the driveway of his grandfather's cabin just outside of town. It was the place Grandpa Joe had planned to live out the rest of his life with their grandmother—the love of his life. But fate had been cruel, and not long after he'd officially turned the reins of King's Finest over to Cole's dad, their grandmother had been diagnosed with terminal cancer. She'd only gotten to spend a few months truly enjoying the old place.

Once, Cole had asked his grandfather why he hadn't sold the cabin with all the bad memories of his grandmother being sick. He'd simply smiled and said, "Your grandmother likes it here, so this is where we'll stay." He'd never asked about it again. But he had to admit that whenever he visited, it reminded him of his sweet grandmother, too. How she'd loved nature and animals. And how much she loved going out on the lake.

Before Cole reached the front door, Grandpa Joe opened it.

"How'd you know I was here?" Cole asked.

"I can still hear pretty good." The old man chuckled. "You can hear that thing coming down the road from a mile away with that souped-up engine of yours."

Fair point.

"You wanted to see me, Gramps. Thinking of renovating the old place?" Cole glanced around the cabin. The kitchen was a little dated, but everything was still in good shape. It was nothing that would bother his grandfather. Unless… "You're not selling the cabin, are you?"

"They'll be carrying me out of here feet first." His grandfather eyed him.

"Okay, Pops. Forget I mentioned it." Cole chuckled. "What can I do for you, sir?"

"Actually, this is about what I can do for you." His grandfather rubbed his chin, his expression suddenly serious. "Can I get you a drink?"

"Got a beer?"

"Sure 'nuff." His grandfather grabbed two beers from the small fridge behind the bar, then joined Cole on the sofa. They opened their beers and sipped them in silence. Finally, his grandfather spoke, a pained look in his eyes. "I owe you an apology, son."

"For what?" Cole turned toward his grandfather.

Grandpa Joe sighed heavily. "When you decided you didn't want to go to college, I thought you were just being lazy. I didn't understand the struggles you were having with school. I should've been more supportive. But at the time, I thought you just needed a little tough love. That's why I gave you the ultimatum that if you didn't go to college, you couldn't work in the company. I thought it'd push you to go to school like your brothers. To tap into all of the potential I've always known was there."

"We don't need to talk about this again, Gramps." Cole frowned, taking another sip of his beer.

"Yes, we do." The old man emphasized each word, his

voice shaky. "Because the ultimatum was my idea, and I was wrong. And when Milo Lockwood took you under his wing and you were helping him build his business, I was hot under the collar. It felt like a rejection of our family and everything we've built with King's Finest."

"It wasn't. I just knew college wasn't right for me then. Being forced out of the company made me grow up and figure things out. Like what it was I was good at and enjoyed doing. When Milo gave me a shot as his apprentice... I found my place in the world. It wasn't about you at all, Gramps."

"Guess that's part of the problem." His grandfather pushed his smudged glasses up the bridge of his nose. "You made your decision without regard for the family or the company I'd been working to build since I was sixteen years old. At the time, I thought that was damn selfish of you."

"You aren't alone in that," Cole said, thinking of his brother Max.

"Maybe. But I was wrong to begrudge your decision to go out on your own and do what makes you happy, son. You've done far better for yourself than any of us could've imagined. And I can't tell you how incredibly proud of you I am for that, son." Grandpa Joe patted Cole's knee, his voice filled with love and pride.

"Thanks, Gramps. That means a lot."

"I'll let you in on a little secret." His grandfather set down his beer and turned to Cole more fully. "The reason I took you walking away from the company so hard is because from the time you were just a wee thing...you were the one who most reminded me of me." He chuckled. "You looked just like me. You had my confidence and swagger. My smart-ass mouth." They both laughed. "I'd envisioned you leading the company into the future long after I'm gone."

"But I'm the fourth in line," Cole said.

"Don't matter." His grandfather chuckled. "You're the visionary of the family. You've got drive and ingenuity. You're a natural-born leader and one hell of a businessman. Look at what you've done with your own company. Was I wrong?"

"Guess not." Cole drained the last of his beer. "But Blake's doing a hell of a job. He'll make a great CEO when the time comes."

"He is, and he will indeed," Grandpa Joe agreed. "I'm mighty proud of him and of *all* of you, son," Grandpa Joe reiterated.

"Thanks, Gramps." Cole bumped a gentle shoulder against his grandfather's.

"I just wish your grandmother had lived to see how everything turned out." The old man heaved a sigh as he ran a hand over his smooth head. "Dixon Bazemore and I were talking about that at the wedding. It was a beautiful, heartfelt ceremony. A happy day for both of our families. But it hurt like hell that our girls didn't live to see the day our two grandchildren would stand up there at that altar and get married."

"I've been thinking a lot about Gram, too. I wish she could've been there."

"Dixon gave Quinn two of his wife's most treasured jewelry pieces. Her engagement ring, which became part of Quinn's engagement ring. And the diamond necklace Dixon gave his wife for their fiftieth anniversary. Quinn wore it during the ceremony. It was a great way to make his late wife part of his granddaughter's wedding day." Gramps sighed. "I wish I'd had the foresight to do something like that for your brothers' and sister's weddings. I didn't, but I won't make the same mistake with you." He waggled a finger.

"Hate to disappoint you, Pops, but there isn't a wedding in my future."

It was the kind of statement Cole usually made smugly. But saying it now made his chest feel hollow. Like there was a hole where his heart should be.

"Isn't there?" His grandfather furrowed his wiry brows. "'Cause you've sure seemed sweet on Milo's granddaughter these past few months."

Cole frowned, his throat suddenly dry.

"Ren is great. Smart, beautiful, sweet, hardworking, determined…she can be stubborn as hell." He laughed bitterly, then sighed. "But she and her son…they deserve someone… I don't know…*better* than me, I guess."

"And what *exactly* would make someone better for her, Cole?"

"Renee is a brilliant scientist with double PhDs. She's made important discoveries that are having a real impact in the world, and I'm…"

"A brilliant businessman who has forged his own path. You're building an empire, Cole. Creating your very own legacy. Impacting this town and this state in real, measurable ways. More importantly, you care deeply for Renee and her child. I see it in your eyes whenever you're with them." His grandfather smiled. "Reminds me of the way my eyes lit up whenever I was around your grandmother. The question is, what are you going to do about it?"

"I've been on my own so long, Gramps. What if I'm not capable of changing?"

"Has Renee asked you to change?"

"No, of course not."

"Then why do you think she expects you to?" His grandfather folded his arms.

"I'm not a traditional kind of guy."

"That dog won't hunt," his grandfather said. "Renee was married to a 'traditional kind of guy.' Didn't work out too well. Maybe what she needs is someone unconventional. Whatever you think your faults are, Cole, you're a good man, son. You've been there for Renee, helping her through this every step of the way. Even though you want that land for yourself." Gramps squeezed his arm. "Not many men—not even good ones—would do that. It's obvious you love the girl."

"I do." Cole didn't hesitate. For the past few days he'd been pondering the depth of his feelings for her. Just as before, his relationship with Renee had touched him in a way no one else ever had. "I love Ren and Mercer. I'd do anything for them. That's why I want what's best for them. Even if that isn't me."

"Seems to me, you make them just as happy as they make you. And I'd venture that there ain't a man out there who'll care for them, protect them and love them the way you do. They're pretty damn lucky to have you in their lives."

Cole's grandfather's words hit him. Made him think of all the times he'd shared with Renee and Mercer. And of all the things he'd done to ensure they were safe and happy. He thought of all the emotions that had been building in his chest these past months. And how miserable he'd been without them these past few days.

Commitment had always seemed scary. Because what if he screwed up? What if he chose the wrong person? He loved his family, and they'd resolved their differences. But their failure to understand him and to accept him for who he was earlier in his life…it had scarred him. Made him feel as if he was the only person he could rely on. The only person he could trust.

But as he sat there now, all he could think of was how devastated he would be if Ren and Mercer walked out of his life. That loss was a much scarier prospect than any of his concerns about entering a long-term commitment.

"Thanks, Gramps." Cole hugged his grandfather, then stood quickly. "I need to talk to Renee."

She'd been avoiding him since they'd come back from Max and Quinn's wedding, when he'd blown it by not telling her how he really felt. He hadn't wanted to push. But now he really needed to speak with her. To be honest about his feelings.

"That a boy. But there's one more thing…the reason I invited you here." His grandfather chuckled, slowly rising to his feet, too. "Can't give you the business, but I can give you something else." He reached behind the bar and produced a small box.

"What's this?" Cole slid open the old matchbox and studied its contents. "Gramps, is this…? I can't—"

"Yes, you can." Grandpa Joe patted his shoulder. "Hope it brings you as much luck as it brought us."

Cole bearhugged his grandfather. "Thanks, Gramps."

"All right, all right. Don't you have somewhere you need to be right now?"

"Yes, sir." Cole shoved the box Grandpa Joe had given him into his pocket, then clapped a hand on the old man's shoulder. "I do."

He had to see Ren. But there were two stops he needed to make first.

Twenty-Four

Renee sat at her desk sorting through the invoices to be paid. For now, there were plenty of expenses and zero income. But she'd done her research and was prepared to absorb the costs. She'd banked enough to keep the farm going for at least a year without tapping into her savings.

Still, her plan was coming along nicely. The plants were healthy and strong, and several of the small crops had begun to bear fruit. The chicken enclosure and roost had been built, and she was now the proud mama of a small flock of baby chicks. She smiled, thinking of how sweet and gentle Mercer had been with the tiny little bundles of yellow fuzz. It would be about six months before they'd be ready to begin laying eggs. In the meantime, he'd get to bond with them.

Ren glanced up at the sound of Cole's Ram TRX pulling into his driveway. Mercer was asleep, or else he'd have his little face pressed to the office window saying *Vroom*.

Every evening when she heard Cole come home, she practically held her breath.

Part of her hoped Cole wouldn't knock on her door. Part of her hoped he would.

Ren sat frozen after the slam of the truck door, her heart beating a bit faster as she strained to hear the crunch of gravel beneath his feet as he took the path between their houses. But after a few minutes, there was only silence.

Renee nibbled on her lower lip and heaved a sigh. When her cell phone started playing "(Sittin' On) the Dock of the Bay" by Otis Redding, it startled her. A photo of her grandfather with his wide grin filled the screen, accompanying his favorite song. She checked her watch. It was after eight in the evening. Her grandfather had usually settled in to watch his favorite TV shows for the night. He and her grandmother rarely called at this hour.

"Hey, Grandad. Everything okay?"

"It is, sweetheart. For you, especially." He chuckled.

"I don't understand."

"Cole pulled his bid for the property, so if you still want the farm, it's yours. Congratulations."

"I don't understand," Ren repeated. "When did this happen?"

"He left here about an hour ago."

Ren sat frozen, barely able to believe what her grandfather was saying.

Why would Cole withdraw his bid after investing months of work into this deal?

"Thought you'd be happy to hear the news," her grandfather said, his voice tinged with concern. "This is still what you want, isn't it?"

"Yes, of course. I'm thrilled by the news, Grandad. Really. I'm just…surprised, that's all." Ren got up from the desk. She rubbed the back of her neck as she paced the floor, glancing out the window toward Cole's house. "Did Cole say *why* he withdrew his offer?"

There was a pause more pregnant than Zora.

"You won, sweetheart," her grandfather said finally. "So why does it matter why?"

"I don't know, Gramps." Ren's voice broke and her vision clouded. She sucked in a deep breath, then sighed. "It just does."

"Cole said he had a change of heart. That he agreed with you about the farm being part of our family's legacy. He said that after watching you work so passionately to revive the farm, he realized it was in good hands. He doesn't want to interfere with that. In fact, once he completes the renovations on Bea's house, he'll sell the place to you at a fair price, if that's what you want."

Cole was going to sell her the place?

In the beginning, that was exactly what she'd hoped for. But now, she couldn't imagine not looking out her window and knowing he was there.

"What about his plans to build his luxury community?"

"Says he'll build a scaled-down version on the plot of land that was his second option. And he's going to push the county to hurry those plans to replace that bridge into town, since it'll impact his new development. So it's a win for everyone."

"And exactly what you've been hoping for." Renee laughed softly. "You always were a sly old devil when it came to getting Cole to do the right thing. I see it's still working."

"What makes you think he changed his mind because of me?" her grandfather asked. "And what makes you think Cole is the only one I use those tricks on?" Her grandfather chuckled again. "Now, I have to go. Your grandmother paused our favorite show so I could make this call, and now she's giving me that evil eye of hers."

"I am not! We love you, sweetheart!" her grandmother shouted in the background. "Congratulations!"

"Thanks, Gran!" Ren bade them good-night and ended the call.

She sat back against her chair, one hand over her mouth. Her heart thudded in her chest. She'd done it. The rest was just a formality. Ren would soon be the owner of the land that had been in her family for three generations. And she planned to restore it and make it even better. Something that would last another three generations. A legacy for her son and any other children she might have.

Not that there were any prospects of that.

Ren walked over to the window facing Cole's house. It was about half an hour before sunset and the sky was beautiful, streaked with pinks and oranges, the silhouette of the Smoky Mountains in the distance. This felt right. Being here in Magnolia Lake on her family's land...this was *exactly* where she and Mercer belonged.

So why did she feel heartbroken?

You know exactly why.

Ren toyed with the locket on her neck. It was the only jewelry from her ex-husband she still wore, because it held the most adorable photo of Mercer as a baby.

She couldn't stop thinking of what Cole had done. The sacrifice he'd made.

"You really miss him, don't you, honey?" Her mother's soft voice came from behind her.

Ren nodded, looking out of the window longingly.

Evelyn stood beside her and slipped an arm around her waist, their heads together. "Mercer does, too. He comes to this window all the time and says, *Vroom!*"

Fat tears fell on Ren's cheeks. She swiped at them angrily. "This is all my fault. I shouldn't have pushed him into this experiment. Then we'd still be friends, and everyone would be happy."

"You were never happy just being Cole's friend, honey." Her mom wiped her tears. "You were just willing to accept his friendship."

Ren pressed a hand to her mouth, the tears falling harder. Her mother was right. She'd been lying to herself and to Cole from the very start when she'd declared she'd only wanted a physical relationship.

"Cole didn't walk away from you, honey. You're the one who asked for space. So go talk to him. This time, be honest about how you feel. At least he'll know the truth and you two can decide where to go from there." Her mother hugged her and patted her back. "I'm going to bed. But I'm here, and I've got Mercer. So if I don't see you later tonight... I'll see you in the morning." Her mother smiled, then walked toward the stairs.

Ren stood there, unsure of what she should do. Her heart ached at the thought of another rejection from Cole. But what was the point of an experiment, except to keep trying different approaches until you found the one that worked?

She hurried up the stairs and prepared to do just that.

Cole stood back and admired the paint job in his new master bedroom suite. His crew had done the work of remodeling the bedroom and adding an en suite bathroom. They'd done meticulous tilework in the bathroom and refinished the plaster in the old house. But he'd wanted to paint this room himself.

Milo had started him off as a painter when he was just a kid. Every now and again, he liked to do a paint job in one of the long-term flips he lived in, to remember how he'd started.

Cole cleaned the rollers in the sink. Then he stripped off his grimy clothing and took a long, hot shower. He lathered his body and washed the grit from his hair.

Cole turned off the water and heard a faint knocking

sound. He stood still and listened but didn't hear it again. God, he hoped it wasn't the plumbing in this old house. He hadn't budgeted for that in the renovation plan. Cole toweled himself off, then walked into the bedroom. He couldn't help glancing over at Ren's house. Her bedroom light wasn't on.

Then he noticed movement below. It was Ren. She had her phone to her ear as she took the path from his place back to hers. He knocked on the window, but she didn't hear him. Cole huffed.

Maybe Ren had just come to say thank you because he'd retracted his bid on the property. Or maybe she'd come to say she was prepared to resume their friendship but wanted nothing more. He hoped like hell it was Option #3.

There was only one way to find out.

Cole glanced around his bedroom, which was a mess after the painting and remodeling. Then he gazed over at the balcony off Ren's bedroom. His mouth curved in a smile.

It was probably a terrible idea. But Ren was an amazing woman and his best friend. He loved her and Mercer, and he'd screwed up by not telling Ren that when he'd had the chance. So he was prepared to go big, because Ren deserved one more grand gesture.

Ren poured herself a little of the King's Finest peach brandy that she kept stocked for her mother. She'd gone over to Cole's house, knowing he was there. She'd knocked three times, and had even tried calling him, but he hadn't answered.

Was Cole upset about giving up the land deal?

Her phone rang, and a photo she'd taken of Cole and Mercer filled her screen, both of their faces stretched wide with happy grins that made her smile every time she saw it.

Ren answered the phone as quickly as she could. "Cole, hi."

"Hello, sweetheart." She could hear the smile in his voice. "It's so good to hear your voice again."

"Yours, too." Ren nodded, her eyes pricking with tears. "Cole, I'm so sorry. I—"

"Why don't you come to your balcony door and tell me all about it."

"You climbed the trellis?" she asked, but he'd already ended the call. "Hello?"

Ren hurried up to her room and opened the balcony door. Cole was standing there with a wide grin.

"What were you thinking?" Ren slapped his arm. "You could've fallen and hurt yourself."

"That should tell you how badly I needed to see you, beautiful." Cole stroked her cheek, his eyes filled with a warmth that seeped into her skin.

She'd missed this man. Missed her lover and her friend. The days they'd been apart felt like an eternity.

Ren held a finger up to her lips and tugged Cole inside her room. She closed the balcony door. "Why did you need to see me?"

"I was in the shower when you came over to my place. I knocked on the window as you were leaving, but you didn't hear me." He squeezed her hand. "Why'd you come to see me?"

"To thank you for what you did by walking away from the deal. And for what you told my grandfather about the farm being in good hands with me. I don't know what prompted you to walk away but—"

"Yes, you do." Cole's mouth quirked in a half smile as he cupped her cheek. His dark eyes locked with hers.

"So you really did walk away from the deal for me." Ren studied Cole's face. "I can't thank you enough. This means everything to me."

"And you, Ren, mean everything to me."

Ren's heart squeezed in her chest, and her eyes stung with tears for the second time tonight.

"I have a confession to make." Ren wrapped her arms around herself. "When I said I would be satisfied with a no-strings, casual relationship, I was lying to you and to myself." She sighed. "Because it isn't true. I am very much in love with you, Cole. I think I always have been."

He pulled her closer, a soft smile curving his sensuous lips. "Do you know why I agreed to this experiment of yours?"

"Because you were afraid I'd start seeing Leonard Dawson?" She grinned. "Spoiler alert—I wouldn't have."

"Okay, that was part of it," he admitted with a chuckle, then sighed. "Imagining you with someone else… Honestly, Ren, it was pure torture. And since you came back, I haven't wanted to be with anyone but you. It was kind of a new concept for me. So I needed to understand why."

"Did you find your answer?" Ren looped her arms around Cole's neck as she gazed up at him.

"I did." Cole cradled her face. "Because I'm in love with you, too. And for me, no other woman in the world compares to you, Ren. These past few months, we've built a genuine friendship and become an important part of each other's lives. The highlight of my week is the time I get to spend with you and Mercer. Because I'm happier with both of you in my life. I don't ever want to go back to a life that doesn't include you. Because the two of you…" His voice was shaky and his eyes filled with emotion. "You *and* Mercer mean everything to me now. And I don't *ever* want that to change."

"Really?" Ren's glasses were foggy, and tears of joy rolled down her cheeks.

"Really." Cole lifted her chin. "I love you and Mercer,

Ren. And I want us to be a family…officially." He clutched her hand as he met her gaze. "Marry me."

"What?" She stared at him, wide-eyed. Her heart felt as if it was beating out of her chest. "You're not serious… are you?"

Cole reached into the back pocket of his jeans and pulled out a ring box. He opened it, revealing a gorgeous vintage sapphire-and-diamond art deco–style engagement ring.

Ren gasped and pressed her fingertips to her mouth. "Cole. It's beautiful."

"This ring belonged to my grandmother, Ren. My grandfather gave it to me because, like my mother and sister, he realized how very much I am in love with you. That being with you makes me happier than I have ever been. It just took me a minute to work through my issues and to realize how much I want a life with you."

Cole removed the ring from the box and turned it so she could read the inscription inside.

To my darling, Ren. I love you forever and always.

"It's perfect." Warm tears streamed down her face.

Cole pressed a soft, lingering kiss to her mouth.

"Marry me, Ren. Please. Because you mean the world to me. And I don't ever want to be without you again."

"Yes, I'll marry you, Cole." Ren nodded, tears flowing down her face. "Because I don't ever want to be without you again, either."

Cole captured her mouth in a kiss.

Tears ran down her face, and her heart felt full, even as a zing of electricity shot down her spine, setting every nerve ending in her body on fire.

The kiss was filled with love: passionate, yet tender. It was everything she wanted. Because *Cole* was everything she wanted.

Epilogue

Three and a half months later

Cole stepped out of his Jaguar F-Type and handed the valet the keys. King's Finest Family Restaurant was a family-style restaurant, so valets wouldn't be the norm. But Savannah, Quinn and Iris had thought it would be fun to do a formal grand opening, complete with a red carpet and Tennessee celebrities like Dade Willis, whose latest song was blazing up the country charts.

A line had already begun to form on the sidewalk outside the restaurant—a full hour before the doors opened to the public. Both locals and out-of-towners were eager to be part of King's Finest Family Restaurant.

Cole handed the valet his keys, then offered his fiancée his hand, helping her out of the car. Ren looked gorgeous in a sleeveless black jumpsuit with a flouncy ruffle down one side and black ballet flats. They stopped, smiling for the photographers, before continuing inside.

"Have I told you that the second you put that thing on, I haven't been able to think of anything but how quickly I'll be able to get you out of it?"

"Cole Abbott." Ren elbowed him, laughing. "This is a *family* restaurant."

"Okay, all right," he grumbled. "But we're staying two hours tops. Then you, me and that sexy-ass black jumpsuit have a date back at my place."

"You're on." She squeezed his hand.

Cole dropped a kiss on Ren's lips, and she smiled.

"You two again with the PDA?" Parker clutched Kayleigh's hand. His brother wore a black suit and tie. He pushed his black eyeglasses up the bridge of his nose.

"Pay no mind to the PDA police here. You two are adorable." Kayleigh shook her head. Her red curls, pulled into a high ponytail, waved behind her.

She wore a pretty black dress with an unusual design. "My husband's bark is worse than his bite." Kayleigh tapped Parker's chest with her crystal-studded black leather Alexander McQueen bag.

"This place looks incredible, Cole." Parker glanced around at the interior of the restaurant.

"I can hardly believe this was once my run-down old jewelry-and-consignment shop." Kayleigh took in the wall of floor-to-ceiling windows that spanned the front of the restaurant, bathing the space with natural light.

Cole's construction team had done a hell of a job on the restoration of the building. The exposed brick paid homage to the original restaurant owned by his maternal grandpa Gus. The seating was a mix of high-top tables, traditional tables and bench seating—all designed by his brother-in-law and built locally by Dallas's company, Hamilton Haus.

Quinn had worked feverishly with local tradesmen, retailers and farmers to source the lighting and other design materials as well as all of the food they served. Ren's farm would be the source for many of the restaurant's organic fruits and vegetables starting the following year.

The shelves were stocked with spirits from King's Finest and other local distilleries. The wines were supplied by a variety of local vineyards.

"I'm proud of the way it all turned out." Cole led his siblings through the space, giving them a mini-tour of the restaurant. "Most importantly, I'm glad that Mom is pleased with it. This is her baby."

"Look at her. She's beaming," Kayleigh said. "I can't wait to see the plans for my inn."

"It'll be amazing, of course." Cole grinned.

The inn was slated to be built for Kayleigh the following year. It would be situated on a plot of land once owned by her family and recently gifted back to her by his father, Duke.

After the tour, they gathered at the back of the restaurant where Iris was putting some final touches on the stage decorations.

Zora was videoconferencing Dallas's mother, Tish, who was watching their infant daughter, Ella.

"Ella is so adorable." Ren pressed a hand to her chest. "She looks just like you, Zora. Yet, she has many of her dad's features."

"She's the perfect combination." Zora smiled at Dallas lovingly.

"Just like us, babe." Dallas kissed his wife.

"More of the PDA?" Parker complained.

Zora elbowed her brother in the ribs, and he laughed.

"Thank you all for coming a little earlier," Duke said, his arm around his wife's waist. "I thought it would be nice if we had a private family toast before the restaurant opens."

Their mother looked gorgeous in a sparkly, floor-length dress in a deep burgundy. And she was beaming with pride.

"You all know how much this venture means to me. I just wanted to thank you all for your support and your contributions in making this happen," Iris said. "But nothing makes me happier than seeing each of you having found your soulmates and starting families of your own. And I honestly couldn't have picked more perfect matches for each of you, if I'd tried. And believe me, I tried."

They all laughed as one of the servers brought them all glasses of champagne.

"Duke and I are truly blessed to have all of you in our lives," Iris continued, her eyes welling with tears.

"Thank you so much, Iris." Savannah hugged her and everyone else chimed in their thanks, too.

"I was an only child and so was Duke," Grandpa Joe said. "We wanted more kids but couldn't have them. So I would never have imagined that I'd one day be surrounded by family like this." His grandfather got choked up and placed a hand over his heart. "I love each and every one of you, more than words can say."

"So before your mother and grandfather start with the waterworks again…" his father teased, handing Iris a drink. "I'd like to propose a toast."

He raised his glass, and everyone else did, too.

"To your mother—the most incredible woman I've ever known. Thank you for your love, patience and wisdom. And for supporting me and King's Finest all these years. It is our honor to now support you as you pursue your dreams." Duke turned toward the rest of them. "And to this group of amazing, accomplished people who I am so proud to know and even prouder to call family. Whether our bond is by blood or marriage, we are truly grateful to have you in our lives."

His father's voice broke with emotion, and everyone

teased him. He laughed, wiping the corners of his eyes. "Thank you for being part of our world. I can't wait to see all that you have yet to accomplish. To family."

"To family." They echoed, holding their glasses up and clinking them together.

"Now, I want you all to see the menu." Iris nodded to one of the servers who unveiled the large menu board on the wall.

They'd known she'd planned to incorporate their family's recipes and share them with the world. But they hadn't known that their names would be incorporated into each of the signature dishes they'd either contributed or inspired—including Ren's Chicken and Dumplings, Cole's Slaw Burger, Quinn's Peach Cobbler, Parker's Old Fashioned and Zora's One-Two Punch.

It was a surprise to all of them and a testament to their mother's love for her family.

"That was incredibly sweet of your mom." Ren dabbed beneath her eyes, trying her best not to ruin her makeup. "I can't believe she included me. Our wedding isn't until next summer."

"You and Mercer are already family, babe." Cole kissed the hand that bore his grandmother's engagement ring.

An older man approached him. "Excuse me, are you Cole Abbott?"

Cole didn't know the man, but something about him seemed familiar. "Yes, sir. But the restaurant still isn't open to the public for another...twenty minutes."

"I know," the man said. "But I was hoping the two of us could talk."

"Can I help you with something?" Cole asked.

"Actually, I was hoping we could help each other."

Cole raised a brow and exchanged a look with Ren. He assessed the man. "I'm sorry, but now isn't the best time to talk business. This is a special night for our family. Especially for my mother." He pulled a card from his wallet and handed it to the man. "Why don't you call my office next week?"

The man studied the card for a moment and then smiled, as if he knew something Cole didn't. It made him uneasy. He slipped his hand into Ren's, threading their fingers.

"Actually, that's why I came here tonight. I thought it would be the best time to introduce myself to the entire family." The man's light brown skin crinkled around his eyes.

Cole couldn't shake the feeling he'd seen him somewhere before. "And why is that, Mr....?"

"Valentine." A deep, almost mischievous smile curved one side of the man's mouth. "*Abbott* Valentine of Valentine Vineyards."

"Ahh." Cole nodded knowingly. "If this is about supplying the restaurant... I'm pretty sure my mother and sister-in-law have already lined up all of their vendors for now."

"And I'm one of them." The man nodded toward a bottle of wine passing by on a serving tray. "Two weeks ago, I bought Richardson Vineyards, lock, stock and barrel. Your next delivery will bear the new label. I just thought I should introduce myself and give you all a heads-up."

"I hadn't heard." Cole still regarded the man suspiciously. "Congrats on acquiring the vineyard, Mr. Valentine. I'll let my mother know—"

"Actually, I was hoping to meet your family. Especially your grandfather, Joseph." The man looked less cocky. There was a hint of discomfort in his dark eyes as they scanned the room.

"And why is that, Mr. Valentine?" Cole asked again.

"I suppose there is no delicate way to say this." The man sighed heavily, then straightened his tie. He glanced around the space surreptitiously. "I'm his...brother."

"My grandfather is an only child. Just like my father." Cole stood taller, clenching his jaw.

He had no idea what kind of game this man was running, but he would gladly escort his happy ass to the door. There was no way he'd let this man ruin his mother's special night.

"Joseph was his mother's only child," the man clarified. "But not our father's. And thanks to you and the ancestry registry you joined, I finally know who my real father was—your great-grandfather King Abbott. That makes me your grandfather's half brother."

Cole and Ren looked at each other. Her eyes went wide, and his heart was racing.

Shit.

Three months ago, Renee had decided to join an ancestry registry to try to locate Wilhelmina's daughter. Cole had always thought it would be cool and interesting to learn more about his family roots, so he'd joined the registry, too. He'd never imagined that *he'd* be the one to find a long-lost relative.

"Hey, don't I know you?" Cole's grandfather walked over, a glass of bourbon in his hand as he rubbed his chin and tried to place the man.

"Hello, Joseph." The man held out his hand, which trembled slightly.

"So I do know you!" Gramps said, narrowing his gaze as he shook it. "Now don't tell me. Just give me a minute to place you."

"Pops," Cole said gently. "This man... Abbott Valentine...he says he's your—"

"Brother," the man said, still clutching Joseph's hand. "I'm your half brother. And I could really use your help."

* * * * *

COMING SOON!

We really hope you enjoyed reading this book.
If you're looking for more romance, be sure to
head to the shops when new books are
available on

Thursday 6th January

To see which titles are coming soon, please visit

millsandboon.co.uk/nextmonth

MILLS & BOON

MILLS & BOON

THE HEART OF ROMANCE

A ROMANCE FOR EVERY READER

MODERN

Prepare to be swept off your feet by sophisticated, sexy and seductive heroes, in some of the world's most glamourous and romantic locations, where power and passion collide.

HISTORICAL

Escape with historical heroes from time gone by. Whether your passion is for wicked Regency Rakes, muscled Vikings or rugged Highlanders, awake the romance of the past.

MEDICAL

Set your pulse racing with dedicated, delectable doctors in the high-pressure world of medicine, where emotions run high and passion, comfort and love are the best medicine.

True Love

Celebrate true love with tender stories of heartfelt romance, from the rush of falling in love to the joy a new baby can bring, and a focus on the emotional heart of a relationship.

Desire

Indulge in secrets and scandal, intense drama and plenty of sizzling hot action with powerful and passionate heroes who have it all: wealth, status, good looks…everything but the right woman.

HEROES

Experience all the excitement of a gripping thriller, with an intense romance at its heart. Resourceful, true-to-life women and strong, fearless me face danger and desire - a killer combination!

To see which titles are coming soon, please visit

millsandboon.co.uk/nextmonth

We Love
Romance
with MILLS & BOON

Available at
weloveromance.com

Romance

For exclusive extracts, competitions
and special offers, find us online:

f facebook.com/millsandboon

🐦 @MillsandBoon

📷 @MillsandBoonUK

Get in touch on 01413 063232

For all the latest titles coming soon, visit
millsandboon.co.uk/nextmonth

MILLS & BOON
A ROMANCE FOR EVERY READER

- **FREE** delivery direct to your door

- **EXCLUSIVE** offers every month

- **SAVE** up to 25% on pre-paid subscriptions

SUBSCRIBE AND SAVE

millsandboon.co.uk/Subscribe

WANT EVEN MORE
ROMANCE?
SUBSCRIBE AND SAVE TODAY!

'Mills & Boon books, the perfect way to escape for an hour or so.'

MISS W. DYER

'Excellent service, promptly delivered and very good subscription choices.'

MISS A. PEARSON

'You get fantastic special offers and the chance to get books before they hit the shops.'

MRS V. HALL

Visit millsandboon.co.uk/Subscribe and save on brand new books.

JOIN THE
MILLS & BOON
BOOKCLUB

* **FREE** delivery direct to your door

* **EXCLUSIVE** offers every month

* **EXCITING** rewards programme

50% OFF YOUR FIRST PARCEL

Join today at
Millsandboon.co.uk/Bookclub

JOIN US ON SOCIAL MEDIA!

Stay up to date with our latest releases, author
news and gossip, special offers and discounts, and
all the behind-the-scenes action
from Mills & Boon...

 millsandboon

 millsandboonuk

 millsandboon

It might just be true love...

GET YOUR ROMANCE FIX!

MILLS & BOON
— *blog* —

Get the latest romance news, exclusive author interviews, story extracts and much more!

blog.millsandboon.co.uk

MILLS & BOON
Desire

Indulge in secrets and scandal, intense drama and plenty of sizzling hot action with powerful and passionate heroes who have it all: wealth, status, good looks…everything but the right woman.

Four Desire stories published every month, find them all at:

millsandboon.co.uk

MILLS & BOON
MODERN
Power and Passion

Prepare to be swept off your feet by
sophisticated, sexy and seductive heroes, in
some of the world's most glamourous and
romantic locations, where power and
passion collide.

ght Modern stories published every month, find them all at:
millsandboon.co.uk/Modern

MILLS & BOON
MEDICAL
Pulse-Racing Passion

Set your pulse racing with dedicated, delectable doctors in the high-pressure world of medicine, where emotions run high and passion, comfort and love are the best medicine.

Eight Medical stories published every month, find them all

millsandboon.co.uk

MILLS & BOON
True Love
Romance from the Heart

Celebrate true love with tender stories of heartfelt romance, from the rush of falling in love to the joy a new baby can bring, and a focus on the emotional heart of a relationship.

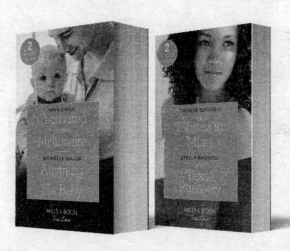

Four True Love stories published every month, find them all at:

millsandboon.co.uk/TrueLove